TESTING FRIENDSHIP

MADISON BOLIN

Editing and design by Jansina of Rivershore Books

Cover photos by Allyssa Sayers (front) and Vadim Sadovski (back) on Unsplash

Library of Congress Control Number: 2023915859

ISBN: 978-1-63522-209-8

Printed in the United States of America
10 9 8 7 6 5 4 3 2 1

Rivershore Books
8982 Van Buren St. NE • Minneapolis, MN 55434
612-208-3434 • info@rivershorebooks.com

To Mom, Dad, and Brother:

I dedicate this book to my original and best friends forever. You have stood by me through every joy and hardship I've endured. You have shown me the joy writing brings to myself and to others. Without you, I would never have found one of my greatest passions. Thank you!

Love Always,
Me

Fall Semester
Sophomore Year
2014

CHAPTER 1

It was the first day of a new school year, tenth grade. It's refreshing to not be the scared, little freshmen anymore, but we're still decently low on the food chain for high school. Juniors and seniors above us would have better seats at the sporting games, lunches off campus, and their stereotypical, high school superiority over the sophomores and freshmen.

My name is Allison Sky Manex.

This sounds like the beginning of a Junie B. Jones book.

The reason I tell you my middle name is because my friends call me Sky or Alli a lot of the time. Speaking of my friends, I should give you a heads up on my four besties: Evelynn, Chelsea, Hayden, and Rose. We've been friends since elementary school and have grown up having sleepovers and talking about boys, complaining about our parents, and sharing our dreams since the beginning.

Chelsea Barlow is on the volleyball team. She loves working out and helps keep us in shape by staying active when we hang out. She doesn't believe in taking the escalator at the mall.

My guilty pleasure is using the escalator whenever she isn't around.

1

Lastly, I can't forget to mention that Chelsea is absolutely boy crazy. You catch onto it pretty quickly once you've hung out with her more than two times.

Hayden Windlet is the funniest person I have ever met. She always has us laughing until we cry. She's also into sports like Chelsea. Hayden is on the softball team. She is one of the few who was on varsity as a freshman. I'm sure college scouts will be recruiting her by junior year.

Rose Bailey is the quietest of us. Our school focuses a lot on STEM (science, technology, engineering, and math). Rose wants them to focus on STEAM instead (adding in the A for arts). She's an active advocate, as she should be. She can play any instrument and loves to be involved in our school plays.

Evelynn Appleby is the genius of the group; well of our grade entirely. She takes her studies extremely seriously and is on track to being our class valedictorian when we graduate. She's drop dead gorgeous and will be brutally honest with our choice of fashion, even when we don't ask for it.

Yes, she did choose all our first day outfits like our mothers used to do in elementary school. She is the oldest one in the group, though. She turned sixteen in August and is going to be able to drive us to school every day now.

It's not that I haven't appreciated her mom always driving us, it's just . . . you know . . . not as cool as rolling up with your friends. We won't have to watch what we say, which is the best part. Oh! and we'll get to choose the music too! Well . . . Chelsea will anyway.

Here's what she chose for us to wear on day one: Chelsea is wearing denim shorts that barely made the cut for school dress code, but she likes to push the boundaries. She's wearing a fitted, striped, short sleeve shirt as well. We're pretty sure the school sets their air conditioning to negative twenty below so girls don't wear these petite outfits, but Chelsea doesn't care and Evelynn is her ally. She claims she's a walking furnace, but you can see the hair on her arms stand up from the goosebumps.

I'm wearing denim shorts as well, with an Adidas shirt that is tucked in the front and an army green jacket that Evelynn insisted I wear. It makes me look "tough" in her opinion. Hayden is wearing black jeans and a white V-neck shirt. She'll let Evelynn pick out her outfit, but that doesn't necessarily mean she'll wear it. Rose is wearing a new floral dress she bought yesterday when we were at the mall. Evelynn is wearing a blue, denim skirt, with a rose-colored short sleeved shirt and white sneakers.

Evelynn would like to go into fashion, but her parents are not supportive of that path. They don't think it's a "steady job" and she should keep fashion as a hobby rather than making it a career. Her dream, or rather her parents' dream, is for her to attend Princeton University after high school, ideally on a full ride, academic scholarship. Poor Evelynn is constantly under pressure either from her parents or herself to excel in everything.

That leaves me, I guess. My friends all have something unique about them, whereas I don't feel there is really anything special about me. I'm the second oldest in our group of friends. My birthday is September 29th. I'm not involved in any sports. I work instead. I have been working at Steve's Diner since I was fourteen. I study hard for my grades, getting A's and B's, but I am losing hope of every being able to earn straight A's. On the other hand, I think I'm funny, but I'm not the Class Clown. I'll likely never be voted Class anything in our yearbooks; I'm just very average. My friends would describe me as hard working, loyal, and a good listener.

I'm house broken too. I'm a freaking golden retriever!

"Bridget South better not be in any of my classes this year. If we have gym together one more time, I swear I'm going to start targeting her with the dodge-ball even if she's on my team!" Chelsea started.

"Ugh! I would take Bridget over Scott Harrison. I know he's sweet, but he will not take the hint that I am not interested. I guess he doesn't care either that I have a boyfriend," Evelynn chimed in next.

"I'm looking forward to meeting new people that join the drama club," Rose quietly added.

Hayden agreed with Rose and said she's looking forward to the new girls that will be on the softball team as well. Chelsea disagreed with Hayden. She doesn't like it when the volleyball team gets new girls. She sees them as competition, not only for the volleyball team, but for the boys in our school that come to watch the girls play in their spandex.

"What about you, Sky? Still hoping that Oliver Walker is in French class with you this year?" Evelynn asked, turning around in the front seat of the car so she could see me in the back.

"She's always hoping that he will be in her classes." Chelsea laughed with the other girls as she tickled me.

I fought my friends off and tried defending myself. "Hey, at least I'm consistent! Chelsea here drools over any guy that walks by."

"I'm just appreciating God's beautiful creatures that He has bestowed upon us." We all laughed with and at Chelsea.

Evelynn pulled into the pot-holed parking lot of Greenwood High School twenty minutes before the first period began.

We are never late with her, which I'm thankful for.

We gathered on the front lawn with more of our classmates since it was a nice day out.

My friends and I knew which classes we did and didn't have together already, but we started comparing our schedules with the other students nearby. For whatever reason, it's nice to know ahead of time who is going to be in your classes. I actually have one class with Evelynn and Rose this year, though! I'll also be able to see them all at lunch.

That's better than nothing.

I enjoy social studies and English classes the most. I dread math and science. It seems like most students lean one way or the other with them. For example, Evelynn loves math and hates history. We balance each other that way when we study together, which is nice.

There was chatter amongst all the students on the front lawn and parking lot as everyone was comparing schedules and moaning with disappointment when they too found out they didn't have certain classes together. There were sporadic shrieks from girls as they ran up and hugged one another as if they hadn't seen one another all summer. The guys did their normal half embrace, hand holding, with the pat on the back thing they do.

You know exactly what I'm talking about.

As my friends were talking to the other classmates, I was scanning the area looking for a certain guy in particular. Butterflies fluttered in my stomach the second I saw him. There he was, sitting on the tailgate of his red pick-up truck. His white shirt popped against his sun-kissed skin. His sandy blond hair had been bleached by the sun too. No doubt he spent all his time on his family boat on the lake.

I enjoyed every shirtless photo his mom and friends tagged him in.

He's involved in football, basketball, and track. Hope stirred within me as it did every year wondering if we would have any classes together or not. I struck out last year, but maybe we'd have French class together again.

Every class together would be just fine too, but I don't want to be greedy or anything—haha.

We had eighth grade French together, but not

5

ninth grade. To say I was disappointed was a drastic understatement.

"Are you going to talk to him, or just keep drooling?" *Busted.* Hayden came and stood beside me without me noticing. I wasn't drooling, but I'm surprised Oliver didn't spontaneously combust with how hard I was staring at him.

Even though it's Hayden, I still blushed a little from being caught.

"Nah. There's a lot of people over there already. I'll probably just wait and see if we have any classes as the day goes on."

"So, the same plan you have every year?" she said smiling.

"Yup, keeps the mystery alive," I said.

We both started laughing, knowing full well that if I was a cat, I would lose all nine of my lives because of my curiosity. We turned around to rejoin our friends.

Evelynn's boyfriend Kyle, whom she's been dating for a year now, came up behind her and hugged her. She squealed in surprise and hugged him back once she realized who it was. We all genuinely liked him.

I'm allowed to go on dates, I just haven't had any guys ask me yet.

I know, it's the 21st century. I could ask them myself, but like . . . it's scary! I'll just stick with social media stalking Oliver. If I will it hard enough, he'll realize one day how madly in love with me he is and that he needs to ask me out right that second before another guy swoops me up. Puh-lease!

The ten-minute warning bell rang. In unison, we gathered our backpacks from off the ground and filed in toward our new locker assignments. Our school kept us clustered by our grades. The freshmen have their own locker area, the sophomores have theirs, juniors, seniors, etc. They have always grouped us by our Homerooms. I liked that, though, because my friends and I were near each other.

That is not the case this year. They reorganized all four grades and are now assigning lockers by last names. That makes sense I guess, but why did they have to change it this year?! I'm the only M in our group and that is right in the middle of the alphabet nowhere near my friends.

I found my locker and fidgeted with the lock. I can remember my combination 98% of the time, but I've learned that I still need to write it down in my planner because there are random days when I can't remember it for the life of me. I either have a complete brainfart, or I start to get all my previous locker combinations jumbled.

22-3-18, HIKE!

We'd get our textbooks once we got to our classes, so for now, I put my afternoon class notebooks in my locker and savor how light my backpack would be for these last couple of minutes until next summer.

I headed to Homeroom. I already knew Oliver would not be there because we have the same Homeroom for all four years. The only difference is the seniors who graduate and the new freshmen that come in.

Our teacher greeted us and welcomed us back for the new school year like they all will.

I wonder if they are honestly happy that we're back, or if they fake it like the students do?

Mr. Duncan went over the guidelines, lunch menu, and announcements for the day. Once he finished, we had about seven free minutes to sit on our phones, listen to music, or play a quick game of hangman if we wanted. I checked my phone to see the group text messages that came in from my friends. They're talking about the new freshmen in their classrooms and how bummed Chelsea was that Micah Stranton graduated.

I only had two girls and one male freshman join my Homeroom. There was nothing to report on them. The two girls seemed to know each other, and the guy was keeping to himself waiting for the bell to dismiss us.

I got to start my day off with English, which was nice. My brain would have time to wake up and not have to start doing equations right away. I felt for the girls that had gym right away in the morning. There's nothing like having gym teachers wanting you to be active and sweaty first thing. Here is the order of my classes this semester:

1. LANGUAGE ARTS
2. BIOLOGY (GROSS)
3. STUDY HALL
4. SOCIAL STUDIES
   LUNCH
5. FRENCH III
6. GEOMETRY (GROSSER)
7. GYM
8. PHOTOGRAPHY I

The core classes are standard: language arts, social studies, science, mathematics, and gym. I took photography as an elective this semester so I could take the second portion in the spring semester.

For as large as our school is, they only offer French or Spanish as a foreign language class that we must take. Personally, I wish they would offer American Sign Language, but they don't. I guess it's good they force us to do this, although I don't know how much of it I'll actually remember later in life. Nevertheless,

I chose French because I knew Oliver was going to be taking it. We talked about it once in seventh grade, so my fate was decided then and there!

My plan worked! We had French I together for an entire year. Nothing came of us, though. He didn't ask me out on a date (*not that my parents would have allowed it anyway*), and we didn't date in "secret," where your teachers, classmates, and everyone in the world but your parents know you have a thing for each other. There were no hugs in the hallway or jealous eyes from the girls not dating him. The only longing looks given were from me staring at him.

He still doesn't realize I exist. I bet he just thinks of me as the girl that can't hold a pencil to save her life. In our class together, the heavens opened once for me, and the randomized seating chart placed us next to each other for the month of January. I "accidently dropped my pencil" nearly every other day (*you can't be too obvious you know*) just to watch him bend over, pick it up, and then turn toward me with his ocean blue eyes and his perfect, braces-free smile he flashed out of politeness while he handed it back to me.

The bell rang to dismiss us, snapping me from my memory and back to reality. I picked my backpack up, slung it over my right shoulder, and headed to first period.

So, it begins!

CHAPTER 2

I sighed. My first four classes were a bust. There wasn't even a sign of Oliver in the hallways.

Lame. I guess I still have lunch and four more periods to go.

I met up with my friends and got in line for the hamburgers and hot dogs they were grilling for us as a "Welcome Back Students." I know I spent all summer with my friends, but still, getting to see them at school was like a breath of fresh air. They're the people I can talk to and make jokes with, unlike the other people in my classes that sit there quietly and awkwardly like me.

Immediately the conversations about who was in whose classes started up. We checked over our shoulders and lowered our voices depending on who was around us. Hayden has geometry with Oliver.

Dang, I wish I was her right now.

It's a wonder to me that Chelsea hasn't walked straight up to him yet and been like, "Hey, Allison Manex has been in love with you since 7th grade. Would you ever go out with her?"

Thank god she hasn't, but I can easily see it happening. I don't DARE plant the idea in her head.

My cheeks started to turn a little red just from the thought of her doing that. Luckily nobody noticed because the sun was shining directly on us.

Chelsea led the way to where we were going to sit on the lawn, when I noticed Oliver was in front of us with his friends. Lo and behold, Chelsea set us right next to his group and rigged it, so he and I were kind of facing each other. I both loved and hated her at this moment, and she knew it by the grin on her face. The conversation shifted toward talking about our teachers and complaining about the homework some of us were already assigned.

"Watch out if you have Mrs. Dobrevin for English. We already have to read Shakespeare and memorize old English. Yuck! They talked so weird back then," Chelsea started off. Chelsea would have flunked every English class since elementary if it weren't for Rose helping her with her homework.

"It's a good thing I have Rose and Sky to do my home—I mean help me with my homework!" She laughed at her own joke.

"Don't we always?" Rose elbowed her in the side, and we all joined in laughing.

"Yes, and I love you guys more and more every year for it!" Chelsea said back.

"Speaking of study nights . . ." Evelynn started to say, but our group groaned so loud that even Oliver and his friends looked over at us to see what happened.

Oops.

"Can't we have one day of freedom before jumping into studying for nine months, Evelynn?" Chelsea whined.

"I thought we made a pact that the first weekend of every year is dedicated to eating junk and binging Netflix?" Hayden reminded us. We all agreed and looked at Evelynn with pleading eyes.

Evelynn sighed with defeat. "I guess we technically did make that pact last year. Okay, *after* this weekend we will need to figure out which nights we can study together."

I rolled my eyes, but I still admired her determination and persistence with grades. Honestly, if it weren't for Evelynn pushing us and caring about not only her grades, but our grades too, I know Chelsea and Hayden would be doing much worse and therefore not get to compete in volleyball or softball. I silently thanked her for that.

"Friday night we'll be at Alli's house in our jammies having sexy pillow fights," Chelsea said—way too loudly for our liking!

We all shushed her immediately and looked around to see who heard us.

Great. That's twice Oliver has looked over at us. He probably thinks we're crazy. UGH!

Behind us a group of junior girls were glaring at us indicating their annoyance. Something like that never bothers Chelsea, but it does the rest of us. *A lot.*

"Sexy pillow fights? Count me in!" Kyle walked up with a major smile on his face. He sat down next to Evelynn and kissed her on the cheek.

"Don't even think about it!" Evelynn said, although she was smiling, no doubt happy to see him.

"You might be able to keep me from participating, but you will never be able to keep me from thinking about it." He gave her a certain look with a large smile.

We think they are the cutest couple, and we are already planning their wedding. Chelsea mostly, but Evelynn gives hints as to what she wants and doesn't want as part of her wedding day; although, her taste changes with the seasons so who knows what she'll end up having and doing at her wedding by the time it gets here. I know it's too soon to be taking this seriously, but I can't imagine them breaking up.

I have never met a couple that is as complementary personality wise as these two human beings. If our school had an IT couple, they would be it. However, because we're not part of the "popular" group, they get overlooked. Kyle doesn't care obviously, but Evelynn does. She cares about her image and she cares about their image. She cares about our image. She cares what people think. She cares about her integrity and reputation. She cares deeply and strongly, and I believe it is her greatest strength and weakness.

Have they had sex? No. Do they want to? Yes, although Evelynn is much more hesitant than Kyle. She, nor we for that matter, could imagine her ending up pregnant and not getting to fulfill her college goals immediately post high school. Evelynn wants to wait, and Kyle is perfectly willing to do that. He'd do anything for her and it's a relationship that I envy to have one day.

I noticed Oliver's group of friends getting up to go play catch with a football while we were still on lunch. We could see the seniors arriving back to campus from having "open lunch" where they could leave and get food around town if they wanted. I looked at my friends, who were laughing and talking. I looked at the guys playing catch. I looked around at the other group of friends and classmates as they hung out in their own little worlds with each other.

How strange it is that we all are growing up together, yet we live completely different lives. I will never view high school from a popular viewpoint, or an outcast viewpoint. I'm not on the inside, but I'm not on the outside looking in either. I am floating right here in the middle; most likely to stay here for the next three years. This is my life. It's a good life, but I'm focused more on what I don't have right now. They drill into us that we need to have five- and ten-year life plans. Go to college! Get a job! Be prepared for the events you cannot prepare for that life is going to throw at you when you least expect it! It's so strange. It's like—

"Hey, Sky! Come back to us," Hayden said, waving her hand in front of my face.

I blinked and noticed all my friends were standing with their trays of food to throw away and their backpacks over their shoulders. The rest of the students were filing into school. I apparently didn't hear the bell ring. I quickly gathered my things and stood up to join my friends.

"What were you thinking about?" Rose quietly asked so that I didn't get crap for my wandering mind.

There wasn't any point to whisper, though; the girls were already assuming it was Oliver I was thinking about.

"Guys, guys, guys, let's not assume Sky was thinking about him," Chelsea chimed in. I lived a short moment of relief thinking Chelsea meant it. "She wasn't drooling, so it had to have been about something or someone other than Oliver!" She laughed and the rest of the group joined in.

I'm not bothered by the playfulness of my friends for the most part. We're notorious for picking on each other in a loving manner. Every once in a while, it goes a little too far, but I've been thankful nothing has ever gone *too* far. We've seen it happen to other friends here at school and it is one of the saddest things in my opinion. I can't ever imagine my life without any of these girls in it. I don't even want to imagine what my life would look like without them either.

"Actually Chels, I was thinking about the photo we saw of your dad in his old track uniform. If only those shorts were juuuuust a little shorter!" I cracked, and the girls oh-ed at that; everyone except Chelsea of course who was grossed out and said we needed to change the subject ASAP since we just ate lunch and she wanted to keep it in her stomach.

We all parted ways once we threw our trash away. We went to our lockers to change out our notebooks for the second half of the day. I checked my class schedule for fifth period French class once more. I'm terrified that I'm going to go to the wrong room one day and not be in the correct place.

How embarrassing would that be to start a class that you're not actually in, and then have to get up in front of everyone to leave the room and go to the correct class! No thank you!!

I checked my room number three times on my way there. *Room 93. Room 93. Room 93.* I walked in and was relieved to see Bonnie sitting down already. We've had French I and French II together so far, so I knew I was in the correct classroom at least. I sat next to her even though I knew we were about to have to stand right back up and go to our assigned seat that was about to be bestowed upon us.

Oliver Walker was officially not in French III with me, but *he* was . . . Maybe I had seen him in the cafeteria or the hallways, but I'd never had a class with him. In a school our size, it's easy to go through high school never meeting all your classmates. I estimated he stood almost six feet tall, with brunette hair spiked forward. He was wearing what every other boy was wearing on the first day in the middle of August: basketball shorts and a Kansas City Chiefs T-shirt.

I would guess about 90% of people who live in Kansas, though, are Chiefs fans for obvious reasons.

He had about as much muscle to him as the average sophomore boy has. He had that athletic build to him, so I guessed he played sports with his friends. Aside from his red shirt, everything else he wore was black. Black shorts, black socks, shoes, watch, and backpack.

Who is he? How have I never seen him around? Is he new? Is he a foreign exchange student? I hope not, only because that would mean he will be going back to his country after this year.

All my girlfriends took Spanish, so I knew they wouldn't be in class with me. The mysterious boy I had my eyes on took a seat in the back row across the room knowing he wouldn't get to stay there either.

Our teacher, Mrs. Lamb, came in and told us to stand up and take our bags with us. She then proceeded to point to each chair and read our full names aloud to everyone.

I don't know why teachers do that. Maybe they find it amusing or something . . . it's not.

Naturally my name just happened to get called first. *How embarrassing, front row.*

Mrs. Lamb started, "Okay in the first row we have; Allison Sky Manex. Bonnie Monique Grunger. Tyrisha Michelle Jones and Lincoln Kent Scott. In the second row, up front is William John Mantel—"

Have I heard that name before? Somehow it sounds familiar??

I didn't listen to the rest of the names being called. My brain acted like a VHS tape that was done playing and needed to be rewound.

His name has a nice ring to it. William. I like the name. I'm sure everybody calls him Will, but William rolls off the brain. I'm sure it rolls off the tongue quite nicely too! Ope, we made eye contact. Look away Alli! Ope, we did it again!

He did not look thrilled to have to sit up front, but he did smile when we made eye contact the second time.

Whoa, his eyes are blue! But not ocean blue like Oliver's; William's are a brighter blue, like an ice blue.

I'm sure the point of seating charts is to keep the talking level to a minimum, and to have us "branch out and meet new people." Normally I would roll my eyes at the idea of this, but I actually looked forward to this arrangement.

We spent the first twenty minutes having to stand up in front of the class and introduce ourselves in French. Since my seat had an imaginary "pick me first every time" sign on the back of it, Mrs. Lamb made me go first.

My hands shook as I stood from my desk and walked to the front of the classroom. My voice mimicked my hands. It sounded as if I was using a megaphone to amplify my nerves.

"*Bonjour.*" Cue awkward wave to everyone and a mental palm to the face! "*Je m'appelle Allison Manex. J'ai quinze ans. J'ai une mere, un pere, et un petit frere. J'aime passer du temps avec des amis, regarder des filmes, et lire. J'espere etre professeur d'universite.*"

If you're wondering what the heck I said, here it is in English: "Hello. My name is Allison Manex. I am fifteen years old. I have a mother, a father, and a little brother. I like to hang out with my friends, watch movies, and read. I hope to become a college professor."

Mrs. Lamb went in the order of the seating chart, so William was the fifth person to go. He was fidgeting and not making much eye contact with the class either. He mostly stared at our teacher, and you could tell he was nervous, but a cute nervous. *Oh gosh, what did I look like up there in comparison?!*

"*Bonjour. Je m'appelle Will Mantle. J'ai quinze ans. J'aime le football americain, le basketball, et soulever des poids. Ma couleur preferee est le vert et mes vacances preferees sont le 4 juillet.*"

He told us he was also fifteen years old. He liked American football, basketball, and lifting weights. His favorite color was green, and his favorite holiday was the 4th of July.

Interesting! I made mental notes of all these things. It was adorable when he blanked on how to say he lifts weights. He made the motion, and our teacher assisted him.

Once everyone introduced themselves, Mrs. Lamb took over and told us what we would be focusing on this semester. From what I listened to, it'll be a very cultural semester. We're going to read some children's books in French, cook French food, watch some French movies, and listen to French music every day. I think I'm going to enjoy this class. The clock was located to my right, as was William.

I have always had the tendency to watch the clocks during school. Now I'll have something else to look at.

The bell dismissed us, and our class dispersed. Sadly, William and I split almost immediately. He went left and I went right. Now I don't want to sound crazy, but I really did think about him the rest of the day. I wasn't imagining dating him by any means. I was trying to place where I'd heard his name before. It was driving me nuts.

I was looking extra forward to photography because it was the last period of the day, and because I was finally going to have class with my friends! Rose was there first. I came second, and Evelynn sat by us when she arrived. We didn't have much time to talk right away so I couldn't say anything about this William Mantel guy, but luckily there wasn't much to discuss on the first day. Our teacher welcomed us, went over our syllabus, and then said he was done, freeing us to do what we wanted as long as we were quiet. It was perfect.

"Do you guys recognize the name William Mantel?" I asked immediately.

Evelynn shook her head no, but Rose responded, "He and Danny Creston hang out all the time. Danny was in gym with us last year, Alli. Oh! William was also in third grade with us but then his parents moved across town, so he had to change elementary schools."

I snapped my fingers and pointed at Rose, "THAT'S IT! That's where I recognized his name from. He's in my fifth period and it has been driving me nuts trying to place him. Thank you, Rose!"

"He's changed drastically from the glimpse I caught of him as we walked into school today. He came to all our plays last year. He had long shaggy hair that covered his eyes and used to have quite a bit of acne from what I remember. It looks like that cleared up though and he cut his hair. He was almost unrecognizable until I saw him and Danny in the halls together," Rose continued.

I nodded in agreement with what Rose said about him. I made a note to myself to pull out my elementary class pictures and look him up immediately when I got home.

CHAPTER 3

*W*illiam Mantel, there he is in my third-grade class photo, just like Rose said. His hair used to be a lot lighter than what it currently is. I never had a class with him since third grade, at least not that I remembered. He didn't seem to recognize me either from the looks of today, but maybe he's keeping it to himself?

I looked at our 7th–9th grade yearbooks next. Sure enough, his face was full of puberty acne, he was stick thin, and he let his hair grow, and grow, and grow. By freshman year, his hair was on his shoulders.

Thank goodness he cut it.

After I looked him up in the yearbooks, I had a mortifying thought: *OH MY GOSH, what if he is looking me up in the yearbooks right now?!*

I quickly flipped back to my photos even though I'd seen them a million times.

Okay 9th grade isn't atrocious, I guess. I have improved my hairstyling techniques at least. 8th grade was definitely an awkward phase, eww. Good god, the haunting of my 7th grade picture returns. I have picked this photo apart, and every time I see it, I'm still horrified. *Why is my head tilted so far to the right? Why am I smiling so hard? What on earth are my baby hairs doing?!*

I slammed shut my 7th grade yearbook, overly dramatic of course, and laid back on my bed.

I doubt he pulled out his yearbooks and looked me up and here I am, checking them all and racking my brain trying to remember if I even passed him in the hallways over the last few years.

Luckily Mom called me down to supper. My parents wanted to know how the first day of school went for my brother and me.

"Good," we said in unison. Our dad chuckled, and our mom rolled her eyes.

"Okay, so what did you guys do today at school?" she tried again.

My brother, Greyson, and I looked at each other sheepishly. "Nothing," we said in unison again.

Although our dad chuckled, he had that tone in his voice. *You know the one I'm talking about. Where Dad wants to laugh at his children, but he knows that Mom is getting agitated, so he needs to step in because he's "Dad," and for some reason once Dad steps in, that means things are turning serious. Yeah, that tone.*

Greyson went first. "My first day went fine. I don't think it'll be as bad as Allison made middle school out to be." Our parents both looked at me with a disapproving frown, so I glared across the table at my little brother, who decided to keep talking about his day, ignoring the warning in my eyes. "I did get turned around, but Spencer actually went to an 8th grade classroom by accident, so that was funny."

We all chuckled at the image of Greyson's best friend being in the wrong classroom. Of all his friends, Spencer is one of the goofiest, but I think he's my favorite one as well.

"Alli, sweetie, what about you?" Mom asked encouragingly.

I shrugged and started, "It was also fine, nothing exciting. It's nice to not be a freshman anymore. Oh, they did rearrange our locker assignments though. Instead of it being based on your Homeroom, it's alphabetical by last name now, so I'm nowhere near any of my friends." I sulked.

"I think that is a great idea!" Mom said excitedly. "You can meet new people and maybe become friends with them too."

"The fact that Alli even has friends is a miracle, Mom," Greyson said. Dad gave him a look, but it wasn't intimidating enough in my opinion.

"Shut up, gremlin. Mom, its 10th grade; we're all pretty set in our ways. Plus, there aren't that many nice girls in my grade. I'm biased, but my friends are the best ones."

"Your friends are wonderful young women—"

Ugh, she used the saying "young women" again. It makes me cringe when she calls us young women and young ladies. She makes us sound like we're thirty years old or something.

"—but you never know who you could meet. Branching out is a great thing. You guys have been together for ten plus years. Making new friends doesn't mean you're going to be replacing your old ones."

"Zoey Mooring's locker is near mine now; maybe she can help me pierce my belly button like hers."

Dad nearly choked on his drink, Mom paused mid-bite with a petrified look on her face, and Greyson's eyes popped out of his head.

"I'm just kidding guys, sheesh."

"You better be," Dad said sternly, wiping his mustache with a napkin.

After we finished supper—lasagna, it's tradition for the first day of school—I was allowed to head to the park that was two blocks from my house. I love how close all my friends live to me. It's very convenient when it comes to hanging out since we can't drive yet.

I can't wait until I get my license and we have more freedom from our parents. Don't get me wrong, I abso-

lutely love my parents and I really don't mind hanging out with them; however, I don't like having to rely on them and plan my life around their schedules. I'm ready to get past that stage.

I was the second one there; Chelsea beat me. Everyone else wasn't far behind except for Rose. There were kids playing on the playground, so we went over to the swings and hung out there. There were actually a lot of people at the park right now. Some kids were shooting hoops, others were playing catch with a football, and the rest of the people were all on the playground shrieking and yelling.

"Oh my gosh, did you *see* what Kendra was wearing today? I can't believe she wasn't forced to change into her gym clothes. I could never get away with wearing that skirt; teacher's pet much?" Chelsea started immediately once I was in ear shot. She was scrolling on her phone, so I figured she was looking at Kendra's Instagram.

"Why don't you try wearing your mini shorts tomorrow?" I asked.

Chelsea scoffed at the ridiculous yet obvious solution with which she was presented. "Please, I would get caught so quickly and I would be mortified if I had to wear my gym clothes all day," she said in her defense.

"I mean, you could wear them to the football games that are coming up. It's after school hours, and they can't dictate what you wear then," Evelynn chimed in, pleased with her idea.

We all nodded in agreement. Chelsea shrugged, but looked like she was considering it.

"Forget what Kendra was wearing, though, Silas and Jayla are back together again! Seriously, this is like the fourth time they have broken up and gotten back together. They're not meant to be, they're just not. I'm telling you. He needs to dump her and be done with her!" Hayden was letting her jealousy show, although she's not great at being subtle any-way.

"Hayden, come on, Silas is not going to dump Jayla for good, we all know that. You're the only one holding out hope. She's going to string him along like she always has until she either gets bored or finds a senior to hook up with, and even then I'm sure he'll continue to take her back," Evelynn bluntly stated.

"I wish you didn't have a thing for Silas," I spoke up. "Remember what he did back in 7th grade to Miranda?"

"I'm sure he's not the same guy he was in middle school, Alli," Hayden said with a defensive tone.

"Some people can change, but he's been a jerk for-ever. I don't think he's going to be changing anytime soon."

Rose arrived and we were glad to change the sub-ject from Silas and Jayla to anything else. We started talking more about our teachers and what we've heard about their classes. I mentioned how geometry was going to be the death of me, but Evelynn was there to remind us about our upcoming study night sessions.

Our group chat turned into mini group chats as we branched off and talked about the classes we have with each other. I was able to have Rose to myself. Hayden was nearby, but she was kind of a "division line" between the two little groups.

"Hey guess what?" I said to Rose but kept my voice almost to a whisper. Her eyebrows raised in interest, but she didn't need to ask anything for me to continue. "I pulled out my elementary photos and sure enough he was in our 3rd grade class."

"See. I knew he was." She chuckled.

"Who?" Hayden chimed in. I was thankful that she kept her voice quiet to go along with ours.

"William Mantel is in Alli's French class this year," Rose stated in a factual manner to Hayden.

"Oh Will? Yeah, he's a really nice guy. He was in my science class last year and we were partners for a couple group projects," Hayden informed us. "I saw him today while we were passing in the hallway. I barely recognized him. He waved at me, and I thought he was waving to somebody behind me, but he wasn't." She laughed. "I looked and there was nobody there. I told him I didn't recognize him, and he said that he has gotten that a lot today. Then we wished each other a good day and kept going in the directions we were headed," she finished.

"He did mention that he likes weightlifting, football, and basketball," I continued, intrigued to see if Hayden could tell me any more about Will.

No, I like William better than Will. Will is too common for me.

"Don't get him started on the debate between Michael Jordan and LeBron James. Will doesn't usually talk much in class, but that is something that really got him going from what I remember." Hayden chuckled at the memory.

Rose and I looked at each other with wide eyes, and then back to Hayden, unaware that she spoke basketball, let alone NBA.

She laughed at our amusement. "What? Will and I talked a lot about basketball last year. I was bound to pick up a little bit. I can't quote the stats like he can, but I can name more than just those two players if you would like me to."

"What are you guys talking about?" Chelsea and Evelynn joined our conversation again.

"Basketball," I quickly chimed in, hoping they wouldn't mention William at all.

"NBA specifically," Hayden said.

"What about the NBA?" Evelynn asked.

"Just that Michael Jordan has six championships with the Chicago Bulls and averaged 30.12 points per game in the regular season," Hayden said proudly.

She made Chelsea's and Evelynn's jaws drop. Rose, Hayden, and I laughed.

"What the?!" Chelsea asked, shocked as ever. "You speak basketball? Who are you?"

Hayden just shrugged nonchalantly, enjoying the surprise she was able to bestow on her friends. It was glorious.

"Don't forget, Michael Jordan also beat the aliens with Bugs Bunny in *Space Jam* too!" Rose added, making us all giggle.

"The playground is clear; should we go and steal it now?" Hayden suggested.

"Last one there is a rotten egg!!" Chelsea yelled and we all took off running full speed to the stairs. We have a ritual that wherever we are, if that sentence gets yelled, the last person to arrive has to do the chicken dance.

CHAPTER 4

For the first time, I wasn't looking for Oliver on the front lawn before school. I was looking for William instead. Not in like, a stalker way per se, although I did look him up on every social media platform known to us. I didn't friend or follow him yet; I didn't want to be too creepy. Luckily, like most of the guys my age, I was able to view his profiles without having to be his friend first. I learned *a lot* about what he likes from Facebook; for example, he's really big into sports. I wasn't shocked, but I didn't want to assume either. He likes the Chiefs for football and Royals for baseball.

Makes sense considering where we live. For hockey though, I found out he likes the New Jersey Devils. *Mental note to ask how a New Jersey team became of interest to him.*

His favorite comedian seems to be Kevin Hart, but he likes stand-up comedy in general. He had a few videos of skits that people had posted to his wall because they thought of him when they watched it. He "liked" them and made little responses like, "lol," "that's funny," and "that's not me, that's you bro." He likes *How I Met Your Mother* and *The Office*, both series that I have never seen, but I'm always open to new suggestions!

He didn't have many profile pictures. The ones he did have were of him leaning against a few cars, some photos of him and his buddies, and him and a chocolate lab (that's his current profile picture on all his social medias). Looking through the photos he has been tagged in, there seems to be one brunette that has been in his life for a while. The pictures of them go back to them as babies (well, at least back to elementary days). Whoever she is, they're close; she's touching him in all their photos.

I didn't see him on the front lawn with my friends. Luckily me being in my own world and zoning out is a very "Allison" thing to do. I didn't hear the bell ring, but I felt Hayden tug on my arm to get my attention. I looked over at her, and she nodded her head in the direction of the front door where the student body was filing toward. I picked up my purple bag that I've had since fifth grade off the grass and joined my friends.

We separated immediately to go to our lockers. I spun my combination, but I didn't feel confident about having it accurately remembered. Last night I was trying to memorize it while I was lying in bed waiting for sleep to take over, but between replaying French class and trying to memorize my combination, I did not sleep well.

Evelynn so sweetly let me know my tiredness was showing through the minimal makeup I wear. *And by sweet, I mean she said, "Allison, did you stay up all night watching Netflix or something? You look dead."*

"Thanks." She was driving us to school as we talked about the appearance of my face. "I had trouble falling asleep like usual." Which was the truth, and my friends all know I struggle with falling asleep. My mom always told me I have an overactive imagination.

Chelsea told us the dream she had as well. It's one we've heard a few times, but it always makes me smile when she tells it. "I already dreamt I was climbing the rope ladder in gym and my shorts fell off while I was wearing my thong that says Friday, but it was really Monday, and I mooned the entire school!!"

We all laughed because this dream of hers has been recurring throughout the school years, ever since elementary when they introduced the rope. I was just thankful she took the spotlight off me and my outer appearance so we could focus on her inner brainwaves for the rest of the ride to school.

I was anticipating fifth period during periods one through four. When lunch hit, I barely spoke. I was trying to calm my inner self for being nervous, while chastising myself for feeling the way I'm currently feeling. Again, I don't have a crush on him. Yeah, he's very attractive and honestly, I can even say he's hot, but I just met him yesterday!!

Get it together. Focus on what your friends are saying. Rose is speaking about drama class and the upcoming play that she wants to audition for, which is great for her. Nod Allison. Nod. Okay, now drop a "for sure" here so that you're engaging. Good. Good job. Okay Hayden is talk—oh my gosh, there he is!

Before I could stop my brain and eyeballs, they were following him to the trash bin where he dumped his tray of food and put his tray on the conveyor belt for the lunch ladies to wash. I visually followed him back to his seat and realized I was familiar with the people in his friend group. I've had a few classes with all of them, just never with William.

Aww, William must have said something funny because he and his friends are all laughing! I wonder if—

"Sky!" Evelynn was snapping her fingers in front of my face, bringing me back to reality and our table where my friends were staring at me either amused or befuddled. "What the heck are you staring at?!" Evelynn almost demanded.

"I think it's who she's staring at instead, Ev," Chelsea added. I started to blush, giving myself away.

Fantastic, it's only day two and I haven't even talked to him yet, and now I'm busted.

"It's just Oliver. He's at the table next to the spirit poster," Chelsea said in a rather disappointed tone. "Can we take bets on if she will talk to him this year or not?"

I breathed a sigh of relief. I can't believe I hadn't noticed Oliver.

My friends started to place their bets, and I rolled my eyes. Whether they were serious or not, I couldn't quite tell. Rose and Hayden were generous and said I would talk to him within the first two months, whereas Evelynn said not until after the winter formal, and Chelsea of course doesn't think I ever will. She and Evelynn started to go down a rabbit hole at my expense, joking about what kind of scenarios it would take for me to gather the courage needed to speak to Oliver. They also were joking about starting a podcast and having me as a guest and then inviting Oliver to be a surprise guest speaker. That led them to talking about starting a dating podcast and, luckily, we can usually leave it to those two to change the subject and focus their attention on our classmates and who they would like to set up and who they would like to break up.

They were still discussing who would be on their imaginary podcast they'll never create when we finished our lunches. I was trying very hard not to glance over at where William was sitting, and it took a lot more concentration than I expected it to. As I watched the clock tick its way down to dismissing us, I felt something in my stomach. It wasn't anxiety—because believe me, I know what anxiety feels like—this was excitement, anticipation, and butterflies all at once. For fifty-five minutes, I was going to get to sit next to this hot guy and none of my friends would be able to see how often I look at him!

Come on, bell, just ding already. Who knew I would start wishing for class to start?

I beat him to our classroom and eagerly took my seat. The second day of school isn't *quite* as awkward as the first, but it's still up there. As the students filed in, the escalation of chatter went up. It doesn't matter that we have known each other since elementary, it's like the secret code to not speak to each other on the first day unless you're best friends. Bonnie was sitting behind me. We probably wouldn't hang out outside of class, but we're more than bodies that fill a seat, but less than friends. If that makes sense?

"So, third year in a row together, Alli, what are the odds?" she asked me rhetorically.

I chuckled with my response to her, "It is pretty crazy that you, me, Tyler, and Serenity have had all these classes together. I mean, in comparison, the percentage of students taking Spanish and French is probably 70 to 30. There are a couple of classmates here I've never had French with, and of course those two freshmen over there who are advanced somehow. They're probably going to make me look stupid."

Bonnie thankfully laughed in response to my wit which made me feel good. "Right?! Little show-offs."

William appeared and took his seat next to me. *Dang, I missed him coming into the room.* Bonnie caught me off guard when she said his name aloud. "Like Will here." This made me look at him and he looked at us in a questioning manner.

"What about me?" he asked Bonnie but looked between the both of us.

"Oh, Alli and I were just saying how few people take French class, and yet, she and I have had class together for three years now, but we've never had it with you."

He looked at me, and I was naturally just staring at him like a bimbo not saying a word. I did manage to smile at him though and nodded my head in agreement with what she said. He gave a small, cute side smile my way and nodded his head saying that it was strange.

Mrs. Lamb came into the classroom, clearly having just finished her lunch as she wiped what I really, *really* hoped was mustard from her lips.

"Alright, guys and gals, welcome back to day two of French III. I am very happy to see I haven't scared anybody away yet. I figured we would take today and see what you guys know about French culture. You're going to draw a minimum of five items that you feel depict France. Now, keep in mind, you need to be respectful when doing this. This project isn't about being funny, it's about truly seeing how Americans view France from our standpoint. I'm going to pass out the paper you will use to draw on. This is not art class, so do not be shy if your drawings aren't perfect. This is fun! I do recommend starting with a pencil first, but I have crayons, markers, and colored pencils up here as well. You have the entire class period to draw and color. Tomorrow though, you all will present your portraits! If you don't finish during class, you'll need to finish at home."

Bonnie raised her hand and Mrs. Lamb called on her.

"Are we allowed to use our phones while drawing?"

"Yes, you may."

I started thinking immediately what I could draw to symbolize France. I have a better chance of winning the lottery than becoming an artist, so I can't choose anything that is too difficult like Notre Dame. She's gorgeous, sure, but I would try to perfect it and I did not have the time nor the patience for that.

Everyone is probably going to draw the Eiffel Tower, so I don't want to draw that. Hmmm, what else do I know that screams France? Oh! The French flag! Duh.

I started drawing the flag as more ideas rolled through my head; a baguette with cheese, wine, the pink panther, the Fleur de Lis, and the candle that talks from *Beauty and the Beast.*

Lumiere, that's his name!

I glanced over to see what William was drawing. Sure enough, it resembled the Eiffel Tower, but ummm, something looked a little off about his version of it. I think he sensed me looking at his drawing because his perfect head of hair turned my way, and we locked eyes.

Say something, Alli. He's staring at you . . . you need to say something, like NOW!

"What is that?" I asked bluntly and rather rudely, I thought.

Smooth, way to sound like a jerk immediately!!

"It's the Eiffel Tower, can't you tell?" he asked, looking a little bummed at my question.

I need to redeem myself!

"It looks like a misshapen A. Also, she has four legs, I think you only drew three." I mentally punched myself in the face. *I cannot believe I just said that. I just made fun of his attempt at drawing the iconic symbol of France.*

William looked back down at his three-legged tower and chuckled in amusement at my unfriendly first remarks. Relief flooded over me, and I cracked a smile and started laughing with him.

"You're right. I completely forgot the fourth leg! Okay, so I'm not an architect. What are you drawing then?" I showed him what I had drawn so far, and his eyebrows raised in surprise. "Oh, wow. Those are way better ideas than what I have," he said laughing.

I shrugged nonchalantly, acting like he didn't just set the butterflies loose in my stomach with that compliment. "What are you drawing right now?" he asked, curious about my work.

"It's going to be the candle from *Beauty and the Beast*," I answered.

"Nice. Ummm, what's his name?" he asked out loud, but thinking to himself.

"Lumiere," I said with pride.

"Yeah, he's the one. I like him, he's funny." He smiled, and I smiled back at our conversation and the direction it was heading.

"Do you like Disney movies?" I asked him, really hoping he was going to say yes and not think it is childish. It wouldn't be a deal breaker of course, but that would stink. I noticed I was holding my breath a little before he answered.

"Only crazy people don't like Disney. They're the classics of our generation."

I wanted to clap out of sheer joy! I remembered where we were and the fact we basically just met. Instead, I wanted to learn more about his taste in Disney, and just his taste in general. I already Facebook stalked him, so I needed to be *very* careful with what I said.

"What's your favorite movie? Disney movie, well any movie. What do you enjoy watching?" *Solid. Typical Alli, one question turned into multiple.* I looked down at the ground a little embarrassed again. When I looked back up, though, he was smiling gently.

"*Hercules*, no question." It was his turn to be confident and proud of his answer. "Yours?"

"*Lion King*. It has the most powerful ending and a lot of life messages that we can apply to our lives I feel." *I'm such a nerd.* He took my reasons into consideration and nodded his head. He said *Lion King* was his second favorite.

"Which Disney princess would you like to be?" His question surprised me and had me thinking for a moment.

I've never been able to pick between Pocahontas and Belle. I let out a puff of air that he took as a challenge. He chuckled again, and my ears liked the sound.

"Okay, so here's the deal," I began. This made him laugh out loud, and I was smiling in response already. "I love Belle for her intelligence and her unwillingness to settle for Gaston. She doesn't like him for his looks; she wants someone with a brain, not just brawn, and that's really admirable. She's also the only Disney princess that they actually made to be older than a teenager, which is cool. However, Pocahontas is such a free spirit and I really admire that about her as well!! She is one hundred percent herself and unwilling to change for anybody. She wants to live her own life even though she isn't sure what she wants out of it. She's not looking for love, but love finds her." He was smiling and I was giddy about explaining my reasons. "Oh also! She has Grandmother Willow. We all need a Grandmother Willow in our lives," I finished.

"Well said!" Bonnie chimed in. She made me jump on the inside because I forgot there were other people in the room with us.

"Which princess would you be?" I asked him, making the now three of us laugh out loud.

He looked like he was thinking about it. He said Mulan, and he made a pretty solid case I thought.

"She's straight up a badass. She goes to war in her father's place knowing that she could die either in battle or be killed for impersonating a man," he explained.

Go to war in my family member's place. Noted!

Mrs. Lamb came over to where we were talking and reminded us that we needed to be focusing on France, not China. Bonnie went straight back to coloring, and I looked over at William, who was looking at me. He did something that was so subtle yet stuck with me. He turned back to his drawing, but now he brought up his other hand and drew in hiding so I couldn't see any more of it. I snickered to myself and stored the memory away. I got back to work on my own drawing and about finished when our teacher told us to wrap up and be prepared to present our pages tomorrow. I just need to finish coloring my pink panther tonight.

The bell rang and we gathered our backpacks like clockwork. Yesterday he and I went opposite ways, but I needed to go to my locker quick. Out of the excitement of heading to lunch, I realized that I grabbed the wrong notebook. Instead of grabbing my geometry notebook I grabbed my history one. We walked out of the door (he let me go first like a gentleman). I thought we would separate once we hit the main hallway, but we didn't. As we continued walking together, we made small talk.

"What do you have next?" he asked me.

"Oh, I have geometry unfortunately. I accidentally grabbed the wrong notebook though. What about you?"

"I'm headed to English."

"You get to go from French to English? That seems kind of nice. You go from trying to speak a language you don't know, to a language that is natural." I smiled at him.

He shrugged in response. "It's a little easier I guess, but our English language is ... well there's just way too much going on with it. They should have made it simpler. Like they had one chance, and now it's one of the most complex languages in the entire world."

I liked his sense of humor, but I also shared his annoyance too. *I wonder if French people think their language is over-complicated like we do?*

I noticed I was almost to my locker when I realized he and I were still walking next to each other.

On cue, he turned to his right and started spinning a combination.

How did I not put two and two together?! Of course, our lockers are right next to each other. My last name is Manex and his is Mantel!

I started to spin my combination next to his. He looked over at me and laughed, realizing that for the first two days neither of us had seen the other at our locker. *At least, I think that's what he was thinking.*

He shut his locker, and I shut mine. We talked about how they changed the locker assignments and which elementary schools we each went to. He brought up how he went to Northwest Elementary until third grade, then transferred to East Elementary because his parents moved houses. I played dumb as if I didn't know we spent third grade together. Instead, I told him I too went to Northwest Elementary and wondered if we had had any classes together.

"Hmmm, I don't know," he said.

Clearly I was the only one looking through my old yearbooks last night then.

We didn't talk for long because I had to go to the math wing, and he turned to head down the language arts hallway. We said goodbye to each other, but I now looked forward to returning to my locker and hopefully run into him again.

CHAPTER 5

I turned my key and walked into the empty house, took my shoes off, and headed upstairs to my bedroom. I slung my backpack off my shoulder and let it thud against the floor. Normally, like the cool person I am, I would start doing homework immediately so that it's done and out of the way. Instead, I crawled onto my bed, laid on my back, and stared up at my ceiling thinking about William.

I thought about his laugh and his attractive half smile that he's shown me. I pictured his posture and how he tends to check the clock about every fifteen minutes. He seemed like an amazing person. He had this presence around him that was drawing me in.

That's a deep statement to think about after a few days of just seeing him. You've only talked for one class period. I know, it just . . . it just feels—I don't know. I can't even describe to myself how this thing with him feels different . . . special . . . right.

I pulled myself out of the *what if* scenarios I was creating in my head about him. I got out my French drawing so I could finish coloring in my pink panther. It wasn't much of a distraction, however. The entire time I colored, I thought about him more and how I want to learn more about him. I want to learn the deep things about him, not just his favorite color, but like, his faith, his family, his dreams, his goals, what he wants to do after high school. I want to know it all! What makes him tick, what makes him angry, what makes him feel better when he's sad?

You're going to have to step up your game and maybe get his number if you want to learn all of this. How the heck am I going to do that though?!

The rest of my night went by quickly. I read a little for fun. Talked with my parents at supper, and then scrolled through social media where I encountered another conflict . . . adding him.

Is it too soon? How long should I wait? Does he check social media much? It doesn't appear that he really posts very often, but it's hard to tell. What if he doesn't accept my friend request? That would be humiliating! Yup, I better wait a little bit longer before anything. That sounds safer.

I decided not to send any friend requests tonight. Instead, I went to bed early so tomorrow would come faster.

It took me three times as long to get dressed this morning than it normally does. It took me twice as long to do my hair (which I still just decided on a half up-half down hairstyle). As far as makeup, I settled on mascara and a hint of eye liner. I get frustrated doing any eye makeup, so I went for the simple look, only messing up four times before I thought it looked okay enough for the public's viewing.

I don't want to be the person that wishes my life away. I don't want to only look forward to the weekends or when school is over, and I can go home. I want to enjoy my life one day at a time because I've always been told that I need to enjoy my youth, and I'm starting to believe it.

I looked back on how quickly the first ten years of school went for me.

I'm in 10th grade now, I have three years left of mandatory schooling. Three years of getting to hang out with my friends, being as carefree as we want to be. Three years before we have to decide what we're supposed to do with the rest of our lives, so we don't waste our time and money at college. Three years of living with my family, as annoying as they can be at times. Three years = 1,095 days. One thousand days seems like a lot, but when I think about how I've already gone through ten years of school before now, where did that time go?

That's something my parents say a lot too, "Where did the time go?" They say it at every birthday or every special event we celebrate. I don't want my time to just disappear—I want to go with it. I don't want to blink and have it be gone and my brain barely remember what happened. I want to be present for my life.

Now with that internal speech being over, I want fifth period to get here already! I'm sitting in second period doing what I just told myself not to do. I'm watching the clock tick, tick, tick its way around and around, slower and slower.

No offense to plants, like I'm very grateful they give us oxygen and they have to endure photosynthesis unlike humans, but I. Do. Not. Care. I want to learn about French culture. I want to be sitting next to him, "watching" the clock behind his silky, brown hair, while "accidentally" making eye contact every now and then.

I blushed to myself thinking about him. *Okay, get a grip, you're blushing for no reason and you're going to make people think you're even weirder than you already are.*

I focused my attention back on what my teacher was saying. I could feel my brain start drifting again, so I started taking notes like crazy. I was writing everything down, just to stay present. There were still twenty minutes left. I attempted to draw everything that was on the whiteboard next—anything to distract my mind from being distracted.

Finally, lunch time.

As appetizing as Surprise Sloppy Joes sounded, my stomach was starting to twist with anxiety.

Naturally my eyes scanned the crowd while I was waiting in line to get my food, but I didn't see him. I looked out into the crowd where I saw him sitting the other day. His friends were there, but he wasn't.

Maybe he's in the lunch line somewhere?

I fought every muscle in my body that wanted to turn around and look to see if he's somewhere behind me. I kept looking straight ahead at Chelsea. She was talking about something; I just smiled and made the correct facial expressions I needed to as I tried to piece together whatever it was she was telling me.

"So, I was like, no way am I going to do that. That's not fair! But Mrs. Brown was all, 'No Chelsea, you need to be a team player. If most of the group wants to do a 70s theme to your video, you need to include yourself. If you don't, I'll be forced to dock points from your grade.' A wig, Alli, they want me to wear a wig that Trina's grandma wore back in the day. Ugh, I am so disgusted! Wouldn't you be?!"

Gross. That wig has probably been locked in an attic since the 70s. "Eww." I wrinkled my nose in agreement. "I definitely would not want to wear somebody else's wig, family or not."

"Exactly!" Chelsea continued venting as I tried to focus on her and everything she was saying.

We got our food and found our table. Once we sat down, I looked over at his table and sure enough, there he was. He looked so natural and almost even . . . cool.

Alli, he's literally eating a sloppy joe. The Queen herself couldn't make eating this surprise goopy-meat sandwich cool.

"Ugh! Our first home football game and it's against Jefferson." One of Chelsea's friends, Kelsey, was eating lunch with us. She's okay. I don't think

I could ever hang out with her one on one, but she's decent enough to be around.

"Are they good this year?" sweet Rose, who has never been interested in sports, asked Kelsey.

Kelsey looked at Chelsea as if Rose just asked what country we're in. I could already tell that Rose wished she hadn't said anything considering the incredulous look Kelsey was not trying to hide.

"Are they good?! What, are you new here?? They're always good! They always beat us, and they have won the championship back-to-back! Yes . . . they are good," she ended with a sarcastic tone.

I was a little annoyed that Chelsea didn't say anything for Rose, so instead I did. "Well, maybe if we start throwing the ball instead of always trying to run it, we might actually gain some more yardage. Luckily though, none of us are coaches and aren't qualified to make those calls."

That quieted her down enough to have Evelynn take over the conversation. "Well, whoever we're playing, we're going to look stylish doing it! It's a blackout game, so I figured we could pick up shirts to decorate. We can do this at my house tonight or tomorrow. What would work for everyone?"

We all agreed to do it tonight. Evelynn wants this to become a tradition for us. The first home game equals making personal shirts. We'll go to her house, do our homework first—AKA, lay all our books and notebooks out to make it appear we're doing homework, when really, we're researching ideas on designs. Afterwards, we'll eat pizza and then decorate.

We did something very similar to this last year and it was fun. As sophomores, we'll get to move up a section in our student seating. Seniors get the front, then juniors, sophomores, and freshmen are in the very back. Fights have broken out between students before because of this seating arrangement. I would blame it on testosterone, but the girls can be just as crazy, if not worse at times.

Rose won't be able to come over tonight. Evelynn volunteered to make her shirt for her, and Rose was fine with that. The fall musical is going to be here before we know it. The drama club always seems to be behind on everything too. From the way Rose describes it, it sounds super stressful. The decorations rip and tear. Wardrobes aren't close to being finished because somebody keeps measuring wrong, and the lead actors never feel confident enough with their lines until opening night if they're lucky.

Rose has never been the lead in a play, but that's okay. We go and support her anyway. This year they're going to be doing a Nicholas Sparks book, *A Walk to Remember*. Rose says she's glad she isn't the lead because Miranda, who is going to be playing the lead role, will be performing a solo song, and Rose does not want to sing.

She doesn't have stage fright as far as screaming, crying, or dying on stage, but singing is one thing she does not want to do in front of the crowd. I don't blame her; I think it all sounds pretty intense. Our drama students don't get enough support or credit in my little opinion.

The girls and I were brainstorming some creative T-shirt ideas already. It's supposed to be decent weather so that's good for us. If it were going to rain, there wouldn't be any point in wearing them. I guess Kelsey is going to join us. Like I said, she's okay; she's just not someone I want to hang out with alone.

Lunch kept my mind from wandering too far with fake conversations I may or may not have during my next class. We were presenting the drawings we worked on in class yesterday. I finished mine last night with the help of the internet. I may or may not have traced a couple of things from the computer screen for assistance.

Hey, I'm not an idiot. I didn't trace the Mona Lisa considering I can't even draw realistic looking food. I traced some food, the flag blowing, and touched up the pink panther that I didn't finish during class.

Ding. Ding. Ding signals the bell to end the lunch period, and it reminds us we still have half of the school day left to complete. My friends groan, but I don't mind. I'm a little nervous right now. Granted I have to present my less-than-mediocre artistic skills and public speak in front of peers. It's not even regular public speaking, it's literally in a foreign language which makes it even more freaky!

Everyone is feeling the same way you are, Alli. You're not judging them, are you? No. Then they're not judging you. I like to think that, even though the doubt still rises from my stomach into my chest with zero remorse.

Do I wait for him? Is it too soon? Is he going to his locker? Am I being a stalker? I decided to head straight to French class. I don't want to risk seeming creepy. Plus, what if I walked with him and it was pure silence because I couldn't think of anything to say, and he didn't want to talk to me? *Nope! I'm going straight to class!*

I was the second one in the classroom, with Bonnie following closely behind me. She sat down behind me and started chatting immediately.

"How did yours turn out?"

"Ugh. It's okay, I guess. How about yours?" I ask politely, watching the door from my peripheral vision.

"Mine is terrible! Like, I'm SO embarrassed I'm going to have to present this in front of everyone! Can I see yours?"

I shrugged and said sure. I unrolled mine and laid it on my desk so she could see it.

"Oh wow!! Yours is good, Alli! I didn't know you were so good at drawing food in particular. That makes me a little hungry even looking at it," Bonnie complimented.

Since she asked to see mine, I thought it only fair for me to ask back, "Can I see yours?"

"Okay, but it's nowhere near as good as yours is, so don't make fun of it okay?"

"I won't," I assured her.

Bonnie unraveled hers as I rolled mine back up and put the rubber band around it. I saw a figure take their seat next to me and realized William had just gotten here. I think I stared at him with a dumb expression on my face, but he smiled politely and said hi.

Do you know what I did? Do you think I was normal and just said hi back? NO!

Instead of speaking like a human, I felt my throat catch, so I didn't want to have a squeaky voice. I attempted to wave at him and ended up knocking over my notebook, pencil case, and poster just as Lincoln came walking by. My poster caught between his feet, and he accidentally stepped on it. Luckily, I had it rolled inward, so he didn't step on the actual art side, just the blank back side, crushing it.

I'll always be able to remember what his shoe size was from the print it left. He immediately started apologizing. I tried assuring him it wasn't his fault at all. He bent down to pick it up for me. Naturally, I bent forward to pick up my marked poster as well . . . BONK! Our foreheads hit and we both straightened up immediately, rubbing our heads. I was so embarrassed!

Lincoln stepped over it and sat down at his desk. Bonnie was laughing hysterically along with some of our other classmates. William bent down and picked up my drawing, handing it to me with a sympathetic smile.

Mrs. Lamb quieted down the classroom and asked Lincoln and me if either of us needed to get an ice pack from the nurse.

I need to crawl under a rock is what I need to do.

We both said we were fine, and she took that as her cue to get started since there were twenty posters to get through. She asked if there were any volunteers. I felt the wind from the hand behind me shoot into the air.

"Alright Bonnie, you're up first. Show us what you drew and speak in as much French as you can. Tell us what your items are, the colors you used, and why you chose that item to represent France. Go ahead whenever you're ready."

Bonnie went to the front of the class, turned her poster toward the class, and my mouth dropped open. It was really good! I didn't know Bonnie was such an artist; granted, I don't know her really at all. Great, she's one of those people that are incredible at what they do and yet, they don't realize it. Or worse, they fake they're not good at it for compliments. I'm not saying that's what Bonnie was doing, I just know people do that and it's annoying. Anyway, the class admired her work, and she received a very strong applause for her poster and her incredible French accent.

Yeahhhh, I am not following her presentation, no way.

"Okay, who wants to go next?" Silence. "Anybody?" Crickets. "No volunteers then?" It stayed quieter than a cemetery. "Allison, you're up then!"

Of course, I am. With the way my luck is going, my poster will probably spontaneously combust, and I'll burn the school down.

I took a deep breath and tried to calm my nerves before I took the two steps to stand in front of everyone. *Don't look at him, don't look at him, don't look at him,* I repeated over and over to myself.

Well, neither my poster nor I spontaneously combusted, so I consider that a win for today. I also didn't look at William until the very end when I was finishing. I'm glad I waited; his facial expression was very serene, and I wasn't expecting it. It made me feel better. I took my seat and looked over at him. We made eye contact, and I did a silent, but exasperated exhale. He snickered quietly to himself.

People started volunteering after Mrs. Lamb called on two more victims. William was the last one for today. We had two more students to go, but we'll finish them tomorrow. His poster was cute, which I'm sure every guy would hate for us to verbally say. He added a fourth leg to his Eiffel Tower, and he just drew it on so that it was there. He didn't erase anything or try to perfect the fourth leg. You could tell it was out of place, but it was perfect to me. He also counted all the legs in French and stared at me directly when he did. I'm pretty sure I blushed. This felt like an inside joke between us. If it's possible, I think my heart even blushed.

The bell rang, dismissing us once again to go our separate ways, except we weren't going separate ways today.

"Are you putting your poster in your locker?" he asked me as we walked side by side down the crowded hallway.

"Yeah, are you?" I asked back.

"Yeah, I can't risk anybody stepping on it, you know?" He chuckled my way, and I couldn't help but laugh with him. This felt like a second inside joke. *Two in one day? Wow!* I was glad to see he felt comfortable enough to be joking with me.

"I figured the next thing to happen to my poster would be for it to spontaneously combust and burn the entire school down," I half-heartedly joked, but internally I was serious.

"And that would be a bad thing?" he asked, raising his eyebrows.

"Would you like to be the one at fault for the school burning down?!"

"I think you would be considered a legend if that happened." He smiled at me.

"If I'm going to ever be a legend, I think I want it to be for a different reason," I sarcastically, but friendly, responded.

"What would you like to be known for, Alli?" he asked what I considered to be in all seriousness.

If there wasn't moving traffic around me, I would have frozen from the way he said my name. I stuttered over a question I have never thought about. Also, we just went from joking back and forth to what I considered to be a deep question.

Unless I'm overthinking this? Am I overthinking this? I should say something, though! Anything!

"Ummm . . . I . . . umm, I guess I'd like to be known for doing the right thing." *Seriously? That's what came out of my mouth. I want to be a decent person. Wow.*

"That's really cool," William responded.

"Wait, really?" I asked incredulously.

"Well yeah. Most people would say they want to be remembered for some talent they have or the money in their bank account, but you want to do what society needs—kindness."

I would have frozen still a second time from his response had it not been for the sea of people encircling us like sharks. My heart just swelled three sizes. I had no idea how to respond, so I asked him what he would like his legacy to be.

He shrugged saying, "I'm not really sure. I'd like to be true to myself, but I don't really know what that means yet. I can say living the life I want, but I don't really know what I want out of life yet either. Do you want to know a secret?"

I couldn't answer out loud, so I nodded my head, wanting to know what secret he wanted to share with me.

"I've never told anybody this, but I started doing some recordings of myself every year on my birthday. I might continue with those."

He piqued my interest.

Holy cow. There is so much more to this guy than what's on the surface. Video recordings? That is so neat!

"What do you talk about in your videos? When did you start this?"

We had arrived at our lockers when I asked him my questions. He chuckled and seemed a little bit embarrassed even. "Uh, I started these when I was thirteen, so I've only made a few so far. I don't really talk about anything important. I just talk about what is currently happening in my life and anything else that comes to mind really. I think it will be neat when I compile them all together one day."

"That will be really, cool! When do you think you'll do that?"

He shrugged again. He tends to shrug a lot, and he always looks down at the ground when he does it too. "I'm not sure yet. It'll probably be when I'm either bored one weekend, or when I'm retired and wanting to relive my youth. Who knows, though." He shut his locker as the warning bell dinged at us, letting us know we had two minutes to get to our next class or we were going to be tardy.

"Well, you should probably put your stuff away so you're not late to class. I'll see you tomorrow." He waved goodbye and turned around.

"Yeah, see ya!" I watched him walk away, already reliving the conversation we just had in my head.

A video of your own life, how incredible is that?! Maybe I should—Alli snap out of it. You need to get to class.

I quickly shut my brain off and turned my locker combination. I threw my poster in my locker, not caring that I just bent all the corners and smashed the middle. I presented it already and it's going in the recycling bin as soon as I get home anyway. I grabbed what textbooks and notebooks I needed for the rest of the day. After throwing them into my backpack, I slammed my locker shut and started walking as fast as I could to class without running. The bell rang, letting me know I did not make it to class on time. Luckily for me, my geometry teacher is cool and didn't count me tardy for being fifteen seconds late.

Throughout the rest of the day, I couldn't stop thinking about what I would record if I were to make little videos of myself as the years went on too.

What would I say? What would I want to talk about? What would I want to relive? What if other people saw it? Would I be okay with that?

My mind wandered through all of life's questions and answers that I have had up until now. I started replaying old memories in my head. I tried focusing on the good ones, but the bad ones crept in too. *Nope. I would not talk about bad memories. I would focus on the good ones!*

The school bell rang once more, dismissing us. We exploded through the school doors like fireworks. We're still going to Evelynn's tonight, but she was going to run to the store and buy us all our black shirts to make sure we match completely.

I needed to go home first anyway. I needed to check in with my parents, answer their daily question of, "How was school?" with the same answer I give every day in response: "It was fine." It'll be a tradition between parent and child until the end of time.

Once home, I kicked off my shoes onto the rug we wouldn't keep organized for Mom and dropped my backpack next to the staircase. She was in the kitchen talking with Dad. They both turned and smiled at me. "How was your day, sweetie?" Mom asked on cue as if a director had said "action" for a movie.

Now it was my turn to shrug as I grabbed a Pepsi from the fridge. "It was fine." This answer never suffices parents, but my parents have never been pushy people.

"Can I go over to Evelynn's to work on homework and make a T-shirt for this Friday's game?"

"Depends," Dad spoke up now. "Which one are you going to do first?"

"Homework of course," I responded, smiling, saying the answer every parent would want to hear. They knew that too because they were grinning right back.

"Uh huh. Sure," Dad said. "Would you like a ride? I need to run to the grocery store anyway."

"That would be great. Thanks! I need to do something first though. Can we leave in like, fifteen minutes?"

"Yeah, that's fine. I'm going to jump in the shower quick." He stood up, kissed Mom, pointed at me, and headed toward the stairs.

I followed him obnoxiously closely because he hates that, and it makes me laugh every time. At the top of the stairs, you have to choose which direction to go immediately: left, straight, or right. He went left into his bedroom, and I turned right to go into mine. I set my can of pop down on my desk and pulled my phone out. I'm alone, but for some reason, I started getting a little self-conscious. I propped my phone against the lamp that sits on top of my desk. I opened my camera, checked my hair, teeth, nose, and hair again, and then pressed Record.

"Hi, I'm Allison Manex . . . oh I guess that's obvious. I heard about this cool idea from a guy at school named William Mantel. He does this thing where he records himself, so in however many years, he can look back and see where he was in life. I think it's a really incredible idea so I figured I would maybe start this tradition as well . . . soooo let's begin."

CHAPTER 6

I went to my locker before heading to my first class. I noticed William also came to his locker this morning. I finished and decided to turn toward him. My heart rate started to increase, but I was going to do this regardless.

"Hey!" I tried to keep it casual and cool, but my voice squeaked a little from excitement.

"Hey. How's it going?" William smiled and asked in a tone cooler than mine that I hoped to mirror back.

I shrugged at him since he does it nonchalantly all the time. "Oh, you know, same stuff different day."

He smiled at that response, which made my insides warm up a little more. I could feel it creeping up onto my cheeks. I tried to keep any hint of blushing away from him.

"How's it going with you?" I asked back politely, wanting him to do the talking so I wouldn't get tongue-tied and flustered.

"Same. I have history first, well, Homeroom and then history. What do you have?"

"English. Nothing like a little Shakespeare to start the excitement of the day. It's basically a foreign language in itself."

"Well, considering how great of a French speaker you are, I can only imagine you're even better at speaking Shakespearian." He chuckled my way.

"Are you going to the football game Friday night?" *Oh. My. Gosh. Did I seriously just blurt that at him?*

"I'm sorry. I didn't mean to change the subject so abruptly. I guess I'm not great at English either." I gave a pathetic chuckle in the hopes to save any face I had left since mine was starting to get hot from embarrassment.

"Nah, you're good. My buddies and I love football, so we go to every game whether it's home or away. How about you? Are you into football?" he asked as we started walking toward our Homerooms. Since I have English and he has history, we'll be walking the same way for a little bit.

"Yeah, football is cool. I will admit up front, though, I don't know a ton about it, but I do know that when our side yells or cheers, I need to yell or cheer too!" I laughed, being honest with him.

It made him laugh too, which I enjoyed even more than whatever it was that I just said that I forgot already because wow, look at those blue eyes! He laughed as he ran his fingers through his hair. This was the first time I saw his arm raise above his head, and his T-shirt sleeve shortened, exposing his bicep.

Holy. Crap. I don't know why that was such an attractive combination, but wow!

"I'm guessing you're going with your friends?" he asked as he lowered his arm back to his side.

I watched every movement he was making delicately.

Snap out of it!

"Uh, yeah, yeah I have friends." He arched his eyebrows at me, and I realized that wasn't exactly what he was asking me. "I mean . . . I have friends that I go to the football games with. Mmhmm."

Nice recovery . . . not.

"Cool. I figure it's the girls you eat lunch with, right?" he asked another question, but this time I was ready, or so I thought.

"You know where I eat? I mean, in comparison to the entire lunchroom, there's quite a few people. We eat at the same time, but uh, yeah, those are the girls that I eat lunch with and hang out with," I stuttered, tripping over my own tongue.

He only laughed which somehow made my cheeks heat up more, but he didn't make me feel stupid. "Nice. Hayden and I had science together last year. I think I saw you at the school plays too. My friend Morris is in theater."

"Yeah, my friend Rose has performed in all the school plays since elementary. We go and watch the fall and spring plays, so I'm sure it was me you saw. Do you guys go and watch Morris?" I asked, completely surprised by this.

"Just me, the other guys aren't really interested in that kind of thing," he said humbly.

"Supporting their friend kind of thing?" I was a little confused.

He shrugged of course. "Not really their kind of scene."

Boys.

"I suppose they're sticking to what they know, which is football. Am I right?" I asked, shifting the focus back to the upcoming game.

"You are right. Do you want to go together?" he asked me.

This time I literally stopped in my tracks. The guy behind me wasn't happy and hit my shoulder square on as he went around me grumbling.

I stared at William dumbfounded. "What?" I asked him.

I also remembered to put one foot in front of the other because I started moving again.

"I figured since you and your friends are going, we could make it a group thing and meet at the game. Only if you want, though, no pressure."

"Yeah totally," I managed to squeak out.

He smiled his genuine and warm smile. "Cool. I'll see you later." He turned toward his Homeroom, and I stared after him, watching the way his body moved with its own synchrony.

I can't believe I'm going to be sitting with him and his friends at a football game! Well, my friends and I . . . OH NO! Now I have to tell my friends about these plans I just made. What if they get mad and don't want to? What will I tell William? Should I not sit with my friends for one game? HA, no, that's not an option with Evelynn there.

I sit and stew about how I'm going to mention any of this to my friends without them immediately shooting me down, and without them thinking I'm crushing majorly.

I could text the group right now if I wanted, give them a heads up. Mmmm, orrrr, I could wait until lunch and talk to them in person. Nah I better text them.

Me:	Hey guys, I maybe changed our plans a teensy bit for this Friday's game. I'll explain more at lunch.
Chelsea:	Changed how?
Evelynn:	Any deets you could give us right now? You know I like to be prepared.
Hayden:	Sounds good, I'm down for anything!
Rose:	*read message at 8:17 AM*

Well, apparently everyone can check their phones in first period. I was not expecting that.

58

| **Me:** | I agreed for us to sit with a group of guys at the football game is all. |

Let's see if I can downplay this and not make anything a big deal.

Evelynn:	Ummm yes, I want to hear all these details as to who the guys are, who you're talking to etc. OMG is he a senior?!
Hayden:	*thumbs up emoji*
Chelsea:	Spill!!!
Rose:	*read message at 8:32 AM*
Me:	No, he's not a senior, none of them are. I'll explain later.
Chelsea:	At least tell us their names!!

I didn't. I left them hanging and put my phone on silent.

The morning dragged on partly because of me anticipating lunchtime with the girls, and because it's school and it's incredibly boring some days. I went through the lunch line with Rose. She didn't ask about tomorrow's plans, and I was thankful for that, only because then I would have to retell the story again and again by the time everyone arrived for lunch. Instead, we talked about our classes so far and what things teachers have said already that we find incredibly weird.

We sat down at our usual lunch spot, and I couldn't help but to glance over toward William's direction. He wasn't there yet, but a couple of his friends were. Hayden was already there nibbling away on her burger. She too didn't ask any questions, which I was thankful for.

"Alright, Sky, what are these plans you made that involve boys?" Chelsea excitedly set her tray down with a thud, whereas Evelynn glided gracefully into her chair.

Eight pairs of eyes all stared at me and suddenly I became clammy and nervous.

"Do you guys remember I mentioned how William Mantel is in my French class this year?"

Rose and Hayden nodded their heads, Evelynn said yes, and Chelsea said no. "Well, he asked if we wanted to sit with him and his friends at the game is all."

"Count me in, I don't care who we sit by as long as they're not annoying and asking me a lot of questions during it," Hayden spoke first.

"Well, I am always down to hang out with new guys!" We all chuckled at Chelsea's response because we knew she wouldn't be the one to object.

"What? I'm friendly enough," she said in defense, making us all laugh again with how *friendly* we know her to be with guys.

"Oh, yeah that's fine. That could be fun to have a large group at a football game, count Kyle and me in!" Evelynn said with more enthusiasm than I expected.

"I know Morris and Will," Rose, speaking last, stated. "They're pretty funny and super nice. I wouldn't mind hanging out with them either."

Apparently, I was holding my breath because I had to let it out long and silently. "Great, I will let William know when I see him next period!" I said, enthused.

I felt relieved and now I couldn't wait for tomorrow night to be here! The rest of the lunch period was basically gossip. Evelynn caught wind of what some of the other girls in our grade made for T-shirts and Chelsea already knew rumors about who was dating who this year, who broke up over summer, and what senior is supposedly hooking up with a freshman, etc. There was some pretty juicy news.

Naturally, I was the second student to class behind Bonnie. I sat down in front of her, and she immediately started talking about her day. I nodded and said, "Oh yeah," when it seemed the appropriate time. However, I wasn't really listening to her. I was more focused on the fact that I might be asking William for his phone number.

I should ask for it, right? If we're going to meet up, it would be nice to have direct communication in case I can't find him or something? I talked myself into it.

He came in through the door in his basketball shorts and black T-shirt with what I presume is a band that I've never heard of. He smiled at me and dropped his bag onto the ground with a hard thud.

"What do you have, a bag full of bricks?" Bonnie immediately questioned. She must have given up on talking about her day to me, or she finished, and I didn't notice. Either way, now that he was next to me, he was my focus.

"I think I'd rather be carrying those. I have some weights I need to drop off to someone next period," he explained.

I laughed at his answer of course. I think that was an appropriate response on my end. I hope so anyway. Bonnie laughed too, and then made some joke I didn't get, and it seemed like he didn't get the joke either. He was polite though and smiled at Bonnie.

Mrs. Lamb came in, again wiping god knows what off of her face.

She had us warm up by making us turn to the person across from us; in my case, William. We had to introduce ourselves, talk about the weather outside, the day of the week, month, and also what our plans were for the weekend.

He went first, introducing himself as Will, which makes me wonder if that's what I should call him. I like the sound of William. It's formal, but it doesn't sound old. It's not like Richard or George; those names sound old to me.

He spoke with fluency and ease, just as he did when he was presenting yesterday.

Maybe this is how I ask for his phone number? Maybe I should try and sneak my phone number in there, so that I can get his?! Mine turn to speak. "*Bonjour, je m'appelle Alli. Aujourd'hui, nous sommes le jeudi 10 Septembre. Vendredi, je regarderai le match de football américain avec William. J'ai ton numero de telephone?*" I finished and then stared at him, hoping he caught my final sentence. I know I stuttered over it, but I was hoping he caught the gist of what I said.

"What was that last part?" he asked, clearly not understanding.

Awesome, now I have to not only ask in English, but I have to explain what I attempted to say in a foreign language.

"I, uh, I was wondering if I could maybe get your phone number. You know, so I can text you when my friends and I get to the game. I think it would make it easier to find one another. It's totally fine if you don't want to give it to me, though! I'll find you eventually." I rushed the words out and inhaled one large breath.

"Oh, yeah, that's a good idea. Here." Without hesitation, William wrote down his phone number in the corner of his notebook paper. He tore it off and handed it to me freely.

Oh my gosh! He gave it to me. I don't think he was repulsed by me asking, either!

"Awesome!" I exclaimed, a little more enthused than I should have been.

Play it cooler Alli.

"I mean, sweet, thanks. I'll shoot you a text later, so you have my number too." I tried playing it off but couldn't hide anything. He laughed his genuine laugh and his eyes seemed to shine a little brighter to me. I tried to memorize the sight of his smile, but Mrs. Lamb drew my attention away.

I guess it's time to focus on reality instead of him.

Mrs. Lamb finished class about five minutes early. She couldn't dismiss us, because that's against school policy. Instead, she said we could talk to each other in French, or pull our phones out.

Obviously, we pulled our phones out.

This was perfect! I entered William's number into my phone and sent him a text so he would have my number too.

Me:	Hey, it's Alli :) Now you have my number
William:	Awesome! Think Mrs Lamb will make us start texting in French too?
Me:	Gosh I hope not! Who knew that reading, writing, and speaking another language was going to be so much? Unless this is super easy for you and I'm the only one on the struggle bus…

William chuckled at my text, which, in turn, made me chuckle too.

William:	Haha no you're definitely not the only one on the struggle bus. It is a lot to remember. Idk how all these other countries learn English, let alone multiple languages.
Me:	For real tho! I do want to visit France one day, specifically Paris. Do you?

William:	Yeah it's on my list of places to see.
Me:	What else is on your list of places to see? :)

Ding. Ding. Ding. The end of fifth period sounded. I was bummed. I was having fun texting him. I really hoped he continued the conversation and didn't leave me on read.

Come on, chill out girl. You just got his phone number. Don't be too eager like you always are. I coaxed myself to put my phone in my backpack until I got to my next class.

The second I sat down in my seat I whipped out my cell phone. Nothing. Disappointment gripped my chest. As if my phone could read my emotions, it buzzed indicating a text had come in.

Oh my gosh!!

I turned my screen on to see what he said, but he didn't say anything. It was Chelsea messaging the group.

Chelsea:	Here are some more options we could do for shirts in the future for more games or for summer.

I put my phone away and attempted to focus on the screen in front of me. *It's not like you've never had guy friends before. I know, but . . . I've never been so, I don't know, intrigued by a guy. Guy friend. Yes, guy friend, and we're barely even that.*

CHAPTER 7

My friends and I got ready at Evelynn's house. We had pizza, Mountain Dew, Sour Patch Kids, and music blaring. We put on our customized shirts and helped each other with our hair. Evelynn and Chelsea did these cute pigtails. I did my usual half-up, half-down with a bow in it. Rose had hers all the way down, and Hayden had hers in a ponytail with a braid twisting through it. We took maybe a million and three pictures between the five of us.

Finally, it was time for us to leave for the game. I shot William a text saying we're leaving now. He replied with, "Sounds good meet ya there."

Kyle is driving separately. He does have his own group of friends, but sometimes I wonder if he fakes hanging out with guys and just waits for Evelynn to be free. They might not physically be attached at the hip, but they're emotionally attached to one another.

We pulled into the parking lot. It's full of seniors and juniors tailgating. I'm sure they're drinking alcohol, but our school officials seem to be watching them closely.

I wonder if they care, because it seems like seniors can get away with anything.

We got out of the car, headed to the student gate, showed our IDs, and then we headed toward the bleachers. William texted me as we pulled in, saying they were just leaving. They'll be here in about ten or fifteen minutes.

Like me, William has a school permit that allows him to drive to school and home. We're not technically supposed to go anywhere else, but everyone runs some errands or goes to their friends' houses.

Seniors get the front rows of the student section. If more attend, then room is allotted for them. All juniors, sophomores, and freshmen have to back up or else tempers flare quickly. Even our athletic director will make sure seniors get the front rows. That's how "sacred" it is. Although, I'm sure when I'm a senior, I will pride myself on the same privilege.

Getting to the game early makes it a little difficult to judge how much room the upperclassmen will need, but we tend to be gracious to avoid any conflict. One-time, last year, when we were freshmen, the game was so full that most of the freshmen, including us, actually got kicked out of the student section because the bleachers were that full. Rose, Evelynn, and I didn't mind, but Hayden and Chelsea complained about it for an entire week.

We sat down in row J, and I texted William immediately, letting him know that. Now the anticipation really started to build. I was on the very inside, so when the guys got here, I could be next to William since I'm the one who arranged this.

Kyle arrived with his two guy friends and sat with us. His friends, Dion and Anthony, sat behind him in the next row up. Kyle, of course, sat next to Evelynn who was on the outside. It's not that we couldn't have scooted over, but then there wouldn't have been enough room for William and his friends. Plus, I don't think they really minded. We've tried hanging out with Kyle, Dion, and Anthony, but I don't know. Something just wasn't clicking for us, at least me anyway. Even Evelynn isn't a big fan of them, but she tolerates them since she hangs around them more than we have to.

Hayden nudged me and pointed to our right. William and his friends had just arrived and were scanning the crowd for us.

Do I stand up and wave? Do I just wave from my seat? I don't want to look dorky.

I stayed seated but made Hayden wave with me to draw their attention. William saw us waving and gave a wave back in acknowledgment. He turned to his friends and pointed toward where we were sitting. They climbed up the bleachers and then made their way into our row.

"Hi," I said, smiling at William.

"Hey," he said in response. "Alli, these are my friends, Morris, Peter, Danny, and Grant."

I waved at them and remembered the social etiquette would be for me to introduce my friends too.

"Oh right, these are my friends, Hayden, Chelsea, Evelynn, and her boyfriend Kyle."

Everyone waved at each other, and the awkward introductions were now behind us. It turns out Kyle already knew William and his friends.

Everyone sat down, and regular conversation got underway, except for William and me. I couldn't think of what to talk to him about now that he was next to me.

Noticing my uncomfortable quietness, Hayden leaned over to me and whispered into my ear, "Maybe ask him about football and sports." I gently nodded, trying to not make anything more awkward or obvious.

Knowing me, I'm bound to make something awkward.

"So, you're a Chiefs fan?" I asked.

"Yeah, I would feel like a traitor if I liked any other team. Plus, it helps that my dad has always been a Chiefs fan too. It's one of the few things we have in common."

"Nice! Do you guys still watch football together then?" I asked him, genuinely interested.

"Yeah, it's not every Sunday anymore, but it's most of them. If we don't it's usually because I'm at Peter's house, but typically the guys will come over and watch the games at our house. Sometimes we'll be in the basement playing video games while the game is on. Peter brings over a TV or two and we hook them all up."

"Is your mom into football too?"

"Nah." He shrugged and then continued, "I mean, she'll come with Dad to the high school games, but I think it's more to socialize with the other moms that come, you know? She is usually doing her own thing while the game is on, but she sits in the living room with Dad and asks him questions."

"Does that annoy him? Some guys hate when girls ask questions throughout the games." I snickered.

He smiled like he had a secret but didn't want to share it. He shrugged and said, "Sometimes he gets a little annoyed having to explain things over and over every week, but I think overall he enjoys sounding smart."

I laughed and shared my thoughts aloud, "Maybe she does know what's going on, but she wants him to feel smart and so that's why she keeps asking."

A look of shock crossed William's face as he pondered this concept. "Holy crap, Alli . . . I think . . . I think you might be right! I'll have to ask Mom if that's what she's doing."

By now, there were about four minutes left for the teams to warm up before kick-off. William and his friends went to get some food and drinks from the concession stand. He asked if I wanted anything, but I politely said no.

He didn't believe me. "Hayden, what does Alli drink?"

"She likes Pepsi." She winked over at me, and I slightly shook my head at her. I didn't want him to buy me anything.

"Pepsi and popcorn coming up!" he said as they headed down the bleachers.

When they got back, he handed me the items he said he was getting. I had a major smile across my face because I am obsessed with popcorn. It's like, one of my absolute favorite foods besides pizza and those big, soft pretzels.

We stood for the National Anthem and then the game began.

I've gone to sporting events ever since elementary school, because what else is there to do on a Friday night during the school year? This game though, easily has been the most fun game yet! Not only was the actual football game super close and intense, we pulled it out with Nichols throwing thirty-two yards to Durham to score the winning touchdown for us. Finally, we beat Jefferson. I hope Kelsey is satisfied too.

Maybe it's because I had William next to me explaining the calls I didn't understand. Maybe it was because my friends and his friends were really vibing, with Chelsea moving after half-time to sit next to Peter. Maybe it was the overall atmosphere and excitement from the close rivalry, but whatever it was, it was incredible. I didn't want the evening to end. William was fun, and so were his friends. *Unlike Kyle's friends.*

We all were laughing and getting along great! Kyle asked Evelynn if she wanted to join him and his friends after the game, but she declined saying she would rather hang with the girls. We do usually hang out afterwards, but we typically just bum around at Evelynn's eating and talking.

When the three guys took off, Peter asked if we wanted to go back to William's house for a bonfire.

YES! Absolutely yes!

Luckily Chelsea had been flirting up a storm with Peter and spoke on our behalf, "We would love to! We're not doing anything anyway, right?" She turned and looked at us.

I will admit, I was the first to nod my head and agree with Chelsea, not caring if our other friends wanted to go or not. Rose and Hayden seemed interested; Evelynn was a little hesitant. She wasn't sure if Kyle would like her hanging out with all these guys without him.

He's not a controlling boyfriend by any means, and frankly, I could see why the hesitation, but also, it's a Friday night, he's with his friends and she's with hers. Plus, as Chelsea was non-discreetly pointing out, she's the one with a boyfriend, and we won't let her do anything inappropriate. Not that she would. Evelynn is honestly the All-American Girl. It's both her greatest strength and weakness.

"Okay, I'm in too then," she agreed.

"Great! Will, you text Alli your address. We need to run home and grab some things before coming over," Chelsea dictated.

"Sounds good to me," William said. He pulled his phone out and before I had even moved from my spot, my phone vibrated from his incoming text.

The entire drive from the high school to Evelynn's, Chelsea would not shut up about Peter. "He's so cute! Did you see his arms? Oh my god, they were nice. I want to wrap my hands around them! Also, he was hilarious. Did you guys find him funny? Well, even if you didn't, he was cracking me up. I'm so excited I'm going to hang out with him! Well, us I mean. We are going to hang out with them." She corrected herself out loud, but on the inside, she only had one person on her mind at that moment.

Hayden rolled her eyes at Chelsea, but in a playful way. "Wait, this is you excited? No way!"

Chelsea stuck her tongue out and Hayden steered the conversation toward me now. "So, Sky, how did it go with you and Will?"

I could feel myself blush a little. I too wanted to drool over William the way Chelsea was about Peter, but I also didn't want my friends bugging me about my feelings.

Instead, I tried to play it cool in front of the people that knew me best. "He's fun to be around. He makes me laugh and we seem to get along pretty well. Like Chelsea was just saying, he and I have a lot in common too and he's easy to talk to, which I love about him."

"Ooooooo, you're SO crushing!" Chelsea squealed. The rest of the girls joined in with laughter and subtle accusations.

"Maybe I can play Doctor Love and get something going between you two," Evelynn said, rubbing her hands together like an evil scientist.

"No, no, no. We're just going over tonight to hang out. We're still getting to know each other. I don't want anybody trying to make anything happen. Do you hear me?" I pleaded, hoping they took me as seriously as I was being.

"Don't worry, I will make sure Evelynn and Chelsea behave. Besides, it's Chelsea and Peter that we're going to have to look out for anyway," Rose spoke up in my defense. I'm not the one that's known for flirting my way into a new guy's lap the way Chelsea can.

Chelsea seemed to take a playful offense to us teasing her, but by the time we pulled into Evelynn's driveway, Chelsea admitted she was guilty. We were laughing as we got out of the car and went upstairs to Evelynn's room. Lucky for us, her closet has a variety of sizes, colors, and comfortable clothing that she handed to us. We all received a pair of sweatpants and a sweatshirt, just in case.

Since we were planning to spend the night, we had blankets, but Evelynn didn't want the blankets we were going to sleep on to get dirty, so she went to the basement and grabbed a literal tote full for us. We also grabbed some snacks and beverages before getting back into the car to head to William's. Turns out, he lives in the country which I didn't know about him.

"As long as we don't get murdered, I'm okay with being out in the country," Rose chimed in, making us laugh.

From the road, we could see where the bonfire was. It was alive and smelled like a fall candle. We got out of the car and grabbed our blankets.

I checked my phone as we started to walk. I had a text from William that I hadn't read yet.

> **William:** We're out by the fire. Head that way.

We headed in the direction of the fire.

William, Danny, and Morris were around the fire when we got there. They smiled and greeted us. Chelsea was quick to be disappointed, and Danny could tell.

"Don't worry, Peter's just inside making himself a pizza and getting the speaker for some music." Sure enough, Chelsea's smile came rushing back to her face and I swear I heard a sigh of relief escape her lips.

William and his friends had enough chairs for everyone if we wanted. Chelsea opted for the ground, but the rest of us took a seat in a chair. I noticed the stack of wood and wondered if William chopped it all. That would explain his biceps.

"Do you chop all the wood?" I asked.

The guys snickered, and I wondered immediately if they made my question dirty somehow. William chuckled, but he knew I didn't mean anything other than what I asked. *I hope anyway.*

"Yeah, for the most part. My dad does sometimes, but it's mostly my responsibility since I'm the one that burns most of it."

"That's not the only place he keeps his wood," Danny cracked, causing all of us to laugh.

"We're talking about William's wood already? Damn, that was faster than I thought," Peter said coming out with an entire pizza in one hand and a 12 pack of Mountain Dew under the other arm. "Well ladies, I have more than just one 12 pack!"

"You can sit next to me with your 24 pack if you'd like!" Chelsea piped up, laughing at Peter's joke.

Smart. Hence her reasoning for not choosing a chair like the rest of us.

He accepted her offer without hesitation and sat next to her by the fire. He offered the pizza to all of us, but I was full from the pizza and popcorn I ate earlier so I declined.

Some of the guys wanted pizza. Peter passed the cardboard around the circle. My chair was across from William's. The circle went William, Peter, Chelsea, Rose, Evelynn, Me, Hayden, Danny, and Morris.

Peter worked on setting up the speaker so we could have music playing in the background. Morris started off the group conversation by asking us who all our teachers are this year. Evelynn and Danny have science together with Mrs. Tanson, and obviously William and I have French together.

"Do you go by William then? Because that's the only way Alli refers to you?" Evelynn asked for clarification.

"Sir William!" Peter said in a terrible, British accent, making the guys and Chelsea laugh once more.

"My grandma does, but my parents don't call me that. It's pretty much Will all around."

"In the sixth grade, he tried going by Billy, and it was the funniest thing ever. Once in a while we still call him that," Danny spoke, making us laugh at the idea of calling him Billy.

"I like William," I said, smiling toward him.

"Then you may call me William," he said, smiling back at me. I loved the fact that I'd be the only one calling him that. Well, Grandma and I, but that's okay, I'm not worried about Grandma.

After skipping a bunch of songs, trying to find the best playlist, Peter settled on a throwback playlist with classics from the 80s. I recognized some, but not all. The rest of the night was us talking, laughing, singing, and eventually Peter and Chelsea cuddling on the blanket.

The smoke kept the mosquitos away, which was nice aside from the watering of the eyes it caused. The wind wasn't blowing too hard thanks to all the trees that lined the perimeter of the farmland.

We stayed there until almost one in the morning. We were out later than we were supposed to be, but we were having such a great time. Eventually, though, Evelynn's dad texted her saying we need to come home right now.

We packed everything up as Danny worked on killing the fire. The guys were gentlemen and walked us to Evelynn's vehicle with the flashlights from their phones. Peter and Chelsea had already exchanged numbers when they were cuddling. They hugged now and Peter kissed her goodbye on the cheek.

Guess what we'll be hearing about the entire drive home?

I wondered if William would hug me, but he didn't offer. Without thinking, I put my hand up for a high five. He chuckled while everybody else laughed. We slapped hands and I turned away from him immediately because of the redness that was racing to my cheeks.

I did NOT just ask for a high-five?! Well, he didn't leave me hanging, I guess.

CHAPTER 8

Saturday morning, after getting home from Eve-lynn's, I stood in the shower, replaying last night over and over in my head: the football game, sitting next to William on the bleachers, all of us being packed into the student section like sardines, my bare leg touching William's basketball shorts, our shoulders rubbing up against each other as we jumped and cheered throughout the entire game. Then afterwards, when we were sitting across the fire from one another; through the flames, his smile would shine in the darkness that surrounded us. His blue eyes, darker than normal without the sunlight reflecting against them, still sparkled against the hood of his sweatshirt that covered his head. The music, the laughing, and the crackling of the fire danced through my ears once more, as if I was back in time, less than twelve hours ago.

I thanked him last night for having us over, but I wanted a reason to text him. I racked my brain trying to figure out what to say to him, or at least how to word something that wouldn't sound lame.

Me: Thanks for last night again! It was super fun. I hope we can do it again sometime!

I don't know. I can't think of anything better. I pressed send on my phone and anxiously awaited a response from him.

After brushing my hair, blow drying it, and straightening it, he hadn't responded yet.

I sighed. *Maybe he's still sleeping? It is only 10:47 AM right now.*

I've never been great at sleeping in late. Chelsea can sleep until noon or later depending on how late she stays up. It has always amazed me. In fact, Chelsea was still sleeping on Evelynn's bed when the rest of us got up and Evelynn drove us all home.

I made my way downstairs to see what my family was up to. They're in their usual spots. Mom was at the kitchen table reading the newspaper while drinking her coffee. Dad was sitting in his recliner in the living room. He was flipping between reruns of *Friends* and the sports channel. Greyson was already at a park with friends doing whatever it is twelve year olds do.

"How was last night, honey?" Mom asked me as I opened the cupboards to see what there was to eat.

"It was good. After the game we ended up going over to somebody else's house for a little bit," I said, closing the cupboards and walking over to check the fridge.

"Oh fun! Whose house?" Mom asked, setting the newspaper down and giving me her full attention. Not in a nosey way; my parents are lenient and respectful of my personal space. It's something my friends envy about me.

"His name is William. We have French class together," I said, closing the fridge, still empty handed as I went back to check the cupboards once more.

"Who all went to William's?" Dad inquired from the next room over.

"Just me. I ditched my friends and went to hang out alone with William in his bedroom until 1 AM,"

I said. This of course made Mom and me smile, but not so much Dad. "I'm kidding, Dad. All my friends went, and we sat around a bonfire. Then we went back to Evelynn's and passed out immediately."

I shut the cupboards again that I had been rummaging through. I grabbed a chocolate chip granola bar off the counter and sat down at the kitchen table with Mom. I checked my phone once more, but he still hadn't responded.

I decided to go to the basement to kill time. I turned on Netflix and scrolled through the menu screen for about twenty minutes before settling on *Impractical Jokers*: something light and funny to help me attempt to maintain a calm energy.

I'm not sure why this is bothering me so much. It's not like I sent him a text saying, "Hey, I don't know if you felt anything these last couple of days, but I'd really like to get close to you and maybe kiss you if everything goes well enough. I hope we can get married and die of old age together . . . if you want, of course, no pressure!"

Nothing I sent was risky or needy, but still, my leg bounced up and down. He's cute, and we had been having good conversations, and I just wanted to continue that with him.

Chelsea was clearly awake and texting with Peter. She was sending us screenshots of the conversation they were having. It wasn't anything interesting. They're just talking about things they have in common like their favorite foods, sports, and TV shows.

She's excited, just like you are. You're searching for the same thing in William right now and wanting that to be you, so be happy for her!

Just like that, a text came from the person I wanted to hear from.

William: Hey, sorry, I was helping my dad with some things around the barn. Last night was fun!

William: Would you want to come over
and watch a movie or something
today?

*Yes, I do! Oh crap, I need to ask my parents. I hope
they don't get weird about me going to hang out with him
alone now.*

I figured I should ask before texting him back.
Besides, I needed to give it a little time, so I wouldn't
sound too eager. If I texted back too soon it would
seem like I don't have a life of my own. I didn't want
to come across as somebody that was waiting by my
phone all morning, even though I was.

I walked upstairs to see if my parents had moved.
Mom hadn't—she was still sitting at the kitchen table
reading the paper—but Dad moved to the couch for
his Saturday morning nap he denies every time.

"Would it be okay if I went to William's today to
hang out?" I faced Mom and asked her directly, even
though Dad opened his eyes at the mention of a boy's
name.

"Are all of your friends going back over?" Dad
asked first.

"Not this time; it will just be me," I said, looking
toward Mom with pleading eyes.

"That's fine, dear, as long as you're home for supper."

I jumped up and down with joy, making Mom
smile at my excitement. Dad wasn't smiling, but he
wasn't objecting at least, so I'll take it! I ran up to my
room to get ready for the day and texted William
back to ask what time he wanted to hang out today.

Luckily William was outside when I pulled
into the driveway. I wasn't sure if his family is
a "use-the-front-door-that's-why-it's-there" or a
"just-come-through-the-garage-like-we-always-do"
family.

In case you're wondering, they use the garage 100% of the time. He said if someone uses the front door, they must be trying to break in.

"I still can't believe you live on a farm!" I exclaimed.

None of my friends have ever lived remotely near the edge of town, let alone on an actual acreage (*or however large this really is*).

He softly chuckled and asked if I wanted a tour.

Absolutely!

"Yeah, that'd be cool." I smiled back at him, hoping to sound casual.

He took me to the barn first where they have two horses: Pumpkin and Whiskers.

"Do you ride them?" I asked him, still shocked at how large these animals were in person.

"Yeah. I used to do competitions in the junior rodeo, but I stopped after I broke my collarbone when I was twelve. Now, we just ride them occasionally. Have you ever ridden?" he asked, looking at me curiously.

My eyebrows immediately shot up. "Oh no. No, no, no. I have never ridden anything but a bicycle in my life," I said, afraid, yet slightly excited to see if he would ask me to go sometime. I had a quick image of us riding together on the same saddle, me sitting in his arms and feeling safe while he—*stop it. Come back to reality!*

"Well, we could go sometime if you feel brave enough," was his response. "Here, this is how you pet them."

He called one of the horses over and showed me how to place my hand in front of their nose. I was scared, yet super into this. I never thought I would get to pet a horse.

"Are the cows in the back then?" I asked jokingly.

"They're out in the pasture, yeah," he said without a hint of humor.

"Are, are you serious? Do you guys have cows?!"

William laughed out loud. "Yeah, we have a few chickens too, but other than that, it's just the regular squirrels, rabbits, and ducks that you see in town. We're not huge into the animal side of farm-life, but my sister, Charlotte, shows our bull for 4-H."

"Do you . . . I mean, when your animals die, do you . . ."

"Eat them?" he finished my question for me. "Would you be disgusted if I said yes?"

I thought about it, and it made me sad, but at the same time, they are animals, bred to be eaten. At least here I know they are humanely treated (from what little I'd seen) so that eased my stomach. I'm not a vegetarian, but I do want animals to be treated correctly because they deserve that much from humans. I explained my thought process to him.

"That's fair; I respect your opinion. To answer your original question, though: We don't eat our cows or chickens, and we don't send our horses to the glue factory, either."

I was thankful yet surprised to hear this.

We walked through the grass toward their shed. This is where they store their machines, toys, or what I would call contraptions. The Mantels have four-wheelers, snowmobiles, a motorcycle, and a broken-down 1953 Chevrolet pick-up truck.

William explained when his grandpa comes over, he, his dad, and his grandpa work on it together.

How adorable is that?

Behind the shed, and just a little farther of a walk (north, I think?), a brown and white fuzzy creature appeared. I squealed in delight!

"Ohhh, myyy, gosh! It's so cute! Is it a boy or girl?" I asked through a smile bigger than my face.

William chuckled. "She's a girl. Her name is Cheese."

My smile turned into a puzzled expression. "Cheese? Like dairy cheese? She's not a dairy cow though, is she?"

William was laughing now, and I could tell this wasn't his first time having to explain Cheese's name.

"It's usually less confusing when her brother is standing next to her, and I introduce him first. He's over there, standing by their mother." He pointed. "His name is Mac."

My eyebrows rose in befuddlement again. "Mac? As in, Mac and Cheese?" A small smirk started to form on my lips. "But . . . why?"

"It's simple; I just really like mac and cheese. Also, so does my sister. It was something we agreed on when choosing their names." He said it so modestly and purely that it made me feel all twin calves should be named mac and cheese, or something similar at least.

It was my turn to chuckle now. "So, if you guys have twin calves again, can I name one pop and one corn then?"

"Sure, on one condition of course," he said devilishly.

"Uh-oh, what's the one condition?" I asked, nervous but too curious for my own good.

He shrugged and said, "You just have to assist in the birthing process is all."

Curiosity gone.

I scoffed, unsure if he was being serious or not. "Sorry, I will not be putting that on my resume! Feel free to name them whatever you desire. I will be here afterwards though to watch them wobble around."

He laughed at my unconcealed emotions, clearly amused. "You can pet her if you'd like."

"Seriously?!" I was shocked again.

"Yeah, she's a sweetheart," he explained as he reached through the fence to pet her face while she was eating the grass.

"Her mom or Mac isn't going to . . . charge us like an angry bull or something will they?"

Still laughing at me, which I rather took pride in being able to make him laugh, even if it's at my expense, he said, "No, but their bull of a dad might."

My hand had barely left my side, but I yanked it back quickly and whipped my head around out of fear so quickly that I lost my balance. William had to steady me.

The loudest laugh escaped his perfect lips. It sounded like music to me, but I didn't have time to take it in, I was still worried about the cow dad charging me!

"I'm sorry, I'm kidding! I'm only kidding, Alli. You're perfectly safe. Their dad really is over there, but he's safely locked in his area. He won't come charging, I promise."

I nodded but didn't say anything. It was more that I couldn't say anything; I could only glance down at his hand that was still holding my arm when he reached out to steady me. When he saw me looking at it, he let go and looked embarrassed.

He cleared his throat and asked if I wanted to pet Cheese for real this time. I did.

I can't believe I am petting a baby cow! An adorable, fuzzy, red-and-white calf. Ew!! She just licked me. Oh, that's gross. Yup, I'm done. I'm too "city" for cow tongue. Cats and dogs can lick me. Sorry Cheese, another time.

I yanked my hand back when her tongue came for me again, making William laugh at me, but this time I was able to enjoy it.

"Is there anything else you would like to see? Otherwise, we can head in if you want," he offered, giving me the choice to decide what to do.

I tried to play it cool again, because truthfully, my nerves exploded like a bomb going off inside of me.

What is there to do inside? Are we going to have enough to talk about? What if we just sit in awkward silence?

"Yeah, we can go inside."

I think I played that off casually enough. He seems okay with everything. Not even a hint of nerves from what I can tell.

"Watch your step," he said, as he led us toward the house. I followed in his footsteps, not wanting to trip. *How embarrassing would that be??*

I asked him if he likes being out here on the farm, or if he wishes he was closer to his friends. He explained that when he was younger, it was a lot more inconvenient. His parents didn't always have the time to take him over to his friends' houses, and their parents didn't want to have to drive their children out to the country either. He says he wouldn't trade it now. He loves being able to drive and ride what he wants up the gravel roads and through the creek in the back. He feels he's able to do a lot more out here than he could in town, with fewer regulations being enforced by the city.

We came in through the garage, directly into a mudroom where he took his shoes off; I followed suit. The mudroom was off the kitchen where Mrs. Mantel was cleaning. I could see whom I presumed to be his younger sister in the living room watching some show on Nickelodeon that I don't recognize.

"Mom, this is my friend Alli, Alli this is my mom, Jenny."

I would have shaken her hand, but her cleaning glove was soapy and wet, so I waved a shy greeting instead and said hi.

She seemed nice and apologized for the mess in her perfectly spotless house. The little girl from the living room went bug-eyed when she saw her brother had brought home a girl.

"Ooooo, William has a girlfriend!" she sang.

"Alli, this is my little sister Charlotte. She knows how to play the annoying card and the innocent card simultaneously. I wish my parents would see her for what she really is, a weasel."

Charlotte rolled her eyes at her older brother.

"Charlotte, this is my friiiiend," (*oof, he really emphasized the friend word*) "Alli. We have class together."

She smiled at me and stuck her tongue out at her older brother. I couldn't help but chuckle at their interaction, and of course, the fact that he called her a weasel.

"It's good you're just friends. I can't imagine anybody wanting to purposefully date my brother!"

"Alright, Charlotte, that's enough. It was nice meeting you dear. Please, make yourself at home." His mom gave another perfect smile as we started walking through the house.

Wow, for being a farmhouse, this house is a lot more elegant than I thought it would be.

There were chandeliers and floor-to-ceiling windows with curtains. Don't even get me started on the gorgeous furniture as well.

"Your house is beautiful," I said, looking around at everything as I walked with him.

"Thanks. Mom's a realtor so she's into interior decorating and keeping everything tidy. It's kind of annoying actually. Even though we're not selling our house, we always have to keep our rooms clean, just in case you know, the President or the Emperor of Japan swings through Kansas or something." His sarcasm made me laugh.

"I mean, you never know though. When the President stopped by our house two years ago, we weren't prepared," I said, making him laugh again.

Ugh, I love his laugh.

The next room we came through was part office, part library, and intimidating with the amount of political and law books I saw. This must be his dad.

I know, I'm such a detective.

He had the same facial features and hair color as William. Plus, he was the only man in the house I'd seen.

"Alli, this is my dad, Tom. Dad, this is Alli, a friend from school."

"Pleasure to meet you, Alli. Is that short for something?" he said, standing and extending his hand to me.

"Hi. Yes, it's short for Allison actually. Your house is stun—"

The phone started ringing and it was attached to an invisible earpiece in Tom's ear. He answered it immediately and held up his index finger to us. I didn't think anything of it. William tapped my elbow and indicated for us to leave. I felt a little rude, but I could also sense some uneasiness too.

We didn't go upstairs, so I never got to see what his bedroom looked like. I'm not sure why I was looking forward to that. I think it's because people's bedrooms are their sacred space. As teenagers, it's how we decorate and express ourselves besides the clothes we wear or the music we listen to.

Anyway, after meeting his dad, we headed to the basement, which was basically a mini house under their house. It had two bedrooms, a bathroom, a refrigerator, microwave, pool table, all the gaming consoles, and of course a massive TV with surround sound. There was an entire wall dedicated to DVDs. You could tell William's movies and Charlotte's movies were mixed together, but it was alphabetical at least.

Holy crap, they have a legit movie theater popcorn and pop machine!

"Wow. This feels like an actual movie theater. This is incredible!" I said, baffled.

"We can watch a movie if you'd like, otherwise we have darts, pool, cards, board games, and more."

I looked around, unsure which to choose from. I decided to go with a movie in case I couldn't think of anything to talk to him about. A movie is a great excuse for silence.

"I vote movie, but we don't have to," I said, looking at him; he was watching me ponder.

"Sounds good to me. If you want to choose a movie, I'll get the popcorn started. That is, if you want any." He looked at me, already knowing what my answer would be.

"Popcorn would be great! What are you in the mood to watch?" I asked, not wanting to choose something he would feel he's suffering through.

"Oh no, you get to choose. I'm down for whatever. Also, help yourself to the pop machine and candy too if you want."

I chose Sour Patch Kids and a cherry Pepsi from the machine. As I crinkled open the candy, I started looking through the movies. There had to be over two hundred to choose from.

I wanted to choose *Beauty and the Beast* since we did meet in French class and it's set in France but instead, I chose *The Dark Knight Rises*. It's not a girly choice, and I figured this would be considered one of William's movies and not Charlotte's.

Uh-oh, do I sit on the couch or the oversized chair? Does he have a normal spot that he prefers? Is it presumptuous of me to take the couch since it technically can seat three people, but there are only two of us?

I took the couch because it had a blanket; a fleece cow print blanket to be exact.

Cute!

I like watching movies with blankets no matter what time of year it is. Plus, since we were in a basement, it was cooler.

"I'm surprised this blanket is cow print and isn't a mac and cheese blanket," I joked.

"Oh, the mac and cheese is my comforter in my bedroom," he said in response, very serious.

My mouth fell open in shock, but then I realized he was kidding again.

I have to stop believing everything he says! I love the way his face can change from serious to joking in a nanosecond, though, even if it's at my expense.

"Excellent movie choice," he said, taking it from me and putting it into the DVD player. He pressed about seven buttons before everything was set up and turned on.

The popcorn was finished and smelled delicious! He pulled out two popcorn containers and filled them up. He handed me mine and then sat on the oversized chair. Disappointment washed through me.

I tried to not talk through the movie because I didn't want to be annoying, but I did have a few questions here and there. He answered every one without a hint of irritation too, which I greatly appreciated.

When the movie was over, he asked what else I wanted to do, but after checking the clock on my phone, I knew I needed to head home for supper. I was bummed about leaving, but I'd had a great time.

I hope he had fun with me.

He was a gentleman and walked me back through the house to the mudroom so I could put my shoes on. He even walked me out to my car.

As we walked, I asked if he was sixteen.

"Not yet, but my birthday is actually next week," he said.

"Really? What day?"

"The 19th."

"Do you have any plans or traditions for your birthday?" I asked, curious and wanting to know everything about him.

He shrugged. "Monday, Mom will take me to the DOT so I can hopefully get my license. Otherwise, we don't really do much. I'll go out to eat with my family, that's really our only tradition now. I'll have a bonfire of course, but that's standard no matter the occasion."

"That's awesome! I hope you get your license on your birthday. I'm terrified of not passing the driver's test." Anxiety crept into my stomach at the thought.

"I'm sure you'll do great," he said encouragingly. "Would you and your friends want to come over for the bonfire?"

"Absolutely!" I eagerly stated, making him chuckle at my excitement. "I mean, I'll double check with everyone, but I don't think we have anything going on."

"Sounds good," he said as we arrived at my car.

Things got a little awkward for me here suddenly. I wasn't sure if there was anything more he wanted to talk about, or if I was dragging out my exit too long. I told him I should get going and he didn't stop me. I got into my car and when I shut my door, he waved goodbye.

He turned around to head back inside once my car started. I drove down their long driveway, reliving my afternoon with him already. This was our first time hanging out, and it was perfect!

CHAPTER 9

Sunday morning, I laid on my bed, listening to the ceiling fan that was rotating around and around, beating to its own electric, rhythmic hum. It created the cool air that hugged me as I hid under my blankets. I'm rarely awake before my mom comes in to wake me up for church.

These last two nights have been wonderful. It has been so easy to talk and joke with William. It's as if we have known each other longer than we have. He's laidback, easy going, laughs with sincerity, and can handle and dish out sarcasm like a champ. Everything about him, or at least what I know so far, is black or white, but not in a bad way. It's black or white in the sense of whether he wants to or not type of way. If he wants to go here or there he will; if he doesn't, he passes. He's living his life for himself and not trying to appease everyone else, which I admire and could learn from.

Tap. Tap. Tap. "Sweetie, it's time to get up. We're leaving for church in about thirty minutes," Mom gently cooed.

She has this special power where she can word things harmlessly, but also let us know that it's not an option either by the tone she uses.

"Yup, Mom, I'm up," I said in acknowledgement. I pushed the navy comforter off me and swung my lanky legs over the edge. I walked to my closet and started pushing the racks of clothes to the right as I mentally sorted through them. The hanger squeaked across the metal rod like a melody that represented my indecisiveness.

How do I have an entire closet and dresser full of clothes, and yet nothing acceptable enough to wear to church that isn't overly dressy, or too casual for the congregation to not judge me?

Funny isn't it; the concept of wearing our Sunday best? Like Jesus actually cares what we wear to church, and yet all parents make their kids dress up so we look presentable to the other humans sitting across from us. Society is so weird.

I put on dark, non-holey jeans, and decided on a sage green, lacey top. I put my hair up in a pony-tail thinking to myself it would have to do for today.

I went to the bathroom since Greyson wasn't in there yet. I heard Mom knocking on his door again as I was getting dressed. He has yet to move from his bed.

I brushed my teeth and put on mascara and lip gloss. Simple is my favorite look.

I was pretty MIA yesterday from the group chat with my friends. Not once did I look at my phone until I got home. There wasn't anything I really missed. Chelsea was talking about volleyball and Peter (naturally), and Hayden was discussing how bored she was at her family's reunion. She was getting a lot of personal questions from strangers she's told are technically her relatives.

> **Hayden:** I've never seen these people in the 15 years of my life I've been alive!

Chelsea: right?? My aunt is always listing people I've never heard of and then she acts like I'm the one being rude when I tell her I don't know who Arthur McHenry III is in our family. Also! we don't even have a first or second Arthur in our family!

Evelynn was quiet surprisingly, but that was because she and Kyle had plans last night.

Speaking of plans, I needed to tell them about William's birthday bonfire for next Saturday. I didn't mind waiting, though. I knew they were going to bombard me with questions.

I feel bad during and after church sometimes when I catch myself not paying attention whatsoever, like today for example. Yes, the pastor was talking about good stuff, but I couldn't tell you what he was talking about. Yes, I at least sang along and bowed my head when we were supposed to, but I'm sure I looked delayed to anybody that may have been watching me.

Although, if all our heads are supposed to be bowed, hopefully nobody will be watching me, because then they wouldn't be paying attention either.

I couldn't help but imagine what school would be like tomorrow. I hoped things wouldn't be awkward. My brain took me down a series of fake scenarios.

What if he had a bad time but didn't want to tell me? I could try texting him today to test the waters. I feel like he had fun though. We laughed a lot together and I don't think he was faking it. We didn't sit near each other, so that couldn't have been too awkward for him, right? Unless he wanted to sit next to me but wasn't sure how I would have responded? No, no! I had asked him where he wanted to sit, and he didn't care, so I left the door open for him to sit on the couch with me and he chose not to.

The other thing I was thinking about in church was what and how to tell my friends. I worried about what they may say in front of him—specifically Chelsea, because she goes too far too often and crosses boundaries with everybody. It would be horrifying if she made William feel uncomfortable and that be the cause of him not wanting to hang out with me ever again.

I know I'll have to tell them at some point, so I might as well do it now.

I pulled my phone out from the sweatshirt I changed into the second we got home.

> **Me:** I hung out with William yesterday. His birthday is next week so he's having a bonfire. He invited all of us again so I said we'd be there.

Deep breath and . . . send. Of course, Chelsea is the first one to respond.

> **Chelsea:** details now and YES! I for sure will be there!!
>
> **Rose:** Nice! Did you have fun?
>
> **Hayden:** what did you guys do?

I waited for about a minute or two to see if Evelynn was going to chime in any second, but she did not. She must still be at church or eating lunch with her family.

> **Me:** Yeah it was fun. We looked at the horses and cows he has on his farm. Then he introduced me to his family, and we went downstairs and watched a movie. It

was a good time. His house btw is absolutely amazing!

Hayden: aww what are the animals' names??

Chelsea: you met his family?!?! Sky! You guys know I hung out with Peter yesterday too, and neither of us went to each other's houses to meet the family. This might be serious!

Evelynn: Hang on Chels, it might not be serious yet. Sky, did you sit on the same couch? Or separate?

Me: We sat on opposite couches. Nothing about yesterday was a big deal. So, who wants to go to the bonfire with Chelsea and me?

Rose: I'll go

Evelynn: Uh-huh suuure. Also, I should be good too. Do you think Will would mind if I brought Kyle?

Me: I can ask him

Hayden: I'll have to check with my parents first. I can't remember if we have anything going on or not.

Evelynn: You didn't really give many details either on what you guys talked about by the way. Was any of it awkward?

Me: It wasn't awkward. It was fun. His horses names are Pumpkin and Whiskers, and his cow had twin calves that they named Mac and Cheese. They're

Me:	adorable! Otherwise, his family seems nice and typical. He has a little sister about Greyson's age. Then, like I said, we went to the basement and watched Batman. He has a real popcorn machine, so he made popcorn for us. Maybe you guys can see it next weekend when we're there.
Me:	Was that sufficient enough?
Chelsea:	Aww he remembered your love for popcorn!! How sweet is he?
Evelynn:	I'll accept it. Why Mac and Cheese?
Me:	He said he likes mac and cheese and so does his sister, so they agreed on the names together. Then I joked that if they ever have another set of twins, if I could name them pop and corn!
Chelsea:	OMG you guys are naming your future baby calves already!

Hayden and Evelynn responded with laughing emojis again to Chelsea's text. I on the other hand told her she needs to slow her horses.

Get it? Slow your horses, because he lives on a farm and has horses? HAH. Good one, self.

Me:	Alright guys, any other questions?
Hayden:	I'm waiting to see if Evelynn and Chelsea have any more questions to grill you on
Me:	LOL thanks Hayden

Chelsea: nah I think I'm good. I can't wait for next weekend now!!

Evelynn: Yes, Chels, we all know you're excited to see Peter. Sky, it sounds like it was a great time, and I look forward to seeing where this goes for you both! Now, what are you going to wear tomorrow to school since you guys just had your first "alone time" together. It needs to be cute! It needs to say, "Hey, I'm willing to be more than friends, but I don't need to get sent home to change." You know?

Me: That would be in Chelsea's wardrobe lol. I don't know. I think I'm good with what I have. Thank you though.

Evelynn: This is true! Okay, at least wear jean shorts and a cute top, not a sweatshirt!

Chelsea: hey, I haven't been sent home yet this year to change!

Rose: We've only been in school for 2 weeks. There's still plenty of opportunities for you haha

Me: But it's cold in our school I don't have the tolerance nor the experience that Chelsea has...with being cold I mean.

Hayden: Nobody has the tolerance nor experience that Chelsea has!

Chelsea: Okay you guys! Stop making me sound like a cold slut sheesh. It's also not my fault that my body temperature runs warm and I'm able to handle the air conditioning system in our school better than you all!

Hayden: Call it what you want lol.

Evelynn: Okay fine Alli, you can wear a cute sweatshirt for the first half of the day. But at lunch you have to remove it and not wear it during French class at least!

Me: Aye aye captain.

I almost didn't text Evelynn in the morning to stick it to her, but then I thought about her logic a little more and realized, as she usually is, she was right. I should look cute today.

I sent her a mirror picture of what I planned to wear. I had on my dark, denim shorts, with a white-and-mustard-yellow striped shirt. I had my navy sweatshirt too. Sitting in a hot class is miserable, but being cold the entire time isn't any better. I have on white sandals, a discreet bracelet, and my simple little rose-gold elephant necklace that I wear every day.

Evelynn: cute! I have a couple tweaks and want to fix your hair, but otherwise, you look hot!

I will gladly take her help with my hair today. I don't know how she does her own hair every day and makes it look amazing.

My other friends complimented me when they got into the car with Evelynn and me. I blushed at all the attention, though, and wanted somebody to change the subject.

Reliable Chelsea did, and finally, it was not about Peter. This morning she was on the subject of volleyball and how practice has been going.

"Also, Peter is going to be giving me a ride home today after practice."

Oh, never mind, I thought too soon.

I tried dishing back to her what she was dishing out to me yesterday over text message, "Ooooo do you think you and Peter are going to start dating soon?!" I mocked.

"I hope so! We have plans to hang out tomorrow before he drops me off at home. It won't be too long, but still, just getting to see him outside of school will be nice!" she said all mushy and in her own world.

I was not expecting that to be her answer. She didn't see Evelynn and me make eye contact before we started smiling in secret with one another.

We pulled into our usual parking area and got out of the car. It was another beautiful morning, so we were going to hang out on the lawn before the bell rang.

Evelynn's tweaks involved me tucking the front part of my shirt in, and then she "fixed" my hair by adding a braid on the side and pulling some baby hairs forward. She also made me put on her lip gloss.

"You can reapply after lunch. This is just in case you see him at your locker in the morning," she explained.

For what feels like the first time since seventh grade, I wasn't searching the terrain for Oliver Walker; however, I did notice him, and couldn't help but glance back at him twice on my hunt for the other one.

I hadn't seen William in the mornings before class started yet. I should ask him where he hangs out.

Or I could not be creepy and not worry about it. That's an option too.

I didn't see William until lunchtime. All morning I had been rolling around in my head what I was going to say to him when I got the opportunity anyway. I decided I would reiterate how much fun I had hanging out with him, and that I was looking forward to his birthday bonfire this weekend.

As we finished the lunch period, I dumped the meatloaf (*I think the school is only advertising it as that, so we don't call the health inspector on them*) I did not finish into the trash can. I waved goodbye to my friends as they headed to their lockers, and I eagerly walked to mine.

Be cool, be cool, be cool! I reminded myself as I was spinning my locker combination. I could see out of my right peripheral that William was also at his locker, turning his lock too.

I was starting to chicken out. I had planned to walk straight up to his locker when I finished at mine, but suddenly, my confidence plummeted.

Come on, he's not going to reject you and think you're disgusting all of a sudden! Um we don't actually know that. He very well could. If he were, he wouldn't be approaching you right now, would he?

I turned to my right and saw him smile when I looked. It instantly made me smile and my butterflies took flight again in my stomach.

"Hey," he said with his casual tone. A word I hear all the time, but it has taken on a new feeling when it comes from him.

"Hey!" I croaked out embarrassingly. I coughed and tapped my chest, trying to cover it. I tried again. "Hey," I said normally.

"You ready for Mademoiselle Lamb?"

"*Je suis prete,*" I said in response. I tried to make it sound sexy, but I don't think he took it that way. He smiled politely. "Oh, I said, I am ready, in case you weren't sure. Unless you knew that, and now I'm sounding conceited. Which I'm not meaning to, I just—"

"Alli, breathe. I knew what you said, I just wasn't able to come up with something clever enough besides

frais. Which means cool by the way, in case you weren't

sure," he said, winking at me playfully.

I smiled in response now, but I had to look the opposite way; I was beginning to blush too, and I didn't want him to see it.

Stupid blushing.

On our walk to class, I brought up the bonfire this weekend. I told Evelynn I would ask if Kyle could join; William said that was fine.

Once we got to class, we didn't have much time to talk to one another. Mrs. Lamb was busy teaching us and making us practice aloud with a partner. She felt the need to change the partner situation up on us. We've always practiced with the person sitting across from us, but today she had us practicing with the person behind us. That means I was paired with Bonnie, who corrected me on every single mistake I made. William didn't miss his chance to shoot me a sympathetic glance.

After class, he walked with me to my locker. He didn't need anything from his, but I wanted to put my French book back and grab my geometry book.

Of course, my worst subject has the heaviest, thickest book ever made in the history of time!

"If you ever want help with your geometry home-work, we could work on it together," he offered, making me freeze in shock.

"Really?!" I half hopped out of excitement.

I could always use the additional help. I won-der what Evelynn would say if I told her I was going to have William help me with math instead of her.

Evelynn is great and all, but she ends up taking over my homework and doing it for me. Don't get me wrong, I really don't mind that, it's just, when I have to take the tests, I don't have her there to talk me through everything.

"Sure. I'm not as smart as your friend Evelynn, but I'm willing to help you with math if you could help me with history. Then we both could help each other with French if you wanted."

"Yes. Yes, I want!" I wasn't even embarrassed this time for my excitement. It made him smile with his sweet, wonderful smile.

"Sounds good. Would you like to start next week? I'll hopefully have my license. We could do it at the library, or I could come over to your place, so you don't have to come out to the farm on your school permit."

William Mantel, at my house? Studying with me? Around my family? Oh, yikes, I don't like the last part of this vision, but at some point, you have to get that first introduction out of the way. Although, knowing my dad and brother, it will continuously be awkward. Ugh! But I still want him to come over.

"Yeah, let's wait until next week. That is, if you don't mind giving me a ride? Luckily, I turn sixteen soon as well."

"Wait, when's your birthday?" he asked, surprised.

"It's September 29th."

"Oh, dang, I didn't realize we were that close in age. That's cool, we can celebrate you this weekend as well!"

"Sure, as long as you're the primary focus though," I said with a huge smile on my face.

We started to walk down the hall to where we branched off to go our separate ways. I'd see him one more time before school lets out. Everyone goes to their lockers to grab all the books and notebooks they need for homework.

Speaking of homework, I'll need to let Evelynn know about the whole math tutoring situation.

We said our goodbyes and I headed to geometry. It was getting harder and harder to focus on math when I couldn't help but daydream about William and me studying together.

Study. Remember you're going to just be studying together. Yeah, but what if, while we were studying, I look up to see him watching me, and a strand of hair falls in front of my face, and then he tucks it behind my ear, accidentally touching my cheek too as we're inches apart from each other —

"Allison?" Mr. Anderson called my name, snapping me out of my imagination.

"Uh, yes?" I said in response, trying frantically to figure out what the heck he'd been talking about for the last twenty minutes while I'd been in my own world.

"What's the answer to the problem?" he said, pointing to the whiteboard.

I looked at it completely lost and with zero indication as to what the answer could be.

"Um, forty-two?" My classmates chuckled at my incredibly wrong answer.

"Not even close; now pay attention," he said politely yet with a stern, teacher tone that you can tell he's acquired over the years.

I nodded, forcing myself to pay closer attention. It was very, very difficult.

I needed gym to get over so I could go to photography class and talk with Evelynn.

"He is totally wanting to hang out with you one on one again!" Evelynn shrieked when I told her the news that I thought would upset her.

"So, you're not mad?" I asked cautiously, yet relieved and thrilled by her response.

"I mean, you may want me to check over your homework just in case he's wrong, but otherwise, no, I'm super excited for you! Are you starting today? Do I need to drop you off somewhere special? Do the rest of the girls know yet?" she rambled off her questions faster than I could process, let alone answer.

I tried to answer them in the order she asked them. "No, we're not going to start today. Since his birthday is coming up shortly, and my birthday is just around the corner, we're going to wait a week, so I won't need to be dropped off anywhere. I haven't yet told Hayden or Chelsea yet, this all just happened. I'll talk about it on the drive home."

"Tell us what on the drive home?" Rose quietly snuck up on us. Since she doesn't have a loud, booming voice, she didn't scare-scare me, but the sudden presence of a human made me jump. Especially because of the topic I was talking about.

"Nothing big," I said with a small smile to try and downplay it.

"Nothing big," Evelynn said in a voice that apparently was supposed to mimic mine. "She has a DATE with William!" she shrieked.

"It's not a date!" I said, looking over my shoulder hoping that nobody else heard her. "We're just going to study together is all."

"So, a study date?" Rose said playfully, bumping my arm.

"That's exactly what it is!" Evelynn chimed in again.

"Not. That's exactly what it is not. Now I really don't want you guys making a big deal about this, please," I said with pleading eyes. I knew Rose and Hayden wouldn't, but I was nervous about Evelynn and Chelsea blowing everything out of proportion.

"It's okay to be nervous, you know? I remember when Kyle and I first started hanging out—"

Our teacher interrupted the story we've heard from Evelynn a hundred times already. I love her, but I was glad when Mr. Kanoah began class. Today's lecture was on light and shadows. We got to go outside for a bit to play with our cameras while the sun was out.

As a small treat, even though he wasn't supposed to, Mr. Kanoah let us out of class a few minutes before the bell rang. I thought I would see William at his locker, but I didn't. I couldn't wait any longer or else my friends would come to hunt me down, wondering why I wasn't outside with them yet.

Chelsea and Hayden hadn't shown up yet. Evelynn wanted to bring up the topic of William again, but I didn't want to talk about this out in the open.

What if he happened to walk by while I was talking with my friends? I wouldn't want him to think I'm gossiping about him.

"I see Chelsea and Hayden coming; now seriously, please don't say anything or make them jump to any conclusions alright?" I had put my hands on both of her shoulders so that she knew I was dead serious.

"Alright, alright. We'll see how everything goes between you two and 'studying,'" she said with a wink.

Chelsea came bounding up to us faster than normal, with the biggest smile I think I have ever seen on her face. "Peter and I are officially official! He's my boyfriend!"

Well, luckily this will trump my news that isn't really news in the first place.

"What!" the three of us shrieked in unison. It's surprising, yet not surprising at the same time.

"Tell us everything," Evelynn demanded.

Peter didn't do anything romantic, like what you might see in a romance movie. There weren't any flowers, chocolates, or doves that flew out of her locker when she opened it. Instead, he handed her a little note saying that he finds her gorgeous, funny, and he has had a really great time hanging out with her. When she finished reading the note, she looked at him, and he popped the question, which she cheerfully, loudly, and very Chelsea-like, said yes to.

"And here we are!" Chelsea said, concluding her story as we pulled into Hayden's driveway to drop her off first.

I was thankful Chelsea was able to make her story last as impressively long as she did. It saved me from having to re-explain myself.

CHAPTER 10

William and I started falling into a routine. I wouldn't see him in the morning before classes started. After lunch we would meet at our lockers, discard our morning backpack contents, replace the new weight with our second-half of the day books and notebooks, walk to class together, and then go our separate ways until the end of the day.

Once home, he and I would text, continuing any conversations or thoughts that we figured the other one would find interesting. Whether he actually found my topics interesting or not, he always texted back and was great at keeping the conversation flowing. We would text deep into the night at times, until one of us fell asleep first, causing the other person to wait up longer and then text, "Are you still up?" to which, one of us wouldn't reply, and then the other would fall asleep. Nine out of ten times, it was me texting him if he were still awake, even though I knew he wouldn't be, but he always continued the conversation the next morning where we left off.

We talk about anything and everything now. It's cliché, but I really feel I have known him much, much longer than a few short weeks. I can now find him in the crowded hallways without needing to see his face. I know his height, his backpack, his walk, how he swings his arms when he moves; I guarantee if I were blindfolded and I had to pick him out of a line of guys by the sound of his voice, I would be able to. I know him up to the point of touch. We haven't hugged; the closest we've gotten to anything intimate is us high fiving twice now.

I eventually texted the group about our future study sessions that I'm hoping will happen, and naturally they all agreed that William probably wants to be more than just friends, but I'm really, REALLY trying to not get ahead of myself or get my hopes up.

I've been trying desperately to control my thoughts, but I will catch myself daydreaming about him during school or when I'm at home with my family. I've also dreamt of him practically every night this week. Nothing weird, but I haven't told him, or my friends either for that matter, about the dreams. We're always doing something different in my dreams.

The first dream, which I will take to my grave because nobody can ever find this out, he and I were riding his cows, Mac and Cheese. That's not soooo weird, except we were riding them through some church (which I expect to have been Notre Dame), and then we ended up on some rainbow still riding the cows. When we reached the bottom of the rainbow and dismounted, he, sure enough, reached his hand up and wanted a high five from me.

Seriously? I can't even get a hug in my own dream?!

This week dragged on yet flew by at the same time. It was now Friday, football night. It's a home game which is nice because then we don't have to bother with traveling and Evelynn has enough time to get us ready. Plus, we don't have to worry about where we're going to sit in our opponent's stadium when they give us like five bleachers for our entire student section.

Peter and Chelsea have been hanging out all week long, so we haven't really seen or heard from her except in the car rides to and from school and at lunchtime. I think she's forcing herself to sit with us because Peter wants to have some guy time and that's what lunch is for in her mind. I know she'd be sitting next to him though if he asked her.

I would if William asked me.

It has also become routine that we all sit together at the games. My friends and I are always there before the guys, but we know how many seats to save for all of us. Rose is the only one absent because she's in our pep band. They sit at the end of the field, so we don't get to talk to her at the games ever. I think Morris is more disappointed about that than anyone.

William and I always sit next to each other; it's my favorite part about the games. He's more generous than he needs to be, but he buys me popcorn and a Pepsi every time. This allows the door to open for my friends to tease me afterwards, but I honestly don't even mind it. I've been having too much fun to care!

This game was intense. We went into double overtime but ended up losing. Of course, a lot of our student section felt the refs were making terrible and one-sided calls. I don't know enough details about football to know if they were being unfair, or if we were being biased on our home turf. I'm sure it's some of both. It was a tough loss regardless and left our side of the stands quiet.

After the game, Peter and Chelsea informed us they were going to hang out. Peter left it as an open invitation for the rest of us to join if we wanted but knowing Chelsea, and being able to read the look she gave us, it was in fact, not truly an open invitation.

William declined first. He said he needed to get up early and do some chores before spending the day with his family for his upcoming birthday. His grandparents were coming down too. He thought he'd be able to work on the pick-up truck some more.

He was excited for it, and it made my heart happy to see him light up when he talked about it.

As far as the bonfire for tomorrow, it turned out there was a major chance for it to thunderstorm all day, but he said if we don't have the bonfire, we can move the party inside to his basement. I'm thankful he didn't cancel it all together.

The rest of us verbally declined Peter's offer. There were some things I wanted to do tonight in preparation for tomorrow anyway. I needed to figure out what I'm wearing (without telling Evelynn I have no idea what I'm going to wear). It also greatly depends on if we're inside or outside. If we're outside, it's going to be muggy and humid, and if we're inside, well, who knows what we'll end up doing.

Not to mention, I've been desperately trying to figure out what to get William for a gift, despite his request to not get him anything. I'm kind of running out of time.

I know, I know, if he says he doesn't want a gift I should respect that decision. But at the same time, I love getting my friends gifts and I would like to get him something. Boys are
so hard to shop for, though!

He lives on a farm, and I know nothing about anything farm related so that's out of the question for me. His parents are financially secure, so I know he doesn't need anything.

Think, Alli, think. What would he like to have for fun? I don't know, maybe a board game? Ugh, that sounds lame or like something his grandparents would give him. What about something sports related? It's too late to order anything online and I've seen he has a ton of Chiefs apparel already. He wears a different sports shirt almost every other day, whether it's the NFL, Royals, Jayhawks, or our high school. I don't know. I'll see if any of my friends have some ideas because I'm desperate now.

Luckily my phone was on vibrate and I was able to sleep through the textbook Chelsea sent to us at 2:43 AM via text message. She recapped, in every detail possible, what she and Peter did last night. They went bowling after the football game until 12:30 AM. Chelsea lied to her parents saying she was hanging out with us since she figured she would be out late. Peter walked Chelsea home from the bowling alley since neither of them have a car or school permit. Chelsea probably could have called her older sister to come and pick her up, but she doesn't trust Rebecca half the time. Chelsea also didn't want to get grounded with the party being tomorrow (well I guess today now).

He kissed her goodnight. That kiss led to another, and then another, and then I was visually seeing things in my head I didn't need to because of the number of details she included about their first make-out session.

"Eww," I started texting back, but decided against that. Instead, I opted for, "Wow, I felt like I was practically there from the intensity of your text." This caused the group to laugh, including Chelsea.

Chelsea:	Ok, maybe that was a little TMI, but omg, it was such a wonderful night. I can't wait for tonight! It's going to be so much fun!
Hayden:	my phone shows it's going to be storming tonight.
Rose:	so, does mine
Me:	William said we'll be in his basement if the bonfire gets rained out
Evelynn:	What's everyone going to wear?

Hayden: *sends a picture of her in her pjs she's currently wearing* I'll probably throw some jeans on instead though, otherwise, nothing crazy for me

Chelsea: I haven't even thought about what I'm wearing tonight. CRAP!

Evelynn: Alli, what are you planning to wear? First birthday party we don't want to overdo it, but also, we can't underdo it either.

Me: We?

Evelynn: Yes, WE! I'm not going to let you blow this opportunity.

Hayden: my sympathies to you Sky

Me: one condition Evelynn, you take us to Wal-Mart soon so I can try and find a gift for him. Then I'll let you dress me up, but I am going to be wearing a pair of my jean shorts, no skirts.

Evelynn: Deal, but we're swinging by Target too then. Who else wants to go with us?

Everyone but Hayden opted to ride along. It's hard to pass up a shopping trip in this town. Besides parks, bike trails, and housing, we're pretty much a shopping and eating kind of town. All the small surrounding towns come here on the weekends to shop, making everywhere crowded. My parents avoid shopping on the weekends as much as humanly possible. They'd rather go when it's 8:00 at night on a Tuesday to avoid the crowds.

We went to Target first where Chelsea and Eve-lynn bought a few new items. Chelsea bought a short floral summer dress that was on sale. She planned to wear it that night. She also bought some new crop tops and a pair of leggings.

Evelynn bought new shoes, dresses, tops, and some new underwear as well. She was going to wear jeans, the new white-and-navy floral shirt she just bought, with the new sandals she purchased today too.

Considering what I wear, and the amount of thrift shopping I do, her closet is like a mall to me. That's the great thing about having so many girlfriends and being relatively the same size: new outfit possibilities are endless. We're always mixing and matching from each other's closets.

Walking around Target gave me more of an idea of what to do for a present. However, I'm waiting until we go to Wal-Mart before purchasing anything. I'm going to go with a food basket option. I'll buy a bunch of stuff I already know he eats. Not to sound ungrateful, but I know how it goes when somebody gives you a gift and you have no use for it. You feel you have to keep the item out of obligation so when they come over, they can see it and feel like they got you something you love.

Here's what I bought him from Wal-Mart: four boxes of Kraft Mac and Cheese, a bag of pistachios, teriyaki beef jerky, plain pringles, and extra cheesy goldfish. I also bought him some light blue and white Gatorades because he drinks that stuff more than anything else. The last item I purchased was not edible; it was a black bandana because a lot of the guys at the football games wear them. I'm not sure if he'll like it, but it was also $2 so I won't be out anything if he throws it away.

Feeling satisfied with my gift, we walked around a little bit longer looking at random things but there wasn't anything else we wanted to add to my cart. I checked out and we made a plan for the rest of the day. Evelynn was going to drop us all off at our houses so we could pack our overnight bags and gather anything we wanted to wear or bring tonight.

She said she'd pick us all up in an hour and a half starting with Rose. It sounded like a good plan to me. She offered for me to leave all the food items in her car so she could wrap it for me. Her obsession with wrapping gifts comes in handy a lot for me.

This morning I talked to Mom about my plans for tonight. She knew we were going to William's but were going to spend the night at Evelynn's afterwards. However, and I think she did this just to be sure I wasn't lying about spending the night at a guy's house, she said she was going to be the one to pick me up from Evelynn's at 9:00 AM for church. I accepted her terms without any hesitation.

When I got home from shopping, I ran upstairs and started packing my bag. I started in the bathroom with the items I use every morning: toothbrush, deodorant, body spray, etc. There's no need for makeup; Evelynn has anything and everything when it comes to that department.

Next, I moved into my bedroom and started deciding what I wanted to wear. I put on the jean shorts I said I was going to wear tonight but then I wasn't sure what else I needed. I didn't know what I needed for shoes since I didn't know what shirt I'd be wearing. I'm always cold so I knew I would need a jacket or a sweatshirt regardless of whether we would be outside or inside. I tried to remember what the other girls owned, but I settled on my army green jacket.

I wasn't worried about pajamas because I could wear a T-shirt and shorts from Evelynn, if need be, so that was easy.

Well, that didn't take as long as I thought it would. Unless, that is, I'm forgetting something! Am I?

I went through the evening again in my head and decided that I should pack some more layers in case the storm holds off and we end up having a bonfire after all.

> **Evelynn:** text me when you're all ready, that way I can pick you guys up sooner if need be.
>
> **Me, Hayden, & Rose:** ready

About twenty minutes later, Chelsea was finally ready.

When we all got back to her house, I expressed my appreciation for her wrapping job on my food basket. We know her house as if it were our own, every light switch, creak in the floor, etc. We have navigated every nook and cranny of this house during our hide and seek crusades over the years. We rush up the stairs and I'm sure we sound like a stampede of laughing hyenas to her parents.

Once in the secrecy of her bedroom, we threw our bags on the ground and proceeded to turn on the music to drown out our conversation to any listening ears; also, everything's better with music in my opinion.

We stick to the classics typically when we get ready together: "Bye Bye Bye," "Yeah," "Hit Me Baby One More Time," "Hips Don't Lie," and so on. Every now and then, depending on who's in charge of the music, we'll play more current hits.

Rose and Hayden were ready. Hayden wanted Evelynn to braid her hair. Evelynn was going to do her makeup and then she would assist the rest of us. Since I needed Evelynn's assistance with what to wear from her closet, my hair, and my makeup, I'd need the most attention. Chelsea had the dress from

Target she was wearing, and she was going to curl her hair for tonight. She's self-sufficient when it comes to getting ready on her own.

As Evelynn was braiding Hayden's hair, I was flipping through her wardrobe over and over, pulling out the shirts I liked. I pulled out a green-and-beige quarter sleeve shirt. It was fitted in the waist and came down below the beltline of my jeans. I also pulled out a burgundy long sleeve shirt that had lace detail around the V-neckline and down the sleeves, all the way to the cuffs that wrapped tightly around the wrists. The last option I pulled out was a white, see-through shirt I would wear over a tank top. It was slightly off the shoulder since it had a wider neckline. It had a V-neck outlined in lace as well, but it was not remotely as deep as the burgundy shirt. It had lace sleeves and I've always been a huge fan of this shirt.

Evelynn immediately nixed the burgundy top. She pulled out a long, dark gray shirt that had open shoulders crisscrossing with shiny silver bead work. She pulled out a navy halter top that I rejected immediately, because I would not be comfortable wearing something that revealing tonight.

Chelsea was also helping and pulling out the shirts she likes of Evelynn's. Chelsea and I have different chest sizes and completely different tastes when it comes to clothing. I made faces at every option Chelsea showed me. I was conscious of Evelynn watching my reactions, so I tried to watch my facial expressions. I didn't want to look too disgusted considering Evelynn wears all these shirts daily.

Chelsea pulled out a brown leather tank top that had dark brown buttons all the way up the middle. I said no immediately, so she showed me this tank top that had spaghetti straps, with an empire waistline. It hung lower than the bottom of my shorts, so I didn't like that. It's something you should wear with jeans. I'm not a fan when my shirts make me look like I'm not wearing any pants. Getting annoyed, she pulled out another tank top that was lavender with small floral patterns on it. I immediately nixed that one as well. She hung it back on the rack with a sigh.

"Fine, I'll show you one more option, Alli, but then I give up if you don't like it!" Chelsea said. It was a tan "shirt" that was extremely open; it crisscrossed deep by the belly button, so you definitely needed to wear a tank top underneath. It's not something I normally would wear, but I've also never tried it on either. I told her I would at least try it on. That satisfied her and Evelynn.

I tried on every shirt that was handed to me from the selection. We narrowed it down to three options: the dark gray one with the crisscrossing throughout the open sleeves, the white top with lace sleeves, and then the green-and-beige quarter sleeve shirt. Chelsea still voted for all of hers that never got chosen, but luckily with Rose and Hayden wanting me to be comfortable, they voted on the white shirt that won me over too.

Once I was dressed, Evelynn worked on my hair and makeup. I requested she keep it as natural as possible.

"Natural to you is only mascara," she said as she put primer on my face.

"Well . . . yeah!" was all I could manage as my rebuttal. There was no point in attempting to stand my ground when she was the one in control of making my face look good.

Thankfully she held true to my request and didn't overdo the eye shadow in particular. She curled my hair and braided two side braids that connected in the back but were hidden somehow. I protested the lip gloss, though, because I felt like that would be too much with a full face of makeup already and my hair curled.

I feel like I'm going to be attending some formal event rather than a night with friends. It was making me nervous, as if I was overdressed in comparison to what I usually look like. I didn't want to come across as a different person to William.

We needed to swing by Kyle's house and pick him up before heading to William's. Thankfully Evelynn's parents let us borrow their suburban for tonight.

The second Kyle opened the car door, it started downpouring. Evelynn was white knuckling the steering wheel now with the wipers going full blast as we headed out of town. She shushed us because she needed to concentrate and couldn't with our babbling. She finally relaxed when we turned onto the gravel road toward the farm.

Well, I'm glad somebody is calming down. I wish I could!

My nerves started to increase, my fingertips were tingling, and my heart was getting louder and louder. I swore Rose could hear it since she was sitting next to me.

When we hit the gravel road, I texted William that we were almost there. Sticking to his word, he was waiting for us in the garage and laughed as we all ran for shelter.

"Glad you guys could make it. Could you see the road at all?" he asked politely, looking at Evelynn who tried to play it cool.

She shrugged and said it was a little hard at times, but nothing she couldn't handle. Kyle raised his eyebrows at her, and we all started laughing, which clearly insulted Evelynn.

"Hey, we made it okay," she said defensively.

"I'm glad you guys got here safe," he said, landing his gaze on mine, making me gulp.

"My mom is a stickler on dirty shoes, so please take them off in the mudroom, and then we'll head down to the basement," he instructed us and we complied.

I must admit, I took pride in not being the one ooh-ing and aww-ing this time as we walked through his house. Don't get me wrong, I was still utterly impressed to the max at his gorgeous farmhouse, but I felt special in knowing that of our group, I was the only one that had been here and knew my way around.

Danny, Peter, and Morris were here already. Morris and Danny were shooting pool, while Peter was throwing darts. It appeared that that was also what William was doing before we arrived. I realized Grant wasn't here and asked if he was coming later. William explained Grant's mom was going to drop him off after he got done with work at the grocery store.

When Peter saw Chelsea, he put the darts down which was smart because Chelsea was already bounding her way up to him for an embrace. Everyone shook their heads in disbelief and that made us laugh together. The laughter from the group pulled Chelsea and Peter out of their little world to re-engage with us.

"Do you guys want anything?" William offered considerately. He pointed to the pop dispenser, the popcorn machine, and the candy area. He winked at me when he mentioned the popcorn. I blushed and looked away. He said there were more snacks down here in the cupboards and that pizza was going to be here in about half an hour or so.

At first it was a little awkward because we weren't sure where to sit or what to do with ourselves since the guys were finishing their own games. I didn't mind watching William play darts. I got to watch him concentrate and watch his arm flex and contract from his throwing motion. He looked like a natural athlete to me.

My friends and I sat on the couches. We talked to each other a little bit, but we mostly watched Chelsea and Peter flirt with the other. He let her throw a couple of times, but she was embarrassed about not being good at it. Chelsea gets easily frustrated at herself when she isn't immediately good at something.

"WIIIILLLLLL!! Your pizza is here. Come up and get it!" Charlotte shouted down the stairs over the music.

"Here, will you finish the game up for me?" William asked me, not waiting for me to stammer my way to the no I was looking for. "Don't worry, there's no possible way for Peter to win no matter what you throw. He's been a little distracted," William said loud enough for everyone to hear. This caused Peter and Chelsea to smile mischievously. Chelsea was proud. You could hear her internal cheering from across the room.

Once again, we all were laughing. Shortly after, we were sitting in a circle enjoying the pizza, music, laughs, and company of one another. Even Kyle was having a good time joking with the other guys. Evelynn was very happy to see him socializing. I enjoyed my time sitting next to William and getting to talk with him.

"How was time with your grandparents?" I asked.

"It was good. Mom cooked lunch and we were able to eat outside before it started raining. Oh, my grandma makes these incredible fudge bites, you should have some. They're over there on the counter next to the microwave."

"I'll make sure to grab one after the pizza," I responded, smiling at his enthusiasm for fudge bites. "Did they get you anything, or do your grandparents not do that? Mine don't; there are too many grandkids, which is fine with me. I'd rather they not."

He let out a soft chuckle. "Grandma can't help but to always buy me a new game. Sometimes they're outrageous games I've never heard of, but this year she got me an NFL Monopoly game. Grandpa got me a new basketball. If it hadn't been raining, we would have shot some hoops together."

I didn't bring the present in! "Oh crud!" I gasped out loud.

"What is it?" he asked, concern forming on his face.

"Oh nothing. I, uh, well I have something for you, I just left it in the car. I'll be right back!" I put my plate down and quickly got up.

"Ev, is your car unlocked? I forgot my . . . thing."

"It should be but take my keys just in case. It's probably still pouring," she said, tossing her keys my way.

I fumbled them and had to pick them up off the ground. This thing is heavier than a janitor's key set! I ran up the stairs, ignoring William's protests saying I better not have gotten him a gift.

It was 100% still pouring outside as I ran through the rain, trying to avoid every puddle. I grabbed the present from the back, not worrying too much if it got wet since Evelynn wrapped it so well. I hustled back inside. I used caution on the basement stairs so I wouldn't trip and die which would inadvertently leave a sour memory for his birthdays to come.

What a buzzkill that would be.

"Here you go!" I excitedly handed him my gift.

"You really shouldn't have."

"She did though. Open it!" Evelynn said with the same enthusiasm I had. Her love language is Gifts, so it doesn't matter who's receiving or giving, she loves being a part of moments like these.

Grant came down the stairs right as William was lifting his hands to open the gift. This caused William to pause and be the generous, courteous host he is by letting Grant know about the pizza and fudge bites. Grant in return was asking how everything had been and luckily Evelynn being Evelynn was there to "assist" in reclaiming his attention.

"Will is about to open his present from Alli. Grab some pizza and have a seat so we can see what she got him!"

Either he is a good actor, or he genuinely loved the gift I got him. I whole-heartedly choose to believe it was the latter.

"Alli! These are great! They won't last at all, but I love all these items, especially the mac and cheese. I'm digging the handkerchief. I'll put it in my Jeep tomorrow, so I won't forget to wear it at the games."

He stood up and motioned for me to stand too, so I did, nervously.

"Thank you," he said in a gentle but grateful tone. And then it happened: he hugged me!

Wow his arms feel nice! Firm and sturdy. Definitely able to overpower me if he wanted to.

I could smell his shampoo and the fresh linen scent from his shirt. My thoughts and emotions were on fire right now. Then I remembered that all my friends and his friends were there watching us, and my face instantly became warm.

He let me go, smiling sheepishly at my blushing face. "Now, I have something for your birthday," he said casually.

My jaw dropped all the way to the floor.

No seriously, I had to pick it up off of the ground. It was heavier than Evelynn's keys!

"Wh . . . what?" I stammered, turning toward my friends; they were all cackling like crazy. Even William's friends were getting a kick out of this.

Did they know? Were they in on this?

William too was laughing and showing off his incredible smile at the expense of my perplexity and bewilderment. "Your birthday is shortly after mine, and I did say this would be a joint party."

He flexed his eyebrows up and then nodded at me playfully yet mysteriously.

When William turned to walk toward a door in the back of the room, I turned toward my friends with the same shocked and baffled expression.

"Sky!" Chelsea tried to choke out between laughs. "I wish you could see your face right now!" She held her side and pointed at me as she continued laughing. Hayden and Evelynn were filming this whole ordeal. I was too stunned to object. William came back holding a large gift bag and told me to sit down. My legs managed to oblige as I sat back down in my original spot.

"I'm going to pull your gifts out one by one," he instructed. I nodded in response . . . I think.

The first items he pulled out were two blocks of cheese: Swiss and Colby Jack. My brain and face immediately were confused, and the room cracked up once again.

I remembered what my parents had ingrained in me as a child: "Always show gratitude toward any gift you are given, no matter how big or small it may be."

I regained my manners and some of my composure to thank him. "Mmm, I do enjoy cheese. Thank you for thinking of me." More laughs from the crowd.

"This is to be eaten with the cheese," he said, pulling out a giant loaf/baguette of white bread.

"I am always down for a good carb and dairy indulgence," I said more enthusiastically.

That's not a lie either.

He smiled, pulling out the next item. "To wash it down, here's some non-alcoholic, white grape sparkling juice."

A candle was the next item produced. Here is when I found out that Evelynn had been involved and my friends did in fact know about this surprise. He wasn't sure what scents I liked, or what kind of cheese I liked to eat (or if I even liked sparkling juice). The candle he had bought was purple and said tropical sunrise on it. If I had ever been to some place tropical, I would assume it smells amazing like this.

"I'll explain the candle at the end." Moving onto the next gift, what he pulled from the bag stumped me. It was a fleur de lis (the flower of life in French) keychain. It was small, and gold with little rhinestones on it.

"Holy cow, William! This is all amazing, but you can't possibly have more stuff in there can you?"

He laughed, informing me he had two more items to give me. He made me close my eyes for the next one. "Put your hands out," he instructed me, and I obeyed. Something plush and soft was set in my hands, like a stuffed animal or something. "OK, you can open them."

My eyes flew open to reveal a pink stuffed animal in my hands. "Awww, it's a pink bobcat!" I said, putting my nose to its nose for a split second.

He laughed again and corrected me, "Actually it's a panther."

My jaw dropped to the floor again as it finally dawned on me what he was doing.

He's recreating everything I drew on my French assignment. These are all the items I drew because they "represent" France to me. I. Can't. Even!! This is the sweetest thing on the planet!!

"I have one more item in here. Can you guess what it is?" he asked, testing me.

"Is it the French flag?" I asked. A quick wave of doubt swept through my mind until I looked into his eyes.

His smile said the answer before his lips. "Yes. Imported from France itself." He pulled out a little French flag on a stick; something that you would get at a Fourth of July parade (but in that case it would be an American flag obviously).

"Evelynn also said that you already own *Beauty and the Beast*. I got you the candle to represent the candlestick guy," he explained.

"I love this. Thank you!" I stood up and wrapped my arms around him now for an even bigger hug than before.

I will never forget this night for as long as I live!

"Alright, alright. Enough with the hugging, let's get back to partying," Danny piped up, making everyone clap.

The rest of the night was so much fun! We had contests for everything, and it turns out, his guy friends are as competitive as my friends are. The guys beat us in pool, but we whooped them in darts. Grant and Kyle had a belching contest; Grant won, and Evelynn was grossed out. We played charades and Rose and Morris were naturally the best actors, even without saying anything. Peter and Chelsea had an arm-wrestling match. It was then up for debate on who let the other win.

We watched a movie called *Role Models*. It was kind of funny. I was focused on the fact I was next to William on the couch. We were sharing the same blanket, but we weren't cuddling. However, throughout the movie, as everyone shifted around, my entire right arm was pressed against his! I could even feel his laugh rumble through him.

Unfortunately, as soon as the movie ended, we had to get going. It was practically midnight, and we would be lucky if we made it back to Evelynn's without getting scolded for staying out too late. It was going to be a late night staying up and talking.

CHAPTER 11

William wasn't going to be in French class today. His mom was taking him to get his driver's license. They were going out to lunch and spending the quality time parents want with their children, especially when we hit the milestone ages. I understand this, because my mom is doing the exact same thing with me in ten days for my birthday.

I texted him last night that I would like to wish him happy birthday in person before he leaves for the day. He said he would meet me by my locker before Homeroom, which made my heart happy.

"Hey!" he said, greeting me where he said he would.

I had arrived first and was rifling around in my locker trying to look busy and not appear as though I was waiting around for somebody.

"Hey birthday boy! Happy birthday!" I greeted, opening my arms for a hug which he returned. This was now our third hug in three days. "Wow, you look so much older now than when I saw you on Saturday!" I said playfully surprised, yet sarcastically.

"That's what my mom said, except she was serious," he said, adjusting his backpack and looking a little embarrassed. It was adorable.

"How are Mom and Dad doing now that their oldest is practically street legal?" I asked.

"Dad gave me the responsibility lecture last night. Mom cried Saturday night, Sunday morning, and this morning too. I guarantee when she picks me up today, she's going to cry then too."

"It's a mother's right," I said in a small defense.

"Oh, I get that, it's just, awkward and sad to see your mom cry, even if it's for a happy reason."

Awww! How sweet!

"Yeah, I feel you. My parents aren't overly emotional people, so if they do show something, it's like, 'whoa, they're expressing emotions,' and then I have to figure out how to react," I said in response, thinking about my parents and the rare times I've seen them sad. They are positive and proud parents more than anything. They're proud of Greyson and me, but not like, brag on social media all the time proud. Thank goodness.

The ten-minute warning bell dinged, and we ignored it. This entire morning, I was mustering the courage to ask him a question but wasn't sure how to approach it without sounding weird or needy. My anxiety being itself last night was making me wonder if he was only being nice about studying together when we talked about it last week. I hoped he was serious and wanted to.

The only way you'll find out is if you ask him. I mean, I could wait to see if he brings it up himself. You could yeah, or you could ask him right now and get this over with. Fine, I'll ask!

"Would you still want to study together this week? I mean, that is, if you get your license and all."

"Are you starting to doubt me, Allison?" he asked, surprising me with my full name and faking offense.

"Well, I haven't actually ridden in a car with you yet. You could be a crazy driver and I wouldn't even know it."

"Let's make a deal," he said, intriguing me.

"What's the deal?" I asked, suspiciously.

"Ohhhhh no. You either accept it and find out, or you decline it and never know," he said, grinning at me, making me unable to say no to his excited eyes.

"Alright, deal. Now tell me." My curiosity will always get the best of me.

"*If* I get my license today, you let me pick you up and take you somewhere. However, the catch is, if at any time, you say 'whoa' or grab the 'oh shit handle' even once, you have to back our trailer bed into the barn."

My jaw didn't hit the floor, but it started to crack open. I didn't know what to expect from him, but this wasn't it!

"*Me*! Back in a trailer?! Are you nuts?"

"If I were you, I wouldn't blow it then," he said, grinning at me again, trapping me in his stare.

My heart started beating faster and my palms started to get clammy as I was holding my backpack. I gripped the right strap tighter, and now it was my turn to squirm where I was standing. He raised his eyebrow at me, waiting for me to say something out loud.

"Okay, okay, it's still a deal. If I do either of those things, then I will attempt to back a trailer in. But I am warning you, you do *not* want to see this, nor would your dad!"

"I suggest sitting on your hands," he said with a wink. I rolled my eyes at him and bit my lip, making him laugh out loud.

The five-minute warning bell sounded, making everyone at their lockers stir, even us. Our Home-rooms weren't near each other, so we didn't walk together long. We parted ways shortly after and I wished him good luck at the DOT. He said he would text me immediately if the deal was still on or not. I told him I couldn't wait. Although I was being a tiny bit sarcastic when I said it.

I started to picture it again, him and I, driving around in his jeep at night, listening to music and going into the country to look at the stars and talk.

Yeah, I hope he does get his license today!

William: The deal is on. I got my license!

Me: OMG CONGRATULATIONS!

You're a free man now!

William: It's a good thing I didn't make this bet with mom. Three times while I was driving us to lunch, she freaked out next to me making me think I was going to hit something, or someone! I wasn't even close.

Me: Yeah my mom is the same way. We've lived in this town my entire life and she still thinks she needs to give me directions on how to get across town. She also likes to use the 'oh crap handle,' but she does that when dad drives too.

William: lol parents. Does 8:13 PM work?

Me: 8:13?

William: Yeah 8:13

Me: hahaha sure, 8:13 PM works for me. I'll be ready at 8:00 though, just in case.

William: sounds like a plan! I hope you didn't have too much fun in French class without me ;)

Me: I could never!

That's the truth too. In these first few weeks of school, William has made this year my favorite one yet. I look forward to coming to school every day. Even though we only have one class together. It's fun getting to talk to him at our lockers, and it's even exciting when I get to see him at lunch despite our paths not really crossing.

I know this will sound silly but seeing him at lunch reminds me he is real and I'm not imagining him. I'm not making up this connection we have, our shared interests and our similar sense of humor. With girlfriends, sometimes it kind of feels like a competition; with William though . . . it's just tranquil and easy.

I'm sure it was the anticipation of 8:13 getting here or maybe because William was gone for half of the day, but today *dragged* on forever. I knew he'd want to know what he missed in class today, but honestly, I don't even know what to tell him. We practiced reading something, some important French document thingy from way back in the day. We also worked on our pronunciation. Bonnie did great at correcting me again. I suppose he would like to know that fun detail.

I told the girls at lunch that William got his license and that he was coming over tonight so we could hang out. Here's how the conversation went:

"Wait! Is he going to meet your family tonight?!" Evelynn asked first.

"I hope not, but Mom and Dad might insist on meeting him first before letting me go with him unfortunately." I groaned at the very possible idea.

"What are you guys going to do?" Hayden asked.

I shrugged. "I don't know honestly. He just said he's going to pick me up and drive me somewhere."

"Oh my god, Alli! What if he's going to take you parking? Or ask you to be his girlfriend?!" Chelsea started shrieking and I had to shush her because a couple of the surrounding tables were looking at us.

"Shhh! Chelsea, I seriously doubt that is what he has planned for tonight."

Although, what if he did? No, I can't go down that road right now. I'm already nervous as is!

"What's parking?" Rose asked.

"Oh, it's where you drive to some secluded place and fool around. Some people only make out, others will go all the way and have sex in their cars," Chelsea explained without missing a beat.

Rose blushed, embarrassed she had asked in the first place.

"I should ask Peter if he has any idea. Then I can give you a heads up," Chelsea said, pulling her phone out to text him.

"No, Chelsea, don't do that. Don't meddle. Whatever they do or don't do tonight is none of our business, and you shouldn't get to know before Sky does." I flashed Evelynn a very, very thankful smile and she smiled back.

"But I'll tell her immediately!" Chelsea tried defending, but she had already put her phone down on the table.

"Evelynn is right; let's let Sky tell us . . . the second they're done hanging out tonight, might I add," Hayden said, staring at me, but flashing her eyebrows up and down at me.

"Alright, alright; I won't ask," she said in her bummed tone.

I was grateful. Plus, I didn't want to hear it from Chelsea; I wanted it to come from him.

Me being me, I was ready to go at 7:00 PM. Since I wasn't sure what we were going to be doing, I decided to wear jean shorts and a fitted, simple white T-shirt. I had my deep red jacket in case of bugs or freezing air conditioning. I wore my white Converse because I'm not a big fan of sandals; I like my socks.

"When this boy gets here, I want you to invite him inside so we can meet him," my dad said at supper.

"His name is William, Dad," I said, rolling my eyes and internally groaning.

"Yeah, Clyde, I'm sure he's a nice, young man if Alli is friends with him," Mom said in my defense.

"What are you kids planning to do at . . . what time did he say? 8:15 at night?" Dad inquired.

"8:13," I corrected him. "I don't know, we're just going to hang out and do homework." I shrugged.

I really don't want him making a big deal about this and embarrassing me in front of William.

"Mmhmm," Dad mumbled, but he dropped the twenty questions.

Mom changed the subject and focused on Greyson instead who was doing his own homework. It gave me the opportunity to sneak back up to my bedroom and wait in peace, away from any parental questioning they may think of later.

At exactly 8:13 PM (even though I had been looking out my window since 7:45), he pulled up to the curb and got out of his jeep. He was walking up to the front door when I was coming down the stairs with my backpack on.

I answered the door, trying not to sound winded from moving so quickly down the stairs. "Hi!" I greeted.

"Hey. Mind if I pop in quick?" he asked.

My smile fell, but I opened the door wider and motioned for him to come inside. "Come in at your own risk," I said, making him smile. "My parents want to meet you anyway."

"And I would like to meet them too. After all, you've met my parents; it's only fair," he said, winking.

"Ughhh," I groaned, making him laugh at my expense.

I could already hear my parents coming to the door, so I knew I didn't need to inform them that William had arrived.

"Hi, you must be William. I'm Nancy and this is my husband, Clyde," my mother greeted warmly, offering her hand to shake his, which he accepted. "Do you go by William?" she asked.

He shook my father's hand next as he responded to Mom's question. "Alli seems to be the only one that calls me William. Well, I guess my grandma does too, but everyone else, including my parents, call me Will. I respond to either, though," he said smiling a very sincere and gentleman-like smile.

"I heard you just got your license." Dad worded it as a statement rather than a congratulatory sentence.

"Yes sir, I did."

"And you feel you're a safe driver?" Dad questioned next, looking William up and down, making my heartbeat faster and my palms perspire.

"Why yes sir, I have been driving our tractors and vehicles out on the farm since I was ten years old," he responded without hesitation.

Dad seemed pleased enough with his response. He nodded and said, "Good," before turning toward me and repeating that I needed to be home no later than 10:00 PM.

"You kids have fun!" Mom said encouragingly, probably trying to ease everyone. She was also trying to ease me with the wink she gave me as she turned around and followed Dad back to the living room.

"Are you ready?" William said, turning to me, perfectly intact after the interrogation.

"That was so awkward," I whispered as we walked to his jeep.

Of course, nothing seemed to ever faze him. He shrugged and said he thought it went well and my parents seemed like nice, caring people.

"You weren't fazed at all by my dad sizing you up and questioning your driving skills?" I asked, surprised.

"Nah. That's just a concerned father trying to make sure his daughter stays safe as she heads out with a sixteen-year-old boy who just got his license. It makes sense to me."

"Okay, by that statement, you are *not* sixteen years old—maybe forty-six!" I responded, laughing.

"As a forty-six year old would do, let me get the door for you, Miss." He professionally opened the door as if he were a butler or doorman in New York City or somewhere.

"Ewww. Don't ever call me Miss, and you definitely do not have to open the door for me. I am a strong, independent woman, *sir*!" I retorted, laughing and making him laugh too. I eagerly took the hand he offered to me as I climbed into the seat, though.

When I was in the vehicle, and William was walking around to the driver's side, I looked back at my house and noticed my parents had gone to the front window to watch us. I was so embarrassed, but I knew he would get a kick out of it, so I pointed to my parents.

"Oh my gosh, my parents watched that whole thing."

"I know. That's why I played it up," he said laughing.

"Are you serious?!" I said in disbelief.

"Sirius Black I am," he joked, referencing *Harry Potter*, which I love.

I noticed the black bandana I had gotten him for his birthday was hanging around his rearview mirror.

"Hey, I recognize that," I said, pointing to the piece of fabric.

"Yeah, I got it for my birthday from someone special and I wanted her to know," he said looking over at me.

Pretty sure if a heart could literally melt, mine just did!

We drove around for about thirty minutes all over town. It was a nice, seventy-degree night, so we had the windows down and the music playing.

Just as I envisioned.

He started taking some back roads I was not familiar with, and eventually we ended up at a private property sign. He put the car in park, and I looked over at him confused.

"We're walking from here," he said putting his hand on the car handle to get out.

"What? This is private property," I said not budging an inch.

"I'm not going to get you in trouble on our first night out together. This is the Ross' property. They let my dad and I fish here whenever we want. It's okay that we're here," he reassured me.

Apparently, I trust him more than I thought at this point, because once he said those words, I relaxed and got out of the jeep to follow him.

We didn't have to walk very far. He also didn't hold my hand to guide me as I thought maybe he would. The land opened into a beautiful, hilly area with tall grass, and a decent size lake in the middle of it. That's where we landed.

William laid out a blanket he had brought for us and lit four of those citronella candles to keep the mosquitos and other bugs away.

Hopefully these work because otherwise, I'll get eaten alive and swell up.

I set my bag down on the blanket and then I sat cross legged and looked at him. He joined shortly and now we sat next to each other, on a blanket, near a lake, with the sun setting off in the distance.

What if he does ask me to be his girlfriend? Man, I wish I had sprayed myself with some body mist before I left the house. Do I smell okay?

"What did I miss in French class today?" he asked, pulling out a notebook from his backpack.

"Not much. We practiced reading aloud to work on our pronunciation," I said.

I tried remembering earlier what I was going to tell him when I figured he would ask me this question. I think I was missing one more item, but I'm not sure what it could be anymore. I did know we didn't have any homework. No homework means less to remember and that's my favorite part about school.

I pulled out my English notebook because I needed to brainstorm an outline for a paper I'm writing on the study of women empowerment. The woman I chose to write about was Cleopatra.

He asked me what I was going to work on, and I told him, which led us to start comparing current society to previous decades. We talked for over an hour without working on our actual homework. It was so cool to get to hear things from a guy's perspective. We started on women's rights and then we kept spiraling into abortion, death penalty, etc. I looked down at my phone because my group chat was blowing up. It was already 9:45 PM.

"Oh crud, it's getting close to 10:00," I said in a disappointed tone.

"We should get going. I don't want to get you in trouble," he said, blowing out the candles and packing up his backpack.

I stood up and helped him fold the blanket we were on. Our fingers touched as we got closer together when folding. He pulled away and finished folding on his own. He asked if I would carry two of the candles while he carried two as well, that way we wouldn't spill the melted wax inside.

We walked back to his jeep in silence, but not awkward silence; I was content. In the car, he turned on the radio and by the time we pulled into my driveway, we both had been singing along and I was comfortable singing—not great, I might add—with him.

This was an incredible night.

He pulled into the driveway since he wasn't staying long and then he surprised me when he also got out of his car.

He's walking me to the door!

We didn't speak as we walked to my front door. I wasn't going to say anything; I wanted him to speak first.

"So, be honest, how was my driving?" he said with a knowing grin. Not once was I ever nervous about his driving. He followed every law correctly. Whether he did that for me tonight only, or if this is how he regularly drives, I'd have to see.

"You are a very good driver, and I was never tempted to use the handle at all," I said smiling with gratification.

"Good. I want you to feel safe with me," he said in all seriousness. It made me catch my breath. He could sense it too, so he tried lightening the mood with the next thing he said.

"This was fun," he simply stated. I nodded in agreement. "Next time, though, we should probably actually work on some homework."

"I agree. I will need help with math; Thursday maybe?" I asked him with hope in my voice.

"Thursday should work for me," he said with his gentle smile.

"Cool!" I said, still waiting to see if he would do anything while we were on the porch.

Maybe a kiss on the cheek or something?

"I'll see you tomorrow at school, Alli," he said, opening his arms up for a hug.

I graciously accepted the hug, but I couldn't help feeling the amount of disappointment that coursed through me.

When he got into his Jeep, I waved goodbye and opened the familiar handle. I saw his lights flash as he turned to head toward his house. I walked up the stairs to my bedroom, unsure of how I currently felt at that moment. Internally I wished a little more had happened tonight, but I still had a wonderful time.

Maybe it will, maybe it won't, but for now, just enjoy the time you're spending with him. It's easier said than done but try not to get too caught up in your feelings. You know that's almost impossible right? Yes, but let's still try to attempt this at least, deal? Deal.

I set my backpack on the ground quietly and pulled out the Cleopatra notes I had. I really did need to brainstorm ideas before I went to bed, but tonight gave me some inspiration. Ideas poured out of me and onto the paper. Afterwards, I brushed my teeth and fell asleep easier than I thought I would be able to.

CHAPTER 12

"Haaaaaappppy Birthday, to you!" Mom came into my bedroom, dressed for work, with a cupcake and a single, burning candle on it. She proceeded to sing the entire birthday song as I awkwardly sat there trying to wake up.

"Thanks, Mom," I said as I reached for the cupcake to blow out the candle.

"Ah ah!" Mom said, making me hold the air in my lungs instead of exhaling. "You need to make a wish first! It doesn't matter if you're one or ninety-nine, you always make a wish on your birthday."

I thought about it longer than I realized I would.

What do I want this year? Good grades? Always. Good friends? I already have those. A boyfriend? I mean, I've wished every year that Oliver would ask me out, and he never has. Yeah, but this year, you have met William. I don't want to screw anything up either. I guess my wish will be this: I wish for new adventures and memories that will last a lifetime. Vague but safe.

"What did you wish for?" Mom asked immediately once I blew the candle out.

I obviously wasn't going to tell her my true wish.

"If I say it, it won't come true, Mom."

She smiled a knowing smile in my direction. "I love you, sweetie," she said, reaching over to tuck a piece of hair behind my ear before getting up from the bed.

"I love you too," and I meant it.

Since I was now fully awake, I decided to get out of bed and start getting ready for the day. I typically never have made a big deal about my birthday and how I dressed on it, but today feels different.

Because you're going to be seeing a certain boy, duh!

I mean, yes, if I'm being honest with myself, which clearly, I am, it has everything to do with seeing William. That and I'm starting to take some more pride in my appearance now that I'm getting out of my horrendous and morbidly awkward pre-teen years. I shudder at the memory of my 8th grade self; that was only two years ago.

I was choosing between a dress, or white jeans. *Dress says, "Look at me, there's a special occasion, let's draw attention to that." Whereas, white jeans and a cute shirt says, "She's looking cute today, maybe something special is going on, or maybe she just wanted to go white instead of denim is all."*

I chose the white jeans with a tan tank top and slate-blue cardigan for when I'm inside with the air conditioning. I almost spiced it up and went with tan wedges that I have, but I opted for my tan sandals because the wedges would have been too much for high school in my opinion.

To each their own on whatever it is they want to wear to school, but my school is nothing like the movies. Nobody, except Evelynn and that's only for important functions, wears heels to school.

I wore my hair half up-half down like usual, but I curled my ends and used some hair spray from my mom's bathroom to try and hold it in place for a day. For jewelry, I always have my elephant necklace on, but I opted to add a dainty gold bracelet and my little gold, hoop earrings.

Wow, I actually look kind of good today.

I mentally complimented myself and headed downstairs for some breakfast. As I ate my Cheerios, I started responding to the Happy Birthday texts from my friends and relatives.

> **Chelsea:** Did you ask your parents about having the guys over on Saturday for your party?

We all know she's asking because she wants to see Peter every second she can, but also, of course I want to see William and his friends as well. Things between all of us have been going well, and honestly, I really do enjoy his friends! I like being around them, but I'll always prefer my alone time with him over anything.

> **Me:** I asked Mom this morning, and she said she would talk to Dad. I'll let you know when I know.
>
> **Evelynn:** I have a backup plan in case the guys do come!
>
> **Hayden:** Of course you do
>
> **Evelynn:** Well, I don't think the guys are going to want to watch chick flicks if we ever want them to hang out with us again.
>
> **Hayden:** ummm, I don't want to watch chick flicks, but I'm forced to

141

Me:	I was thinking maybe we could go to the splash park or the falls?
Chelsea:	Ooooh, I like the splash park idea! It'd be a fun place to get wet!
Hayden:	Of course you do
Chelsea:	What? NO. Not like that, at least, that's not what I was originally thinking!!
Hayden:	suuuure you weren't.
Rose:	*read message at 7:13 AM*
Chelsea:	well since you mentioned it though. LOL
Evelynn:	Let's plan more at lunch when sexual innuendos aren't being discussed via text. Sky, did Will text you happy birthday?
Me:	No
Evelynn:	no worries! Maybe he's waiting to tell you in person!
Me:	Yeah maybe.

I hope so. Technically he already surprised me at his party, so I shouldn't get my hopes up. I can't help it though, it's too easy to picture these imaginary scenarios.

Evelynn:	I'll see you ladies soon!

William was leaning against my locker as I walked up to it.

He was smiling his beautiful and soft smile that made my face warm.

"Hey, happy birthday," he greeted me warmly.

I full on blushed under his gaze. "Thank you," I practically whispered. I cleared my throat and thanked him with a little more confidence and appreciation.

In response, he laughed at my correction, which made me blush harder, but I was already fidgeting with my combination and my hair was luckily covering the side of my face that he was standing next to.

"Are you getting your license today?" he asked.

"Unfortunately, I can't go until Saturday. My parents couldn't take today off," I said totally bummed, which he sympathized with.

"Aw, I'm sorry. I'd take you there if I could, you know."

"Thank you. I appreciate that."

"I could always drive you guys too if you'd like," he offered, unprompted.

This caught me off guard and made me stutter, "Th-thank you. I'm sure I'll take you up on that offer sometime."

"Sounds good," he said, smiling softly again. "What are you doing for your birthday?"

"Tonight, I'll go out to eat with my family. Then on Saturday I'm going to have the girls over and cause some mayhem around town." I hesitated to say the next part, but he picked up on it.

"What is it?"

"Um, well . . . I was wondering if maybe you guys would like to join us? I was debating on whether I should say anything or not. Anyway, you can think about it, unless you already know, then you can tell me too, but if you don't know and need to talk to the guys first, I totally understand you know?" I inhaled deeply, realizing I barely breathed during that entire spiel.

As always, this caused William to remind me to breathe, but he also put his hand on top of my left shoulder. "We'll be there. You can count on us." He smiled.

He asked if I was ready to head to class, and I was. I slung my backpack over my right shoulder and shut my locker. I took my rightful place next to him as we walked, talked, and my favorite thing: laughed with one another.

Friday seemed to fly by, and before I knew it, we were at the football game again. We are playing at home tonight, which is always nice. We barely won this game. Being in the student body and chanting back at the other team is one of my favorite things about going to high school sporting events. The Dragons thought they had won, but we made a last-second play, throwing the ball to Scott, who ran it seventy-two yards for the winning touchdown.

I couldn't see who it was, if it were high school students or adults, but some people got into a brawl or something as we all were exiting the stadium. The school resource officers, and other people were trying to break it up. I don't like being around that kind of thing, so my friends and I hightailed it out of there to the parking lot as fast as we could.

Luckily, William and his friends weren't into that either because they stayed with us and avoided it all. Peter was the only one who wanted to see what was happening, but Grant was dragging him by his shirt to keep him moving.

"Are you going to give us any details about tomorrow night?" William asked me as we were walking.

Everybody could hear, he wasn't only directing it toward me, so Evelynn spoke first.

"Nope. You're going to have to wait and see what we have planned. And Chelsea," she said, hard side eyeing her, "you cannot tell Peter anything."

"Hey, I haven't spilled any details. Give me some credit," she defended herself.

"That's because you don't know most of the plans either," Hayden said, poking Chelsea. We could tell this bothered Chelsea.

"She's kidding Chels," I said, trying to reassure my friend before her feelings got hurt from the joke. "Nothing has been kept from you."

"Ohhh, so does that mean you ladies don't even know what we're doing tomorrow?" William asked, catching onto my word choice.

My face gave me away, I know it did, but I tried to backpedal, "Oh, no, we do know what we're going to do, it's just, Chelsea hasn't heard the official plan yet is all. But no, tomorrow is totally planned."

"Wait, why don't I know the official plan?!" Chelsea squawked. "And Evelynn, I thought we weren't telling Sky what the plans were??"

"What? You guys are scheming, and I'm not included?" I exclaimed. It was my turn for my jaw to drop open.

"Can everyone chill?!" Evelynn piped up as the guys and Hayden were all laughing at the mass confusion unfolding. "Chelsea and Alli, we will talk in the car and sort everything out. Guys, you are free to go. William, Alli will text you what you need to know tomorrow after getting her license. Now, save the questions for later. We need to get going!" She took charge, ushering the girls toward my car and making the shoo-ing motion toward the four guys that were with us.

"I will await thy text m'lady," William said, bowing and turning away. He didn't see it because I covered my eyes, but they were rolling. I was smiling though. I'm always smiling because of him.

Saturday morning, we were the fourth people in line at the DOT for me to get my license. Evelynn told me what shirt I should wear, even though all you see of it is my collar.

I am over the moon excited to have my license officially! I technically have a car already, even though I haven't seen it yet. I think Dad was trying to psych me out because he was talking about it being a brown, rusted piece of work and how it was his first car when he was sixteen.

At least I hope he's kidding . . .

We pulled up to a storage unit and Dad unlocked the padlock. He slid the loud and creaky red door open to reveal a green, four-door, 1999, Chevy Malibu.

A giant smile spread across my lips at the sight of my first car! "Oh my gosh! Wow!!" I exclaimed, running my hand across the hood to the driver's door. It was unlocked, and I got in. Dad got in the passenger side next to me and pulled the key out of his pocket.

He wouldn't give it to me at first. "Now, do you remember our deal?"

"Yeah, I do," I said, not looking at him as I ran my fingers back and forth across the steering wheel, envisioning the open road ahead of me.

At least I think I do. I'm sure it's about safety and stuff.

"Allison," he said in his stern dad voice. "I'm serious. Driving is going to be one of your largest responsibilities in life; it can also mean death too," he said, pinning me to my seat with his stare.

"I know. I know," I said.

I meant it too. I knew that driving was a major deal. Driver's Ed drilled into us the death and paralyzed statistics of young and old drivers. Between drunk drivers, motorcycle accidents, and animals darting out in front of you, it's a wonder anybody would even want to drive honestly!

"I promise I will be as safe as I can be," I said in a gentle, but honest tone.

This seemed to satisfy him because he gave me the key and I stuck it into the ignition. It turned over easily and started smoothly which made me happy! The radio was kept off, and Dad didn't say much on the ride home so I could stay focused. Even though I'd been driving for two years now with a legal adult, this felt different, more real.

It literally feels like a rite of passage. This is both thrilling and terrifying. Driving really does give you the power of life and death. Should humans actually be allowed this right? Stop thinking about this and just focus on getting home safely.

After slightly driving over the curb, I parked in the street and turned her off. Obviously, I'm going to give her a name, I just needed to see her before I could really decide on one.

"I can't believe my baby has her own car and can legally drive all by herself!" Mom said, greeting us at the door and throwing her arms around me. I hugged her back and thanked her.

I was itching for 6:00 to roll around, even though my friends had been over at my house since 2:00 in the afternoon. The guys are going to be coming over at 6:30. The reason I needed six o'clock to get here was because my friends decided to gang up on me and hold me hostage!

Okay, it's not exactly like that. They told me one plan so that I would be satisfied with what I thought was going to happen, and it turns out, they planned an entirely secret night instead! Can you believe that? Yes. Yeah, well . . . I can too. I just wish I had gotten to be involved with the planning against myself.

The guys rolled up in William's Jeep. He's the only one of his friends that can drive until December, but he doesn't mind. He said he trusts himself more than he trusts them driving.

Apparently the first thing we were going to do was play car tag in town. One car hides somewhere in city limits and sends pictures to the other car that is the one doing the tagging. The pictures have to have enough clues in them to show where we're hiding, but not enough to completely give it away. You're also allowed to move once you send the picture, but only within a certain radius. If you move, you have to send more pictures. Once the other car finds you, they tag you, and then they get to go and hide.

We have never gotten to play this in vehicles, only on our bikes. Being in cars was a lot more fun. The guys located us too easily on the first try. We had a harder time finding them, but after four pictures, we found them near our high school. We did this for over an hour until we grew tired of it.

I didn't know this was going to be the final hiding space, but when we hid again, we hid at a playground that had a little splash pad built into it. It's tiny, but we were fortunate to be the only ones there at 7:30 at night. The mosquitos weren't bad tonight which was fortunate because we got out of the car and were sitting on the playground, waiting for the guys to come and find us.

When we saw the headlights of his jeep pull up, we stayed as still and flat as we could on the playground equipment as we watched their confused expressions when they saw our empty car. Of all of us, the quietest one, Rose, gave us away by laughing uncontrollably at Morris' expression of confusion.

At first it seemed a little silly to have eight high school students hanging around the splash park, but once we got going, we couldn't stop laughing and having a great time. For whatever reason, having all of us getting gradually more and more wet by splashing one another was a sight and memory to keep in the "happy thoughts vault."

The laughing was contagious, and the connection William and I made that night was golden. We officially crossed the awkward beginning stages of friendship into a comfortable, harmonious, and solid friendship. Through William's playful hands on me, and the smiles we exchanged all night, I could feel he felt the same.

CHAPTER 13

I went for a walk by myself on a cold, fall night in late November. I didn't want to sit in my room and stare at my ceiling anymore while I thought about William. He was all I seemed to think about anymore. I saw the way other girls looked at him when we walked down the hallways. They smiled at him as he walked by, but then they turned their glaring eyes toward me.

It feels like we have almost everything in common. Big stuff too, not like, oh, both of our favorite colors are blue. We agree that mental health in America is undervalued, and we believe in working for our money, not just having our parents give it to us. We have discussed a few of the taboo topics like politics and is it okay to marry your fourth cousin if you had no idea they're your fourth cousin. We have similar interests such as being outdoors, music, and we enjoy driving around together. The list can go on, but I'm sure you get the point.

I love my girlfriends, I do, but man, all I want to do is spend my time with him. He's one of the easiest people to be around. He makes me feel at ease, like I don't have to prove anything to him, I can be my complete and total self.

Don't act like you don't try and show off for him every now and then.

That's true, I do, but luckily when I botch something, I don't feel embarrassed. Yes, he laughs at me, but I'm already laughing at myself too so it's okay. That connection with someone of the opposite sex is rare. At least for me it's rare. He's the first guy friend I've had like this, and it kind of scares me.

The New Year's Dance is coming up; I really want to ask him to go with me. Currently there isn't any other boy I would want to go with.

What if Oliver asks you this year? Please! He's never taken an interest in me; I can't imagine this would be the year considering we have zero classes together. He's not just going to walk up to me and ask out of the blue. Besides, I'm sure he's already had multiple girls ask him anyway. I doubt I stand a chance.

I'm going with my girlfriends, but that's not a surprise. Evelynn and Kyle are going obviously. Peter and Chelsea are too; well, Chelsea is still deciding on how to ask Peter, but we all know he will say yes to her. It makes perfect sense that William and I would go together. Right?

Okay, I think I'm going to do it! Tomorrow, after school, I'm asking him. I'm just going to ask him straight out if he would want to go to the dance with me. I hope this pep talk works . . .

I was restless that night. I tossed and turned thinking about how tomorrow might go.

What if he says no? What if he says no, and it's so awkward he doesn't want to be friends anymore? What if he says yes, though? Do I really have a chance? What's special about me? I'm just your average girl. I'm 5'6" with strawberry blonde hair and hazel eyes. I hover around 118 pounds. I can run kind of fast, and I'm decently coordinated when it comes to sports. Then again, I feel most girls at my school are at least somewhat coordinated with balls.

Hah! Some girls more than others, haha, but anyway. We're friends, yes, but maybe this is crossing the friendship line? There's no point in trying to deny my feelings for him. I'm 1000% crushing on William John Mantel and everyone knows it, but does he? What if he does know it? What if he does realize it, and has been ignoring it on purpose this entire time because he doesn't want to be more? Do I want to cross that line? What if he only says yes so he doesn't hurt my feelings and we have a terrible time? This could change everything between us! Or it could change nothing, I guess. Come on, Alli, it's just one friend asking another friend to a dance. Yeah, but I want to be more than friends. Maybe this could lead to dating?

Now I'm getting ahead of myself! I need to slow down and wait to see what he says when I ask. I try to will my body and mind into accepting the darkness of sleep.

I must have fallen asleep shortly after because I woke up remembering an annoying dream I had that I didn't like. Long story short, William was surrounded by girls swooning over him, while I was watching from far away, disgusted with what I saw. The worst part of my dream was when he purposefully made eye contact with me and flashed a knowing smile toward me. He knew how bothered I was, but he didn't care, and that crushed me.

"Dang, did you stay up all night or something?" Evelynn asked me immediately when she saw me.

"How can you tell?" I asked rhetorically.

"Do you want to talk about it?" Rose asked in her sweet, caring voice.

"No, not really. I just had trouble falling asleep, and then my mind created a stupid dream that I didn't like."

"What was it about?" Chelsea now inquired.

"I can't really remember," I lied. "It left me with a weird feeling, so I'm glad I can't remember the details of it." This was partially true. They say you can never remember the very beginning of your dreams.

Whoever "they" are. The specialist people I guess like psychiatrists or dream analyst scientists.

Now that it's getting colder out, as winter encroaches upon us, we have all gravitated toward sitting inside before the school day starts. We find a table that is open, but we generally sit at the same table we do for lunch. We're typically there early enough to get our spot, but occasionally, it becomes occupied by different classmates and that annoys me more than it should.

That's our unassigned assigned table.

Where William sits changes daily. Sometimes he and his friends are there early enough to grab a table, other times, they arrive close enough to Homeroom time that I don't get to see him.

Today they were early, and I spotted them sitting at a table near the windows. It's all the way across the room from us, but I felt my gaze constantly gravitating toward him.

Naturally, my friends noticed and called me out for it.

"Sky, are you going to ask him to the dance yet?" Chelsea started.

"Seriously though, we all know you're dying to go with him. You should just ask him already and get it over with. Besides, I can't imagine he would have more fun with anyone other than you," Hayden chimed in this time.

"I'm going with Morris," Rose said, making us all turn to her in surprise.

"Wait, who asked who?" Evelynn said, shifting her focus on Rose for a minute.

"I asked him."

"When?" I asked, surprised too.

"About two weeks ago now."

"Two weeks! You've known for two weeks that you're going with Morris, and you haven't said anything? Do you already have a dress too?" Evelynn exclaimed.

Rose didn't say anything, she looked away, embarrassed about getting "caught." She started to smirk a little though.

"Oh my god, Rose! How could you shop for your dress and not tell us?!" This hurt Evelynn.

"I was with my mom, and we found the perfect one. I had to get it then and there, but I'll still go with you guys when you want to go."

"We will need to go soon. We don't want everything to be picked over by the time we get there," Evelynn said, taking charge as always. "But we'll get back to that, we need to focus on getting Alli to ask William."

"I plan on asking him today," I said, trying to convince them.

"Uh-huh," Chelsea mumbled. "I'll believe it when I ask you at lunch how it went." All the girls nodded in agreement with her.

As if on cue, the school bell rang, making us gather our stuff and get started on our day of learning. I was relieved until I remembered this meant I was going to see him in about fifteen seconds at our lockers.

Okay, you rehearsed this a thousand times last night. Keep it short and simple. Just say, "William, would you want to go to the New Year's Dance with me?" then it's over!

"Hey Alli!" William smiled as he approached me.
Gosh his smile is contagious.

"Hey William, how are you?"

"Eh, I'm okay, I've been studying for my biology test I was telling you about, so hopefully that goes well," he said, shrugging nonchalantly.

I should ask him right now. Right this second. Yes, now would be a great time, because I won't see him until French class, and then if he says no, hopefully any awkwardness would settle by then and we could still be normal—

"Alli?"

My head snapped up at the sound of his voice. "Hmmm, what?"

"What's on your mind?" he asked genuinely, making me freeze solid.

"Oh, umm, I'm just thinking about this weird dream I had last night, sorry. You'll do great on your test, you always do!"

"What was your dream about? If I was in it, I hope I didn't do anything too weird or creepy," he said jokingly.

I let out a deep, fake laugh because of how spot on he was, but I was not about to tell him that.

"You might have been in it, but I can't really remember. I just woke up with this weird feeling. It's no biggie, it was all just a dream." I told him the same thing I basically told my friends, trying to downplay the dream, while I mustered the courage to ask him.

Okay . . . I guess, here goes nothing!

I shut my locker and turned toward him. He was ready to walk with me and I guess I was doing this now.

"I, uh . . . I was wondering if—"

"Hey Will! I've been looking for you!" Just then Natasha Bert bounced up to our lockers. Well, technically she bounced up to him.

What the heck does she want?!

"Hi Natasha, what's up?" asked William.

"I was wondering if we could walk to Homeroom together and go over our biology notes? I need to get some last-minute cram time in before our test, but I'm stuck on a couple of the questions. I was hoping you would be able to help me with them?" she said with a smile I was jealous of.

"Yeah, sure. I can try to help. There are a couple of things I'm not sure about though, forewarning. Alli, I'll catch you later. Text me if you remember anything about your dream," William said, turning his back and walking in the opposite direction of me.

"B-bye." I stumbled and awkwardly waved my hand toward his back. I caught the last look Natasha gave me before she and William headed toward their Homeroom.

This is not happening?! She doesn't want to ask you science questions, William, are you that naïve?! She's going to ask him to the dance, and he'll probably say yes. I mean, Natasha is good looking; even I have to give her that. Plus, she's popular so why would he ever say no? I blew it. I didn't ask him soon enough and now he's going to go with some other girl, a bimbo too for that matter.

She once asked me what an Orange-uh-tan was. I didn't understand what she was asking so she tried explaining it to me, "You know, they have red hair, look like gorillas, but are different."

"You mean . . . an orangutan?"

"Yeah, that thing!"

I can't remember the face I made at her, but she has never liked me since.

You could almost call her baboon! Haha! Okay, back to suffering.

This was a catastrophe! I was tempted to text him on my way to class and ask him what questions she had, but I didn't think I was ready to have my fears confirmed quite yet, so instead I texted him, "Good luck on your test! See you after lunch!"

I did, however, text my friends what happened, and my phone blew up with responses of support. They were telling me things like, "She's not going to ask him." "Even if she asked him, I'm sure he's going to say no." "You should text him right now and explain that you were going to ask him until she rudely interrupted!"

I considered texting him again, and asking him, but I really didn't want to ask him via text. I also wasn't sure if I was going to be able to wait half of a day either.

I put my phone in my pocket as my brain ran wild imagining and picturing things I didn't want to. I pictured William and Natasha dancing together, William holding her around her waist and Natasha having her arms wrapped around his neck, leaning in very close to his face.

I tried to focus on my class, but I couldn't. We were watching a Chinese movie in Chinese with English subtitles. It was about an emperor that had three wives and wanted a fourth one; something that doesn't fly here in the United States, unless you live in Utah, I guess. All I could picture, though, was William as the emperor, and all these different women surrounding him, swooning over him, and touching him like in my dream.

Gag.

I couldn't bear waiting any longer. The clock ticked so slowly that I thought the hands weren't even moving sometimes. FINALLY, the bell for lunch rang! I shot out of my seat and practically ran to my locker to wait for William to show up. For a moment I thought maybe he had gone straight to lunch, but eventually I saw him making his way toward our lockers.

This is it, moment of truth.

"Hi!" I said. I sounded like I had just run a marathon or something; William didn't seem to notice thankfully. He grinned at me and fiddled with his locker combination until he got it open.

"Hi," he simply said, with no indication of anything out of the ordinary.

I didn't want to seem weird or *too* eager, so I asked how his test went first.

"It wasn't too bad. There were a few questions I had no idea about, but other than that I think I did okay."

"Did talking with Natasha help at all?"

Here it comes.

I held my breath, anticipating what he was about to tell me. I was hoping he'd tell me she strictly talked about biology, but this entire morning, I had been fearing the worst.

"Not really, no. We talked about some potential questions that might appear on the test, but then she ... um, well she changed subjects, and talked about something else."

Something else like what; the dance? Please tell me what else she talked about with you.

It didn't seem like he was going to go any further, so instead, I prompted him for more details as I stared at him intensely.

If I ever needed the power to read somebody's mind, this would be it.

"Other things like what?" I couldn't breathe regularly.

Maybe ignorance really is bliss? Maybe I should tell him I don't want to know. Yeah right, you can't bear not knowing.

"She asked me to the New Year's Dance." He said it so calmly. Like it wasn't a big deal at all.

I knew it. It probably isn't a big deal to him either. Why would such a cute guy ever worry about not being asked to a dance?

My heart sank immediately, but there was one more piece of information I needed to know: his answer.

"And ... what did you say?" I asked, deflated.

I held my breath once more though. I held it so hard I swear I could hear my lungs asking me to breathe for the life of them, but I couldn't let it out just yet.

"I told her that I'm not into that sort of thing; school dances I mean. But I thanked her for asking me."

He told Natasha Bert no?!

"How did she respond?"

"Honestly, she seemed surprised. She tried to convince me it would be a great time with her and her friends, saying how much fun they had last year and how this is going to be even better, but I told her I was sorry. Luckily for me, Mrs. O'Connell started handing out the tests and telling everyone to be quiet."

We made our way to the lunch line, but I wasn't very hungry due to my nervous system being on edge all day. My lunch tray was pretty empty when I went to pay and that caused the lunch lady to frown. She didn't say anything thankfully; that would have been embarrassing.

We parted ways after paying. He went to sit with his friends, and I went to sit with mine. My head was swimming from my inner dialogue.

He told her no, so he's not spoken for, but he also said he doesn't like school dances, so would he go if I asked? I would like to think so. I hope he feels differently about me than he does Natasha. However, I would bet no guy has ever turned her down. What if she keeps persisting and eventually, he says yes?

Great, all my fears from last night are coming back. I know some of his friends are obviously going; over half of them to be exact. I wonder if that would make a difference to him. Although, I would assume he already knows they're going. UGH, this sucks! Is today too soon, I mean he JUST said no to freaking Natasha Bert!

I ate my lunch, mostly in silence, while I listened to my friends talk.

"Peter loves food, so I was thinking maybe asking him somehow with food. Or maybe I could do something with basketballs since that's his favorite sport. Oh, I know! How does this sound? We have a Marvel marathon with pizza and Mountain Dew, and while we're watching *The Avengers*, I can ask him. It'll be perfect; he'll be watching a movie he likes, plus he'll have me," she said enthusiastically enough, how could any of us not agree to it?

We already knew there was no possible way he would say no to Chelsea, despite how she asked, but we didn't want to spoil her excitement either. She couldn't wait to ask him. She pulled out her phone immediately and was already texting him about plans for their movie night. If she had it her way, they would ditch school and go right now, but we of course advised her against that.

"Fine! I'll see if he's free tonight then," she said, coming to terms with the fact she shouldn't skip school to ask her own boyfriend to the dance.

"So, Alli, what did William tell Natasha?" Hayden asked, changing the attention to me, as all the eyes at my table fell on me putting chips into my mouth.

"Yeah, I cannot believe you left us hanging in the group chat," Chelsea said.

"Chels, I literally just asked him at our lockers before I got my food and sat down here," I defended myself.

"Oh. Regardless, now you know, so spill," she demanded, making me kind of annoyed at her. I don't have it as easy; William and I aren't dating like she is with Peter, so it may not be an obvious yes, and it could be a terrible and awkward no from him.

"He, uh . . . he told her no," I said. They all looked at me with hopeful smiles. "Unfortunately, his reason for telling her no is because he doesn't like school dances. 'He's not into them,' " I said with air quotes. "So, I don't know."

Rose tried to be positive for me. "Hey, you two have become really good friends. Maybe he said no to Natasha because he doesn't know her and doesn't want to be at a dance with someone he barely has talked to. Maybe he would rather go with a good friend instead? Or maybe he would even *go* for a really good friend?"

I shrugged in response to her positivity. I had thought the same things, but I just didn't know.

"You should still ask him," Hayden said flatly. "You won't know until you ask. It's cliche, but it's true." All the girls agreed again and stared at me. I kept nibbling on my food. I stayed quiet as I thought about what I was or wasn't going to do.

I was nervous for French class after lunch. It's not that I don't want to see him, because I always want to, it's just—

It's just what? I'm scared, I guess. I don't want to jeopardize anything between us. Our friendship is very special to me.

Okay, I think I have decided what I'm going to do.

The bell that ended lunch rang. My friends and I gathered our bags and headed our separate ways. Today I just went to class by myself and waited for him. I tried not to stare at the door as I sat with anticipation, but every movement I saw made me look up in reflex.

There he is . . . just look at him. I drank the sight of him in as he came closer.

He saw me and smiled as he made his way to his desk next to me. I was beaming on the inside, but on the outside I was shaking. My heart was beating so hard I swear Bonnie could hear it drumming inside of me.

"Hey again," William said, sitting down. "Were you in a rush to get here?"

Oh, he noticed I didn't wait for him like usual.

"Hey," I said back. "Sorry for not waiting; there was something I needed to do before class."

He nodded in understanding and didn't press for further information. He was either respecting my privacy, or literally didn't care to ask. Either way, I was the one holding this piece of paper tightly in my hand, and I was probably sweating through it by now.

After our teacher came in, I figured it was the best time to give it to him. That way, class would start, and he wouldn't be able to say anything if it was bad.

I'm not sure if I went about this correctly at all, but I needed to get this over with for my own sanity! I plopped the folded up note onto his desk more aggressively than I had intended.

He picked it up and gave me a confused look. As he was unfolding it, I couldn't watch his reaction. Mrs. Lamb started talking to the class. He folded the note up and put it in his pocket. It was a short note, but I wondered if he had read it completely.

Mrs. Lamb informed us that we'd be watching a French documentary. As she was preparing to hit play, he didn't do anything except stare straight ahead. Once the lights went dark, and the movie started, he pulled the note back out. He was either re-reading it or he was hoping it would spontaneously combust.

The note read, "*William, I know you don't like dances, but I was wondering if you would be interested in going with me to the New Year's Dance as friends?*

PS: since I feel like I'm in middle school again with this note, please check one of the following boxes for Yes, No, or Maybe."

I glanced at him, but he wasn't looking at me, and he wasn't smiling either. His facial expressions gave nothing away as he folded up the note and put it in his jeans once more again without marking anything.

What have I done??

I only looked at him two more times during class. I tried hard not to; I wanted to focus solely on the movie like he was, but I couldn't. I was focusing on steadying my breathing and trying to slow my racing heart down once again.

Toward the end of the class William pulled the note back out and unfolded it once more. He clicked his pen and marked a box. He didn't give it back to me, though; instead, he refolded it and tucked it back into his pocket.

Ding. Ding. Ding. We got up like the trained dogs we are and filed out the door. I didn't need to go to my locker. I prepared myself to be able to flee if needed!

"I don't need to go to my locker, I have my geometry book already," I told him.

I awkwardly fidgeted there as I waited for him to either say something or hand me back the crumpled-up piece of paper. I did not have a good feeling.

"Okay," was all he said, still not moving.

I nodded at him in acknowledgement because I didn't know what else I should do or say. I opted to not say anything out of fear of making everything worse than what it already was.

As I turned to head the other way William said my name. I turned back around to face him. He was holding my note for me to take from him. His facial expression still didn't give anything away as I took it from him. Our fingers brushed and I felt it in my toes instantly.

With that finally over with, William turned and headed toward the lockers, while I took a deep breath and unfolded it to see what he marked:

CHAPTER 14

*M*aybe? Maybe! Maybe?! I can't believe he marked *maybe!!*

His answer kept running through my head during the rest of my classes.

Maybe isn't a no, but it's not a yes either. Should I text him now, or should I leave him alone? Am I okay with him not wanting to go with me? Is it just because he doesn't like dancing? What do I do? I decided to wait until I saw him after school to see if he'd say anything.

Ding. Ding. Ding. The final bell sang to us that we were free. This time I didn't rush to my locker. I took my time walking down the crowded hallways. I saw William's back as he rummaged around in his backpack to put away his textbooks and notebooks. I hesitated walking up to my locker, but I had to do this. I spun my locker combination and it unlocked for me. As I opened my locker I looked over at William and we made eye contact.

What is he thinking?

"Hey," I spoke.

"Hey," he responded back. He continued digging around in his locker and pulled out his math textbook and stuffed it into his black backpack.

Is he going to say anything about the dance?

"Are we still on for doing homework together after supper?" I inquired.

"Yeah, that works for me. My place?" he asked.

"Yeah, that's fine," I responded.

He's not going to say anything.

William closed his locker and gave me a slight smile as he turned to leave the school. I wasn't sure how to feel. He didn't say anything about the dance, but at least he still wanted to work on homework together, so that gave me some hope.

Do I pretend like I never asked him and just ignore this whole thing though? Is he expecting me to be the first one to mention it?! No way. The ball is on his side—err, in his court, however that saying goes. I am not going to be the first one to mention it.

I texted Evelynn immediately when I got home and told her everything that happened with William. She was sympathetic, and a great listener. She thought I should still bring it up to William tonight if he never does. That way both he and I could clear the air, be on the same page, and move forward.

I texted William when I finished eating with my family; he let me know that he was finishing up and I could come over any time after seven.

"I'm headed to William's now!" I hollered to my parents who were in the kitchen. They couldn't see me, but I knew Mom could hear me.

"Be back here no later than 9:30," Mom hollered back.

"I will."

They like William. They think that he is a nice young gentleman and is very polite when he comes over to our house. I'm glad they like him too; it keeps them off my back and out of my business since they already trust me and now, they feel they can trust him too.

I pulled into his long driveway and turned the garage door handle. It was open as usual. His family rarely keeps their doors locked. If nobody is home, then they will lock the doors to their house and vehicles. It blows my mind every time. I headed in without knocking. I'd grown close to his mom and sister in the same manner I was with my other friends' parents.

I took my shoes off and saw his parents in the living room watching television, *America's Funniest Home Videos* to be exact.

"Hi Alli!" Charlotte got off the couch and came to give me a hug.

She was a cute little thing. Tiny! She had pretty brown hair like her brother, blue eyes as well, and freckles on her cheeks, nose, and forehead. You could tell they were brother and sister physically. However, William is in this stage of life where he doesn't want his younger sister to ever be near him or his friends because he finds her irritating.

I get it, though. She and my brother are in the same grade, and I wouldn't want him hanging around my friends either. Although, I feel it's a little different with younger brothers than younger sisters. Younger brothers don't want to be involved in the stereotypical "girly" things, while younger sisters don't always mind video games, or paintballing, or whatever.

"Hi sweetie! Will is downstairs; help yourself to anything in the fridge or pantry. You know where it's all at," Mrs. Mantel offered.

I smiled at her and thanked her. My stomach had had butterflies this entire time, so I wasn't in the mood for food, plus I'd just eaten supper. I grabbed a blue Gatorade and headed downstairs.

He was already studying at the table. We exchanged our normal hellos as I sat down and pulled out homework. I started with geometry so he could help me. He's good with numbers and formulas and things of that sort, whereas I'm more of a person who can recall people, places, and events more easily. We balance each other in that aspect.

Things felt awkward almost the entire time with him. Not awkward enough that I couldn't concentrate, but awkward enough that I didn't like it. Things with him have always been natural and easy-going; this isn't. This sucks, and this was exactly what I was completely trying to avoid!

I started packing up my things at 9:08 PM. Neither of us mentioned the dance or the note throughout the entire evening. Remembering Evelynn's words, I figured this was the time to ask him if things were now different because of what I had done.

"William, are we okay? I know I sprung the dance on you, even after you informed me of telling Natasha no; I just thought maybe it would be fun to go as friends."

"I was surprised you asked. Did you ask anyone else to the dance?"

My hopes diminished as I told him I hadn't, just him.

His face was serious as he said his next word, "Good." I was confused, but he smiled my favorite William smile and finished his sentence with, "Because I was holding out, hoping you would ask me."

My jaw dropped open. It literally fell so far open, that he took his index finger and closed my mouth for me because I was utterly speechless.

Hallelujah!!

I smiled the biggest smile at him and asked if he was serious because I couldn't believe it.

He laughed at me and said of course he was serious.

"So, were you lying to Natasha about not liking dances then?"

"Oh no, I didn't lie. I hate dancing, but I figured since all my friends are going, I couldn't think of a better person to go with than one of my best friends."

He said yes!! He had the same logic I had with all our friends going. Awww he even called me one of his best friends too! I'm not quite sure if that means he is friend-zoning me for good, but I am not going to worry about that right now.

I couldn't help but throw my arms around his neck and embrace him. He held me back and it felt as natural as breathing.

"Wait a second," I said, stepping away from his embrace so I could see all of his face.

He cocked his head to the side with a confused expression.

"Why did you mark 'Maybe' then on the note I gave you? Also, why didn't you tell me right away? Ever since I gave you the note you barely spoke to me. I thought maybe I had ruined everything between us . . ."

His lip curled up on one side and he looked at me sheepishly with a shrug. "I just wanted to make you sweat it out a little."

Again, my jaw hit the floor, and he lifted it back into its place with his finger. "Are you serious?"

"Are you mad at me?" he asked, with a slightly pouted lip.

Yes! Well, no, he did say yes after all, plus, look at that pout.

"You have no idea how much I have been sweating this, William John Mantel. If someone had collected my sweat, I probably could have filled a pond with it."

Okay, like that was an attractive comparison to make . . .

He laughed. Of course, he laughed, he got what he wanted and that was for me to wig out like I did.

He's my favorite jerk in the world.

"But really though, I hope I didn't make you too mad, Al. Do you forgive me?" he asked, staring deep into my eyes.

"That depends; are you going to actually dance with me?"

"Poorly, but yes, I will dance with you," he said, smiling at me sincerely now.

I smiled again and threw my arms around him once more. "Then I'm not mad."

I wasn't, and I didn't want to be. I was on cloud nine! I was going to the dance with William, my best friend as well!

Eeeek!!

It's official, all my friends have dates to the dance and now we are going to shop for our dresses! Well Rose is just coming along to hang out since she already has hers.

Evelynn's mom loves seeing her daughter dress up. She wanted her daughter to be involved in beauty pageants, but Evelynn's dad was very opposed to those, so this was the next best thing her mom could enjoy. She offered to drive us all and buy us Starbucks. Needless to say, we were happy to have her tag along.

The mall was busier than we thought it would be, so we hurried to the prom dress shop called *Whitney's Formals*. They sell short dresses for homecoming and other formal events too.

Being in this store makes me excited for next year when we are juniors. You can only go to prom if you're a junior or senior unless you get asked by an upperclassman. I won't be getting asked to prom this year, that's for sure. Of all of us, Chelsea is most likely to be asked, but I don't know if Peter would be happy about that. A later bridge to cross though if it comes to it.

Knowing we wouldn't be going to prom didn't stop us from looking through the gowns though. We talked about what we liked and didn't like, imagining ourselves trying them on. Eventually we made our way to the back of the store where the dresses we needed were.

We each grabbed five dresses that we liked and went into the dressing room. We showed each other every single dress and gave feedback on which ones we liked and which ones we didn't. Traditionally for the New Year's Dance, girls wear short dresses, and then long dresses to prom. *Why we wear short dresses in the middle of winter is beyond me; but we do.*

Evelynn's mom was complimentary to us as we were trying on dresses; she wasn't with her daughter though. She was brutally honest with Evelynn, and it made me cringe. For example, Evelynn liked a gold dress, but her mom said it made her look like a hooker and it didn't complement her daughter's complexion.

Was it my favorite dress she tried on? No, but I would never have told her she looked like a hooker! Also, does her mom have experience being around hookers or something because it literally looked like a regular dress a teenager would wear?

The dress I ended up choosing stopped at my knees. It's fitted, satin, and red with sparkling straps that come up by my neck and then crisscross in the back. Chelsea got a blue, strapless one that came to her knees as well, and Evelynn went with a delicate, white dress that has a halter neckline and beading under the bust. Hayden chose a simple black-and-white dress, but it was cool because it had an ombre effect.

I didn't need any jewelry to go with my dress; I had some at home that I was going to wear. The rest of the girls found some earrings and necklaces for themselves. After finding our dresses and browsing through the prom dresses a little bit more, we went shopping for shoes next.

Exhausted from shopping all afternoon, we went back to Evelynn's house to rest and discuss how we might do our hair for that night. We had ideas, but we needed our dresses to help decide what hairstyle would complement the dress. If it has a back you want to show off, you should wear your hair up, if it doesn't, then you can wear your hair basically however you would like.

CHAPTER 15

We had everything planned on our end; now we needed to let the guys know what our dresses looked like, so they could match us.

It must be easy being the guy for a formal event. You just wear whatever you're told and smile for the pictures.

I sent a picture of my dress to William so he and his mom could find a matching tie. He plans to wear all black with a red tie. I told him he'll look very sharp.

Even if he wore a potato sack, he would still look hot.

Traditionally we go out to eat before a dance, so Chelsea made reservations for supper at our local Italian restaurant *Romano*. Our group consists of ten of us: Evelynn and Kyle, Chelsea and Peter, William and me, Hayden and Rob Knudson, and Rose and Morris. Hopefully Rob doesn't feel too out of place. I only know him by name. I'm not sure if I've ever really seen him at school, even in the hallways. He and Hayden have Homeroom together; they're just friends and aren't looking to be anything more, at least she isn't.

Tonight's the dance! I can't lie, I was a little nervous. I just wanted him to have a good time since he didn't enjoy dancing, and I wanted to make sure I wasn't a lousy "date."

I don't know if I should use that word, even with mental air quotes around it. I'm already adding enough pressure onto myself as is.

To try and calm my nerves, I reminded myself that we were going in with a group of my friends and his, and we all have had a great time hanging out with each other already. This was just going to be another one of those times, except we'd be dressed up, and maybe laughing at each other's dance moves.

Yeah, no pressure.

You know when we're getting ready for an event because we'll have the music blaring from Evelynn's room. We also can't help but shout and scream along with the words the entire time either. Being around my friends helps to calm me.

Even if things get awkward, or he and I run out of things to talk about, at least I'll have my friends to turn to for help.

I'm not usually a fan of the whole, "girls have to go to the bathroom together no matter what," but tonight could open my eyes to a new appreciation for it.

Evelynn had her hair and makeup done before any of us showed up, which wasn't surprising. I was appreciative of it, because I seriously needed help with both, and she was willing to assist wherever needed. I have never worn red lipstick, so seeing it on my pale face really made me feel like a clown at first, but my friends reassured me it didn't look bad at all, it's just not what I'm used to.

"It'll grow on you, I promise," Evelynn said.

And if not, I'll just accidentally wipe it off during supper.

The grandfather clock at the bottom of Evelynn's staircase chimed five times, signaling it was 5:00 PM. The boys were going to start arriving soon for pictures, along with all the moms and a few of the dads who probably wished they were anywhere else but here.

William texted me he and his friends were on their way now to Evelynn's.

Ahhhh! Oh, my goodness!

We were putting our heels on when we heard the doorbell ring. My phone vibrated at the same time; it was a text from William saying they're here.

The girls headed downstairs as I took one more look in the mirror before I went to see him. My hair is loosely curled in that half up-half down style with the top half being in a braided bun. The bottom portion of my hair still falls to my chest in length. I'm terrified my head could catch fire any second, even by smelling a candle, because of how much hairspray Rose used on me.

I headed to the staircase where I could hear the moms. As I walked down the steps I felt as though this was a scene from a movie that only William and I were in. Granted everyone was already busy taking pictures with each other, but still! I found William with my eyes as I took one step after the other; I was going extra slowly in the hopes I wouldn't fall.

His eyes held mine the entire time, and his smile was almost too large for his face. When I got to him, his eyebrows did their archy thing and he gave me an up and down glance. I couldn't help but blush under his gaze.

"Wow . . . you look . . . wow!!" William said, still smiling. I beamed up at him as I too admired his attire. His tie was almost a perfect match for my dress, and he really did look handsome in all black. The dark colors made his blue eyes pop ferociously tonight.

"Thank you," I said, looking down, still blushing. Right then, Charlotte came up to me to give me a hug. I didn't realize she was here with their mom.

"Alli, you look so pretty, like stunning!" Charlotte gushed to me.

"You do look gorgeous dear," Jenny said, giving me a hug.

"Thank you both," I said, smiling at them, and then searching for William once more. He reached out to tuck a loose strand of hair behind my ear.

"Wait, Will. Do that again and hold it!" his mom said, putting her camera up to capture the staged photo.

I will need a copy of this.

My mom was there too with her camera. She told me how beautiful I looked as she hugged me. She wanted all the staged photos that were possible. It was a little embarrassing, but when I looked at William, I could tell he was a lot more uncomfortable than I was. It allowed me to remind him (and myself) to smile, breathe, and relax.

"I don't know where to look. There are cameras everywhere!" he whispered into my ear.

"Focus on your mom. All the other parents are just background noise. It's your mom's camera that matters," I whispered back.

He put his arm around my waist and pulled me closer to him as we gathered for more group pictures. I relished the feeling of his forearm as it brushed against my stomach. I could feel his front side pressed against my back. It was the closest we had been since the time we watched a movie together on his couch.

After the group photos, we made our way to the "presenting of the flowers" pictures. The guys presented their corsages to the girls, and of course we were all ooh-ing and ahh-ing over our flowers. Mine had three roses, two white ones and one red rose in the middle with some silver, sparkling ties hanging down from it. They were perfect!

"Thanks. Mom technically picked them out," he said.

"Either way, I love them. Thank you."

Next the girls attempted to pin our boutonnieres on the guys, which was terrifying to do! The guys have it easy, they just slip the band onto our wrists; we have to try and not draw blood.

I think everyone was holding their breath waiting for someone to get poked, but nobody did thankfully. Kyle faked getting stabbed though. It made everyone laugh besides Evelynn and her mom. She slapped his shoulder out of annoyance, but quickly got over it. She was back to smiling for photos a second later.

Naturally, Evelynn's mom was the director of this photoshoot, telling where all the guys should stand and place their hands, and when to shift into the next pose. My heart couldn't help but beat faster every time William placed his hand on me. The butterflies were still fluttering around in my stomach, and I was praying they would go away soon.

At 5:45 PM, we grabbed our coats and said good-bye to our families as we headed out the door for supper. Our reservation was at 6:00 PM, which gave us an hour before the dance to eat. William was such a gentleman the entire time. He helped me with my jacket, taking it on and off, and he always opened the car door for me. It was a little weird at first, having him do things I could easily do for myself, but I enjoyed the chivalry and one-on-one attention from him.

I, and most of the girls, had the alfredo pasta and breadstick, except Evelynn; she had a salad. The guys had a mixture of ravioli, soup, and who knows what Morris ate, but I could smell it from the other end of the table!

William had a red sauced dish. He tucked about three napkins into his shirt, and also covered his lap with three more napkins, "just to be safe." As the gentlemen were paying our bills, I took my napkin and licked the end of it so I could wipe the corner of William's mouth where he continuously missed a spot of sauce on his own. William didn't seem bothered in the slightest.

Once the guys signed their checks, we loaded back up and headed to the dance. Between the ten of us, we had to take two vehicles. William drove me, Rose, and Morris, while Evelynn drove Kyle, Peter, Chelsea, Hayden, and Rob.

When we arrived at the school gym, we checked our coats in and surveyed the dance floor. The classic "Cupid Shuffle" had just started so we all jumped in and kicked off our night! Apparently, William gets his left and right mixed up when dancing, but we laughed through the whole song, not only at each other, but at our group members too. When the "Cupid Shuffle" ended the DJ turned it into "Yeah" by Usher, which really got the crowd dancing.

After about thirty minutes of upbeat, fast songs, the first slow song of the night came on: "I Don't Dance" by Lee Brice. William and I were both shy about the first slow song. He held his hand out to me like the gentleman he had been all night and I took it. I placed one hand in his, and the other on his shoulder. He placed his in mine, and his other arm around my waist, and we rocked back and forth, staring at each other. He was smiling his gorgeous William smile, and I was thankful it was dark because yet again, my face betrayed me by blushing. He spun me around a couple times, and we couldn't help but laugh at how ungraceful I was.

"Hey, you're supposed to warn me remember!"

"It's more fun that I don't," he said. I didn't tell him this, but he was absolutely right too. I was smiling and laughing every time he spun me, which was a lot.

Evelynn and Kyle were naturals. Chelsea and Peter were practically making out the entire song. Rose and Morris looked about as awkward as I felt, and Rob was not rocking Hayden around in a small circle like the rest of us, he was pushing her around the dance floor like it was 1950 or something.

I found out later his mom made him and his brother take dance lessons growing up. Hayden didn't find that out either until tonight. I couldn't tell if she was bothered or not. During the dance she seemed okay with it, but people were staring at them.

After the slow dance, a couple of us left the gym to get some drinks. William and I spotted Natasha Bert at the same time. We turned to each other and chuckled because of how pissed off she looked at us.

I was beaming on the inside (and probably the outside to be honest). She had a date of course—she would never come to one of these dances without a guy—so I didn't feel bad at all.

The Black-Eyed Peas were playing when we came back into the gym. We found our group and started dancing again. Everyone seemed to be having an awesome time. We were all laughing and smiling and enjoying our time like we were supposed to be. I'm not sure when it happened, but eventually I noticed the butterflies had left my stomach. I wasn't nervous anymore.

The next slow song was "Love Me Like You Do" by Ellie Goulding. Once again William and I embraced one another for the song. I got caught up listening to the lyrics while looking up at him in the dark. We were standing closer together during this song than the first. I could smell the cologne he was wearing mixed with some sweat. His hands were warm, and his breath gently blew on my hair every now and then. That's when the first thought crossed my mind, I wanted to kiss him.

What are you thinking? That's a bad, bad idea. Stop; don't think about that. You're here as friends. Strictly friends.

I knew I was right. Luckily, the song ended soon, and we were all back to jumping around on the dance floor. We took another water break, and I asked William if he was having a good time.

"Yeah, definitely. This was a lot more fun than I thought it would be," he said.

"You didn't think you would have a good time with me?" I jokingly said, shoving his shoulder, but also smiling.

He laughed at me and said, "I don't think I would be having any fun if I were here with anybody else."

Oh, my heart! This night has been amazing and more than I ever expected it to be.

After another hour they played the final song, "Closing Time" by Semisonic. This time I put both of my arms around his neck, and he placed his arms around my waist. To keep my mind from *certain* thoughts I asked him if he and his guy friends had any plans after the dance. He said no, so I invited him over to Evelynn's afterwards.

"Some of us are going to watch a movie if you guys want to join."

He agreed to come. He knew his other guy friends would be down for it too.

The song ended and the dance came to a close. We applauded the DJ; he really did an awesome job.

He dropped me off at Evelynn's. He wanted to run home quick and change out of his nice clothes. I told him we'd leave the front door unlocked for him.

Once inside, we changed into our sweatpants and helped each other remove the hundreds of bobby pins that were lodged into our skulls. We left the movie choice up to Rose. Hayden and I were in charge of food duty, so we popped the popcorn, gathered some pop, and brought down all the candy we could find.

William and Peter came into the kitchen while we were assembling the feast. They helped us carry everything as we descended into the cold basement. William found a place on the oversized recliner chair since the couches were all occupied. Hayden and I handed out the drinks and popcorn.

Rose decided on *Easy A* for the movie. Typically, comedies are a safe choice. Even if it's a stupid movie, like what some of the guys watch.

I was the last one standing when I looked around, debating on where to sit. I noticed the bean bag was unoccupied, but William scooted over and patted the spot next to him. I eagerly accepted, noticing how tight of a fit it was for both of us to be sharing. He put his arm up on the back of the chair and I sat next to him, although I might as well have been on his lap (which I would not have complained about), but we made it work, leaning against one another.

I'm sitting here for the sole purpose of being warm and to enjoy the movie, I lied to myself.

Peter fell asleep about twenty minutes into the movie. Chelsea kept poking him to wake him back up. I noticed Hayden had dozed off as well. Rose kept throwing popcorn at her, but she never stirred.

About halfway through the movie I decided to do what my mind had been tormenting me with. I slid down in the seat a little and rested my head on William's shoulder. I wasn't sure if he would be comfortable with it or not, but he didn't fidget or pull away. Instead, he put his hand on my shoulder, so I looked up at him. He smiled and I smiled back. It was then I had the feeling this is what compatibility must feel like. I know this meant more to me than him, but it was the perfect ending to the perfect night. I could not have been any happier than I was right at that moment.

SPRING SEMESTER

SOPHOMORE YEAR

2015

CHAPTER 16

*A*s William was holding me in his arms, he tilted my face toward his and gently planted the sweetest kiss on my lips. He asked me to be his girlfriend and I said yes. Our kissing intensified. The passion was heating up between us as we discovered the feel of each other's hands on the other's body. Slowly William . . .

Beep. Beep. Beep. Beep. My alarm clock brought me back to consciousness.

Dang. I wanted to see what he was about to do.

I sluggishly rolled out of bed, dreading another Monday of school. I started my everyday ritual of getting ready to look average. I danced into my skinny jeans, pulled on my white sweater, and chose a scarf from my collection.

I headed downstairs to make some toast and eat a banana before school. I'd be driving my friends to school this week, so I ate quickly. Now that I'm sixteen, it's my responsibility to drop Greyson off at school on the days Mom needs me to. Today, thankfully, was not one of those days. I pulled on my brown, tall boots and headed out the door alone.

For months I waited to see if anything was different between William and I after the New Year's Dance. I laser-focused on his texts, language, and body posture. Nothing. His texts were the same; he kept his normal distance, and his touching me had not increased. I was torn between saying something to him or just burying my feelings for him forever.

It doesn't help that I listen to songs like "Can't Fight This Feeling" by REO Speedwagon or basically all of Taylor Swift's songs. "Teardrops on my Guitar" and "You Belong with Me" are the hits from my fantasy life soundtrack. I am disappointed every time I come back to reality where things are still as they have always been.

My friends aren't much help either. They are split in their opinions. Rose and Hayden feel I shouldn't say anything with the risk of ruining a solid friendship, whereas Evelynn and Chelsea are the exact opposite. They think I should be bold and tell William exactly how I feel. I guess I wouldn't have expected anything less from my friends. I know them too well and they know me. I err on the side of caution more than I do confidence.

We're having a girl's week this week. Peter and Chelsea broke up. It sounds like Peter only dated Chelsea because he thought she would have sex with him within the first few months.

Jerk.

With Peter being William's friend, I've been avoiding this topic. I don't want to create conflict with William when this wasn't any of his doing. He also swore to me he didn't know Peter's intentions. Chelsea feels I should be mad at William by association, but I'm not going to do that, so she's annoyed with me currently. Evelynn and Kyle have been fighting over who knows what, and I have my internal conflict going on with my feelings toward William and what to do about them.

This will do us all some good!

In French class, I let William know that my friends and I are doing homework after school together this week. He was fine with that of course.

I decided not to tell William about my feelings for him. I agreed with Rose and Hayden; my friendship with him is more important right now. More and more it's him and I hanging out alone. Every now and then I'll go over when his friends are there, but my girlfriends don't really come with me anymore. Rose has once or twice since she and Morris are close, but Chelsea refuses and I don't blame her. Besides, she has her eyes set on a soon-to-be senior anyway, so she'll be okay.

Near the end of April, I went to the zoo with William's family. This was the first time I spent a long time with his sister and parents. It was about a two-and-a-half-hour car ride, although, with how often Charlotte had to stop for potty breaks, it was probably closer to three hours. I didn't mind though; William and I entertained each other while Charlotte sat in the third row of their suburban by herself. She had her tablet which kept her occupied and she also had headphones, which made her parents happy.

William and I talked about our upcoming junior year, and played tic tac toe and twenty questions. Every now and then, William's mom would chime in with guesses during twenty questions, but William's dad focused on driving and only driving. They had music on technically, but it was turned so low I couldn't hear it.

As we were buying tickets, Charlotte asked the lady at the counter where the penguins were located. They're one of her favorite animals. It turns out, almost all the animals are one of her favorites, haha.

Same girl! Same.

The aquarium was the first place you walked into once you went through the admissions gate. It was dark in there aside from the lights that lit up these monstrous tanks.

Jellyfish have always fascinated me. They had all different species, sizes, and colors here. I was absolutely mesmerized and I couldn't tear my eyes away. It wasn't until William poked me that I realized his family had left the aquarium.

The penguins were the second stop we made, and Charlotte was pressed against the glass. She was fogging the glass up with every breath she took; it was a wonder she could even see. She grabbed my hand and pulled me to the other side where we watched a line of penguins jump from a ledge into the water below. I don't think I'll ever understand how something so natural for them can be so fascinating to us.

It's an entirely other world, or rather, what seems like a simpler world. Then again, animals struggle with finding mates too, and they can be super aggressive about it which I wouldn't like.

Yeah, it would be awful if I had numerous guys fighting for my attention and affection.

I rolled my eyes at my own mental sarcasm.

As we snaked our way through the zoo, Charlotte was as excited as I was. When we would get close to the next animal, she would grab my hand and pull me with her to try and get to the glass first. If William were within reach, I would grab his hand too.

As awesome as they all are, I'm in love with elephants in particular. I raced Charlotte to the elephants when I heard two of them trumpet into the air. We spent extra time with the elephants like we did the penguins so we could watch these beautiful giants.

Throughout our time, I noticed William's dad kept to himself. He would talk with Jenny if she initiated anything, but otherwise he left us alone and never once had his phone out to take any pictures. In fact, the only time I saw his phone was when he had to answer a phone call, then he was on it for at least forty minutes while we wandered through the zoo.

Their mom on the other hand was all about taking pictures of us. Luckily for William and me, she focused mostly on Charlotte since Charlotte wanted pictures of her and all, and I mean *ALL*, of the animals in the zoo. She even wanted a picture with a random, regular rabbit that had made its way into the park.

I was exhausted by the end of the trip. I was ready to go home and not walk for the rest of the weekend. I wanted to sleep and eat, that was it. Charlotte was out like a rock in the backseat. William and I ended up falling asleep as well. We must have hit a large bump because I woke up. I could feel something heavy on my shoulder; William had his head on me and was still asleep. I made eye contact with his dad in the rearview mirror and felt a quick blush spread across my cheeks. I didn't want to disturb William, but I knew I wasn't going to be able to nap anymore either. I closed my eyes and pretended to be asleep for the rest of the drive.

SUMMER BEFORE
JUNIOR YEAR
2015

The school year came to a close, sending us into summer. Let the late-night bonfires, all-night movie marathons, sleepovers, and summer drives begin! I would be able to work more hours at the diner, too, which would help my bank account. We always seem to be short servers.

William would be busy helping his grandpa and dad on his grandfather's farm. He was excited to show me his sexy farmer's tan, and I would be looking forward to seeing his biceps after he'd been bailing hay for three months. He'd put in a lot of hours over the summer, but they had been having a good crop season which was a blessing.

My own grandpa was a farmer, but I never understood what he was talking about when he would discuss his machinery and what they needed to do to the ground to prepare it for the planting and harvesting seasons.

My friends would have their own stuff going on outside of our time together as well. Evelynn's parents liked to pack in a lot of family vacations, and Hayden worked at a jewelry store. Apparently, this is proposal season. Chelsea doesn't have to worry about working; her parents are very generous toward her and her sister, and I'm always envious. Rose is going to a month-long theater camp that she goes to every June. It turns out, Morris will coincidentally be attending this year as well.

On the nights that I'm not with my girls or family, and the nights William isn't with his guy friends or family, he and I enjoy going on our midnight adventures as we call them. We explore the town at night either by walking or driving around. We show each other new music we have discovered and see if the other person likes it too.

My favorite thing to do is go out to his farm, sit under the stars, and talk. I feel like we never run out of anything to discuss, and when we do, we are comfortable in the silence of one another. I like it when we talk about our futures, there's just something about discussing the unknown that is so enticing to me. I wanted to talk about death once but was afraid he would be creeped out by the subject, so I never did. But then, one night, when it was just the two of us, he brought the subject of death up himself.

"Do you ever think about death?" he asked me.

"Yeah. Actually, I feel like I think about it a lot; like more than I probably should," I responded quietly, worried I would taint or disturb the energy around.

"Why do you feel you think about it too much?" he asked inquisitively. His head turned toward me, giving me his undivided attention.

I didn't want to face him when I spoke, so instead I shrugged and continued staring at the stars, wishing I could see beyond the lightyears into heaven before speaking right away. "I've had a lot of people I love die already, and I wonder what life would be like for the people who love me, if I passed away at a young age."

"Speaking as one of those people, it would be very sad, and really hard, but we would keep going like I presume you would want us to, right?" he asked.

I was already replaying the words in my head, "*. . . the people who love me.*" "*Speaking as one of those people.*" *Is he saying he loves me?! Or is he just saying he'd be sad if I died right now?*

"Alli?"

"Hmm? Oh yeah, of course I would want you all to be happy and continue with life. Otherwise I'd be selfish for an unnecessary reason. What about you?"

"Yeah, I'd want my family and friends to move on. I've, uh, I've written a note before."

I now turned to him puzzled and leaned up on one arm to get a better view of him. "What kind of note? Like a suicide note?! William, are you—?"

"Hey, it's okay. I'm not suicidal and I haven't thought about suicide, just an untimely death that nobody may expect. The note is basically like my final words I would leave everyone with if I didn't get the chance to say goodbye in real life, that's all."

"Oh," was all I could manage because my brain was already thinking and processing again. "I like that idea."

"We can only plan so much in this life, but God will make sure His plans are carried out for the best."

I have never heard William talk about religion or anything remotely linked to spirituality. "So, you believe in God and stuff?" I asked, with a hopeful tone.

He chuckled at the changing sound of my voice, "Yeah, is that hard to believe or something?"

I blushed under the blanket of the night. "Well no, I just, you just . . . we've never talked about this kind of thing yet is all."

"There are some things I rarely tend to talk about with anybody, and religion is one of those topics."

"So, why me?"

"Why you what?" he asked.

I laughed at our terrible English. "Why you talk to me about death with I?"

He laughed at my response and smiled. His perfect white teeth were visible in the night, and he shrugged once more. "I don't know," was all he said, but I wasn't going to let him off the hook this easily.

"No really, why me?" I pressed.

He shrugged again and didn't say anything, so I didn't say anything and waited him out. I won, too; he spoke more honestly than I expected.

"You just make me see past this high school life. I know we're only sixteen, but when we hang out, I don't know, I feel—you allow me to be my complete self. People aren't their real selves in high school you know. Everyone is trying to fit in no matter what 'group' they associate with. With you, I'm not trying to fit in or impress you or anything. I just . . . am. I feel like I'm living life rather than trying to get through each day. I guess that's why I feel I can talk about death to you, because I feel so alive. If that makes any sense at all."

My heart swelled and floated higher than a hot air balloon taking flight. I knew we were close, but I never realized he felt the same way! My brain must not have been getting enough oxygen because I couldn't think clearly. The politeness in me knew I needed to respond, but I didn't know how to. All I was able to manage was, "I feel the same way."

Wow, what a lame response to the deepest, most personal thing he has ever said aloud to me!

I could tell he was feeling embarrassed, so he shifted the conversation off himself and onto the future. "I know college is forever away still, but where are you thinking of going?"

"University of Kansas. It's the only college I've considered."

"Why's that?"

I shrugged. "It's close to home, and I hear they have a good psychology program."

"You want to be a shrink?" he asked me.

I smiled. "Yeah, the human brain is fascinating to me. I want to better understand why people do what they do or think what they think. You know? I mean, just look at how different guys and girls are in general. So, yeah, I want to be a therapist and do my best to help people. Maybe after being a therapist, I will become a college professor? I don't know, I haven't really thought that far ahead yet."

"That's really cool. While you're studying all that brainy stuff, maybe you can uncover your strange reasoning for needing the volume setting to always end in a zero or five." He laughed and pushed me.

I was stunned. "You've noticed that?!"

Now he was laughing really hard at me. "Are you kidding me? Why do you think I give you the remote every time we watch something? You can never leave the volume on one setting during a movie. You're constantly adjusting it five notches either way."

"Well, yeah! When nobody is talking the music is blaring at an unnecessary pitch, might I add, and then when people start talking again, it's like they're whispering so I have to turn it back up." I tried to be serious when explaining my reasoning, but I couldn't help but laugh with him. "Well, what about you, mister 'I can't have my food touching, or I just won't eat it!'"

"Hey, that's a legitimately logical thing to be disgusted by."

"No, it's not!"

"Yes, it is! If my gravy runs into the corn, then it's no longer just corn, it's wet-gravy corn. And if my baked beans mix with my mashed potatoes, then forget them. They're a lost cause at that point."

I could barely take a drink from my water bottle without spitting it out from laughing so much. I wanted the heat off me now, so I turned it around and asked him the same question.

"What about you? Where do you see yourself going to college?"

"I don't know. I'm kind of torn between staying close to home, or going somewhere far away from Kansas, like Arizona or Texas maybe."

"Oh wow, really?" Another thing I did not see coming. The idea of William being on the other side of the States did not thrill me. In fact, it made my heart deflate immediately.

"Why?" I couldn't help but ask.

I selfishly wanted to know why one of the best things to ever happen to me wanted to move across the country. There was no masking the dejection in my voice.

"We've been here our whole lives; don't you want to see what and who else is out there?" he asked with a gleam in his eyes.

I shrugged silently in response.

I do want to see what else is out there, but I can't imagine going from living with my family to moving across the United States and barely seeing them except for the holidays.

"Someday, yeah," I said, daring to look back at him. I tried to lighten the mood. "What are you wanting to do then?" I asked, pining for more information even though I was hesitant to see if there were any more surprises he was about to spring on me.

"Criminology," he said confidently.

"You want to deal with sociopaths?" I asked, raising my eyebrows, yet again surprised by his response.

He smirked. "Well if I catch any, I could always send them to you, and you could pick apart their brains."

I tilted my head at the idea because it wasn't an inaccurate assumption, and it would be fascinating!

He laughed at my consideration of what he just said. "Nah," he said, correcting himself from what apparently was a joke. "I'm thinking of either law enforcement or forensics."

"Dead bodies, much better," I joked with him.

We chatted more about what we thought college would be like, and what we hoped for. When midnight rolled around, I told William I needed to get headed home. Before I left him for the night, we planned to have a "Halloween" movie marathon the following night. We said our goodbyes and I was already anticipating tomorrow's moments with him.

However, my first issue was going to be trying to sneak back into the house. We have a Great Dane named Minnie, and she has incredible hearing. She's a tattletale when it comes to me though, I swear. This time I came prepared. I have treats in my car for when I get home to quiet her immediately.

Tomorrow came quickly because it was the weekend and weekends always pass by too fast. William got the movie set up and ready to play while I prepped the seating area. Two blankets apiece because we were keeping the windows open with the breeze blowing through. We had three pillows, one for William and two for me; one to use, and one to hide behind just in case. He brought over the drinks, popcorn, and gummy worms. He pressed play and I snuggled up next to him on the couch. I still knew it didn't mean anything to him, but it felt nice to be physically next to someone I cared so much about.

We laughed at the cheesiness of the movies, but I may or may not have hidden behind the pillow once or twice during the suspenseful parts. William caught me doing it too and laughed at me.

It was getting late once again, and we knew that I needed to get home. As the credits were rolling for *Halloween Three*, William said three words that I was *not* expecting to hear. These three words made my heart stop.

"I met someone."

CHAPTER 17

He what?!
 I sat there, stunned. I couldn't say anything for a moment, I just stared at him. I finally found my voice, although it didn't sound like my voice to me.

"Uhh . . . who? And . . . where?"

And why?!

"Her name is Katherine, but she goes by Kat. Her uncle owns the farm next to my grandpa's apparently. She visits every summer from Pennsylvania, but I've never seen her before. Anyway, a couple of weeks back I was outside helping Grandpa when I saw her walking by his property fence, calling for her horse that got away from her. I helped her find her horse and we just sort of got to talking. We've hung out twice since then."

Twice?! These times he could have been hanging out with me, he was hanging out with some new girl?! Hey, you're not his girlfriend. You don't have the right to be jealous or to dictate who he spends his free time with.

I know my brain was trying to be rational, but I didn't want to be rational right then! I was in shock. I wanted to deny, deny, deny!

"What is she like?" I asked. I was being calm, at least I hoped I was. I didn't want him to know how shredded inside I was.

William smiled.

Why is he smiling right now?

"She's cool. She's down to earth, likes to have fun like us, loves farm animals, and wants to travel the world. She laughs at my jokes, and it seems like we like the same kind of things." He shrugged. "I think you would like her." He looked at me with a hopeful smile.

Hah! Yeah right! Could I ever like a girl that you like? Why don't you man up and tell him your own feelings then? Don't make me laugh either, Self.

"You can meet her if you want. I'm having a bonfire tomorrow night and you're welcome to join us. Bring your friends too if you want."

I honestly had no idea what to tell him. I didn't want to say anything I regretted, and I didn't want to lie to him. Instead, I gathered up my things and told him I really did need to get going. He didn't fight it or ask me anything else. We walked in silence to my car, and it was horribly awkward. *I feel a little nauseous right now, too.*

A raccoon stepped out in front of me, and I swerved hard to the left to miss him. I came to a complete stop and the squealing of my tires echoed in my ears. It was then I started to cry.

Are you crying over a boy? No, I'm not crying over William himself, but more about the situation and all my feelings. Plus, I almost hit a fuzzy, innocent raccoon!

I didn't cry long—about three minutes was all. I'm thankful I was out in the country and didn't have to worry about traffic; plus, it's late anyway. I drove home in the silence and was able to sneak into my house without Minnie waking up my family. I think she could sense my sadness, because she followed me up the stairs and into my bedroom. Normally she sleeps with Greyson, but tonight she didn't.

I don't know how to feel about anything William told me. On one hand, she's from Pennsylvania, so she's not going to be here much longer since it's already the beginning of August. On the other hand, William has been hanging out with another girl, alone, and he thinks I might like her. Which, okay . . .

Maybe she is nice and cool as he says, who am I to judge, right? But gosh, I've never thought of William hanging out with another girl, it has always . . . been me. I've always been his girl. Obviously not in the romantic way, but friendship. Charlotte herself has literally told me he has not hung out alone with a girl since he was in elementary school when their babysitter would bring over her own daughter.

The next morning, I invited my girlfriends over for breakfast so I could fill them in on last night's news.

"I say we go check this girl out." Hayden was all for going to the bonfire tonight.

"I think the main thing to focus on is that she is from Pennsylvania, and she'll be going back there after the summer is up. Whereas, you'll still be here with him, hanging out one on one, and nothing is going to change the 'thing' that you guys have . . . this 'bond,' " stated Rose.

The girls nodded in agreement as they picked at their eggs and crunched on their pieces of toast.

"Count me out for going over there. I still don't want to see Peter," Chelsea said, clearly still upset.

"I won't be able to make it tonight either. Kyle and I have plans," stated Evelynn.

Rose and Hayden agreed they would go with me if I wanted to. I was hesitant for a little while, but eventually everyone but Chelsea talked me into going. Chelsea was trying to talk us out of going; besides, we only had a couple of weeks left of summer and, like Rose said, this Katherine chick was going to be going back to Pennsylvania.

Thank goodness for that.

When we arrived, the guys were trying to get the fire burning steadily. I spotted Kat immediately since she was the only female there. She was wearing jean shorts like all of us, with a white, strapless shirt that showed a little too much chest if you ask me. Her chestnut hair was curled and held back with a silver barrette. She looked great from head to toe, I'll give her that; even her ankle bracelet was adorable with the horseshoes on it.

Dang.

William introduced all of us to her when we arrived. "Kat, this is Rose, Hayden, and Alli. We all go to school together."

We smiled and waved at each other in that awkward, first-time meeting someone way. I was hoping she caught on to the fact my smile didn't say, "I'm genuinely interested in getting to know you." No, it obviously said, "I'm only waving and smiling to be polite for William's sake. I have zero interest in you."

We sat down on our blankets and lawn chairs and got situated by the glowing embers, while the guys finished getting the fire scorching hot in front of us. Rose and I sat in lawn chairs, while Hayden sat on a fleece blanket. We formed a circle around the fire when the guys came and sat down as well. The circle sat like this: Rose, Morris, Grant, Danny, Hayden, Me, Peter, William, and Kat. They were sitting extremely close to each other on a blanket for barely knowing each other.

Hayden started the conversation right up once everyone was situated. "So, Kat, tell us about yourself."

Kat smiled shyly and started telling us where she's from and how she landed here in our town. "I'm from Chesterbrook, Pennsylvania, which is a suburb right outside of Philly. Every summer my little brother and I come to visit my aunt and uncle on their farm from July until the end of August. Their farm is next to Will's grandpa's.

"Um, I'm in love with horses, Paints specifically. I have one, and his name is Abraham, Abe for short. Annnnnnd yeah." She finished by shrugging her shoulders the way William always does.

I grimaced on the inside wondering if they truly have hung out that much she's even picking up on his mannerisms.

"So how did you and Will meet?" Hayden inquired. I glanced a warning shot in her direction because I was nervous William would think I put her up to this.

"I was riding Abe and wanted to see something up close, so I dismounted him. I thought I had his reins tight enough around the fence post, but he got loose, and I couldn't find him. Luckily Will was around. He got a hold of Abe and calmed him down. I have never seen Abe take to a stranger the way he did for you," she said, smiling at William. "I was extremely impressed to say the least. I figured this guy must be decent if my horse could sense it." She looked at William with flirtatious eyes and bit her lower lip.

My palms were stinging with pain. I glanced down to see what was up with them. Turns out, I had curled my hands into fists without realizing how tight they were. My fingernails were digging deeply into the palm of my hands. I uncurled them and stretched out my rigid fingers, allowing the blood to flow freely once again.

"What are some of your interests? What do you like to do with your friends since you live so close to a large city?" Hayden pressed further.

"Ummm, we go shopping a lot, ice skating, binge on movies, watch YouTube. I don't know." She laughed and continued, "I think we do what almost all seventeen year olds do."

"Are you going to be a senior then?" I asked.

"Yup. Will told me you're all going into your junior year."

"That's right. We all can drive now. It's so cool!" Peter stated. He imitated driving a stick shift vehicle even though he literally drives an automatic Ford Focus.

He could drive a hearse, and he still would think he has the coolest car on the road.

Our conversations moved on from Katherine as we discussed what was happening around town and gossiped a little about our classmates. The big news was that Natasha Bert just got dumped by Travis Nyle. She was a sophomore dating a senior, but now he's going off to college and doesn't want to be tied down to a high schooler apparently. At least that's what the rumor mill says.

Despite all the conversations going on, and the guys doing "guy things," I couldn't help but always bring my attention back to William and Kat on that blanket. She would lean in extremely close, and they would whisper back and forth all the while laughing at whatever it was the other person had just said.

My heart ached with jealousy. I received a text from Rose saying that even she is noticing how much I have been staring at him and Kat, so I tried not to. My attention shifted more toward how close Morris and Rose have become throughout the year.

I wonder if they're going to date. Would you not like that? Well obviously, I want Rose to be with a nice guy and Morris does seem genuine. I don't know, it sucked when Peter and Chelsea broke up; I don't want things to be awkward again if another one of my friends and his friends dated and then broke up.

When it got late enough, we all decided to leave about the same time. William told us not to worry about the chairs that were his. His friends gladly left a mess for him to clean up later.

He walked my friends and me to my car so I could drive us back to my house. He hugged all of us, but when he got to me, I didn't want to let go of him. After we got into my car, I noticed Peter was driving the guys home in his car, while William was going to drive Kat back to her aunt and uncle's. *At least, I hope that's where he's taking her directly.* Kat was leaning into William's shoulder so tightly, I almost thought she was sitting on the center console, but I could see her seatbelt was being stretched to its limit.

Really?

I was annoyed and jealous and my friends could tell. Rose and Hayden were great on the drive home, though; they didn't talk about Kat at all, or try to cheer me up by building me up and putting Kat down the way Chelsea and Evelynn would have done. Instead, they talked about the upcoming school year and how we now get to sit rows ahead at the athletic events in the junior section.

And best of all, little miss Katherine won't be there.

I nodded along and commented the occasional, "for sure" here and then when it seemed appropriate, otherwise I focused on driving and internally fought with myself.

Fall Semester

Junior Year

2015

All week my mom kept reminding me school was starting soon and she couldn't believe her oldest child was turning seventeen soon.

It's the exact repeat from last year when I turned sixteen and she couldn't believe it then either. I will not say that to my future children. I won't. I'm breaking the cycle, mark my words, Self.

Speaking of turning seventeen, that means William's birthday is coming up shortly and I haven't decided on what to get him yet. I did the whole food thing last year. By default, athletic stuff is always the way to go, and I'm thinking I'll do that this year.

I laid out a pair of jean shorts and a cute mauve-colored top. It had large flowers on it and open shoulders for the short sleeves. This wouldn't have been allowed in middle school. We weren't allowed to show our shoulders.

Don't want the guys getting aroused over a shoulder! Seriously people, come on. There are bigger issues in the world to worry about.

I had a pair of white sandals I was going to wear with my outfit and then a couple of bracelets Rose made all of us.

I slid into bed and let my mind wander about what could happen during this school year. I really attempted to stay away from thoughts of *him,* so I focused on the classes I was taking: Algebra, Chemistry, History, 11th grade English, Gym, Photography II, and some class that is supposedly going to prepare us for everyday life. Things like how to change a tire, taxes, and other things real adults do. I don't know, it could either be helpful, or it could be lame. I'll have to see.

Eventually, after 284 sheep jumped the fence, I drifted off to dreamland only to be obnoxiously woken by my alarm clock. It's a disgusting reminder that my life is once again controlled by clocks.

Honestly, if it weren't for the fact that we get to move up seats at the athletic events this year, I wouldn't have believed I had advanced grades.

Everything was the exact same as it had been last year. My friends hung out in the morning before school, and William and his friends barely made it to school before Homeroom began.

For the first time in our friendship, I finally became annoyed with William. He voluntarily kept telling me things that I didn't care about. "Kat said this, Kat said that. This is what she's doing in Pennsylvania right now, they don't require students to take a foreign language in high school if they don't want to," and on, and on, and on he would go. At times, I physically had to bite my tongue so I wouldn't tell him how much I do not care.

I know I didn't want to hear about her, and as awful of a friend as this makes me sound, I was waiting for the time to come when they weren't talking anymore. After a few weeks, I realized I hadn't heard him mention Kat, so I decided to go against everything I stood for and ask him about her over text.

Me:	How's Kat?
William:	Idk
Me:	oh . . . did something happen?
William:	she has a boyfriend now so she doesn't talk to me anymore.
Me:	Are you okay?
William:	I'm fine. She should have given me a heads up she was seeing somebody else back home but whatever.

I didn't press any further because right then I was opening my Facebook to creep on her profile and sure enough, she's Facebook official with a guy from her school. According to the pictures she had posted of her and Mr. Devan, they had been hanging out before she came to Kansas for a couple of months.

I wonder if this Devan guy knew about William? Maybe I should message him? NO, no, we're not going to meddle like that. William would be so pissed at me if I did.

With Thanksgiving almost here he seemed to be in good spirits again, so I was thankful about that. Things felt back to normal between him and I. The two of us hung out without him constantly checking his phone. We laughed the way we always had and everything in my world was right again.

Morris and Rose officially started dating. Morris is a good guy so I was happy for them. I see her a little more now since she hangs out with William, me, and the rest of the guys.

Speaking of new couples, it was brought to my attention one day at lunch that apparently a lot of people in school think he and I are dating. We're not obviously, and now I must try twice as hard to not get wrapped up in my own fantasy world. We have our bond as Rose calls it. My friends remind me how special and rare it is between a guy and girl. I know they're trying to make me feel better, but the reminder doesn't always help.

For a year now, I've been trying to squash my feelings for him, so I don't keep getting my hopes up. I want to be able to hang out with him and not remember every curve of his body or the way his arms look when his sleeve rides up without him even trying. And his eyes—ugh, I *love* his eyes—I feel like I drown in them when he gives me his full attention.

With it also being late in November, the school started to advertise the New Year's Dance. On Wednesday, Rebecca Clinkon came up to William's locker as we were emptying our backpacks after a long day.

"Hi Will!"

"Hey Rebecca, how are you?"

"I'm great. Say you don't have a girlfriend, do you?"

WOW. Okay . . .

William hates this question; it makes him feel awkward when people wonder if he and I are dating. I was at his house once when his uncle was over and stated he didn't know that William and I were finally dating. I had never seen William blush, but he turned scarlet red, and informed his uncle that we're simply good friends.

"Uh, no I don't." William's words brought me back to present day.

"Good! I was wondering if you would go to the New Year's Dance with me then. I'm single, and you're single, it's perfect!"

"Oh, um, sorry but I'm, I'm actually already going with someone."

What?! This is news to me. Awful news.

"Who?" Rebecca asked, clearly bummed.

I held onto my locker for support from this wave of shock rushing through me.

"Well," he started, "she hasn't asked me yet technically, but it's kind of a tradition we go to this dance together." He looked at me as he said this.

I swear my heart just flew out of my chest! I didn't care she was standing there getting rejected. The joy coursing through my veins out trumped any sympathy I should have had for Rebecca.

William wants to go to the dance with me, again!

Rebecca quickly realized he was referring to me. She glared at us and spoke one word as she turned and walked away. "Whatever."

Naturally, he and I turned to each other and started to laugh.

"You do realize this is now the second time you've been asked to the New Year's Dance by a popular girl, right?" I said in almost a sad voice, mentally comparing myself after just experiencing an incredible high of excitement.

He shrugged and scrunched his face. "Their popularity won't make up for the loss of fun I would be having."

"Oh, so you just expect me to ask you this year?" I attempted a straight and serious face but failed.

"Well yeah, you did such a good job last year with the whole note thing."

"Uh, don't remind me! That was so embarrassing!" I smiled and blushed still thinking about it.

William laughed at me. "I can never let you forget that. So, Allison Manex, where's my invite?"

It was my turn to have a little fun with his emotions. "I actually hate telling you this way, but I, umm, I'm already going with somebody," I said, looking down at my feet.

I glanced up to see his reaction, it was perfect. His face went from smiling and joking to straight, and if I'm not mistaken a bit of disappointment.

"Oh," he said, running his fingers through his hair, "I didn't know you had a date already. Who are you going with?"

I bit my lower lip, already feeling guilty for making him feel bad. "Well, I haven't actually asked him yet, but umm, it's tradition that he and I go together, especially since we had so much fun last year," I said, smiling at him.

He smiled back in recognition. "Oh, you jerk! That was good!"

"What, you think I couldn't have asked anybody else?" I faked being wounded by his words.

"On the contrary, I was worried you didn't want to go with me. That really sucked for a minute, Al," he said with genuine honesty that pulled my heartstrings.

"Trust me, William, you're the only guy I want to go with to the New Year's Dance." I stared into his eyes hoping he could feel what I was feeling at that moment.

He reached out toward my face and tucked another strand of loose hair behind my ear. His proximity to me made me hold my breath.

"Well partner, I reckon it won't be as much fun to dosey doe alone," he said softly.

"I reckon not," I whispered, holding his gaze as he pulled away.

"Ready to leave now?" He snapped back to his usual voice and closed his locker.

Did he feel anything just then?

The next day I decided to ask him since we already knew we were going with each other. I wrote him the same note I did last year, except this time I said, "Since this is tradition you already know the drill. Would you go to the New Year's Dance with me? Mark yes, no, or yes, because I'm not giving you a maybe option this year." I smiled and chuckled to myself as I folded it up.

We have French IV together this year. It's still after lunch, which I like. When he got to class, I went up to him and handed him my note. Because of the random seating chart, we're across the room from each other.

I didn't realize it until I sat back down in my seat, but I wasn't nervous. In fact, I felt an emotion normal people feel when their body isn't sweating, or their heart stays in their chest; I felt confident.

He opened it immediately, read it, laughed out loud, marked his answer, folded it back up, and walked it back over to me. I eagerly opened it with steady hands to see which answer he marked.

___ YES

___ No

✗ YES, BECAUSE I'M NOT
giVing YOU A MAYBE
OPTiON THiS YEAR

Yay! Let the dance tradition continue!

CHAPTER 18

During the second semester of my Everyday Skills class, we got assigned a project I considered fun. We were partnered up, and for the entire month of March, we visited with a lot of people from our town. We met with people of all ages, different economic statuses, levels of education, and occupations.

I was partnered with Bryce Vinton. We were never friends, but we went to the same elementary school and had a couple classes together in middle school, so he wasn't a stranger. Sometimes I think about how odd it is to have so many people in my graduating class, and yet, some of them, I never have had a class with, therefore, I've never met them. Whereas, with Bryce, I've had multiple classes with him and see him all the time around school.

I can't imagine small schools where everyone knows everything about everybody . . . yikes! Talk about not feeling like you have any privacy.

Bryce and I had to come up with interview questions, pre-approved by our teacher of course, to learn more about people in our own town. I believe the point of this is to open our eyes to diversity and struggles that everyone in all areas of life encounter.

My partner was not at all thrilled about this project. The nursing home in particular didn't sit well with him. I wondered if it was because he had a grandparent pass away in a nursing home or something, but I didn't ask.

I, on the other hand, found people fascinating and couldn't wait for these interviews. We worked together in class on creating the questions we wanted to ask, and then when March 1st came around, we scheduled times to meet with twenty different people from our community. It's a large project and it's going to be time-consuming, but this is for our final that is due in May.

Bryce and I exchanged phone numbers since we were going to need to meet outside of class a lot. He was on the track team and had practice every day after school, plus track meets over the weekend "unofficially." When he's not at practice, he works like I do. No wonder we have about two months to work on this project. The nice part is that during our Skills period, we are allowed to travel and interview during that time frame, so that should help us.

The first person we agreed to interview was one of the most successful people in our town. His name is Curt Pennington, and he is the owner of a car dealership. Curt's company has been ranked number one Best New and Used Car Dealership across the United States of America for the last four years.

That is impressive.

My parents have traded a couple cars in for used vehicles and they have enjoyed the service provided to them. They allowed me to quote them in my paper as a primary source.

I dressed in nice, dark blue jeans, a white, sleeveless top, a cream-colored blazer, and white heels.

"Dang, you look hot, Alli," Bryce said as we walked to his truck so we could drive to the dealership.

His compliment caught me off guard and made me blush.

"Oh—why, uh, thank you. You don't look bad either. Your tie is a nice touch," I said.

I hoped he took my compliment genuinely too, because he did look sharp in his black jeans, black button up shirt, and blue tie.

"My mom made me wear it. I think it's stupid," he said, starting his truck.

It started more quietly than I thought it would considering the lift he has on it. I assumed its roar would have matched its "ferocious appearance."

"No, it looks good. Do you wear ties much?"

"Are you kidding? The only reason I have this tie is because it matched Payton's dress for the New Year's Dance; we went to together," he explained.

"Oh, Payton Winser?" For some reason, I was a little surprised he went to the dance with her. She's not good friends with Natasha Bert, but they run in the same group most of the time. "Are you guys, like . . . together?" I asked him, unsure if I was over-stepping our acquaintance line.

He shrugged nonchalantly. "We're more like friends with benefits." He kept his eyes on the road as he made a left turn at the green light.

"Do you want to be more?" I asked, prying a little. My curiosity was getting the better of me.

He laughed out loud. "No. No, I don't think she's my type. At least not somebody that I would want to date anyway."

"Why not?" I cocked my head to the side in confusion.

He looked over at me and gave me a side smirk. "You're not going to like my answer," he said with no humor in his voice.

"That's okay. I don't need to like your answer," I said back to him, which made his smirk grow into a smile.

"The reason we're friends with benefits is because we have sex, and its pretty good sex too. Other than that, when she wants to cuddle and talk, I'm never interested in anything she has to say." He looked over at me to see my reaction.

I raised my eyebrows in surprise at how direct he was. I didn't know what to say at first, so I didn't say anything.

"See, I told you you wouldn't like my answer," he said.

"Hey at least you were honest, and like I said, I don't need to like your answer. Does she know you feel that way?" I asked.

"Are you secret friends with her or something? Are you gonna, like, run off and tell her all of this?" he asked, glancing over at me warily.

"No. I haven't talked to Payton since middle school when we were in the same science class and had to be partners on something. I just had a friend that dated a guy and then he dumped her because she wouldn't do that stuff with him. I thought it was super douchey. That's all."

"That stuff? You mean sex, sexual intercourse, or putting out?" he asked, clearly now making fun of me.

"If you must word it like that, yes. Yes, I am referring to sex," I said, folding my arms and staring out my window.

"Have you ever had sex?" he asked me as we pulled into the parking lot of the car dealership.

My jaw dropped to the floor of his truck. I was mortified that he just asked me that! I could feel the heat in my cheeks turning my face red. I jumped out of his truck and slammed the door shut behind me. I started storming toward the front door, until he called my name.

"Hey Alli!"

I reluctantly turned around after pausing for a few seconds to gather myself. My hands were tight fists as I faced him. "What?!"

"Do you want your notebook?" he asked with a grin.

I stomped my feet up to him and ripped the notebook from his hand without saying anything. I turned back around to head toward the front door again, wanting to get away from him, but he stayed on my heels the entire time. I thought he was going to attempt to pry an answer out of me, but he didn't say a word. When I glanced at him over my shoulder, he was still smirking and I re-clenched my fists, digging my fingernails into my palms on purpose.

I knew I needed to pull myself together before we met with Curt. I took a few deep breaths as we sat in the waiting area for guests. Bryce got up to get himself a cup of coffee and asked if I wanted any. I didn't say anything, I just looked up and then looked away still annoyed. He got the hint. I heard him chuckle to himself. He came back with a single cup for himself.

"Curt is ready for you," his assistant said, smiling at us and walking us toward his office.

We walked through the large, double glass doors. They were clear on the top and bottom, but frosted in the middle to instill privacy for anybody who is seven foot or shorter. Everything in his office was crystal clear. He had a see-through desk, coffee table, the mouse for his computer, and windows for the walls. Even this massive picture of his family was crystal. Their eyes followed you anywhere you went, too; I wasn't a fan of that. It felt like they were moving inside the frame, and it was creeping me out.

Curt Pennington stood up from his desk and came to greet us. We both shook his massive hand, which, wouldn't you know it, he had a crystal ring on too.

"Hello Mr. Pennington," Bryce and I greeted him in unison. That annoyed me, causing me to glance at him while he was smiling his stupid smile back at me.

"How do you do?" Mr. Pennington greeted us back warmly. He motioned for us to sit on the couch across from his desk. It was a single couch, so I was sitting closer to Bryce than I wanted to be, but I attempted to ignore the proximity.

Curt half-sat on his desk across from us and luckily assisted us with getting the conversation flowing. "So, have you guys ever interviewed somebody before?" he asked with a knowing smile.

"No," we both started in unison again. I fought the urge to look at him this time.

Mr. Pennington laughed, and it seemed to relax Bryce, but I still felt on edge. "Well, I'll make this easy on you guys. Let's start with your names."

Bryce looked at me, allowing me to answer first. "I'm Alli Manex."

"And I'm Bryce Vinton. If you remember, my partner and I emailed you the questions ahead of time. If there are any that you do not want to answer, please let us know, and we will gladly proceed with the interview."

I gawked at how professional he sounded considering what we were talking about in his truck less than fifteen minutes ago! Mr. Pennington seemed impressed as well because he raised his left eyebrow in appeasement.

I asked if we could record the interview and Mr. Pennington agreed to let us. I decided to let Bryce do the asking of the questions while I wrote. To my shock, Bryce knew a lot more about business than I ever thought a seventeen year old would. I'm fairly sure Mr. Pennington was about to offer Bryce a job as a car salesman. He was that impressed. As was I, to be honest.

As I was writing down the answers, Bryce thought of additional questions to ask. It was quite fascinating to listen to even though I didn't understand 98% of it. I felt like a fly on the wall observing these two.

As we were walking back to his truck, I couldn't help but ask where he learned all that business talk.

"My dad is co-owner of the Quick Parts store in Bashton. He talks business all the time with me because he wants me to take over for him when he retires."

"Do you want to?" I asked, climbing into the passenger seat, and shutting my door at a normal speed this time.

"Huh," he said, pausing in the middle of fastening his seatbelt. He looked over at me with a questioning look on his face.

"What?" I asked, confused myself now.

"Nobody has ever asked me if I *want* to take over the business. They always ask me *when* I'm going to take it over."

"Do you not want to, then? Follow in his shoes I mean?" I asked, not sure if I was hitting a nerve or if I should change this subject all together.

"You know, Alli, you ask a *lot* of questions," he said, chuckling to himself.

"I'm a curious cat," I said, shrugging and putting my hands in the air, pretending I had claws.

"Curiosity kills the cat, you know."

"And yet, here I am." I smiled back at him.

"So, have you had sex?" he said, turning to me again, making my jaw drop to the floor once more.

"Are you serious?!" my voice went up a few octaves because of my annoyance for him.

I cannot believe he's asking me this again!

"Why do you want to know so bad whether I have or not?"

"I told you I have," he said, shrugging.

"So? That doesn't mean I need to disclose my personal life to you." I crossed my arms again out of frustration.

What a buzzkill. And to THINK I was impressed with him back at the interview.

"So, you haven't."

"I never said that," I defended myself.

"Oh, so you have?" he asked in a surprised tone that I didn't appreciate either.

"Whether I have or have not is of no concern to you," I scolded, turning my body to face out the window.

Of course, he was now laughing at me. "What are you from the 1940s or something? Who talks like that?" He was now laughing hysterically.

"Why do you want to know?" I asked, trying to hold my angry face, but it was getting hard because of all the laughing he was doing. I was being drawn to laugh with him, even at my expense.

"I'm a curious cat," he said, winking at me, which again, surprised the heck out of me.

"Well, you're just going to have to stay curious for all I care. That's not something I am going to talk about with you ever; so, drop it," I said sternly, trying not to smile to show how serious I was being.

"You seem worth the wait." He didn't say anything the rest of the drive to school, and I was too dumbfounded to speak either.

Is he . . . is he flirting with me? What? What did he mean by that?

"Would you go on a date with me?" I smiled as I read his text again. I texted him back yes with a smiley face.

"Awesome. I'll pick you up at 7:30 Saturday night."

Oh, my goodness, I'm about to go on a date! Like a real date date. This isn't like when William and I have gone as friends to the New Year's Dance, this is different.

Dad was hesitant to let me go, but Mom finally convinced him it was time to let me date. I facetimed my friends immediately afterwards to tell them the news. They were ecstatic for me. I told them I didn't know any details yet because he hadn't told me, so we started brainstorming some potential ideas. With it being April, it's not super warm out yet. I wondered if we would go bowling or to a movie? Rose thought maybe we would have a picnic, but I didn't take Bryce for being one to plan picnics.

Then again, he has been consistently surprising.

"Have you mentioned this to William yet?" Hayden asked me.

I figured she was going to bring him up. "No, I haven't. I don't really know what to tell him exactly. Bryce and I have been talking for two months, but obviously nothing serious has happened, and this is only the first date."

"Well, you could start with telling him that you're going on a date," Hayden suggested the obvious. "Maybe that will shock him into realizing that there are other guys that want to pursue you in that manner, instead of only keeping you in the friend-zone?"

I shrugged at the idea, wishing it would be like that.

"Maybe," was all I responded with.

Chelsea was blunt on the other hand with her thoughts. "Sky, I want to be honest with you. I think if anything were going to happen between you and William, I feel that it would have happened by now. It's been over a year and all that's happened is you having a not-so-secret, hard-core crush. Give another guy a chance. Bryce is funny and really, really cute! I think you might be surprised that you *could* like another guy whose name isn't William."

Evelynn silently nodded in agreement.

I'm sure they've talked about this with each other when I haven't been around them.

Hayden and Rose didn't say anything, though. Whether they felt the same way, I couldn't tell.

And maybe they're right. Maybe I really do need to branch out and see who else is out there. After all, William did with that Kat chick last summer.

As sucky as it is, I feel there is truth in regard to what Chelsea said. Unfortunately, I still have hope that something could happen between us, but maybe for now, I *should* give my attention to another guy. After all, Bryce and I have been having some nice conversations and we've been working on our giant Everyday Skills project since February technically, so it has been a while.

I started to let my heart and mind open to the idea of pursuing somebody else.

"I think you need to outright tell Will your feelings and get an honest answer from him," Evelynn stated, now that the door had been opened. "Tell him exactly how you feel and that you want to be more than friends with him, and if not, then you're pursuing Bryce and it's Will's loss!"

"That is so much easier said than done, Evelynn," I said.

I can't just outright demand to know his feelings . . . can I?

"Yeah, it is, but it's also more freeing than you could imagine too, Sky. Like, imagine if you and Will talked about the giant elephant in the room. Whether it's a good or bad talk, at least it would finally be out in the open. Then you can move forward down either path. And, either way, *we* are going to be here for you."

I know my friends mean well. They were probably tired of me always drooling over William and never doing anything about it. I told them I needed to think about all of this, and they understood. I ended the call, and then fell back on my bed, exhausted from all the emotions and internal conflicts I have dealt with for the last year and however many months.

It was Friday night, and I was staying in with my family so we could have pizza and game night.

I debated whether I should text, call, or see William in person to talk with him. I knew that by texting I wouldn't be able to gauge his true reaction since it's behind a screen. Calling might be too weird since I didn't have much to tell him aside from my news. In person, well, I'm always down to see him and we're always hanging out anyway. I texted William to ask what he's doing tonight. My in-person option might not work if he's with his friends or spending time with his own family.

Me: What are you up to tonight?

William: Going to watch the track meet. Are you coming?

Oh yeah, I forgot Bryce mentioned that. He invited me to come and watch him.

Me: Nah, staying in with my family tonight. My weasel has a new game he wants us to try out. Want to do something after the meet?

William: Sure. Want me to come to your place since I'm out already?

Me: Yeah that works.

I reminded him to come in through the basement door when he got here. It was about 10:30 PM when he texted me he was on his way. My nerves accelerated like an airplane taking off.

He came in, bringing the frigid air with him. "Gosh it's cold out tonight."

"There's a blanket under the ottoman if you need one, otherwise I can make you some hot chocolate if you'd like," I offered.

"Nah that's okay, the blanket should be enough. How was game night?"

"Terrible, my brother kicked our butts."

William laughed, knowing how competitive my family can be with games, especially my brother and me.

"Want to play?" I asked, holding Yahtzee in my hands. "I need to redeem my honor," I said, smiling. He couldn't see my knees shaking, but I wondered if my fingers would give me away during the game.

He laughed at my joke and agreed to play Yahtzee. I turn on the television so we can have some background noise. The movie *The Hunger Games* was on, so I left it on that.

We sat down and started rolling the dice. I asked him about the track meet tonight, and he informed me that our girls won the meet, and our guys placed third.

Sweet, large straight!

We talked about other things, and I decided I better get this over with before I chickened out. That could happen too easily, and I really did want to have this talk with him.

My turn to roll the dice. I shook the cup with the dice and rolled. We looked down to see what I rolled, and as I picked the dice back up to roll again, I blurted out, "I'm going on a date with Bryce Vinton tomorrow." I stopped shaking the dice and peeked up at him.

His face didn't show much. "Bryce from the track team?"

I nodded my head yes to let him know that's the Bryce I was referring to.

His face still didn't have much expression to it, which I thought was kind of interesting.

I was trying to read every little thought he might be thinking.

Is that jealousy? Surprise? Is he bothered? Is he excited for me?

"What is it?" I asked him after he didn't respond in what I considered to be a normal manner.

"Umm, I guess I'm just kind of surprised you're going out with Bryce of all people." He kept his eyes on the dice and didn't look at me.

"What do you mean?" I pressed.

He shrugged. "I don't know. I don't really know Bryce, but from the things I heard, he can be a dick is all and I don't want him to be a dick to you."

Is he going to try and talk me out of this?

I watched him look anywhere but at me as I spoke, "I guess I won't really know unless I give him a chance. Unless . . . you don't think I should go out with him?"

He hesitated again before speaking, "No . . . you're probably right. What are you guys going to do?"

"I'm not sure; he said he won't tell me until he picks me up."

"Well I hope you have a good time, but Alli, if he is a jerk, promise you'll tell me okay?" William said, making my heart leap into my throat so I could only nod in response to his request.

We are going to an indoor ice-skating rink! I was so excited because I had only done this once when I was a lot younger. That surprised Bryce. I told him I had never gone skiing before either. I finally made his jaw drop this time. He told me skiing is something I need to experience at least once in my life.

That's what everyone says when I tell them I have never skied, so maybe it's true?

We got to the ice rink and put on our skates. I stood up and felt like a new-born deer. I wobbled during my first few steps and almost fell over, but luckily Bryce caught me and steadied me.

We got onto the ice and Bryce was thankfully holding on to me. Eventually I was able to stand on my own without his assistance. He was a natural. He never faltered the entire time. I, however, fell at least five times, and my butt had the bruises to show for it!

"You know, they have those plastic things you can push around to help you stay up?" he said after helping me stand back up after my fifth doozy.

"I try not to be prideful, but I'd rather fall than use that thing," I said, making him laugh while I felt the warmth of his hand in mine.

"I'd be more than happy to massage your ass too," he said with a wink and his flirtatious smile.

"I'm sure you would be!" I laughed and shook my head playfully at him.

He held my hand the rest of the time we were on the ice. Despite falling and the bruises, I had a wonderful time with him! We both were laughing all night, the music was great, and it was nice to be this comfortable with someone new, even if I made a fool of myself by falling. Sure, he was laughing at me, but I was laughing at me too.

Bryce and I were officially boyfriend and girl-friend on April 16th. We hung out a lot, but I still hung out with William one-on-one too. Bryce didn't like me hanging out with William alone and we argued a couple times about it. He claimed the entire school thought there was something going on between William and I, so he's not crazy for thinking there could be. I tried explaining how he and I are just good friends and nothing more, but he was still bothered by it. There didn't seem to be anything I could say to change his mind about it either. It felt like a losing battle.

Bryce would take me on real dates and always planned them, which was fun. Other times, we would have chill nights where we worked on homework together. I met his family not long after we started dating. He has two older brothers and one younger, so his mom loved having another female in the house with her.

He was different from William in a lot of ways. He made me feel special, made me laugh in an altered way, and cuddling felt differently with him than with William.

I guess everything feels different with Bryce because it means something to him and me; it isn't one sided anymore.

Interestingly enough, William texted me after the first few dates I had with Bryce wanting to make sure nothing happened, or that Bryce didn't treat me inappropriately somehow. I kept reassuring him that Bryce had been very kind to me and I hadn't felt pressured to do anything.

In July, we had been together for three months. It wasn't long or anything, but it was the longest (and only) relationship I had been in up until then. Things started to change between Bryce and me. Since it was summer, I started getting busier with work and spending more free time with my friends as well as with him.

One night Bryce and I were hanging out at his place, but he wasn't being his usual laughing, self. He seemed distant, and scatter-brained.

"Are you okay, Bryce? It seems like something is on your mind," I asked him.

"Um, yeah, I guess for the most part, but I need to be honest about something. Do you remember when we were in my truck, and we were talking about Payton and me?"

"Yeah?" My stomach started to sink to the floor. My mind was already racing to where this was probably headed.

"I, uh, well . . . I don't want to be a douche, but I want to go back to being friends with benefits with Payton. I just don't want to do it while I have a girlfriend, you know?"

I couldn't say I was shocked, because I knew he was missing sex, and I always made it clear when we were making out that I didn't want to go any further. He pushed sometimes, but for the most part, and to his credit, he always respected my boundaries.

"Oh . . . I see." I hesitated before I continued. "Would you want to like, stay friends and still hang out at all?" I asked him, staring at the ground with a lump in my throat.

"Truthfully? I'm not one to be friends with my exes. I don't know how other people do it. I hope you don't fault me for that."

"No. No I don't fault you, Bryce. I appreciate the honesty, I just—I thought we were having fun together. Like I thought you enjoyed hanging out with me and being around me?"

"You are fun. You make me laugh and I like being around you, I just want more, and I know you don't. Unless . . . would you want to . . . you know, now?" he asked seriously.

I raised my eyebrows at him in surprise. "No. I don't want to have sex with you right now. I mean, maybe in the future, but if that's the only reason you want to stay with me, then I'd rather we break it off."

I wasn't completely appalled because again, I respected his honesty, and this seemed like a cleaner break than what other people tend to get.

"That's fair, I just figured I'd try. The worst you could do was say no one more time," he said, not looking surprised at all either. "Can I tell you something, Alli?"

I nodded.

"If you never talk to Will about your feelings for him, then you're always going to be hurting yourself. I knew you had feelings for him before we dated, and I can feel it now. Talk to him," he said, bumping against my shoulder with his.

I was speechless! *Am I seriously this obvious? Do I wear a flashing sign on my forehead that says, "I'm in love with William Mantel"?*

"Yeah. That's what my friends have always said too. Are you sure you don't want to be just friends? You're doing well at it so far." I attempted a playful smile.

"Nah, Payton gets jealous too easily." He chuckled mostly to himself.

"Understandable."

"Well, uh, I think seeing other people would be best for us then." He stood up and opened his arms for a hug. I stood up too and he gave me a hug goodbye.

"I'll see ya around, Alli."

I was at his house, so I had to be the one to leave. I picked my keys up from the coffee table and told him I'd see him around too. I opened the front door and left without looking behind me.

I laid on my bed, processing everything that just went down with Bryce, I couldn't help but notice that I wasn't feeling devastated.

Shouldn't I be completely bummed that my first boyfriend just broke up with me?

I dug deep to really listen to what I was feeling in that moment, and the word that summed me up was not at all what I was expecting. I felt . . . free. I felt lighter realizing Bryce was only a cover up this entire time, and he knew that too.

Sorry, Bryce. I really didn't mean to do that to you, but I have a feeling you'll be just fine.

I hated being in my room right now. I wanted to do something, so I decided to drive around while listening to music. It's my default now. I waited seventeen years to be able to leave (almost) whenever I want to.

After driving around town for an hour I realized I was on William's side of town. All I needed to do was take a left and I would head down the gravel road to his house. I called his number and he answered. My clock said it was 11:23 PM, so I hoped I didn't wake him.

"Hey Al, what's up?"

"Hey, are you home right now?"

"I am, is everything okay?" he asked.

"Would it be okay if I came over?" I was already heading toward his place.

"Yeah of course. My parents are asleep, so just let me know when you're here and I will come and let you in."

"Okay . . ." I paused for a second. "I'm here."

"Wow, that was quick! I'll come upstairs."

I parked in front of his house and got out of my car. He came up to me, but he didn't have his usual smile on his gorgeous face. He can hear what I say even when I stay silent. He knew something happened between Bryce and me and that's why I was here.

He didn't ask me anything; he didn't have to. Instead, he opened his arms and I automatically stepped into them, wrapping my arms around his back. He held me, putting one hand at the base of my head and the other around my backside.

I needed this.

William didn't pull away, even well after a regular hug should end. Instead, he waited for when I was ready; eventually I reluctantly peeled myself away.

I walked over to their front porch and sat down on the top step. I never noticed how nice of a porch they had because I have never once used their front door.

William sat down next to me, still silent. He patiently waited for me to say whatever was on my mind.

"Bryce broke up with me," I finally whispered.

"What? Why?" He was surprised by this information.

Because I'm in love with you and everyone in the entire state of Kansas knows it.

I shrugged. "He wants to have sex and I don't, so he asked if I was willing to be friends with benefits and I said no." I was playing with my shoestring, not wanting to look him in the face.

"He broke up with you because you didn't want to have sex? What an ass!" William said in a semi-serious way, but also in a voice that only he could pull off, making me chuckle.

"In all seriousness though, Alli, you're an amazing person. Any guy would be lucky to be with you," William said, causing me to look up at him.

But do you want to be with me?

These words came to mind instinctively. They crept back up on me, my feelings for him that I had been suppressing while I was dating my first boyfriend. They've always been there, and I feel they are always going to be there. I was sitting here with him; he had his arm around my shoulder consoling me over a guy that could never compare to him. The only place I wanted to be was here with William. All those times that everything felt different with Bryce was because I always kept thinking about William and how everything Bryce and I did, I had wished I was doing with William, and that wasn't fair to Bryce. I'm not mad at Bryce at all. In fact, I feel like I should almost go and apologize to him even.

Heh, well maybe I don't feel that bad. He'll be okay, he's got Payton to comfort him after all.

We sat there in silence as I thought about all my feelings. He broke my thoughts with a question he had no idea the complexity of.

"Are you okay?" he whispered.

I stayed silent, wondering how to answer this. I know he was asking if I was okay about the Bryce break up thing, and the answer to that was easily yes.

"No," I said truthfully.

I'm not okay. It's even worse when he hugs me tighter for saying that.

I need to do this. I need to finally get this out in the open. I can't keep carrying the weight of this inside of me.

For the first time in our friendship history, I called him Will instead of William. I'm not sure why I did. It could be because my heart and mind were frantically fighting against each other. My heart wanted me to tell him, but my mind was telling me not to, pleading with me not to tell him. His name just came out that way, and honestly, it was probably the last thing I should have been focusing on when I spoke my next words.

"Will—there's something I need to tell you . . ."

CHAPTER 19

*A*m I seriously about to tell him? Why is my heart beating so loud? Can he hear it? He's just staring at me . . . god he's attractive, I just want to wrap myself up in his arms and . . . focus, Alli!

"What is it, Alli?"

Oh god, oh god, oh god!!!

"I . . . umm, mmmm, I . . ."

"You're making me nervous. What's up?"

I can't look at him. I think my heart moved into my throat. Where's my breath?

"I . . . ummm, I'm okay that Bryce and I broke up," I stammered out.

"Okay . . . well that's good. I'm glad to hear—"

"Because I like you," I spat out.

Holy hell, I actually said it. I told William how I felt! Why is he looking down? Why isn't he saying anything? He's not looking at me now. Oh my god, what have I done? My heart is about to leap out of my throat now! I'm going to throw up. This is how he's going to remember me. His former best friend that threw up on him.

"Um . . . William? Could you . . . could you say something?" I begged him with my eyes to speak, to say literally anything!

William stood up and took a couple steps away from the porch, his back to me. He leaned on the railing and crossed his arms, but not for long. He didn't seem to know what to do with his arms or hands right now.

"I know," he said.

I was confused. I wasn't expecting that kind of response. "What?"

"I know, you like me, Alli. I know you. I know when you're anxious, or happy, or upset but trying to not let people know you're upset. And I know when you are attracted to someone. So yeah, I know."

I raised my eyebrows in shock.

What the heck? If he knew, why hasn't he said anything?

"So, for like a year and a half you have known, but you haven't said anything?" I desperately wanted him to say that he liked me back, or that he wanted us to try and be more than friends. I wanted this so badly!

William looked at me but looked away. He touched his face, and then put his hands in his pockets.

"No, because you're my best friend and I don't ever want to hurt you. I can't . . . I can't stomach the idea of not having you in my life. If we dated, and something terrible happened where we weren't in each other's lives anymore, I don't think I could handle that. You are the closest person to me, even above my friends. You're beautiful, and funny, and I love the time we spend together and I value our friendship so much I don't want to risk losing what we have now by us dating. You know?" He looked anywhere but at me when he spoke. "Does that make sense?"

I could see the painful truth in his eyes as he spoke. My heart went from my throat straight to the pit of my stomach in a nanosecond. I felt like I had just swallowed an anvil.

You are not going to cry, Alli. Do you hear me?

I nodded my head in acknowledgement at William and stood up.

I need to leave.

With a pained expression, he didn't try to stop me, he only said, "I'm sorry, Al."

I could tell he meant it, but it didn't make it hurt any less right now.

"No, don't be," I managed to choke out.

I needed to go; tears were starting to form, and I couldn't let William see them.

"I'm going to go." I didn't look back as I walked to my car. William might have said something, but I wasn't listening. The tears started escaping as soon as I sat behind the wheel.

Rose was the first to contact me after a couple of days. I didn't tell anybody because I wasn't ready. She found out from Morris. He was wondering where I was Monday night when William and his friends were hanging out and I was absent.

She came over and we went for a walk. Talking to her about it made me feel as though the anvil was being lifted off me.

"I told him I liked him, and he responded saying he already knew and didn't want to risk losing our friendship." I replayed the scene from my memory aloud to Rose.

She thought about her response for a minute before speaking. "It sucks. I'm sorry. Let yourself feel your emotions, though. Don't try to contain them. I don't want you to accidentally take them out on Will. Make sure you take time and listen to yourself and your own emotions. If you need to grieve, grieve. Some people would probably say you and him never dated and you shouldn't be sad, but I disagree. We all have different connections and diverse levels of connections with one another. Who's to say we can't grieve for something we wanted but didn't get? It's kind of like when people interview for jobs, and they don't get it. They wanted it, prepped for it, interviewed for it, and then they received a phone call or letter of rejection from that company and they're sad, you know? I don't know if it's too soon to bring up, but I do know that all this time, you too had been wrestling with the idea of saying anything out of fear of messing things up and losing him."

I nodded in agreement, listening to a different side of Rose I wasn't used to hearing.

It's true, I was scared of telling him my feelings for fear I would screw up our friendship, but I also figured if he did like me back, which he didn't make clear his feelings last night, but IF he did, then wouldn't it be something we should talk about together?

"I know you're hurting right now Sky, and I hate to see you hurting, but I think he just needs time to process everything too, now that it's out in the open I mean. I'm not saying you two won't date in the future, but he is also scared of losing you, so in a way, I kind of view it as you both being in the same boat." She shrugged and continued. "I don't think that helped, but I hope you find a little comfort in the fact that he would rather have you in his life more than anything."

When you're this close with somebody, someone is bound to get hurt at some point or another. I've hurt my friends many times and they have always forgiven me and have loved me regardless.

I somehow felt better and worse all at the same time. Better because I think he and I will be okay even though I'm still feeling what I'm feeling, but also, the sensation of not just wanting him, but needing him is an entirely new level of emotions I didn't realize were brewing on the inside of me either. I want to date him. I want to be more than what we are, but in the end, I just need him to be in my life, and if that's friendship, then so be it.

Even though my heart still felt like it needed to be surgically repaired, I couldn't stand not being around William. I was frustrated at my emotions, hurt by his thought process, and yet all I wanted was to be near him because I missed him.

Is that twisted?

After wallowing for a couple of days, and us not speaking in French class, I couldn't stand the awkwardness anymore. I texted him asking if he would meet me at the park we always hang out at.

I was nervous and awkwardly shy as he walked up to the swing I was on. I could tell he was, too, this being our first time talking since "that night."

"Hi," I said to him when he sat down on the swing next to mine.

"Hey," he said back, looking at the ground. "How are you?"

I shrugged my shoulders. Of course, I was still feeling all the feels, but I also knew he felt terrible too and I didn't want that.

"I'll be fine," I said with a slight smile. "How are you?" I asked, hoping he would give me an honest answer and not something he thinks I want to hear.

He shrugged too. "I've been worried about you."

My heart thumped harder from those words. "Really?" I asked, not able to hide my surprise.

He looked at me befuddled. "Of course. I didn't know if it was okay or not to reach out to you, so I waited, hoping you would reach out."

I was stunned by his answer; all I could do was stare at him with my mouth ajar, but no sound escaped.

"Why do you look so surprised by that?" he asked, cocking his head to the right.

"I just . . ." I stammered, trying to remember how to form words again. "I can't believe how alike we can be on this, and yet, we both have different opinions and it's just confusing and sucky and I also understand your hesitation too which is also annoying because we're practically the same person!" I inhaled deeply and caught my breath while I wiped my eye, trying to act like I had a quick itch and not cry again.

"Interesting," was what he responded with. I thought he would continue, but he didn't. Instead, he rocked back and forth on the swing, examining his feet like he just realized he had two of them for the first time in his life.

After what seemed like minutes of silence, but in reality, was twenty seconds, I spoke, breaking the silence. "Interesting? Really? Can I get a little more than that right now, please."

"Sorry," he said. He stood up and motioned for me to stand too. He wrapped me in a strong embrace which was what I needed from him.

"You're right though, Alli," he spoke while hugging me. I could feel his breath from his words thump against his chest as he spoke. "We are practically the same person, which is why it scares me if we were to be more than friends. I'm truly sorry I can't explain it better, but I just don't think it would end well. You might be willing to risk that, but I just . . . I can't and I'm sorry." He hugged me tighter and I tightened my grip on him, and on reality as well.

I finally pulled away from him so I could look into the eyes I loved. "I understand, William John. I don't 100% agree, but I understand at least."

"Does this mean we are okay then?" he almost whispered. I could tell he had been holding his breath for once.

"I would sure like us to be," I said, causing a smile to appear on his perfect lips. The lips I desperately want to kiss. Seeing him smile made me smile automatically in response.

"There's the smile I've missed," he said.

My body started to relax finally.

I think I can live with this, as long as THIS is always there.

CHAPTER 20

The summer was coming to a close as I mentally prepared myself for senior year.

It doesn't feel real.

Things between William and I have been good, though, so that helps. I'm continuously coping and working toward accepting that a friendship with him might be all I ever get to have. I'm just grateful when we hang out or text, that everything seems to be normal again for the most part.

William and I were hanging out in his basement, just the two of us. We were sitting on the same couch, but we left a seat in between us. I was curled up under a blanket as usual, wishing he would move closer to me and warm me up with his personal body heat. We were talking about what we think our last year of high school will be like.

"I can't believe our senior year is a week away. It just doesn't seem like it should be here already!" I exclaimed.

"Yeah, it is crazy, but I think post high school life is going to be awesome," he said, sending a reassuring smile my way.

"How so?" I asked, curious about his thoughts.

"Everything is our last. Last first day, last seasons for sports, last New Year's Dance." He made a silly face at that because he knows how much I love to dance, and yes, I am bummed about how our school dances are coming to an end forever.

I playfully kicked him with my foot, exposing it to the cold, and to his fast hands. He grabbed it and started to tickle me. I shrieked with surprise and from the tingling sensation that comes with being tickled. I don't enjoy being tickled at all, but of course when he does it, it's not as torturous. I kicked and tried to fight his strong hands off my ankle, but he overpowered me.

Eventually the "torturing" ceased. As I was curling myself tightly under the blanket, he said something that shocked me. "How about I ask you this year?"

What?! Of course. A thousand times yes!

My heart was doing cartwheels! I tried to play it off nonchalantly, but he knew how excited he just made me.

"Yeah, that'd be okay," I said, shrugging. We laughed together at my attempt but I failed to hide my giddiness.

"What class are you looking the most forward to?" I asked him.

"Probably Yearbook. I've always been told it's an easy A which are my favorite types of classes. How about you?

"Psychology," we said in unison. We laughed together again.

"You're wanting to be a therapist, Alli, of course I know what your favorite class is going to be." He laughed at me.

He does know me. I love the way he lights up when he laughs! I love how his eyes crinkle in the corners. He makes everything seem effortless and almost inhumanly perfect.

"Um correction, it's actually going to be AP Psychology. Thank you very much. I'm worried it's going to be hard, though. What if I don't do well and it deters me from wanting to go into this field? I don't know what I would do as a backup plan."

I looked down at the ground as the worry lines between my eyebrows formed. This wasn't the first time I'd had this thought, but it was the first time I'd said it out loud to someone.

"Hey," he said as he scooted closer so he could wrap his arms around my shoulders and pull me in for a hug. I silently inhaled his comforting scent.

God I want to kiss him so badly even though we just talked about needing to be friends. It's just when he holds me like he does, I want to melt into him through every crevice.

"First off, you're going to do great in all your classes because you always have. Secondly, even if you change your mind about what career path you decide to go into, you're going to be great wherever you end up. No matter what you're doing, you always give it your all, and that's what is going to make you successful in this life."

Okay, wow . . . I was not expecting that to come from him. I figured he was going to make a joke and try to make me laugh the way he normally does, but this, this was deep, and real . . . and dang it, why doesn't he see how good we are together?! How easy all of this is and could be.

I wrapped my arms around him for a deep and tight hug. He squeezed me back in response and we sat there like that for longer than normal. I could feel him starting to stir, so I released him. As I pulled back, I stared into his eyes that were only inches from mine. My impulsive thoughts took over and I leaned in and kissed him.

He didn't pull away immediately. Instead, I felt his hand slide up from my shoulder onto the back of my neck. He pulled me in closer and deepened our kiss. We were kissing for a minute before he pulled himself backwards. He quickly moved back to his original spot as he cleared his throat and wiped his bottom lip with his thumb slowly before speaking. "Whoa . . . Al, umm . . . we really shouldn't do that, cuddling is one thing, but kissing is not a good idea . . ."

My heart rate was attempting to slow back to normal.

"I . . . I'm sorry. I can't believe I did that." I bit my lower lip that was still damp from his. "Are you mad?" I asked nervously.

He inhaled, but shook his head no. "No, it's just . . . we shouldn't, it will only complicate things."

"You're right. I'm really sorry." I looked down at my hands that were playing with each other. *I can't help but notice he didn't pull away immediately either though when I kissed him . . .*

"It's fine . . . so um, do you want to shoot pool or something?" he asked, trying to change the subject and get back to normal.

I could sense his discomfort and knew if he had something in his hands to occupy his mind, then he would be more at ease. "Yeah. I've been practicing, so you better watch out," I joked, trying to lighten the environment around us.

"Have you now?" He perked up at the idea of a challenge.

"Oh, for sure! I've been sneaking into your house and practicing while you all slept," I said, clearly joking.

"Well then I guess I'll tell my dad we need to start putting locks on the windows too."

"Mmmm, I've learned how to pick those as well so you can't stop me. Mwahaha."

"In that case, electric fence it is!" he said, laughing, and I laughed with him.

He kicked my butt as he always does, but I think I have gotten a little better over the summer for as much as we've played.

On the drive home, I replayed our kiss a million times. The heat of his lips on mine, the strength from his hand pulling my face in closer. I got so many goosebumps I turned my heater on in the car for a little bit.

Wow! That was—wow! Wait ... should I tell my friends? They are totally going to freak out. Nah, I'm not going to tell them. I want this to be another shared secret between him and I.

I laugh and smile all giddy-like to myself on the rest of the drive home.

The night before school, our parents allowed us girls to have a sleepover.

I hosted the slumber party in my basement under the rule that lights must be off no later than 10:00 PM. Of course, we will have the lights turned off, but that doesn't mean we have to be asleep at 10:00. Believe me, we won't be.

"I dumped Rowan," Chelsea started the conversation with a bang. I can't say I was shocked, but oddly, I expected him to dump her since he's the one off at college.

"Why?" Hayden asked what we all were wondering.

"Well, he dumped me technically," she corrected, and I suppressed a small chuckle on the inside from my pride wanting to be right. "It was pretty mutual actually. It's not a big deal. He's hot and all, but with him going to be in North Carolina, long distance was going to be way too hard on me." She shrugged.

"Are you okay?" sweet Rose asked sincerely.

"Oh, she's most definitely okay. She's a smoking hot, single, senior volleyball player." Evelynn snapped her fingers and waved her arms, hyping

Chelsea who was doing a dance move I wish I could do with my legs and butt. "She's got options and choices. Yes girl!" Evelynn stated. I joined in cheering for my friend, happy to be reminded Chelsea will in fact be okay.

"Speaking of boyfriends," Chelsea turned her gaze to Rose who didn't seem to be paying attention because she was typing on her phone. She looked up and blushed under the hard stare of our eyes. "How's Morris?"

She tucked a loose strand of hair behind her ear and blushed a little like I do. "He's good. He's playing video games right now with the guys," she said, glancing my way. I too knew this information.

"Have you guys, you know?!" Chelsea raised her eyebrows in the "we want to know your secrets because we're your best friends" kind of way.

"Oh Chels, stop," I said, as Rose looked back down and blushed even harder this time. We knew they hadn't—well, I guess nothing had been verified, technically.

"Hey, we shouldn't assume anything," Chelsea said, defending her intrusive question. "Because if you guys have, I just want to make sure you're using protection," Chelsea said, still teasing Rose.

"Good thing if we ever need protection, we can just come to Chelsea instead of the pharmacy for condoms," Hayden chimed in, throwing a pillow at Chelsea who responded by throwing it back. This caused Greyson to yell down the stairs at us to shut up. We being loud, but it's hard not to be when you're having to defend yourself from four other pillows coming at you with full force.

Once we wiped the tears of laughter from our eyes, we decided to put on some movie Evelynn chose. It's literally about these girlfriends that start senior year of high school together. I couldn't tell you the name of it because we weren't actually watching it; it was background noise for us as we flipped through some magazines, listened to the outfits Evelynn was choosing for us, and scrolled through our phones.

This is perfect. This is us, I thought to myself as I looked around at my friends. *I wouldn't want to spend my last night of summer with any other people than those sitting in my basement with me. Well . . . except for one person in particular.*

Fall Semester Senior Year

2016

My friends and I pulled into our usual parking space for the last first time.

How weird.

We got out of Evelynn's vehicle and started walking toward a shaded area under an old tree. It wasn't even 8:00 AM yet and the humidity was ridiculous! It was going to be scorching hot today. Thank goodness I'd be inside all day.

Evelynn was complaining about how the humidity was going to start making her hair frizz, while Chelsea was not wanting to smell from sweating.

"If you smell, I have you covered," Evelynn said. The fact she has enough room in her locker for her books, notebooks, spare school supplies, perfume, deodorant, make up, and more is astonishing.

Although, if the school saw how organized she kept it, I wouldn't be surprised if they forced all of us to be that tidy.

I wasn't really listening to my friends; I was too busy trying to take in the sight of everyone on this day. One of the popular groups of females had underclassmen taking photos of them. Some of the guys were playing catch with a football as they always did, acting as though nothing was different today.

I wonder if most of our classmates are feeling the same thing today: bittersweetness, sadness, fear, joy, apprehension? I'm sure everyone is feeling something; it'd just be interesting if we all took a poll to see what the majority is. There's the future therapist in me coming out again, haha. William would laugh with and at me if he had heard what I was thinking.

Hayden was snapping her fingers in front of my face as I came crashing back to reality. The bell was ringing for us to head inside for Homeroom. I've never been so aware of this building until now. I was taking in all the banners, lockers, and just everyone.

I headed to the same locker for the third year in a row. I spun the familiar combination. *Click.* As I stocked my locker full of unused notebooks,

William popped up beside me. I could smell him before I turned to confirm it was him. I smiled at him as I closed my locker and threw my bag over my shoulder.

"Are you ready?" he asked me.

"Ready as I'll ever be I guess." He knew I was anxious about this year, so he leaned over and gave me a hug for comfort. Naturally, my heart picked up speed at his touch.

"Try to relax. It's senior year, we get front row at every event we go to. The underclassmen are going to move out of the way for us, and we have complete and total domination rights!" He grinned his perfect teeth at me.

I rolled my eyes in response because I couldn't think of anything witty enough to say at the moment.

We started walking down the same hallway together when I asked him if he knew any of the freshmen that were going to be in his Homeroom.

"You mean freshmeat," he tried correcting me. I smiled, but I was not going to call them that. He continued, "No idea. Mrs. Stanley passed out the sheet of paper with their names on it, and we all were supposed to write a little note to them, but I didn't read their names, and if I did, I definitely forgot them over the summer. What about you?"

"I recognized one name because it's Bonnie's little sister; other than that, no idea."

"I wonder if Bonnie is taking French class this year?" he thought aloud to himself.

"She is," I confirmed with confidence. "She tried really hard to get me to take it with her, but I was adamant about only wanting to take the four required years for college."

College was a touchy subject to me when it came to William. He hadn't fully decided yet on which southern state he wanted to disappear to. He was leaning toward the University of Texas, but he hadn't applied yet.

Our walk together was coming to a close. William wrapped up the conversation. "Well, best of luck to her and Mrs. Lamb! As for us, let's go kick senior year's ass!" William said excitedly, squeezing my hand as he went right, and I went left.

I knew I would see him later today, and it was impractical for me to desire this, but I wished we had every class together so we could spend more time talking and hanging out. Since neither of us are taking French this year, we don't have a single class together except for lunch (which I consider a human need, not a class).

Once I was seated in my chair, I pulled out my class schedule and looked at it for the 80th time this week. Aside from AP Psychology class, I am also taking AP Sociology, American Government II, Animal Science, English Literature IV, Journalism, and Gym of course. Also another perk of being a senior is that instead of Study Hall, we get Open Campus where we can leave for the period. I have fulfilled my math requirements, so I opted to not take math this year, despite my mom's protest.

No math = greatest year ever!

William thinks his classes will be pretty easy as well. We still plan to do homework together like always. Lucky for me, he won't have to watch me struggle with math anymore; but naturally he's disappointed. I think it will be fun that I'm taking Journalism and he's going to do Yearbook this year. We can search for stories together. He can take the photos that I will print in the school newspaper.

Yeah, senior year may just kick ass after all.

I looked around the room at the three new freshmen who appeared terrified.

I remember when that was me, I think to myself as I confidently walked down the familiar hallway.

CHAPTER 21

I took my place next to him on his couch. I fluffed the blanket and made sure it covered all our toes. For me, there's nothing worse than having cold feet, literally and figuratively, but mostly literally. He naturally made enough popcorn for everyone, but he always makes it for me because he knows my love for it. I'm sure when I'm fifty years old, my heart is going to hate me for the amount of butter and salt I'll have consumed by then, but I'll worry about it later.

Rose and Morris are also sharing a blanket on the love seat, but they're not sitting as close as William and I are. That's Rose, though; she's shy in general, and won't be showing any public displays of affection, even in front of her friends.

We voted to watch a scary movie tonight. We've been watching a lot of comedy and superhero movies. We're wanting to change it up, plus it's October, and that means the entire month is "spooky season." Grant chose *The Conjuring*. He said it's extremely scary.

I'm glad I'm sitting next to William. His presence alone makes me feel safe and more at ease.

I was an absolute baby throughout this movie and William was enjoying every second of it! I couldn't help it. I was covering my eyes with the blanket during a lot of scenes. William would hold me a little tighter when I was scared and I 100% leaned into him.

Once, when a suspenseful scene was taking place and the music was building, making my heartbeat faster and faster, he grabbed my shoulders and screamed, making me jump out of my skin! If I were a cat, I would have been on the ceiling with my claws dug into the rafters.

"WILLIAM JOHN!" I screamed with fright. Aside from Rose and myself, everyone else in the room thought it was hilarious to hear me scream. I was shooting daggers at him with my eyes. All he had to do was smile at me, which he did, and I internally forgave him, although I didn't want him to know it immediately.

"Oooooooo, she's dropping the first and middle name on you!" Danny laughed.

"Dang right!" I said, lightly attempting not to let William pull me back next to him, but also, of course, relishing him reaching and tugging me as well.

Through his laughter, he tried to apologize, "I'm sorry, really! Come on, sit back. I promise I won't do it again."

I gave him a hard side eye while still acting as if I didn't want to be near him anymore. "No way; you're totally going to do it again."

He tried to compose his face, but he was struggling to keep his face serious. His smile kept breaking through.

"No, really. I truly promise. If I do it again, you can . . . get revenge at some point."

This piqued my interest, "What kind of revenge?" I asked. Everyone was also more interested in his answer than they were in the movie too.

"Whatever you deem is fair in return." He smirked without showing teeth.

I took the deal. "Deal. You better believe me when I say I'm exceptionally good at revenge!"

I tried to sound as threatening as I could. I even raised my right eyebrow at him to show my seriousness. My friends laughed at me, and I could tell William was trying to take me seriously, but I didn't even take myself seriously. There isn't anything I would purposefully do to hurt or get back at him, and everyone on earth knew it.

"Noted," was his response. He tapped my previous spot next to him, and I, without a second thought, leaned back into his body, snuggling up next to his warmth and steady beating heart.

As usual, William and I were doing homework after school one evening. I was working on Animal Science. My homework consisted of me imagining, planning, designing, and managing my own prairie field. I had to figure out what types of animals, insects, plants, bushes, trees, etc. I would include and my reasoning behind them.

He was supposed to be working on his English paper, but his phone kept notifying us his Snapchat was blowing up. I tried to ignore it, but after a while, I couldn't focus on my own thoughts, all I could hear was his phone chiming from notification after notification.

He was sitting across from me, but I could feel his leg shaking with anticipation. After what was maybe two minutes, he picked his phone back up, took a picture, and then set it down again so he could "focus."

Finally, after fifteen more minutes of his constant leg bouncing, chuckling to himself, and my annoyance that had been building the entire time, I asked him who the heck he was snapping so much.

"Just someone from my Yearbook class," he said, preparing to take a picture of himself to send back.

My eyebrows came together, confused. He doesn't even snap me this much, let alone his guy friends. It must be a girl.

"Is it a girl?" I asked directly.

"Yeah," was all he said.

Another sensitive area for me. It was rough on me when he was talking to that Kat girl from Pennsylvania. Jealousy I didn't realize was inside of me came out during that time. I didn't like that side of me, and I don't want to see it again.

"Gotcha," was all I said in response, but I could feel my agitation growing. I continued with my homework, but it was getting harder to concentrate on when William's phone wouldn't shut off from notifications.

Finally, I couldn't take it. I snapped at him with ice in my voice.

"William . . . seriously?"

"What?" He looked up, surprised as I was from the tone I'd just used with him.

"What do you mean 'what?' This entire time you've done nothing except laugh to yourself and be on your phone. Are you even going to do your homework or are you just going to sit on Snapchat all night? Because I can leave if that's the case. I can go upstairs if you want privacy or something."

I immediately felt terrible for what came out of my mouth. I had never snapped like that, especially toward him; maybe in a joking manner, but there wasn't an ounce of joking this time.

"Alright, alright, I'll put my phone down. Sheesh," William said, laying his phone down so the screen wasn't facing up anymore.

"Can you also put it on silent? It has been driving me nuts," I asked. I attempted to make my voice sound a little kinder, but I didn't do a particularly good job at it.

He didn't say anything, but he picked his phone back up, clicked the down volume button a couple times, and then turned it back over. His phone was silent, and now so was he.

Great.

After twenty minutes of pure silence, he started to pack up his stuff.

"I'm going to get going. I'm not really getting anything done," he said flatly.

Obviously . . .

"Alright, I'll see you tomorrow," I said in a sad tone. I felt bad that I upset him.

"See ya."

He never looked at me when he packed his back-pack and took off.

Thanksgiving was approaching quickly. The leaves were changing and falling, the grass was dying, and the temperature was dipping at nighttime. My friends and William's wanted to do something fall-ish outside, so we decided on having one last bonfire before the snow in Kansas started.

Naturally, William hosted the fire out at his place. William's mom made sure we had enough blankets to sit on and wrap ourselves with. The temperature at 9:00 PM was thirty-five degrees, but that wasn't going to deter us.

The thermoses of hot chocolate made their way around as I took in everyone around the glowing fire; my friends, William's friends (whom I now consid-ered to be my friends too), and William. I wanted to remember this night forever. All of us sitting here, laughing, and reminiscing on elementary, middle school, and high school.

We shared embarrassing stories of each other we swore we would never share. Peter shared the story of how he, William, and Danny went to McDonald's and poor Danny got diarrhea from it. Peter and William couldn't help but laugh at the memory of Danny stinking up McDonald's bathroom. Danny has never gone back to that McDonald's since.

Evelynn shared the story of her and Hayden walking through the library while it was packed full of students, and as they were about to leave through the double doors Hayden wasn't paying attention to where she was looking, and she went SMACK into the metal pole that divided the doors. The entire library looked over at the noise her head made upon contact. Evelynn cried laughing at the attention Hayden drew toward them while Hayden hugged the pole she had just run into, not understanding how she didn't see it. The librarian ushered them out so they would quit being a "disturbance" to everyone else.

William brought up the time he and I were walking on a bike trail late at night during the summer when I wanted to take a rest, so we sat down on the cold ground. A baby snake came slithering out of the grass, watching us closely as we did with it. I thought it was adorable and William joked about how large its mom probably was in comparison. On cue, momma snake came flying out of the grass toward us and we both stood up and started running scared.

"That was seriously terrifying." I shudder still at the memory.

I wasn't about to get bitten by a snake. No thank you.

"You should have tried out for the track team with how fast you ran!" William teased. "I swear if she kept pace, her mile time would have been five minutes or less."

I stuck my tongue out at him as we both laughed at the memory, and our friends joined in laughing with us.

Rose wanted us to play a game, so we started with Make Me Laugh. I was awful. All anybody had to do was look at me and I would laugh. Peter pretended to give a lap dance to Danny, which was hysterical. Hayden pretended that she was Jack and Rose from the Titanic, which made our Rose burst out laughing from Hayden's poor acting skills.

"Hey! I was able to make you laugh and you still guessed what I was doing and were correct. It clearly wasn't *that* poor of an acting job," Hayden defended. She flipped her hair trying to act even more dramatically, which caused us to continue laughing.

Only a couple more people went after Hayden did. We grew tired of that game and decided to stop. Throughout the night William kept checking his phone and seemed to be texting someone, which I thought was odd because all his friends were here, and I knew he wasn't texting his parents or sister this late. At 10:33 PM, I found out who he was texting; actually, we all found out because that's when *she* arrived.

William got up from sitting next to me to greet her as she walked toward us. She got dropped off by someone, but whoever dropped her off drove away. I looked at my friends and they had a confused expression on their faces as well.

"Sky, who is that?" Evelynn asked me.

"I have no idea," I said. I was squinting, trying to figure out who this person was.

Do I know her? Is she in our grade? Has she been at his locker, and I just never noticed? No, that would be impossible of course.

William and the mystery girl were near the fire now. William introduced all of us.

"Everyone, this is Casey Fittzen, she's in my yearbook class." We all said hi in unison.

William came back and sat down next to me, but I had to move over because there wasn't enough room, having added Casey to our circle. She separated William and me as she sat between us, which of course I thought was rude.

Evelynn was the first one to start questioning this Casey chick. I had questions of my own, but they weren't for her, they were for William.

Why is she here? How old is she? Are you two talking, talking? Why did you have to invite her to this bonfire? What is with you and bringing random girls to these bonfires anyway?!

"Wow, you look young. How old are you?" Evelynn asked immediately.

William gave Evelynn "the look."

It's true; she does look young.

"Sixteen, but I'm a sophomore," she said, smiling at Evelynn, not at all fazed by a group of strangers.

He's talking to a sophomore?

"Who dropped you off?" Hayden now asked.

"Oh, that was my friend," she answered coolly.

"You don't drive?" Hayden asked a follow up question.

"I have my license; I just don't have a car yet. Sometimes I use my parents', but my dad works the graveyard shift, and we only have one family vehicle."

I couldn't do anything except stare at her and take in her features and the persona she was giving off. I hadn't stood up next to her yet, but she seemed like she was shorter than me. When she was walking next to William, she didn't seem to reach the same height on his body as I do. It appeared she had dark brown, if not black hair. It's hard to tell since it's so dark outside and the fire doesn't give me the best of light to judge hair color. Not to mention she had a stocking cap on too like some of us. She had a nice fading tan from the summer sun like William gets. The fire was complementing her complexion and it was giving me envy as people who tan easily always do.

Casey was all sorts of smiles and even her teeth were nice, straight, and super white against the glow of the fire too. We didn't play any more games as a group; instead, we got the stuff for s'mores out and started roasting marshmallows. I caught at least seven of my marshmallows on fire because I wasn't paying any attention to them. Rose started cooking my marshmallows for me so I could eat a decent s'more.

Casey and William talked quietly with each other, laughing, and snickering like they already had secrets, but every now and then, he would chime into the group conversation. I sat there stunned and completely caught off guard. This must have been who he was snapchatting the other night when we were doing homework.

Well, when I was the one doing homework.

I tried not to stare, but I'm sure everyone could tell I was. Well, everyone except William and Casey; they were wrapped up in their own little world.

When midnight rolled around, we were all cold enough that we were ready to take off from the farm. Luckily, Casey was getting up to leave as well.

Good.

"Is your friend coming to pick you up, Casey?" I asked her, as we were all folding our blankets (well the females were, not the guys).

"Actually, I'm going to take her home," William chimed in.

Super . . .

"Okay, I could take her if she needs a ride, then you wouldn't need to go all the way into town when I'm already headed that way," I offered, but William declined immediately.

"It's okay. I don't mind," he said.

Casey was looking up to him and smiling in what I considered to be admiration.

I'm sure it is cool to have a hot senior guy drive you home at midnight.

I smiled a fake smile in return. It disappeared the second I turned my back toward them. My friends talked about this new girl the entire ride back to my house. They asked if I knew anything about her. I didn't, not in the slightest.

"I'm sure she's just a fling," Evelynn tried to be positive for me.

"I mean, they might not even have a thing. We don't know that for sure," Rose tried to reason, but we all looked at her in disbelief.

"I'm just saying," she said, holding her hands up in her own defense.

"She's sixteen, and he's eighteen, I'm sure they really don't have much in common anyway. He's a senior and she still has two and a half years of high school left," Hayden stated her thoughts as well.

I appreciated my friends being in my corner, but nothing they said made me feel any better. Casey wasn't from out of state; she lived in town. She went to the same school, and they had class together. They were going to see each other every single day, and that's a fact. An awful, horrible fact, that I couldn't change.

CHAPTER 22

Everything was changing and it was changing fast! William and I weren't hanging out as much now because he'd been hanging out with Casey a lot, and alone too. I knew he liked her. He hadn't said anything yet, but I could tell. He was different when she showed up. He and I would be talking at our lockers, then Casey would appear, and somehow, he'd smile more and laugh more, even though nothing she said was funny.

Well, at least to me it's not funny. It's also not funny how often he has been walking her to her classes.

He still sits next to me on the couch when we watch a movie together, so I'm thankful for that. I've been treasuring all our alone time. When he and I do get to hang out alone, I never bring up Casey's name. I want to know things, but I also don't. My brain makes up its own scenarios enough as is; I'm not sure if I want to know reality too. He has been more considerate with not being on his phone as much when we're together, which I really appreciate.

It was almost December and they were advertising once again for the New Year's Dance, William's and my tradition. After this, there would only be our senior prom dance left in April, and then graduation.

"How about I ask you this year?" His words replayed

inside of my memory. A memory I had been clinging to ever since he spoke it.

I had been looking at dresses on Pinterest and online longer than Evelynn had been this year, and that's saying something.

William and I had plans to hang out tonight since he was with Casey last night.

He and I were at our lockers preparing for the first half of the day. I grabbed my English, Sociology, and Psychology books and notebooks. William reached for his World History, Economics, and Pre-Calculus textbooks. I'm sure it's pathetic, but I have his schedule memorized. In my defense, though, we each only have six actual classes. Otherwise, we have an open campus and gym that takes up the other two periods.

"Can today go any slower?" William said, looking over at me.

"We *just* got here; don't jinx it and make it go any slower!" I said, leaning over and pushing his face in the other direction.

"You ready to see your crazy cousin this weekend?" he asked me.

I probably shouldn't have, but I told him all the crazy things that happen when my cousin Mike comes over. He's thirty-six going on sixteen. I don't know if he has ever taken anything serious in his life. He's funny, but I don't think he'll ever grow up. One time when he was supposed to be watching our younger cousins, he let my little brother and our other cousin Drake split a liter of pop. *A liter!!* He justified it by saying the two boys were technically supposed to share it with everyone and they didn't. He then encouraged the boys to have a belching contest. The adults were not happy when they heard what was going on in the other room and saw the empty bottle laying on the floor with spilled pop on the carpet. The worst part was that my parents were upset at *me* for not stopping Greyson, which I thought was unfair.

"I don't know. I never know what Mike is going to do or say, or if he's even going to show up. He always says he's coming, but half the time he never does, so who knows? What about you?"

"Yeah, we're going over to my grandparents' to play games and watch the hockey game of course. It's typically a good time as long as the grandparents are feeling well. Last year Grandpa wasn't doing so well, and it was sad to see."

Awww, you can easily see sadness in his eyes from thinking about his grandpa's health. He is so sweet.

"How's he doing?" I asked, concern in my voice.

"He's been doing better. I talked with him on the phone the other day after school and he said he's been feeling better and has some more energy and stuff."

"That's good!" I said, smiling over at him; he too was smiling.

I could see Casey coming down the aisle and I internally groaned.

Naturally, she was all smiles and practically bouncing as she glided toward us, well toward William, her desired target.

I didn't want to be around these two, so I reminded him about the arcade tonight and what time I'd pick him up. He was nodding in response just as Casey started to say his name. He turned around and his face lit up. I shut my locker and took off in the opposite direction so I could escape her voice.

I blame William because the day really dragged on. I knew he would jinx it, but finally the last bell rang, setting us all free. I headed to my locker to grab all the textbooks and notebooks I'd need for the weekend.

I was waiting for William to show up to his locker, but I didn't see him. I waited almost fifteen minutes before giving up.

Maybe he's talking with a teacher, or has already left? I bet he's at Casey's locker.

I internally battled with myself. Should I wait a little longer? Should I text or call him to see where he's at? Should I go into the dreaded sophomore hallway to look for him? I decided against all of it and headed to the parking lot to go home. I should be feeling better than I was considering I didn't have to wake up early tomorrow or go to any boring classes, but instead, I felt as though . . . well honestly, I didn't know what I was feeling, but I knew it didn't feel right. Hanging out with my best friend tonight would help though!

Our plans were to go to the arcade that is downtown near the capital. I love seeing our capital; her design is stunning. I don't particularly enjoy driving downtown because of the traffic, and it's not something that ever interests my girlfriends, but William is always up for it. After the arcade and walking around the capital, I'm guessing we'll just go back to his house and play games or something. I texted him telling him I'd be at his house no later than 7:10 PM. He didn't respond by the time I left my house.

I drove to his house and was there at 7:03. His Jeep wasn't in the driveway though.

That's weird.

I called him while I was sitting outside his house. After it rang for what felt like forever, it went to voicemail, "Hey, it's Alli. Where are you? It's 7:20. I guess call me as soon as you get this."

Where is he?

My car radio said 7:45 now. I'd been sitting outside his house for forty-two minutes. If he didn't live out in the country, I bet his neighbors would have called the cops because I'd been loitering for so long. No text or call from him. I finally saw some headlights coming at me.

Yup, that's him.

As he was pulling into his driveway, I started to get out of my car at the same time William did . . . and Casey.

What? Why is he with her? Did he bring her along so she can go downtown with us?

Again, another stare down between the three of us. Nobody was saying anything, so I started first.

"I tried calling you." I was staring at William with a confused expression on my face.

Casey was looking back and forth between me, William, and her shoes. I barely looked over at her, though; my focus was on him.

William looked down at his keys, then back to me. "I'm sorry, my phone . . . died."

Since when does William lie to me?! Of course, his phone was on, if it were dead, it would have gone straight to voicemail, but it didn't.

I didn't call him out on it; instead I asked about going to the arcade, "Are we still on for tonight?" I glanced over at Casey, and she was looking at me too.

I honestly could have laughed at myself for asking this question aloud. My brain beat me to the punch.

Of course, you're not. He's hanging out with Casey again. He forgot about you.

"Ummm . . . well . . . actually . . ." William was stammering and shifting uncomfortably. "Casey and I have plans for tonight." He was looking anywhere but at me.

He was really nervous. If I weren't fuming right now, I would think it was kind of cute, him standing there, squirming under my anger. But this wasn't cute. This was nowhere in the realm of cute, not this time. I was so angry at him!

I didn't say anything. I didn't want to say something I would regret. Instead, I gritted my teeth and nodded at him. I turned to get back into my vehicle when I heard William: "Al . . ."

We both knew there wasn't anything he could say, though. I paused to see if there was something he was going to try and say, but he only stared at the ground. I peeked over at Casey; she was watching me with an expression on her face that I considered to be a slight smirk.

Is she smirking at this, or did I read her face wrong? Either way, this isn't her fault, this was William's fault for forgetting about our plans.

For the second time, I got into my car and drove home crying from his house.

I waited outside my house until my face wasn't so blotchy and red from the fountain of never-ending tears that came out of it. Obviously, I didn't want my parents to know I had just been crying. Once I thought I looked decent enough, I went in and headed for the basement. I put on *Peter Pan* because it's one of the few Disney movies that isn't romantic.

About fifteen minutes into it, my phone vibrated, indicating a text message. *William??* My breath caught in my chest hoping it was from him. My heart fell; it was from a number I didn't have in my phone.

> **Unknown Number:**   Hey this is Casey. I just wanted you to know that William feels terrible about tonight. You should text him and forgive him. We forgot you had plans together. You guys can hang out another time. ☺

Wait, what? Why is she saying, "we forgot?" Did she know he and I had plans tonight? Also, why does she have my number??

I didn't text her back. I wasn't really sure what to tell her, plus, I preferred to talk with William directly instead of through a third party.

"Hi Boyfriend!" she said with the biggest smile.

My heart stopped. Like I swear it literally skipped a beat.

Boyfriend? What. The. F—. My jaw dropped, my eyes bulged from their sockets, and my eyebrows were probably past the hairline on my head from being raised so high.

I watched William freeze and his back tense up as he was about to reach for his final notebook. He was staring at the ground but then he glanced over at Casey. Afterwards, he sneaked a peek at me. He had an apologetic, "oh crap" look on his face.

Casey chimed in after a long, awkward silence between the three of us. "Oh, I guess you didn't tell her yet . . ."

I was too stunned to speak or even think.

"No, I, uh . . . hadn't yet," William mumbled out. He was looking anywhere but at me again.

How come you can't seem to look at me anymore? No. no. no. This is not happening!

"Ohhhh . . . oops. Sorry." Casey looked directly at me, rocking back and forth on her heels.

Are you actually though? That smile on your face doesn't seem to match your words.

I swallowed my heart. "Oh . . . that's . . . nice. I'm happy for you guys."

"Thanks!" Casey said, eagerly lacing her fingers through his. "William asked me after you left. He was SO nervous. It was adorable."

William didn't say anything, nor did he look anywhere in my direction. I could tell he felt extremely awkward.

"I bet he was," I said, looking at him. He avoided my gaze. "Nice. Well . . . I uh, I'll see you guys around." I closed my locker and almost sprinted away.

These last few days had really sucked. William had a girlfriend, and it wasn't me. I clutched my sides as I walked through the crowded hallways. I was hoping my arms could hold everything inside of me until I sat down.

Time with my family was much needed. I was able to escape (for the most part) from my thoughts about William and what had been going on.

On Saturday I hung out with Hayden and Rose and told them what had happened. They were sympathetic and helped try to get my mind away from the drama and hard feelings.

Sunday wasn't as easy. I knew that I would be seeing him tomorrow, and as always, part of me was excited to see him, and the other part was anxious. At 2:18 in the afternoon my phone vibrated. It was William wondering about hanging out tonight and working on some homework together.

> **William:** Want to hang out after supper? You and me?
>
> **Me:** You're not going to forget again, are you?
>
> *Harsh.*
>
> **William:** No I promise.

I didn't text him back for about twenty minutes. I wanted him to think about what he did to me, but I already knew that I would say yes to him. I'd always spend time together with him if I could.

> **Me:** Sure.
>
> **William:** Want me to come there?
>
> **Me:** Sure.

I repeated myself.

I saved a little homework just in case William had some he needed to work on tonight. He texted me letting me know he was on his way. Naturally, I told him the backdoor was open when he got here. I was reading *The Pact* by Jodi Picoult when he came in. I drank in the sight of him when I saw him; his clothes, his smell, all of it was so familiar, but the air around him was heavy with change.

We exchanged "heys." He slipped out of his shoes and sat on the rocking chair. Normally he sits next to me if I'm on the couch like I am now, but I think he was being cautious.

"So . . ." he said, folding his hands together.

I wanted to clear the air immediately; I hate tension. "What happened the other night?"

He sucked in some air; he knew this was coming, though. He bit his lower lip before saying his next words, "I am really, really sorry. I just forgot about the arcade."

"You mean, you forgot about me?" It was more of a rhetorical question.

"Yeah, I guess. I am really sorry."

I knew he was. I could read it in his eyes, and I should have left it at that.

"It's not just the arcade though, you lied to me too, about your phone being dead. It wasn't."

Again, he inhaled air so that his lungs could breathe and give his mind a little extra time to think.

"I'm sorry too for that, it was the first thing that came to my mind to try and ease what I did. There's no excuse, and I'm not trying to give you one either. I thoroughly and royally screwed up, and I truly hope you can forgive me." He got down from the rocking chair and came to kneel in front of me as though he was worshiping the Queen of England or somebody of high status.

I shook my head at him and tried to curb the smile and amusement that was building inside of me.

When I still didn't say anything to him, he slowly inched forward and wrapped his arms around my legs and clung onto them. This made me laugh out loud at his absurdness.

Of course, I would forgive him, but talking about the other night still reminded me of how much he hurt me. I tried to say this as a joke, but it didn't come out right.

"Thank god your girlfriend texted me on your behalf though."

My words made him pull away from hugging my legs. He sat back on the rocking chair away from me.

"Please don't bring Casey into this. She was just trying to help; this wasn't her fault."

I sighed. "I know, you're right, it was not her fault. I am curious why she has my number though? Her text really caught me off guard."

"She was just trying to help you and me. She felt terrible about that night as well. She thinks you blame her for all of this."

"She does?" I asked.

"Yeah, she thinks you don't like her," he spoke.

"Why does she think that?" I asked curiously.

"Well, for one, you barely look at her and you hardly acknowledge her when she's around. Like how many times has she been at our lockers, and you shut yours so you can walk away from us? She wants you to accept her and to accept that she's a part of our group now. I told her all your great qualities and then you basically shunned her immediately."

I refrained from telling him about the weird vibes I'd been getting from her staring at me.

"I mean, I'm not exactly looking for a new friend right now. She's in your life, but I didn't think she needed to be very involved in mine."

"I'm not saying you need to be best friends with her, but everyone could use another friend, Alli; you're not limited to a certain number."

"Speaking of friends, is she okay with you having a girl best friend?" I was terrified of what his answer could be.

He looked away again. I even double checked the wall behind me to make sure there wasn't something abnormal growing out of it considering how much he had been staring at it. There wasn't anything on the wall but empty space, just like I was starting to feel between William and me.

I could see him carefully choosing the words he was going to say, but nothing came out of his mouth, so I spoke first, again.

"You don't need to sugarcoat it, just tell me. Tell me that she doesn't like the relationship we have."

"She's just . . . yeah, she is a little uncomfortable with me having a female best friend. It's kind of hard on her at the moment."

Awww, I love it when he says that we're best friends. I rarely hear it, and lately haven't felt it from him.

"Why is she uncomfortable with it?" I asked.

"Because . . . she knows about your feelings for me." William said this looking only at his hands this time as his thumbs continuously bounced off each other.

He told her that?! My jaw dropped open once again. I'm pretty sure in this year alone, I've hit jaw dropping records.

"You told her about that?" I asked in disbelief. "Why? Why on earth would you tell her that?"

"Because I tell her everything. I have since the first day I met her," he said in a matter-of-fact tone.

"What else have you told her about me? Any other personal stuff, huh?" Again, anger was spitting off my tongue.

"Nothing. She asked if you have ever liked me, and I wasn't going to keep that from her."

I was standing now while he was sitting. I ran my fingers through my hair, visibly frustrated and trying to think rationally.

"Girls don't actually want to know the real answer to that question. She was testing you to see what you would say. She was hoping you would have said no to all of it. That's the answer she was looking for."

He stared at me with a confused expression but he responded with, "Well, regardless of the answer she was looking for, I went with the truth."

"What else did you tell her about us?" I asked in an accusatory tone.

He stood up now, shaking his head in frustration. "I don't know," he said, shrugging. "Just that you and I are close and have a history of hanging out together a lot I think. I won't lie, Al; she does kind of prefer if I, uh, don't really hang out with you alone."

My voice was shaking when I asked my next question, "And . . . what did you say to that?"

"I told her she doesn't need to worry about you and I, and that I don't think it's fair to our friendship if we stopped hanging out."

I breathed the biggest sigh of relief! I didn't realize how intensely I was holding my breath in. He took his right hand and rubbed my left shoulder in a comforting motion. Instead, I walked into his arms for a hug. He hugged me back and I noticed that a tear had escaped from my eye onto his shirt.

We sat in silence for a little bit after this, neither one of us knowing what to say.

"This got complicated. I miss how it used to be. Everything with you and I was so easy, you know? We could just hang out alone, and not have to worry about anything, or anyone for that matter. All our friends understand it. They understand us," I said.

I gestured at the air between him and I. We were both sitting on the couch next to one another like we always have. Not cuddling, just sitting near the other.

"I know, but it is different. I have Casey and her feelings to consider too. It's hard trying to split my time between you and her, my friends, our group of friends, family, and school in general as well."

I never thought about how much he probably is juggling.

"I'm sorry. I never gave it any thought how much you're juggling right now. I know I haven't made it any easier on you either."

"Casey feels concerned that she has to 'share me with another girl,' " he said with air quotations.

This made me nervous. "But I'm not just any girl, William. I thought . . . I mean, I'm your best friend, you just reminded me of that a little bit ago," I stammered.

"And you are . . . it's just . . . well she's my best friend too and I want to make her happy as well. I like her a lot. I've never had feelings like this for anyone, ever, and I know you don't want to hear that, but yes. That's how I feel." He said it all in one breath and was finally able to get it off his chest.

Yeah, this is not what I want to hear. Obviously, I want him to be happy, I mean duh, he's my friend, my BEST friend! I want nothing more than for him to be happy. I just don't want to lose him because he found happiness somewhere else.

"What are we going to do?" I asked him, even though I knew he wasn't going to have any clue either.

He rubbed the back of his neck, thinking. "I really don't know. Maybe we can hang out all together more often? But you have to understand, I'm going to want my alone time with Casey too."

I can understand that. I don't like it one bit, but I can at least understand.

"And with me too, right?" I asked, fearing he could change his mind at any second.

"Yeah, with you too. I just don't know if I can give you as much alone time as we had before Casey, and again, I hope you can understand. I mean if the roles were reversed, I would understand you spending more time with your boyfriend than me."

I considered his words, and he was right again. I could understand where he was coming from.

"Could I ask a favor of you?" he asked hesitantly, reaching out for my right hand and holding it in his.

I was nervous and only nodded yes in response.

"I mean this nicely, because again, I've told Casey how great of a person you are, and she's a great person too. Could you . . . maybe attempt to befriend her? Again, I'm not saying you guys need to have slumber parties or anything, but I just want her to feel welcomed by all my friends, but most importantly by you. As my best friend, Al, would you do this for me?" He bit his lower lip, and I could easily sense how much this question had been weighing on him.

Be friends with her? He wants me to be friends with a girl he just told me he has never had such strong feelings for. Ugh, how am I possibly going to be able to do this? Well . . . you love him, right? Yes, so much. And you want him to be happy right? Yes, of course. Well, right now Casey brings him happiness, but he didn't say she was his sole purpose for happiness, he still wants your friendship, and this would mean a lot to him if you did try and befriend her to the best of your abilities. Okay . . . fine . . . I will attempt to befriend her for the sake of mine and William's friendship.

He didn't say anything as I was thinking to myself, but I finally spoke, breaking the silence between us.

"Yes. I will try to be friends with Casey and make her feel more welcomed. I understand she'll be around a lot more and that's something I need to adjust to." I watched his face go from scared to pure delight. He smiled so large and bright and then threw his arms around my neck for an embrace. I graciously hugged him back.

"Thank you! You're the best. This means a lot to me."

Yeah . . . I can tell it really does.

"You're welcome," I said, rubbing his back as we finished up hugging.

We pulled away from one another and I didn't want the joy in the room to disappear, so I suggested we not do homework and do something fun instead.

"Well, I think it's safe to say that we are not going to be getting any homework done tonight, so what do you say? Are you up for losing some Yahtzee?" I asked him, forcing a smile to try and lighten the air between us once again.

"I'm pretty sure your record indicates that you are the one that is used to losing. I know how to roll large straights." He smiled back.

"You're just lucky!" I said, shoving him out of the way so I could make my way to the closet filled with games.

After Yahtzee, which he naturally beat me at, we played two rounds of Candy Land and then needed to call it a night. After all, it is Sunday, and we have school tomorrow.

As I was picking up the board game pieces, he was stuffing his backpack with the supplies he brought over but never used. I thought playing the games would help, but the second it was time to say good-bye again, it didn't feel normal. Sure, I'll still *see* him tomorrow, but like I said earlier, things are different now and it really sucks. We hugged goodbye, and I dragged the hug out a little longer than normal, but he let me. I'm sure he knew I needed it, and I hoped he needed it too. Friend to friend if nothing more.

CHAPTER 23

Naturally, Casey was at William's locker. It was hard seeing them together; I didn't know if I could get used to it. Every time I saw her touching him, I became overwhelmed with jealousy, sadness, and a third emotion that I couldn't put my finger on, but I didn't like it. She was always touching him in some sort of way. They were either holding hands, kissing, or she would be running her fingers through his hair; everything I wanted to be doing but couldn't. My friends would probably think I'm paranoid, but I swear every time she sees me coming, she always amplifies her touching.

Okay, here goes nothing, I thought to myself as I said hi to Casey and William.

"Hey guys," I said.

"Hey Alli!" William said with excitement while Casey said hi and wrapped her fingers through his.

"I like your shoes, Casey, where did you get them?" I attempted.

"Thanks. I got them at American Eagle. Your . . . um, fingernails look well groomed," she said in what I think was an attempt at a compliment.

"Oh, uh, thanks. I clip them myself," I said, looking at the ground.

"Yes. It shows," she said with a smirk.

Awkward silence fell between us, but when I looked back up at William he was smiling and winked at me. I know he could tell I was trying, and I appreciated his acknowledgement.

"Well William, should we get going?" Casey asked, leaving me stunned at the fact that she used his full name like I do.

She calls him William now? When did she start that? That's my and Grandma's thing.

"Yeah. I'll see you later, Al," he said, touching my forearm as they walked by me. Casey glanced back over her shoulder giving a not so happy expression.

Lunch today was chicken nuggets and buttered noodles. *My favorite!*

Our table consisted of Rose, Evelynn, me, Hayden, Chelsea, Sabrina, and Tanya (Rose's friends). Sabrina brought up the New Year's Dance.

I'm glad my friends get excited about this stuff the way I do. I'm not sure what I would do if my friends didn't like going to the dances with me. I literally wouldn't have anyone to go with.

I had to miss Junior Prom while they all went. I know my parents had been planning the vacation to Hawaii for a while, but I wished they wouldn't have surprised Greyson and me with it. Well, that's not true, the surprise part was great, the nonrefundable hotel and passes weren't because of the dates we were going to be gone. My friends expressed their sadness that I wouldn't be at prom with them, but they also told me how jealous they were that they wouldn't be in Hawaii.

On the bright side, I'll be here for Senior Prom and I have William to go with to the New Year's Dance since he told me he was going to ask me this year!

Evelynn is going with Kyle; Chelsea is going with a junior named Roscoe. I guess they have gym together. Even though the girls are supposed to ask the guys, Hayden was asked by one of our classmates named Andrew, and Rose of course is going with Morris; that leaves William and me.

The girls were talking about how they asked or were going to ask their guys to the dance.

"Alli, who are you going to ask to the dance?" Tanya asked, trying to include me in the conversation since I'd been quiet.

"William Mantel said he was going to ask me this year, since I asked him the last two," I explained.

"Oh duh, I should have known since you guys are dating after all," Tanya said, dipping her nuggets in some barbeque sauce.

The conversation I loathe. I hate explaining that he and I aren't dating even though we're together all the time. I get how it must look to the outside world but being reminded of reality sucks.

"Actually, Will is dating a sophomore. Can you believe that?" Chelsea happily dished the news, but I gave her a side-eyed glare.

"No!" Tanya and Sabrina said in unison, shooting me a sympathetic look.

I couldn't get a thought in before Chelsea started explaining more to them.

"Oh yeah. They have Yearbook together, that's how they met. Typically, sophomores can't even get into that class, but I guess this year, hardly anybody wanted to be in it so they opened it up to underclassmen." She shrugged but continued. "Will and Alli have been friends for three years now, and he's only known this other girl for a couple of months. Like the other night, Alli and Will were supposed to go to the arcade—"

"Okay Chelsea, that's enough!" I half shouted, trying to stop her before she started replaying the worst night of my life to people that I don't want to know my business.

My abrupt and harsh voice made Tanya and Sabrina jump in surprise; they were leaning forward toward Chelsea, hanging on to her words. They repositioned in their seats and avoided making eye contact with me.

"Sorry. Got a little carried away," Chelsea apologized and took a bite of her noodles.

I collected myself so I didn't come off as a jerk again before speaking.

"Yes, William is dating an underclassman, but I know that he is going to be asking me to the dance. We've already talked about it."

Everyone at the table looked genuinely surprised and I hated it. I didn't like being the center of the conversation and I was really hoping that one of my friends, not Chelsea, could step in and change the topic. I raised an eyebrow at Evelynn because she's someone who can think and act quickly when needed.

"Uh, Sabrina, have you applied yet to any colleges?" Evelynn took my cue easily and I gave her a gracious half smile. She nodded understandingly.

"Oh no, now you've done it!" Tanya moaned while Sabrina took a deep breath and exhaled loudly, clearly stressed.

"I have applied to—" she started listing all the big named colleges she has applied to but hasn't heard back from.

I stopped listening though, because I was in my own head again, plus college also isn't my favorite subject either. I'm excited to leave high school, but these first few months of senior year have already flown by. I only have one more semester left with my friends, and that's sad and scary when I stop and think about it. Who knows how much is going to change in just a few months? I guess I can relate to Sabrina being stressed out, although I applied to the University of Kansas and have been accepted. I didn't have a back-up college in mind and thankfully, I didn't need one.

The bell rang, dismissing us from lunch. Rose asked me if I could come with her real quick. I gave her a puzzling look because this was the one time during the day, I got to see William at his locker and not have to worry about Casey showing up. I didn't object though, because I was wondering what was up. Maybe she and Morris had a fight or something?

She pulled me off to the side in the hallway as our group dispersed their separate ways.

"What's up?" I asked her.

She was fidgeting with her fingers. "I, uh, I was just wondering when you and William had decided you were going to the dance together?"

"Back in August. Why?"

She bit her lip and looked up at me. She was now playing with her hair, clearly uncomfortable.

Great, she knows something I don't and doesn't want to tell me.

"Rose," I said gently. I could tell this was already hard enough on her. "What is it?"

"Well . . . it's just, the other night Morris and I were bowling with Will and Casey, and well . . . when we were there, he uh . . . he asked her if she wanted to go to the New Year's Dance with him."

I thought my entire lunch was going to come back up. I was sick to my stomach at that very moment. Worry was written all over Rose's face, but I couldn't comfort her because I was the one feeling like I was about to throw up.

"Alli? You're turning extra pale, maybe you should sit down for a minute or go lay down in the nurse's office," she said, holding onto my arm as I didn't move a muscle.

"Yeah. Nurse's office. Good," was all I managed to piece together. Without talking, Rose walked with me to see Mrs. Delton, our head nurse.

"Mrs. Delton, I think Alli needs to lay down for a while. She's not feeling very well," Rose explained as

I was already lying down on one of the beds they had for students.

"Oh dear! You don't look well at all. Do you think you're going to throw up?" she asked tenderly.

I could only nod and that was enough for her to rush behind her desk and grab a trash can.

"Thank you, Rose. You can head to class; I will look out for her now," Mrs. Delton politely dismissed her.

I had my eyes shut when Rose said she hoped I felt better soon. I didn't acknowledge her because I knew this wasn't going to be something that passed quickly.

"Do you think it was something you ate, honey?" Mrs. Delton asked me.

I only nodded once again, too afraid to open my mouth.

"I've always thought they put too much butter in those noodles for you young people. Just because you're young doesn't mean your bodies can tolerate it any better than an old person like me." She brought me a blanket and I gladly put it over my face. "Now you lay here, and we will see if you feel well enough to go to class."

I attempted to calm my mind and stomach with deep breaths, but I was having a lot of flashbacks that were tearing at my insides. I was remembering our first two dances together; how night and day different they were. Sophomore year I was *so* nervous around him. I watched everything I said and tried not to make a fool of myself. Junior year though, I had taken my place at his side. Being around him was as natural as breathing for me. I no longer worried about looking stupid, but instead, enjoyed doing stupid things with him.

It hurts. It hurts that he asked *her* to *our* dance. I feel as though I'm being replaced, and that's a new hurt that I haven't experienced; one that feels as though it's just beginning. It still hurts remembering how a few nights ago he had forgotten our plans to go to the arcade because he was with her. And now, it hurts that I didn't hear this from him. In fact, the last few big pieces of information I have received haven't come from him.

Will he ever tell me anything himself?

I wiped quickly at the tears that were sneaking from my eyes. How embarrassing to be crying at school! Thank goodness I was hidden under a blanket.

After thirty minutes, Mrs. Delton asked if I was feeling well enough to go to class.

No.

"Yeah," I said instead. I have things to do and notes to take. I went to my locker and loaded up every book and notebook I needed for the second half so I wouldn't have to come back to my locker until the end of the day. I headed to Psychology for the remaining twenty minutes.

When I was in my final class of the day, I watched the clock like a hawk. With five minutes left of class I packed up my things and zipped my bag shut despite the annoyed glare I received from my teacher.

Ding. Ding. Ding. I rushed to my locker to try and beat William. For the first time, I was hoping that he went to Casey's locker. I never imagined I would have thought those words.

I tried hustling, shoving my books and notebooks into my bag, but all that did was cause me to drop my entire backpack. As I was picking up my contents, I heard William say hi to me. I didn't look up. I could see his shoes in my peripheral vision. I gathered everything I needed and quickly, overdramatically, shut my locker louder than necessary. I didn't dare look at his face though. I couldn't yet.

"Alli—" he hollered behind me, but I was hustling toward the doors to leave.

I didn't look back.

"Al!" his voice was closer now as I got outside. "Hey, slow down." He caught up to me and pulled on my arm to slow me down. I jerked it away. "What is going on with you?" He pulled me around to face him, but I still wouldn't look at him.

He put his hand under my chin and gently made me look at him. I could feel the strength in his warm fingers and hear the desperation in his voice, trying to get me to talk to him.

"Would you please look at me," he asked in a more even-toned breath. I finally caved and looked into his ice-blue eyes. "Tell me," he stated.

"Tell you what?" I said, even though we both knew my dramatic exit meant something.

"What did I do this time, Alli?" he said, sounding a little annoyed, which sent me over the edge.

Excuse me! Don't you dare give me attitude, not after what you just did.

I swallowed and looked at him. "I heard about your bowling endeavors."

"Okay . . . and?" William asked, shrugging. He still had a confused look on his face. He hadn't put the pieces together yet.

"And? Annnnd?! You asked Casey to the New Year's Dance. *Our* New Year's Dance!" I said, throwing my hands up in the air at him. I was trying to keep my voice down, but I could see people looking over at us because I wasn't being successful.

He inhaled loudly and adjusted his backpack on his shoulder. "What did you expect, she's my girlfriend," he said.

"I *know* she's your girlfriend, believe me I get that! But you were the one that told me you would ask me to the dance this year. Remember, when school started? You said, and I quote, 'how about I ask you this year.' "

I could see William thinking. There it was, his face lit up when he remembered that moment. That incredibly special, exciting moment that meant the world to me, and apparently only to me.

"Oh ... gosh ... Al ..." he stammered but couldn't find any words to say.

Yeah, I bet the concrete is fascinating to stare at. I raised my eyebrows at him this time. Waiting to see what he could possibly say now.

"I'm sorry. I did say that ... but things are different now. You know?"

I shook my head at him in disbelief.

"I'm really sorry," he said in an attempt for me to forgive him yet again. I saw Casey headed this way.

Nope, I am not doing this with her here. She doesn't need to see this.

"Yeah, you've been saying that a lot lately. I need to go," I said, moving around him so I could head to my car and get as far away from him as possible.

I heard Casey ask, "William, babe, what's wrong?" but I never stopped to look back. As I opened the driver's side door to get into my car, I realized I had forgotten my government book.

Screw it, I'm not going back, and stop calling him William.

I liked my job. My coworkers were fun, and work kept me busy physically and mentally, which I appreciated. My boss Steve was the definition of a teddy bear and had owned his restaurant for almost thirty-five years. He was intimidating in my interview, but once I started to work with him, I realized there was nothing scary about him. Aside from the fact he had the right to fire me, but I wasn't too worried about that.

Casey and three of her friends came in with thirty minutes to closing. Kim was waiting on the other table in the restaurant, so I took Casey's table. They were snickering as I came up to take their drink order.

"Hey guys, what can I get you to drink?" I asked.

Casey's friend, Destiny, asked if we had Coke.

"Sorry, we don't. We have Pepsi products."

"Well that sucks. Do you have Mello Yello?" she asked.

"No, but we have Mountain Dew," I said.

"Nope. I don't want that. Do you have Orange Fanta?" she asked next, looking at her friends while they chuckled.

"Sorry, that's a Coke product too, but we have Sunkist," I said, shifting my weight from one foot to the other.

"Ew, definitely not. I really would like a Coke," she said, looking at me with a smile.

"I'm sorry, we just don't have Coca Cola products."

"Alright fine . . . I guess I'll just have water then since this place isn't very accommodating," Destiny said.

I looked at Casey next who was sitting on the outside of the booth like Destiny was. "Yeah, we're really Coca Cola people so I'll just have water as well."

I nodded in acknowledgement while the other two girls ordered Diet Pepsi and Mountain Dew. I went to the back to get their drinks while they looked over our menu.

I brought their drinks to their table and asked if they were ready to order.

"I asked for a lemon in my water," Destiny spoke when I handed the drinks out. "Can you fetch me one?"

"Sure." I went to the back to grab a lemon slice. I put it on a tiny plate and brought it back out to her.

When I gave it to her, the girl that ordered the Diet Pepsi spoke next. "I asked for Pepsi, and this is definitely Diet. Do you think I need to be drinking diet pop or something?" she asked, staring at me while the others glared at me.

I was taken aback by her comment. I apologized, and told her I would go and get her regular Pepsi.

"Good," she responded.

Once I brought out the new beverage, I asked the girls if they were ready to order and they were. I took their orders and as I turned to head back to the kitchen, I heard a cup fall and liquid splash onto the ground. I turned around and noticed it was Casey's drink.

"Oops! Sorry, Alli," Casey said.

"You might want to mop that up before somebody slips and sues this place," Destiny said.

I went to where we kept our mop buckets and brought out a "Caution Wet Floor" sign. I told Casey I would go and get her another water. I went to the kitchen, entered their orders, and brought out a new water. Next, I went back and got a mop bucket and started mopping up the spilled water.

As I was mopping, the table of sophomores were talking about the New Year's Dance.

"William is going to *love* me in my dress! Alli, do you want to see a picture of it?"

I responded with sure. "Yeah, that's a pretty dress. I'm sure it will look really nice," I said, complimenting the photo she showed me.

"Will is constantly telling Casey how beautiful she is. They're absolutely adorable together!" Desitny cooed.

"You know, if you can get a date, you could come with us if you wanted," Casey said, smiling at her backhanded invitation while her friends once again were giggling amongst each other.

"Thank you for the offer, but I have plans in place already," I explained what I thought was an innocent enough explanation.

"We get it, you think you're better than us," the regular Pepsi girl said, sounding offended.

"Oh, that's definitely not what I meant by any means," I stuttered.

"No, no, we totally get it," Casey said.

The bell rang, indicating their food was up. I wheeled the mop bucket back to where I was going to dump the excess water, thankful to get away from the misunderstanding. I washed my hands and then brought them their food.

"FINALLY! It took long enough," Destiny exclaimed.

"Is there anything else I can get you guys right now?" I asked as I always do.

Mountain Dew girl chimed in, "We literally just got our food."

I didn't say anything; I was becoming extremely agitated. I left them in peace while I went to the back to complain to my coworkers who had been listening to everything these girls had said since they came in.

I checked back in with their table and Casey's fries were apparently cold, so I had Derek make some fresh ones that I brought out to her.

"How could they be cold?" he asked me in the back.

"I don't know. I think she just waited too long to eat them." I shrugged.

When it appeared the girls were almost finished with their food, I asked them if they needed any boxes, but they didn't. I asked if they were all going to be on separate checks and Destiny responded with, "Obviously, do you think we're rich or something?"

I didn't mean to, but I rolled my eyes at her comment. Oops.

I handed them their individual checks and started collecting their plates from the table. When I came back, they had their credit cards ready. I took them to the computer and entered them one by one. I brought back their credit cards with the receipts they need to sign. They left immediately after signing. I have never been more grateful to see a table leave. As I was cleaning their dirty table, I collected their now signed slips and noticed not one of them left a tip and the Pepsi girl even wrote, "poor service" on hers. Anger burned within me.

Is this really the sweet Casey that has great qualities William was referring to? Her friends were awful, but Casey wasn't much better either. Should I tell him about this?

Dave, Kim, Derek, and I left work together. I got into my own car and headed home.

Today has been a long day, and I still have homework to do. Like I'm going to be able to focus my thoughts and opinions on how tenure affects teacher quality.

I was working on my paper when suddenly, my basement door came flying open, and in walked William.

Yikes . . . he's pissed. Why is he so mad?

"What the hell, Alli?! Casey called me crying and asked to see me. She said that you were extremely rude to her and her friends at Steve's Diner." His eyes were shooting daggers at me, while his hands were trying to find a place to land.

WHAT?!

"WHAT?!" I repeated my thought out loud. "Did she seriously say that?" I asked, absolutely stunned.

"Yes! She and her friends told me you were basically a bitch to them the entire time and especially toward Casey. She told me she even invited you to go the dance with us and you laughed in her face."

My jaw dropped to the floor in utter disbelief.

I tried to defend myself, "William, that's ... like ... none of that is true! How could you think I would treat her and her friends like that, especially while I was at work?! Also, I wasn't rude to them, they were the ones that had me running around with my head cut off and they didn't even tip me at the end."

"Stop lying, Alli. Casey told me the only thing that was requested was her getting warmer fries and that you barely would do that for her. She also said that they all tipped generously because they came in so close to closing time. God, how could you treat her like this? Just because you're jealous doesn't—"

"Jealous?! This isn't about jealousy! She's completely lying to you right now and trying to make me look like the bad guy here when I have been doing exactly what you asked of me. I have been attempting to be friends with her!" I snapped at him.

Thankfully, my parents were on a date right now, otherwise the yelling may have been concerning to them. I wondered if Greyson was going to come downstairs or not though.

Hopefully not.

He threw his hands up out of frustration like he always does. "I can not believe you're saying this about her, Alli. Until you apologize to Casey, don't talk to me!" He stormed out, leaving me gawking after him.

I sat there until I heard my parents' footsteps above me. It snapped me out of replaying everything that just went down with my supposed best friend. I realized my hands had been shaking this entire time.

I knew I was right about the weird vibes I had been getting from her. She has never liked me.

I tried to focus my thoughts back on my paper, but all I kept doing was re-reading the same paragraph over and over. I wasn't going to be able to write this tonight, so I gave up and went to bed, avoiding Greyson and my parents.

William was serious. He hadn't texted me back for two days now when I'd tried contacting him asking if he and I could talk or hang out. I texted Casey and asked her if we could meet. She said she would but I needed to come over to her house.

I was both nervous and angry to talk to Casey. I wanted to confront her and ask why she completely lied to William about what happened at the diner, but I didn't want to snap and have her running to William claiming I was an actual bitch.

I texted her I was outside and she came out to my car so we could talk.

I had no idea how to start, so I started with the hardest question that needed the largest explanation. "How could you tell William that I was rude to you and your friends when I wasn't?"

"Look, I have one thing to say to you and I didn't want to do it over text message. This needs to be said face to face so that you can fully understand. William is *my* boyfriend not yours. I know you have feelings for him, but you need to know that I'm the number one person in his life. I'm not going to be friends with any girl that has feelings for my guy. He's in love with me, not you, do you get that?"

Again, I was stunned into silence. She didn't let me respond before she continued. "I will get you out of William's life, one way or another." With that, she got out of my car and went back inside. I still sat there stunned, attempting to process what she just said.

He'd never believe me if I told him she said this to me. He didn't believe me last time. Why didn't I think to record this conversation with her?! Is she, is she turning him against me? Is her plan actually working?!

He'd been avoiding his locker really well. I didn't see him at lunch, or in the hallways. I started to wonder if he was even at school at all.

I started going to my locker after every single period. I was even tardy to some of my classes because I waited there for so long. On Thursday, I finally got lucky between 6th and 7th period. He started to retreat when he saw me waiting for him.

"William!" I hollered.

He froze but turned around to face me finally. I hadn't moved, I just stared at him, waiting to see if he was going to come back, or if he was going to leave me hanging. I caught a break; he turned back around and came to his locker.

"Hi," was all I managed to say to him.

He didn't say anything, though. He opened his locker and emptied his backpack.

"I'll apologize to Casey," I said after his continuous silent treatment.

At least this finally got a response. "Good," he said, grabbing his backpack and leaving immediately.

I jumped when his locker slammed shut. The intense air from it blew my hair back.

Casey was headed toward us, and as pissed off at her as I was, I needed him to hear me apologize.

I swallowed every ounce of pride in me before speaking. "Casey, I . . . umm . . . I'm sorry for how I treated you the other night at the diner. It had been a long day and work didn't help, but that's not an excuse."

She continued staring at me, not giving any signs of acknowledgement of my apology, so I continued.

"Maybe we all could go to the dance together? It was a good idea you had."

I thought she would say something in response. After all, she had all the guts in the world to speak to me the way she did in my car. She didn't say anything. No physical words came out of her mouth. Instead, she gave me a head nod in acknowledgement.

A head nod? Really?

"Ready babe?" she asked him. He said he was, and they both left without speaking to me.

I shook my head, fuming.

Whatever, this better smooth things over between him and me, that's all I care about.

I got a call from Casey that night. I hesitated answering it so I ignored it.

This entire time William has been wanting me to be friends with the most vile person I have ever met. The worst part is, he doesn't even see this side of her!

Casey called again and I ignored it. She called immediately once more, so I finally answered. I knew I needed to be careful in case she was with William.

"Hello?" I asked, trying to sound like my normal self.

"Don't for a second even think I want you to go with us to the dance," was all she said before hanging up.

What am I going to do?! How do I get William to see who she really is without jeopardizing my friendship with him??

CHAPTER 24

William stopped answering every text I sent him. He also didn't come to his locker as often as he used to. I figured I should take the hint and back off a little. It was hard, though. The more space he tried to put between us, the more I wanted to fill it and show him that we could make this work and we could just be friends despite my feelings.

If only my feelings had an off switch I could just flip. Would that make things better? Could we go back to being like we used to then? Also, I still don't know what to do about Casey. She made it clear she wants me out of his life. What scares me are the lengths she may be willing to go to as well to make sure this happens. I can't even think about this right now; it's making me feel sick.

I still hung out with my girlfriends in my spare time, but I'd also started to hang out with some of my coworkers too. They're a couple of years older, but they're fun. They're attending the local community college. Some of them plan to go onto a university afterwards, but not all of them.

Derek Tannek was one of the cooks for the diner. He was a senior in high school like me; however, he attended a small school in the next town over. His mom preferred the smaller school district, and he hated it ever since elementary school. He's a brown-haired, brown-eyed kind of guy, with dimples. He had been working at the diner since he was fifteen, so I've worked with him for a few years now. I like talking with him. He's easy to joke around with and he likes to have fun, which is nice; especially when it's slow at work.

I was working the closing shift with him on Wednesday night. It's technically my responsibility to put all the chairs up and mop the floor, but he always helps me so I can get out of there sooner. I have always appreciated it, and tonight in particular I appreciated it even more. This gave me some alone time with him so I could ask him a question that I'd been wrestling with for the last two weeks.

He was putting all the chairs on the tables, seat down of course, while I was filling the mop bucket with soap and water. We were talking about how his school's football team did this year in comparison to ours. We're not in the same class for sports since Greenwood High is at least twice if not three times as large as his.

His school lost in the regular season, whereas my team made it to the semi-finals. Both he and I shared the mutual feeling of sentiment knowing this was our last football season as high schoolers.

The same thing I talked to William about at the beginning of our season.

"Oh well, now it's on to spring sports!" he said excitedly.

"How come you didn't wrestle this year?" I asked him.

"I was going to, but Mom has been working doubles almost all year, and I figured I should help with finances. Besides, I don't think I'm good enough to get a scholarship to college anyway, and I need the money I'm making here to help pay for college as well," he explained.

I knew he came from a single-parent household. I can't imagine if my dad left Greyson and me the way his dad left Derek and his three younger brothers. Derek says he's glad his dad isn't in his life, but I suspect he's masking his sadness with anger.

"You're going to Greenwood Community College, right? You're planning to stay here?" I asked. I don't want him to start thinking about the what ifs of wrestling and where he could have been if his father had stuck around.

"Yeah, I'll stay here in town, then I can still work here and live at home to help out," he said, putting the last chair up on the bar.

I wheeled the mop bucket to the back corner so I could work from the back of the store to the front door. He went to the cash register to count it down and make sure the balances matched.

It grew silent as I mustered the courage to ask my question. He was busy counting, and I didn't want to disrupt him. Not to mention, if I did make anything awkward, I didn't want to have to spend another half an hour around him in silence or something.

I finished mopping and was pouring the bucket of nasty water down the drain. We turned off the lights and locked the front door to head home. We were parked next to each other, so we walked together. When we were almost to our cars, I turned to him, figuring it was now or never.

"Derek I was wondering if I could ask you something?" I said, looking down at the ground and fidgeting with my keys in my hand.

I piqued his interest. "Sure," he said.

I was nervous, not because I was afraid he would say no, but because I didn't have a clue what his feelings were toward dances. It wasn't something that we had ever talked about at work.

I always went with William, so I never needed to ask another guy to a dance before.

I don't want Derek to be appalled by me asking him to do something he might think is stupid.

"This probably sounds lame, especially since you don't go to my school, but would you . . . umm . . . go to the New Year's Dance with me? I would buy our tickets and pay for supper before," I added in an attempt to receive a yes from him. Guys do love food.

"What day is it?" he asked.

Oh no, he's going to be busy either as an excuse, or because he really is busy doing anything else but going to a dance at my high school.

I pulled out my phone to double check what I had written in my calendar.

"It's actually on New Year's Eve this year, which is cool. We've never had that before."

"I don't think I have anything going on but let me double check when I get home tonight and I'll text you. Sound good?"

"Yeah, that works for me." I was skeptical on the inside though. If he didn't text me, it could make things weird at work.

Although, I don't want things to be weird at work, and they'll only be weird if I make them weird! But what if he makes it weird? Then I can't control that things are weird and then I'll feel weird because he feels weird and then everyone at work will probably feel the weirdness and wonder what the heck happened between us.

Boy do these thoughts feel familiar. Breathe. Calm your mind and stop thinking about what hasn't happened yet.

I inhaled silently to try and ground my thinking as we said goodnight and headed our separate ways.

When I got home, I debated on going to bed right away in case he either rejected my invitation, or didn't text me, or if I should stay up for a little while and see if he did say anything.

To keep my mind from going down its own rabbit hole, I poured myself a bowl of cereal and opened my agenda to see if I had anything I absolutely needed to have done regarding homework for tomorrow. I had a couple science questions left from today's class. We started doing our homework, but ran out of time, so our teacher said to finish on our own tonight, and then we'll go over the answers tomorrow in class. Normally William and I would have at least texted about homework, but I haven't heard from him all day.

I guess I'll need to try this on my own. But seriously though, why is there math involved in science? They're basically like evil stepsisters to me. They're always ganging up on me even though I'm not in an actual math class this year!

After completely not understanding the first question, I moved onto the second problem, and had no clue what I was doing with that one as well. I was chewing my pencil when I finally gave in and texted William.

> **Me:**   Any chance we could meet early in the morning? I've got some hard science problems I can't figure out.

I put my phone face up so I would know instantly if he responded.

I saw it light up, and I instantly picked up my phone to view the message! It was from Derek saying he doesn't have anything going on the weekend of the dance and would go with me. I was excited he agreed to be my date to the dance, but man I wanted it to be William that texted me back that fast. I thanked Derek for agreeing to go with me and I would let him know when I know more details about times and things.

I gave up on my homework and hoped that William would text me back tonight.

When morning came, I checked my phone immediately to see if I'd missed a text from him. I hadn't. Deflated, I went to school and started my day off with seeing Casey's arms wrapped around him at our lockers. I said hey to them while I got what I needed. William said hi back while Casey glared, not saying anything. He finished first at his locker and wished me a good day.

"Thanks," I said, shocked. "You, you too."

The closer the fall semester came to a close, the less William and I spoke either in person or text. I was starting to go mad with wonder, but I was too terrified to mention it to him in the fear of upsetting him. If he needed space, I would give him space; hopefully then he would see I wasn't being clingy, and we could still hang out together.

Then FINALLY the week before Christmas break, we talked the most in what felt like a long time. We talked a bit at our lockers until Casey came to take him away. We also did homework twice together that week! Things were starting to feel a little like how they used to, and I was excited. We never spoke about the New Year's Dance, but that's okay. We focused on our homework and what we were doing for Christmas this year despite how we do the same things every year with our families.

That's why we call them traditions. Like how our dance used to be a tradition.

"Are you going to your grandparents' on your dad's side?" I asked him.

"Yup. We'll be there on the 23rd and 24th, then we'll head over to Mom's side and spend Christmas day there with them. What about you? Going to your cousin's?" he asked.

"You know it. I will be eating too much ham and mashed potatoes, and then hopefully we will watch a movie so I can fall asleep to it."

"Always falling asleep during movies." He chuckled, and my heart melted. I had not heard him laugh, just the two of us, in way too long. I savored the sound.

"You know it!" I said, playfully shoving him. He smiled and shoved back. I decided since things were going well tonight, I brought up his girlfriend in the hopes he would see it as me being sincere.

"Are you getting Casey anything for Christmas?" I asked with a soft smile on my face to emphasize support.

"Yeah, I'm getting her a jewelry set this year," he said.

"Oh nice!" I scrounged some enthusiasm to put into my voice. "Do you have a picture or something of it?" I asked.

He pulled out his phone to show me, and my eyes went huge. "*Wow*, this is really beautiful," I said, shocked and surprised. It was a necklace, earring, and ring set. It was all rose gold with diamonds in everything.

"Are those real diamonds?" I asked, pulling my eyes away from the picture to look in his.

"Yeah. Casey saw this set at the mall when we went shopping last weekend, so I went back and bought it for her," he explained. "I had zero idea what the lady was talking about. I just told her I wanted what was in the window. Do you think I should have gone with a bigger diamond for the earrings? She said they could have added some more beading to the necklace too if I wanted."

"Definitely not. I'm sure the lady was just try-ing to upsell and make a larger profit. If this is what Casey saw in the window and loved it, then she'll love it as is. I just wouldn't mention to her that you could have gone bigger with the diamonds." I forced out a chuckle. William laughed with me. I couldn't believe how beautiful this set was. I bet it was expensive for someone in high school.

"Good, that's what I was thinking too," he said. He put his phone back in his pocket and we went back to working on our homework.

When he left, I asked if I could have a hug, and he gave me one. I was cherishing this night. Every time we talk, it feels like it will be a while before we get to be "us" again.

Spring Semester
Senior Year
2017

My dress this year was a soft pink color. It was strapless, with the top half completely decked out in rhinestones that flowed into the tulle skirt bottom half. Like the other two years, all my girlfriends and I got ready together. My hair was softly curled, with a rhinestone barrette in it to pull a small chunk away from my face, but otherwise, most of my hair was resting on my shoulders.

Kyle was already at Evelynn's house as we were getting ready. He was downstairs with her dad watching something on TV. Derek was next to show up. He wore a matching pink, button up shirt, with a black tie, and black slacks. I was surprisingly impressed with how he looked. I always found him attractive, but I was extra attracted to him right now.

"You look beautiful, Alli," he said, taking my hand and spinning me around. I wasn't expecting that either, so I tripped over my own feet. Typical, awkward me.

"Thank you. You cleaned up nicely as well," I said in response. He flashed a smile at me and then presented me with a corsage. It was a pink rose with black, sparkling tips. I loved it!

After the pictures we went out to eat at a bar and grill this year. It wasn't anything fancy, but that didn't matter because I enjoyed being there with my friends. Derek was a little shy with the others since he didn't know them, but my girlfriends tried to talk to him, and some of the guys did as well thankfully.

We arrived at our high school and headed into the gymnasium where we could hear the bass from the speakers bumping away. Immediately my eyes were scanning for William, but I hadn't seen him yet.

We all dragged our dates onto the dance floor and started dancing. It was a little awkward at first with Derek, because I wasn't sure if he was comfortable with dancing or not. I also wasn't sure how he wanted to dance in proximity to me.

What was too close? Is this bizarre for him? I wouldn't be questioning myself if I were with William, I would already know.

It only took a few songs before we found our rhythm and got closer as the night went on. I enjoyed slow dancing with him. Turns out he's a confident dancer and wasn't afraid of spinning me around. He even dipped me twice. I'm thankful he was holding onto me tightly, because I was afraid I was going to fall on the ground in front of everybody, but his arms held me.

After the first hour, some of my group took a break and headed to get some drinks.

William!!

He was standing in line to get a drink with Casey and I drank the sight of him in.

God he looks good.

Casey's dress of course was the same one from the photo she showed me that night at the diner. It was a knee-length gown like all of ours. It was white with spaghetti straps, and quite fitted. It definitely was a gorgeous dress. Her spray tan really made the white pop against her skin. She looked stunning.

When they turned around, they saw us waiting in line. We were with Chelsea and Roscoe, so William did the "guy hand-shake thing" with him. Normally I would give him a hug, but with Casey there I decided against it. I waved stupidly instead.

Smooth, Alli, smooth.

William smiled directly at me though and told me I looked beautiful tonight which made my heart flutter in every direction. I introduced Derek to William and even Casey.

"You look really pretty tonight, Casey," I said, in an attempt at sincerity. I needed William to see that I was still trying even after I apologized to her.

And after how hostile she has been toward me. I can't let her think that she's scared me off.

"Thanks, so do you." She smiled at me, but I could tell it was as fake as mine was right now. William's, however, was genuine as he looked between his two girls.

"Even my nails?" I asked, flashing them to Casey. "I actually painted them."

"Yeah, keep up the good work on them," she said before saying goodbye on behalf of her and William.

"Is that the same girl that said her fries were cold?" Derek asked questioningly.

"It sure is," I said.

"Why on earth are you complimenting her? She and her friends were horrible to you that night."

I sighed. "Because life is complicated and sixteen-year-old girls are even more complicated," which Derek agreed easily with.

I only saw William a couple more times throughout the night. Unfortunately, I didn't get a chance to talk to him. He was wrapped up in Casey. It honestly made me sad to see him so happy.

What a friend I am to feel that.

The last two years he was smiling at me when we were the ones slow dancing together and now it's somebody else in his arms. Someone else is making him smile his heart-stopping smile.

"Is he the guy you wish you were here with tonight?" Derek asked me, snapping me out of my thoughts.

"What?" I asked him. My cheeks were blushing, but I don't think he could see them in the dark lighting we were under.

"It's okay if it is. I really don't mind; we're friends after all."

I sighed, remembering that I've never been good at hiding my emotions from people.

"Our sophomore and junior year we went to this dance together, and he was supposed to ask me this year, but naturally, he couldn't. Or he forgot, but either way, I never would have gotten to be here with him."

"That sucks. I'm sorry. Do you want to make him jealous at all?" He had a playful grin on his face.

I smiled in response, but I squinted my eyes at him in suspicion. "That depends, what are you imagining?"

He shrugged his shoulders that were under my hands. "That depends on how far you would want to go? We could dance next to them. We could make out next to them. That's my vote by the way, or I could propose marriage in front of the entire school. You choose."

My mouth dropped open at the last suggestion. I was horrified at the idea and that was exactly the reaction he was going for. We burst out laughing and I told him that it was okay.

"William is obsessed with her. He and Casey would probably be ecstatic if I got engaged so then I would have a boy in my life besides him."

I chuckled, but it was a sad chuckle and Derek could tell. He dipped me again, which instantly took my mind off the thoughts I was having because I was terrified of crashing to the ground again, but it never happened. He always held me tightly.

Our senior dance came to an end.

My friends were going to go back to Chelsea's and play games. I invited Derek, but he had other plans that he invited me to. Derek was going to our coworkers Jayden and Brent's apartment to play games as well. He let me know that I wouldn't be the only female there if I did want to come. I considered it and decided what the heck, it could be fun!

I guess Derek forgot to tell me it was a college party we were going to. The apartment complex that I drove us to was at Greenwood Community College and was crawling with drunken people celebrating

New Year's Eve. I've never been around drunk people, so this was a different scene for me.

We were still in our dance attire, but I didn't stand out considering all the other girls were wearing short dresses.

The first girl we encountered squealed at us as we walked by, "OHHH MY GOSH you guys match, how freaking adorable are you two. Oh, my goodness! Mindy, hey Mindy, look at them! They match!" I smiled at her and kept following Derek down the hallway.

We reached Jayden and Brent's apartment and walked in. Music was blaring, there were about thirty people crammed into the living room and kitchen, and beer cans were everywhere, along with a table set up for a game called Beer Pong.

Whatever that is.

We found Brent and Jayden, and Derek did that thing again guys do when they see their buddies. Both of my coworkers were surprised to see me here.

"Alli, we didn't know you were into this kind of thing. Awesome! Help yourself to anything you want to drink, we're about to start another round of Beer Pong. You all want to play?"

I shook my head and told them that I would watch first. Derek said he'd play the winner; he needed some beer in him first. I didn't know he drank.

"I didn't know you were into this," I said to Derek as he cracked open a can of Coors Light.

"Oh yeah sorry, I guess I should have given you a little more heads up."

You think?!

"Is this cool for you? If not, I don't blame you for not wanting to stay. I can catch a ride back to Chelsea's house to pick up my car," he offered.

"Oh, no it's fine. I've just never been around this, and I've never drank before," I told him.

I had never been embarrassed about it, but suddenly, as I looked at the people around me, I felt as though I was drastically younger than everyone and I didn't like it. Most of these people were only a year or two older than me, but for some reason, they just seemed a lot more . . . responsible isn't the word, but they seemed a lot older? Mature? Cool maybe? I don't know. I don't know what word I'm looking for, but I felt as though I was sticking out like a sore thumb, and I didn't like it.

"Want to try?" He held out his beer for me to try. I took a drink.

That is disgusting!

I puckered my face up and gave it back to him. He laughed at the expression I made.

"Let me go see if there is something fruitier for you."

He asked a girl named Aneeta if she had any Smirnoff Ice or Mike's Hard Lemonade. He came back with a Mike's Hard and opened it for me.

"Here, try this; it tastes just like lemonade."

He was right, it tasted exactly like lemonade. My parents have given me the talk about how dangerous alcohol can be, especially if you don't know your limit. I know drinking and driving is wrong, and we've been shown videos in school about people needing to get their stomachs pumped because of alcohol poisoning. With this in mind, I drank slowly, very slowly.

We watched the game of Beer Pong; it was a simple concept. Jayden and Brent won, so Derek asked if I wanted to be his partner against them. I agreed.

I was awful. I had to drink quite a bit and needed a second drink. I was given another Mike's Hard Lemonade. Derek carried us, but we still lost. I was starting to feel what Derek described as a "buzz." My head started feeling tingly, along with my finger tips, but I felt like I was still in control of myself, so I wasn't worried.

I have never seen Derek so talkative! Maybe it was all the beer he had been drinking, but he was a social butterfly, completely opposite of him tonight at supper. I was thankful he stayed by my side since I didn't really know anyone there. He introduced me to his other friends and some of their girlfriends. It was obvious that I was still in high school, but then again, so was Derek.

He had some interesting friends here. People were making out randomly in front of everybody. Others, well, I can't even describe what they were doing, but they thought it was the most hilarious thing on earth, and I was sucked into it. Whatever was happening was hilarious! These two guys were pretending to joust with one another using whatever they could find around the apartment. We all gave them room, but they were wobbly and kept falling into things even though they were supposed to be going in a straight line toward the other.

Someone noticed the time on the clock reading 11:58 PM. They turned on the television so we could watch the ball drop. We missed it though. We didn't care, we did our own countdown.

"FIVE, FOUR, THREE, TWO, ONE, HAPPY NEW YEAR!!!!" we all shouted in unison. I looked around at everyone kissing each other for New Year's and turned to Derek. He had the same thought and so we kissed to bring in the New Year. We then proceeded to continue kissing, well after everyone else stopped.

I noticed cheering in the background and pulled away from his lips to look around at everybody cheering for us. I was immediately embarrassed, but I didn't feel my face get hot for once. Instead, I thought it was hilarious and I buried my face into Derek's neck laughing as he wrapped his arms around me. I could feel his body laughing in unison with mine.

Jayden wanted Derek to be his partner for another game of Beer Pong. He looked at me to see if it was okay and it was. I wanted him to have fun. I realized I hadn't thought about William this entire night until now.

I wonder what he's doing right now. I'll text him!

Me: Heeeyyyy youuuu whte are kyou doing?

Aneeta came and sat down next to me on the couch. She was wondering if I had a thing for Derek and I told her I didn't; we're just coworkers. Then she asked if I liked anyone, and I told her about William and how he's dating someone. We bonded over that. Turns out she experienced something similar a few years back. I was able to tell her about Casey's true intent on trying get me permanently out of William's life. I think if Aneeta would have met Casey right there and then, she may have thrown a punch on my behalf. It was a great feeling getting to tell my side and not have somebody accuse me of lying!

Me: William!! Hley text mew back

I can't remember if this was my third or fourth lemonade, but I was given one more drink to have. Now I was aware I was intoxicated. I wasn't as bad as some people considering they were passed out on the couches, or ground, but when I went to the bathroom my face was showing definite signs of alcohol consumption. My cheeks were bright red, as well as my eyes, and I looked greatly in need of sleep. Not to mention, I was starting to slur my words and forget things that happened only a couple minutes ago. At some point during the night too, I ended up with Derek's tie around my neck, and I don't remember when that happened.

I don't know where Aneeta went, but I realized I hadn't seen Derek in a while. I found Jayden and asked if he knew where Derek was. He sluggishly pointed toward a bedroom while laughing, telling me he went in there to lay down. I headed that way making sure not to step on the people lying on the ground. I didn't think to knock since Derek was probably sleeping. Instead, I walked right in so I could talk to him.

Oh my god! Derek is naked . . . with Aneeta?!

Aneeta ducked under the covers to hide her face and body. I shut the door because they were nude, and it clicked what they were doing.

They were having sex!!

I felt embarrassed for disturbing them. I came back to the kitchen not sure where to go now. Jayden asked me if I went into the bedroom and I said yes, he laughed in my face and told me he didn't think I would actually go in there. Now I felt even more embarrassed. I looked around, and the room started to spin so I shut my eyes and sat down.

I didn't want to be here anymore. I was exhausted, sweating, and clearly drunk. I didn't want to call my parents because I didn't want to get in trouble. There was only one person I wanted, William. He never texted me back, but I decided to call him anyway. He didn't answer, so I immediately tried again. No answer. I tried a third time and he finally picked up.

"Hi, Alli," he said, probably with annoyance in his voice, but not much was clear to me at this moment.

"Can you get, pick me from where I am?" I stumbled out.

What did I ask?

"What was that?" he asked me confused.

"Can you get me; I don't know where?" I was trying to speak more clearly, but the alcohol was affecting my thought process.

"Have you been drinking?" he asked, concerned.

"Yeah, I have."

"Okay, where are you?"

"Some apartments on campus," I said, trying to be helpful but failing.

"Okay, stay there; I'm coming to pick you up. I'll call you when I'm there," he said.

I wasn't sure about much right now, but all I knew was my best friend was coming to get me. I would have felt more excited, but I was dizzy.

Uh-oh, I think I might puke.

I found my coat and went out into the hallway where it was a little quieter for my head.

After about fifteen minutes, William called me back, asking which apartment complex I'm in since there are multiple on campus. I told him I had no idea and that I would go outside and see if he could find me that way. The cold helped my head feel a little clearer. He asked if I could see his headlights anywhere yet, but I couldn't. He turned the corner, and I told him I could see him, if he saw me. He said he did.

I started walking toward his Wrangler, it was quite the distance from the apartment to the parking lot. He had gotten out of his Jeep and met me halfway. He put his hands on my shoulders to look at me, or maybe steady me, I'm not exactly sure.

"Are you okay?" he asked, concern still in his voice.

I love it when he's concerned. It makes me feel important to him again.

"Yeah, just tired mostly, and hungry," I told him.

"How much have you drank?"

I wasn't sure how to gauge it. I held up my hand indicating three, but I didn't think it had been quite that many, so I slowly put down my fingers. Then I just stared at my hand and giggled.

"Are you going to throw up?" he asked.

"I don't think so," I told him. The nausea had subsided a little.

"Alright let's take you home," he told me.

This terrified me. "No, William please. Can we hang out a little bit, just until I sober up? I don't want to get in trouble. Please can we go back to your house, only for a little bit I swear?"

He looked unsure. He glanced toward his Jeep, then back at me. I tried pleading to him with my eyes. My teeth started to chatter, and my legs started to shake from the cold.

"Okay, we'll go back to my place," he finally said.

I thanked him about six times in ten seconds. We started to walk but I quickly realized I was not steady, and almost fell over. Luckily, William grabbed me before I scuffed my knees. He put his arm around my waist and helped me the rest of the way to his car. He opened the back door, which was weird, but then I realized that Casey was in the passenger seat with an upset look on her face.

Oops.

"Happy New Year Casey!" I said as William was walking around his vehicle.

She didn't say anything to me, but she glared at William as he got into the driver's seat. He explained that he was going to drop Casey off at her house and take me back to his. She protested, but William told her that he'd see her tomorrow. I was overwhelmed with pride for him.

That's right! He's taking care of his friend as he should. Me. That's me he's taking care of. You have not removed me from his life.

Selfishly I laughed about that to myself. Then again, maybe I laughed out loud because Casey turned around in her seat and was glaring at me now.

We pulled up to her house, and William walked her to her door. I watched both of them. Casey was upset, and William was trying to explain his side and make her feel better. They kissed bye, but they didn't look like they parted on the best of terms.

Oops, again.

William didn't say anything on the drive back to his house. I was a little out of it to try and make conversation with him. He helped me inside and we went to his basement where he sat me on the couch and got me a glass of water. I asked if we could have pizza. He said that's fine and went to make one. While it was cooking, I asked him if I ruined his night.

"We were watching *Harry Potter* and celebrating New Year's together," he said. He didn't seem mad at least. Not that I could tell anyway.

"Are you upset with me?" I cautiously asked.

"I'm glad you didn't drive home drunk, but I wish you wouldn't have put yourself in this situation in the first place."

His uncle was an alcoholic and was never allowed to see him or Charlotte. Mr. Mantel wouldn't allow it unless his brother cleaned up, but he never did, and he passed away from liver failure at forty-two.

"Casey's pissed, though," he said.

"Yeah, I figured. I'm sorry about that," I said. "Thank you though. For everything. The water, pizza, picking me up, and being my friend. I like you; you know. No, I love you, William."

Holy crap!! I know you've been drinking but jeez!

I covered my mouth with my hand, not believing I just said that to him. He was saved by the bell of the pizza being done. He didn't look at me and went to get the pizza out of the oven.

A few minutes later he brought down some delicious pepperoni pizza for us. I took about five bites when I had to rush to the bathroom.

Gross. Oh, this toilet is cold. I like that.

William came in, despite my protesting. I didn't want him to see me like this. I was an absolute mess, and smelled, but he held my hair back since it fell out from its barrette. Once I finished throwing up, he got me a pair of his shorts and a T-shirt to sleep in. He texted my mom for me telling her that I was spending the night at Chelsea's and had forgotten to text her because I fell asleep for a little while. He then texted Chelsea to update her, so she could cover for me if necessary.

He is a wonderful human being.

We went back to the couch, but he didn't sit next to me like normal. He pressed play on the *Harry Potter* movie they had been watching. It felt cold without him there. I laid down and passed out almost immediately. I woke up to William shaking me awake. It was about 9:00 AM and William needed to get ready to see Casey. Apparently, she'd been blowing his phone up all morning wondering what happened.

He told me to give his clothes back another time, so I grabbed my dress, heels, and coat; he let me borrow a pair of Charlotte's sandals that happened to fit. I asked what his plans were today with Casey, and he said they're going to have lunch with her parents and then celebrate her brother's birthday.

Other than that, we didn't talk on the way to my car.

As I was opening the door to exit, he turned to me. "Alli, don't do this again," he said with a serious face.

I didn't like his wording. I told him I wouldn't. I got out and watched his taillights flash goodbye as he drove away.

CHAPTER 25

January was ending and I had barely seen William. I'd been hanging out with Derek since the New Year's Dance. Whenever I was with my coworkers we were either drinking or hanging out in somebody's garage.

My girlfriends weren't fans of my coworkers, but I stopped telling them when I was with Derek and the others. I liked the feeling of being around people that didn't really know me. They couldn't tell what I was thinking and couldn't pick up on little signals the way my girls and William always can.

My coworkers wanted to have a good time and were down for anything. It was new and exciting. I felt . . . I don't know, different, more in control with them, even though the alcohol contradicts the control part. It helped clear my mind from thinking about William, school, and the future. All I thought about when I was drinking was the present moment, and the fun I was having.

When William and I do "talk," it's mostly through texting. Our conversations basically go like this:

Me: Can we hang out?

William: Casey and I already have plans.

Me:	When can I see you, it's been forever
William:	I don't know, maybe next week-end?
Me:	You said that last weekend too
William:	Well, I don't know what to tell you. I'm trying to juggle you both.
Me:	Your juggling is really lopsided
William:	Ok

You know how guys get Just Because flowers for their women? I was thinking of getting him a video game as a Just Because gift.

Don't lie to yourself. You want to buy his attention and you know it. Yeah, well, maybe I am, but I'm starting to feel desperate. He liked playing that popular football game, *what's it called . . . Maiden? No, that's not right. Madden! Yeah, I think he'll love it.*

I spent the first weekend of February with Derek, Jayden, Brent, and a couple of girls. My taste for beer was getting better. I could drink a couple cans without wanting to throw up.

What a life accomplishment.

Friday night, the six of us hung out at Jayden and Brent's apartment like we did on New Year's Eve after the dance. We played Beer Pong, Flippy Cup, and some card games. Throughout the night I tried texting William, but he barely responded.

Me:	What's up?
Me:	Whattre you doing?
William:	Hanging out with Casey. You?
Me:	Hangin out with guys toi . . . having funn

William: Drinking?

Me: Maaayyybeer ☺ Want to join?

No response from him.

Saturday was pretty much the same thing. We went out to eat after work. We drove around for a little while, and once we grew tired of that, we went back to Jayden and Brent's apartment and played Beer Pong and *Call of Duty* on their PlayStation. Well, the guys played *Call of Duty*, the rest of us sat around watching them and talking with one another.

I tried texting William again, but he didn't answer any of my three messages I sent him. I even focused on my spelling to make sure I didn't give away that I'd been drinking. No response. I figured he had to be with Casey, because he always texted me when he was with his guy friends.

I decided I would find him myself. Derek didn't want me driving buzzed, so I "compromised" and drank a glass of water first. I took off around 12:30 AM. I drove by Casey's first because it was closer, but I didn't see his Jeep. I headed to his house next, and his Jeep was in the driveway.

I got out of my car and had to steady myself a little more than I expected.

Okay, I should not have driven. How stupid of me! Deep breath Alli. Don't let him know you're feeling the alcohol. I blew in my hand to smell my own breath. *Gross, my breath reeks of beer. Crap, but I just need to SEE him,* I thought to myself. *I just want to see him for five minutes and then I can leave.*

I really missed our time together, because it's been so long since the last time just he and I hung out. I was also feeling anger toward him. I felt he was constantly picking Casey over me. *This is what she told you she wanted and it's working.*

I decided to avoid the garage entrance in case his parents or Charlotte were still up. I went around back and checked the sliding door. It was locked. I reached under the orange rock where they kept their spare key. It's not the first time he and I have used the spare key at each other's houses.

Two years ago, my uncle passed away from a drowning accident. It happened at 1:30 in the morning. When I found out the news I snuck over to William's house and woke him up from sleeping. He stayed up with me all night, not saying anything, just being there with me. It helped more than anything he could have said.

I heard the television, so I figured they were watching a movie or something. I turned the corner and saw *Step Up* was playing, but Casey and William were not watching the movie. They were making out. Like hard core making out, and I caught them off guard. We all were startled!

"Alli, what the hell are you doing here?!" William asked, putting his shirt back on. Casey was hiding under a blanket, probably putting clothing back on as well.

"You weren't answering your text messages, so I thought I would come and see you in person," I slurred a little.

"Kind of busy right now," he said. Casey appeared from under the covers and shot me an angry expression.

"Well, it's not like I've been hogging your clock, that's her job," I said, pointing at Casey.

Oops. That came out jumbled.

"I mean your time. You don't have any of that left to share apparently."

"Seriously?" Casey chimed in, upset.

William shook his head. "Are you drunk?" Was that anger rising in his voice?

"I'm not drunk. I had a drink or two earlier, but I also had water too," I tried to defend.

"So, you drove after you've been drinking, Alli? Are you seriously that stupid?" William screeched.

Casey folded her arms at me and shook her head saying, "Apparently."

"I . . . uhh . . ." I didn't know what to say. Yes, I drove here impaired but I didn't think that I was quite this diminished.

"Come on, I'm taking you home. Casey, stay here. I'll be right back," William said, grabbing my wrist. I started to protest, but I knew better after the look he gave me. I shut up until we were in his vehicle.

"Please don't be mad at me, I only wanted to see you! You have to admit, it has been a long time since we've hung out, or even done homework together," I started.

"I know it has, but I want to spend my time with Casey, and I'm tired of having to apologize for it," he said.

"You don't have to keep saying sorry—"

"Then why am I always the one apologizing?" he asked me.

My mouth dropped open. "What on earth do I need to apologize for?!" I was shocked.

He was driving a bit too fast for my stomach and spinning head.

"How about how crazy you've been acting for starters?" he said, staring directly into my soul. "You've been blowing up my phone even when I'm clearly not responding. You're having Rose ask Morris questions about Casey and me, and tonight, you have yet again, been drinking and putting yourself and others in harm's way!"

Oh wow, he is extremely angry at me.

I shrank into my seat, unable to look into his fiery eyes. I felt like he and I were on repeat with everything we kept saying to each other. I wanted more time with him, he wanted to hang out with Casey, we don't get our time together, I get mad, he apologizes, lather, rinse, and repeat.

"Why are you drinking so much lately?" he asked me next.

His question caught me off guard. I didn't feel like it had been *that* often.

"It makes me feel better. It helps me take my mind off things," I said.

"Things like me?" he asked.

I sighed and tried to explain, "You, me, what we've been going through for months now . . . and our future."

"So, you're drinking because we're not hanging out as much?"

His question made me upset.

"No, it's not because we're not hanging out as much! It's because . . . it's because it dulls my emotions. I'm tired of feeling the way I do."

"How's that?" he asked.

"Forgotten," I whispered.

"I haven't forgotten you. I never could. You should know that," he tried to say.

"Then why isn't it clear to me?" I asked with hurt in my voice.

This time William is the one shaking his head. "I don't know, Alli; I don't know what to do anymore." We drove the rest of the way to my house in silence.

"Thanks for bringing me home," I said, peeking over at him. He was looking out his driver's side window, nodding in acknowledgement. I wanted a hug from him, but I thought it better not to ask for one tonight.

I woke up to a text from William asking to see me after lunch. My heart fluttered with excitement.

We're actually going to hang out today! Maybe last night wasn't so stupid of me after all!

I texted Hayden asking if she could pick me up from my house and drop me off at William's. Unfortunately, I had to explain to her why I needed her to drive me to his house so I could pick up my own vehicle.

"Seriously, Sky?!" she raised her voice, which is extremely rare. I was taken aback. "How could you be that stupid?!"

"Look. I know it was the stupidest thing I have ever done, but I'm not going to do it again. I promise."

"Yeah, says every person that does it again when they say they aren't going to." Her eyes were locked on the road. She wouldn't even look at me.

Again, I shrunk into the passenger seat of somebody else's car.

"William laid into me last night too."

"Good, he and everyone should. Do you realize what could have happened?"

"Of course, I do, Hayden."

"No—apparently you don't, otherwise you wouldn't have done it. You need to stop drinking too. It's dangerous and annoying."

I was stunned into silence. I did not know she would be this upset at me either. "It's what my other friends are into," I said in a pathetic attempt to justify my actions.

"Then get new friends, or better yet just come back to hanging out with your real friends, full time."

"Speaking of that, William wants to hang out today finally," I said, glancing over at her.

Her facial features softened immediately. "Really?" She was as surprised as I knew she would be.

"Yeah. We're meeting after lunch today." Excitement crept back into my voice as I imagined what we would do or say, one-on-one.

I hope it's just him and me anyway.

"Wow. Well, let me know how it goes," she said, pulling into his driveway.

His Jeep was gone, and it didn't appear anybody else was home right now. I was thankful for that. I wondered what William told his parents when they saw my car at his place, but not me.

William wanted to meet me at the park by my house, so I walked over there and took my place on a picnic table. It was an odd February day. The sun was poking through the clouds, and the temperature was in the thirties, when normally it's in the single digits, or below zero. I wore a sweatshirt with a long-sleeved shirt underneath and my white beanie with the fluff ball on top that William gave to me last year for my birthday.

He told me to meet him at 1:00 PM, but it was eight minutes past when I last checked my phone. Finally, at 1:15 he rolled up. It was unusual for him to be late when he knows somebody is waiting for him.

That's okay. He's here now.

He walked up in his jeans and black Nike sweatshirt.

That's a new sweatshirt.

Something seemed off about him. I couldn't put my finger on it. I felt it in my gut though.

Doesn't he want to hang out with me? If he does, why does he not seem happy to see me? Is he still upset about last night? Why does he look so tired?

I started to get an uneasy feeling about this. We exchanged Hi's and I tried to be cheerful, but his facial expression had a seriousness yet sadness to it.

After a few minutes of quietness I asked, "Why do I get the feeling that we're not actually hanging out today?"

He had difficulty looking into my eyes when talking to me, but that wasn't new. "I've done a lot of thinking about what happened last night. You put yourself and others' lives at risk when you drank and drove to my house. You've been hurting yourself to drown out your emotions, and that's not healthy at all." This was practically identical to what he said to me last night.

"It won't happen again, I swear. It was stupid of me, and I know that. Hayden ripped into me today too about it, as she should have," I explained.

"It better not happen again, for the safety of everyone, but if it does . . ." He took a deep breath to fill his lungs before saying the second half of his sentence. "I'm not going to be there for you anymore."

My heart and mind froze at his words.

What does he mean he won't "be there for me anymore"? He can't be saying what I think he is . . . can he?

I was frozen solid, I couldn't speak, I couldn't ask him to clarify, but he could tell I was confused, so he kept going.

"I can't do this anymore with you, Al. I can't watch you hurt yourself because of your feelings for me. Last night, you said you're drinking so you can numb the pain and stop thinking about us, that's not okay. That's not healthy."

"I didn't realize you were so concerned about my health?" It was a little snarky, but he had repeated that to me three times and I couldn't help to think he was hiding behind that phrase.

He flashed an angry look toward me and stood up from the bench he was sitting on across from me. "Of course, I'm concerned about you. I care about you."

"So, you care about my health so much that you don't ever want to hang out with me? I'm pretty sure emotional feelings fall under health, and if you're that concerned, you would hang out with me."

"See, that, right there. That's why I can't do this anymore. I can't be responsible for your health; mental, physical, or emotional anymore. It's taking its own toll on me! It's too hard for me to juggle you and Casey anymore. It's not fair to any of us. I'm constantly disappointing you and that's hard to watch. I know I've been an ass to you, and I really am sorry. Casey was pissed last night too—"

"Who cares what Casey was feeling last night. I needed you; I needed my best friend." I slammed my hands on the table and stood up in anger too.

"I care. I love her and I never wanted to feel like I was going to have to pick between the two of you—"

"And all of a sudden you feel you need to pick between her or me now?" There was a sinking feeling entering my gut because I already knew who he was going to choose, and it wasn't me.

She is getting exactly what she wanted and he doesn't even know it.

"Look, this isn't easy," he said, but I scoffed at him. "But I do think it's for the best . . . for all of us," he finished.

My heart was slowly ripping apart with every word he kept saying. My eyes were filling with tears. I tried not to let them, but it was impossible.

"I stayed up all night trying to think of what I could do to make this easier on us, but I couldn't come up with anything better. I'm sorry. I am very, very sorry," he spoke slowly.

"I have done everything, *everything* you have asked of me. I have given you space. I have acknowledged that I haven't made it easy on you while you've juggled your time between her and me. I have *tried* to be friends with Casey. I invited her to the movies with my friends and me. I've offered to drive her to school. Hell, I even asked if she wanted to have supper with me, just her and me, and not once, William! Not once, has she ever taken me up on any of my offers."

"She's shy. She's intimidated by you," he defended his girlfriend.

"She's not shy! She's manipulative and you can't even see it! I never told you this since you didn't believe the truth about when she and her friends came to Steve's Diner. I asked to speak with her about what happened before I apologized to her, like you demanded of me, and do you know what she told me? No, you don't and you're probably not going to believe me either, but I *swear* to you, she said that her goal is to get me out of your life and that is exactly what she has done!"

The tears were coming down my cheeks now.

He didn't say anything for a minute, but then he spoke, "You're right . . . I don't believe you, Allison. This isn't Casey's doing, this is yours."

Everything in me felt as though it had come to an abrupt halt.

Am I even breathing? Is my heart pumping blood like it should be? Am I supposed to do something to make my heart beat? No, wait, it does that on its own, thankfully.

He nodded his head at my silence. "This is for the best." With those final words, he turned to head back to his Jeep, leaving me to pick up every piece of my heart and soul he had just shattered.

CHAPTER 26

February

The rest of the month was a blur. For two weeks I didn't see William. He wasn't with his guy friends in the morning, I didn't see him at lunch, and he must have been using Casey's locker for his books because he never came to his own. He also wouldn't answer any of my text messages or phone calls. Finally, on the last Thursday of February, William was at his own locker in the morning.

What do I say? Should I say anything? Did he just need time to think about things? I know he's been ignoring me, but I don't know, maybe enough time has passed, and things have settled down for him? I guess I'll try.

"Hey," I said as I slowly spun the combination to my locker, keeping my eyes on him. William was deep in his locker, so maybe he didn't hear me. I tried again, "William, hey."

He zipped up his bag and shut his locker, facing me. He shook his head at me and said, "Don't." Then he turned around and left me with my jaw and heart on the floor.

He really meant what he said . . . but how? We were inseparable. We were best friends. We were Alli and William, for crying out loud. WERE, Alli, you WERE Alli and William, but not anymore.

I told my friends at lunch what had happened with him this morning and I started to cry at school. I quickly put an end to it and asked them if we could hang out tonight so I could tell them the whole story without the eyes and ears of everybody in the lunchroom. They agreed and would all come over to my house after school.

I'd been debating on what to do with the video game I got him. I thought about returning it, but I threw away the receipt. I could give it to one of his friends, but that might be weird. I decided to still give him the game, but I needed to figure out how without him trying to return it.

I put the game in his locker after lunch. I knew his combination by heart of course. I attached a little note saying, *"I know you love this game, and I bought it for you back in January. I can't return it, so you'll just have to enjoy it. I hope you have a good day."* I stuck it on the front cover and set it there for him to find later.

The last bell dismissed us for the day and the only thing I wanted was to get home as soon as possible. It was about the only thing I wanted anymore. At least at home I know I won't see William or Casey, and I can try and distract myself more than I can when I'm at school.

I saw him out of the corner of my eye. I froze, not sure if I should hurry and leave or wait to see his reaction. He opened his locker, and his eyebrows revealed his confusion. I didn't sign my name, but he knew immediately it was from me. He took the note off and turned toward me.

He's going to talk to me!

"Thanks," he said, giving me a microscopic, side smile.

As if on cue, Casey arrived. "Hey my most won-derful boyfriend!" she said, giving me her permanent smirk as she spoke. "Is that one of the video games you like? Who is it from?"

He hesitated for a moment, "Oh, uh . . . it's from Morris. He's letting me borrow it."

"Aww, that was thoughtful of him. Maybe you can teach me how to play it tonight," Casey exclaimed, kissing him on the cheek.

"I don't think you'll like it, but we can try it," Wil-liam said in response.

I watched him slip my note into his pocket before Casey could see it. I closed my locker to get the hell out of there.

March

The month dragged on forever. It was hard seeing William around school, but even harder trying to not talk to him. He and Casey pissed me off one day in particular. It was before first period, and I was gath-ering my books from my locker. Not only could I see them out of the corner of my eye, but I could hear them smacking lips too. They were standing next to his locker holding each other and kissing. I slammed my locker so loud it made the entire row of people look at me, including Casey and William.

"Seriously?! Get a room," I screeched at them. They didn't say anything. Casey leaned into him even harder as she smiled widely in my direction, clearly taking pleasure in my outburst while William looked down at me, embarrassed I had made a scene, I'm sure. I stormed off to Sociology. William kept the touching to a minimum after my outburst at least, but I still had to see and listen to them. I wished he would go back to using her locker.

I hate the fact that I barely want to see him. Everything I loved I now resent. I hate that our lockers are next to each other. I hate that we have the same route in the hallway. I hate not being able to talk to him, and I also hate that I feel this way too. It's not fair that I am suffering and he isn't even fazed.

I barely drink anymore though when I'm with my coworkers. I still hang out with Derek, Jayden, and Brent, but if they are drinking, I will only have one and then I cut myself off.

I'm getting better at not giving into peer pressure from them. I'm proud of myself for that. Plus, after Hayden and William got super angry with me, it did in fact make me realize I hadn't been coping well.

I'm seeing a therapist now too. My parents had noticed my mood changes and how William wasn't around anymore. Since I wouldn't talk to my parents about what was going on, they wanted me to talk to a professional.

He uses my full name during our sessions, which I hate of course. When adults who don't know you refer to you by your full name, I don't know, it just always rubs me wrong. It's as if they're somehow looking down on me.

I'd use his full name if I could, but his name is literally Earl, so he doesn't have a nickname. Earl is married with three sons (at least according to the picture on his end table, next to the chair he sits in across from me). If it weren't for his wife, I'm not sure he would have much insight into how an eighteen-year-old female who lost her best guy friend to an insanely manipulative sophomore, and who was dealing with the fear of graduating high school and having to make new friends all over, probably feels . . . but whatever. I was only there because my mom's health insurance was covering it, and I knew it would make my parents sleep better at night.

"And how are you sleeping at night?" Earl asked me. These were his typical questions. Anytime I talked about the other people in my life, he always turned the conversation immediately back on me. He wanted to know my personal thoughts and feelings. He thought I was "projecting" my frustrations with William and Casey back onto my parents and the other adults in my life.

"I've been sleeping like a rock with the fan on," I said sarcastically, although mostly true. My sleep wasn't really being affected; I just kept having dreams about *him*. Nightmares really. I don't tell Earl though, because then we'll probably go down the rabbit hole of dreams and I don't want that.

We focused a lot on my relationship with my parents, but particularly my dad and my relationship. With my dad being the prominent male role-model in my life and all. We talked about the similar traits and qualities my dad and William share and what I'm looking for in a future husband.

"Whoa, Earl! I haven't even graduated high school. I'm not looking for a husband yet. I still need to get my college degree and my career going before marriage."

"I'm glad to hear that, Allison, but whether we're conscious of it or not, we constantly are seeking people who share the same qualities as our parents or guardians. We know love by what we have witnessed growing up. You love your friends, right?"

"Yeah."

"When you go to college and you start making new friends, there's a high chance your new friends will remind you a lot of your current friends. You'll make new male friends at college as well. You said William is planning to attend a university in the south somewhere, is that right?"

"Yeah, Arizona or Texas probably."

"Well, when you attend the University of Kansas and start meeting new men, they will probably share a lot of similar traits William has."

Ew, "new men." what a thing to say. Also, does that mean I'm going to meet new guys that will be friends with me and then ditch me once they get a girlfriend? Because I'm definitely avoiding them! Next session he wants to talk about my issues and feelings toward Casey. Joy . . .

April

I still have a gaping hole in my heart from William. I feel like I've lost the other half of myself. I don't even mean that romantically. William was my everything as a friend. We knew what the other was thinking without anything needing to be said. We could read each other better than any parent could read their child. It felt like we spent all our time together, and now it's gone. He has Casey. He has somebody to continue with, but me, I don't have anybody.

Okay, I have my girlfriends, who are trying their best to help me, but they're not William and they never can be. I don't know how to move on from this. It's like I'm being haunted by the ghost of my former best friend, all the while, he's completely alive and well and totally happy with his life while I'm learning to live with all of my broken pieces.

Senior Prom—the last social event before graduation day.

Once again, I needed to find someone to ask to the prom. I just realized that I had never been asked to a dance, I've always done the asking. To quote Chelsea, "You're a strong, independent woman. You don't need any guy to ask you, you can ask any guy you want!"

"Thanks, Chels. I'll probably ask Felix Junk." (It's pronounced like Young, but with a "K" on the end). "We have Sociology together."

"Oh . . . he's . . . cute." She forced a smile and tried to sound supportive.

I mean, he's not ugly by any means. He's a very average, boy next door kind of guy. Like me, honestly, except, I'm the girl version, of course.

"Thanks, I just have no idea how to ask him. Yeah, we know each other and have talked briefly in the classes we've had together, but we're not like friends. We've never associated with each other outside of school."

She shrugged and gave a simple answer. I honestly wasn't sure if she was serious or not at first. "Send him a pizza with 'PROM?' spelled out in pepperoni. The delivery guy can drop it off and you won't even have to watch him open the box."

"Chelsea, that's a good idea!" She was smiling ear to ear in satisfaction.

I went home that night and knew the first thing I would need was his address.

How on earth do I get his address without seeming like a stalker?!

I decided to try an old phonebook my parents hadn't pulled out of the office drawer since the dawn of the world wide web. To my luck, and the luck of a lot of descendants, there was only one family in Greenwood, Kansas with the last name of Junk.

I was nervous to call Geraldo's Pizza Shop.

What if they won't do this for me? What if his parents are cooking supper and they get upset that I sent a pizza? What if he thinks I'm creepy and doesn't even want to go with me? This could be a waste of money doubled with embarrassment.

I mustered the courage and called Geraldo's Pizza Shop anyway. Thankfully, this wasn't the first time they had done this for people. I thanked them graciously, asked if they could write, "From Alli Manex in Sociology," and then tipped generously as well.

Now I wait until tomorrow.

"Hey, Alli, thanks for the pizza last night, it was perfect," Felix said, sitting next to me in class.

I had been sweating all morning waiting for class. "Oh, yeah, no problem. I was afraid I'd upset your parents by spoiling whatever they were planning."

"Oh nah, don't worry about that at all. We were having meatloaf anyway and my dad always cooks it until it's extremely dry, so the pizza was a good save."

I gave him a polite smile, but all the while, I was dying on the inside waiting for him to reveal his answer to my question. He was laying out his notebook and pen on his desk as our teacher was about to start class.

"By the way, Alli, my answer is yes, I'll go with you." He smiled over at me. I sighed aloud in relief which made him chuckle and our teacher asked me if there was anything I needed to get off my chest before we started.

"No, sorry. I'm okay," I said, smiling over at Felix who was silently laughing to himself.

My senior prom dress was navy, fitted, with a flattering square neckline to my face, and a small train that I could bustle before dancing. It had a corset back and exposed boning around my chest and rib cage. It had rose-gold flowers sprinkled throughout. I was absolutely in *love*! I couldn't stop twirling in front of the store's mirror. After Mom and I bought it, I kept trying it on at home up until the night of prom when I could leave the house in it.

My girlfriends and I decided to only tell each other the colors of our dresses and nothing more. We wanted to surprise each other for our last dance. Evelynn and Hayden both wore black dresses. Evelynn's was velvet and fitted to her perfect figure. Hayden's was an A-line made of satin material. It was fitted to her waist, then it flared out. It also had pockets which is really convenient.

Rose's dress was burgundy. It was mermaid style with one shoulder and a herring-bone pattern of sparkle across the entire dress. Chelsea's was ice blue on top that grew into a darker blue the further down you went on the dress. It was sequined from head to toe. She too had a train like mine that we were going to need to bustle once we hit the dance floor. I was jealous she could wear a strapless dress. She has the boobs for it whereas I do not.

To match me, Felix wore a navy tuxedo and a rose gold tie. He looked great in it! Against Evelynn's wishes, Kyle wore a white tuxedo. She said he had always wanted to wear a white tuxedo, but Evelynn never wanted him to.

Good for him to wear what he wanted though.

Morris wore a burgundy suit that matched Rose's dress. It was a slightly different shade, but close enough. The rest of the guys wore black tuxes and a coordinating tie depending on the dress color of their date.

This year we rented a limousine for all of us to ride in together. We had a nice size group to split the cost, otherwise my parents would have made me pay for my portion with my own money. We went to a Thai Cuisine restaurant for something different. Only one other prom group was there when we arrived, which was good because the restaurant didn't have much seating left with two groups taking up most of the chairs.

Felix talked with Kyle a lot throughout the night. Like me, Kyle and Felix didn't hang out outside of school, but they had more mutual friends than Felix and I did. I was happy to see him have somebody besides me to talk to. He was having a good time.

It's as if William and I were still on the same orbit pattern. Who just happened to be in line outside the school when we got out of the limo? *Them!* My eyes found his while her arm wrapped around his body in response. She was wearing a lavender two-piece prom dress with silver beads throughout the bodice. The color really made her dark hair pop in contrast. Yes, she looked beautiful just as she did at the New Year's Dance, I can still admit that.

I *tried* to focus solely on my group the entire night, I really did, but I could sense him I swear. I still felt very in tune with him; like two magnets trying to find one another. When I looked over Felix's shoulder during a slow dance, they were dancing two people away. William and I made eye contact, and oddly enough, he didn't drop his eye contact with me like he'd been doing for the last however many months things have been weird between us. I stared at him back, trying to figure out the expression on his face, and eventually he looked away and focused his attention back on Casey. I inched closer to Felix, and he tightened his grip around me in response.

What was William thinking during our eye contact??

I'm not sure if Felix knew my history with William, but if he did, he never said anything the way Derek did when he noticed me staring at the happy couple all night.

I had an enjoyable time with Felix, and of course my friends, but despite my best effort I was still sad on the inside. I don't think my senior prom is going to be a prominent memory in my brain.

At least I hope it isn't.

CHAPTER 27

May

Our last full month of school had arrived. Commencement would be June 10th and I was beyond ready to graduate. It was something I was nervous about at the beginning of the school year, and I still was, but I was ready. I was done. I was over coming to the same school every single day of my life and having to see and hear him next to me, but not be able to communicate with him.

I had started wishing that he wouldn't even come to his locker anymore, then I wouldn't have to hear her thrill of excitement upon seeing him and endure their constant touching. They walked the halls holding hands, they kissed at his locker, she over touched his body when I was around as if I was going to randomly jump into his arms. Anytime she and I made eye contact I wanted to smack the grin off her face.

Trying to move on from him and pretend he didn't exist anymore had been the hardest thing in my entire life. I'd listened to the sad songs, I'd vented to my girlfriends to the point of exhaustion, and more water had flowed from my eyes than anything Niagara Falls could produce. I cried my way through writing a poem, but at the end, I felt something

I hadn't felt in a long, long time. I felt like maybe I could be okay after all.

WHAT TIME CAN DO

I think it's time,
In fact, I know,
But the hardest part is trying to let go.
We both have our memories to cherish and hold.
I hope one day they will be good enough to be told.
At first, I was mad,
And then I was sad,
But at the end of it all, through the good and the bad,
I will always smile when I look back on what we had.
Moving on isn't easy,
Especially when I think about our time spent together,
It can start to make me queasy.

What you did to me wasn't fair,
I put all my effort into us and it's like you didn't even care.
I can say this,
You taught me a big lesson,
Falling in love can be a deadly weapon.
One thing that I'm proud to say,
The time I spent with you never came unwelcomed.
You will always be a part of my life.
A happy memory,
A good laugh,
A tear or two;
I will never forget you.
I do hope you think of me,
At least once in a blue moon,
I hope our memories will make you smile the way I do.

Earl thought it would be good for me to imagine my life a few years from now and that's where this poem came from. I was imagining my life after college, being on my own and starting my career as an adult. I was trying to visualize being healed. I'd try anything to make this pain go away.

I was shocked William still had me on social media as a friend. I figured she would have made him delete me. I would never admit to my therapist or closest friends how often I creeped on his profiles. Since he hadn't blocked me, all the photos I had taken of him were there, and I still had him tagged, which meant he still potentially could be looking back at them too!

Yeah right; that's just wishful thinking.

During one of my creeping sessions, I was looking through photos of him on Facebook when I saw the newest picture Casey had tagged him in. It was William holding his acceptance letter from the college he had decided to attend.

I CAN NOT BELIEVE THIS! William is going to be attending the University of Kansas with me.

I squealed aloud and danced around my room. Dad poked his head in to make sure everything was okay, and I told him things were great. He was happy to see me smiling.

The next day at school I decided to attempt a conversation with him once again. I knew he'd told me not to, but I couldn't help it. This was huge! I thought after high school I would never see him, but now I'd get the chance to see him around campus, and maybe even have a freshman class with him.

I waited until after lunch when I knew Casey wouldn't be around. "University of Kansas, huh?" I asked him at his locker.

"Yeah," was all he responded with.

"What made you decide to go there?" I asked, desperately trying to continue any form of communication.

"I want to be close to Casey. I can come home any weekend, and she can visit."

Choosing a college based on your high school relationship, classic mistake, but honestly, I'm grateful for this decision right now.

"Did you end up applying to the University of Texas and Arizona?"

"Just Texas. They accepted me in April," he said casually.

I tried to be nonchalant with my voice. I couldn't let the excitement I felt scare him off now. "Are you still looking into forensics?" I asked.

"Yeah, I got into the Criminal Justice program which is the first step," he said, throwing his bag over his shoulder.

"Well congratulations. I am really proud of you," I said, beaming at him.

William cracked a side smile toward me, and my heart reacted to seeing it. He hadn't smiled any kind of smile at me in months. The smile on my face grew even larger and for a split second I thought he would walk with me to class, but he didn't. He told me thank you and headed off toward the library instead of the class he had next.

Graduation parties are happening every weekend from now until post-graduation. I'm not invited to a ton, in comparison to the size of our class, but I have a couple of handfuls I would like to go to, including Derek's. I've only seen him when we work the same shifts. I haven't hung out with him or our coworkers in a while. Partly because it's getting old sitting around and drinking in a garage, but mostly because I've just been busy with my own stuff going on. I'm trying to make sure I do well on my homework, I'm wanting to spend my free time with my girlfriends, and also, I have my therapy sessions I'm going to every Thursday.

Unfortunately, Hayden's and my graduation parties overlap entirely, but otherwise, I'll be able to make it to all my friends' parties. I debated heavily on whether to invite William to mine or not. I figured on one hand it would be normal and I wanted to make sure he knew he was welcomed; on the other hand, I didn't want Casey to find the invite or hear about it and then give him hell, which in turn could cause us to somehow drift further apart.

Like that's possible. Actually, don't even think that because something, somehow could honestly happen considering how my luck has been going.

It was the week before finals and two weeks until we graduated. I couldn't believe this! It was crazy to realize this chapter of my life was about to end. I would no longer be a student at Greenwood High School. I'd no longer see my best friends every single day. I wouldn't be living with my parents anymore.

I don't think people have talked enough about this transitioning period. This had been my entire life for eighteen years, and now I was practically about to be on my own.

I cannot possibly be responsible or mature enough for this! How does society trust any eighteen year old to make adult decisions?! We can barely cook to feed ourselves. That's probably why they still have cafeterias at college, so we don't starve immediately.

For my journalism class, we must write a two-page column reflecting on our memories of high school. This was going to be published in our school paper that would be handed out at graduation, so we need to be professional.

I opened my notebook and realized I had grabbed my science notebook by accident. I asked my teacher if it was okay for me to run to my locker and grab the correct notebook. I spun the combination to my locker without needing to think about it. I could probably do it blindfolded. When I pulled my locker open, a piece of paper fell out and landed on my right foot. Confused, I leaned down and picked it up. On one side was a handwritten note that said,

Poppy,

I don't blame you if you don't want to come, but you are invited.

-Hoppy

The memory of these nicknames instantly flashed through my mind. *Last year, he and I were playing basketball against each other. He was taking it easy on me, but he was still winning. I didn't care, I was enjoying breaking the rules by wrapping my arms around him, giving him a bear hug, and claiming that I was only trying to steal the ball. I didn't care if I was fouling him, and he didn't seem to mind. Every now and then he would grab me around the waist and lift me off the ground when I was going in for a lay-up. We were laughing and having fun like we always did.*

He was shooting around for fun while I went to get a piece of gum from my bag. When I came back onto the court, he was attempting to dunk the ball.

"Nice hops you got!" I shouted at him. He flashed an amused smile at me while I laughed in return, popping my gum.

"Oh yeah? Let's see you try it, Poppy!" he teased back.

"Alright Hoppy, let me show you how it's done!" I took the ball from him and headed back to half court so I could get a solid running start. I started dribbling toward the hoop, but when I got to the free throw line, I picked up the ball, traveled with it, and attempted to "dunk" it.

What that entailed was me overestimating my athletic ability. I knew I wasn't going to be able to reach the rim by any means, but I thought I could get more air than I did. I was able to reach the net, but as I shot the ball, my legs kept going forward while my torso went backwards. I twisted in the air so I wouldn't land on my back and risk hitting my head on the concrete below. Instead, I landed on my left side, hard.

William came sprinting over to me as fast as he could. "Oh my god, Alli! Are you okay?!"

I rolled onto my back and sat up. My left arm was scraped up and my hand was the worst part. "Ow." was all I could manage. I was thankful I didn't hit my head or lose the air out of my lungs, but I was in a lot of pain.

"Come on, let's get you home and cleaned up." He bent down and scooped me up in his arms. I didn't protest.

When we got back to my house, I walked myself inside and we headed upstairs to the bathroom so I could clean my arm and hands. William offered to do it for me, but I protested this time. As gentle as he can be, I was afraid he would rub too hard on my raw skin, and I would look like a baby in front of him.

I joked with him as I washed the dirt and pebbles from my arm. "Maybe I should be Hoppy; did you see how much air I got?"

He laughed, but I could tell he felt bad and was blaming himself. "I think you better stick with Poppy and leave the hops to me, okay?"

"Hoppy and Poppy. I like it."

I flipped over the note and on the back was his graduation invite. I was thrilled yet confused.

This is really from him, right? I mean, he has our nicknames, but who's to say this isn't some prank by Casey and her friends to embarrass me if I show up? Do I ask him about this? Should I verify before I show up? If he doesn't want to be friends, why would he invite me to his graduation party?

I was going to ask him about it. I had too many questions, but the main one I needed answered was, "What does this mean for us?"

Should I invite him to mine then? They're thankfully not on the same day. Mine is on Sunday and his is the Saturday before mine.

I didn't text him. I wanted to talk to him face to face and I decided that after last period, I would. I needed to make this quick, though; I didn't want Casey getting there and interrupting anything.

Does she know about this? I can't imagine she would "allow" this.

Why are people so ridiculous in relationships too? "Allowed." He's eighteen years old, he does not need her permission for his own party! Not to mention, I know him. He wouldn't even have this party if it were up to him. He would have friends over and a bonfire like always.

I packed up my backpack five minutes before I got out of my last class. I know that drives teachers nuts because once one student starts packing up, everyone does, and today, I was *that* person. I didn't care though. I needed to get to my locker as soon as possible in the hopes that William would be there without her attached to him.

I opened my locker, but I didn't put any of my books away. I had to make sure I saw him the second he got here.

There he is! He's alone, good, but I still don't have much time. Ugh, I love the way he walks with his backpack on one shoulder. It would sound crazy outside of my head, but he looks extra attractive the way he carries it! Focus, Alli, focus. I need to make this quick.

I held up the invitation to him so he could see it. "Is this actually from you?"

He fumbled with his locker combination, but he looked over at me with half a smirk. "Of course, it is. I thought the Poppy would give it away."

"Well, it did, but I just needed to make sure, because honestly, I'm confused."

"Look. It's just an invitation to my graduation party. If you don't want to come that's okay, I—"

"No!" I cut him off. "No, of course I want to come, but . . . I thought you didn't want to talk to me? I thought you didn't want to be friends, and last

I checked, people don't invite people to their own party if they're not friends with them."

He looked me in the eyes. "If you want to come, you can. If you don't want to, I understand."

That wasn't an explanation, but I'll take it. "Does Casey know about this?" I made sure to use her name and not make it sound like there was vomit in my mouth as well.

He looked down at the ground and shook his head. "No. She doesn't."

"Why wouldn't you tell her?" I asked, still confused, but giddy knowing he was doing something that may upset her. He invited me because he wanted to and not because she was allowing it.

"If you don't come, I won't have to explain anything to her. If you do, then I'll just tell her the truth."

"And what's the truth?" I asked even though his answer made it obvious.

"That I invited you. Look, you're reading into this way more than you need to. Again, you're invited if you want to come, and I'll see you there if you do. If not, don't worry about it."

I shifted my weight on my feet and noticed Casey was headed our way. I quickly turned toward my locker and put the invitation back in there. William noticed my change of expression and turned to look over his shoulder.

"Hey babe!" she said, wrapping her arms around him and bringing him in for a kiss.

Our conversation was over. I didn't want to risk saying anything more, especially in front of her. I heard him say hi back to her and fiddle with his own backpack, as I did with mine. I gathered what I needed to study for finals and got the heck out of there. I was still confused, but he was right, I was overthinking this. He invited me, he even said it in person, and of course I was going to go!

I practically skipped out to my car. I was beaming from ear to ear. I found it ironic that I *just* wrote a poem accepting how it was time to move on and how I hope he thinks of me in the future, and boom, just like that, he reached out.

Clearly, I need to write more poems if this is what comes out of them.

I raided Evelynn's closet for a dress. I needed to look perfect for his party! My friends were a little skeptical of me going. They don't want me to get my hopes up.

I settled on her maroon (*sorry, I mean wine*) colored dress. It goes to my thighs, but it's on the shorter end. I'll just need to be cautious if I bend over. I'll need to be more lady-like, as my mother always said while I was growing up. The dress also has a high-neck neckline with an open corset in the back. I'm going to dress it down with white sandals. I don't want to go overboard and look unnatural in heels.

Rose got ready at my house with me this morning. We had a couple of graduation parties to stop at before William's. I made Rose drive because I knew if I drove us, I could easily chicken out and decide not to go after all.

She curled my hair and helped apply a little make up on me. Nothing heavy; again, I needed to look nice, but not *desperate nice* you know?

"Alright, Alli, it's time to go," Rose said, checking her hair one more time in the mirror before looking at me.

I was sitting on my bed watching her finish. I was frozen in place. "I . . . I don't think I can do this."

Stupid nerves!! I knew this would happen.

"Of course, you can, Sky," she said, coming to sit on the bed next to me. "We have a couple of stops to make first and hopefully that will ease you into realizing that you *can* do this." She grabbed me by the hand and pulled me onto my feet. "Plus, when we get to his house, I will be with you the entire time. I won't let Casey do anything to stop you from enjoying this. And remember, *he* invited *you*. He wants you there."

I took a deep breath, thanking her for doing this with me. She hugged me, and we headed out the door to our first party. Anna, our classmate, had been in theater with Rose since middle school. Outside of our group, Rose and Anna would hang out occasionally. They both are shy humans, so it's crazy when you watch them perform on stage. They really do become entirely different people. They did a play once where Anna had to go crazy and run around screaming incoherent things on stage. She did amazing! I literally thought she wasn't as put together as she appeared because she made crazy look so natural. Seeing her now, as we talked about graduation, made me realize how many classmates in our grade I don't truly know. All the thoughts and fears that everyone has. It's universal.

We had two more parties to swing by, but we kept these brief. One was Bonnie's from French class. She decided she would like to become a French teacher. Honestly, she'll do great at it too. She's amazing at everything she does. I just hope she has a lot of patience with her future students.

The second was another friend of Rose's. His name was Tucker, and he was in band with her. I felt bad when we got to his house; Tucker didn't seem to have many people at his graduation party, so I was hoping they were all coming later.

We said goodbye to Tucker, which meant it was time to head to William's. Rose checked in with me to make sure I was okay. "If you really don't want to go, we don't have to."

"No. We should," I managed to tell her. I knew if I spoke too much my voice would start shaking like my fingers already were.

If I had been driving right now, I would be clutching the steering wheel until my knuckles were white. Rose would probably have had to pry me off the steering wheel once we arrived.

When we pulled up, there were a lot more vehicles here than there were at Tucker's; about three times as many, if not four.

Maybe we should have invited Tucker to leave his own party and join us? No, he'll be okay; you have other things to worry about.

I managed to open the door when Rose did and got out when she did. She immediately came to my side in a show of support. She didn't take my arm or hand like Chelsea would have. Rose knows how to support by being close in proximity but not making a show of it. I didn't want it to look as though I was here against my will, or that I wasn't invited, because I was.

I was scanning the crowd immediately, but I couldn't see him yet. I was also looking for Casey, but I didn't see her either.

Maybe she's not here yet? HAH, YEAH RIGHT. I can almost sense her presence as much as I can William's.

Morris greeted us with his usual, friendly and large smile. He wrapped Rose in a hug but didn't kiss her. Hugging was about the only PDA they shared.

"Where's William?" I asked after saying hello to Morris.

He pointed toward the garage. "He's in there with his family and guests. A lot of us are hanging out in the shed."

I nodded at him and then turned to Rose. "Should we go say hi?" she asked me. I nodded again in response but didn't say anything.

We started walking toward the garage where we could hear the most talking coming from. I turned back toward Morris because I needed to know before I got there. "Is Casey here?" I asked him, hoping I sounded normal. I didn't want to sound scared, but my fingers hadn't stopped shaking yet.

"Yeah, she doesn't actually leave his side . . . like ever," Morris said with a puzzled expression.

"I've noticed." We continued walking.

I let Rose and Morris do the talking because I wasn't listening. I was silently praying Casey wouldn't do anything once she saw me.

Please don't make a scene, please don't make a scene! Also, please don't throw a drink on me because I borrowed this dress and even I don't want Casey to have to endure Evelynn's wrath if her dress got ruined. Then again . . . no, no, Evelynn is very protective of her clothes.

We stepped into the garage and my eyes locked with William's. A smile crept onto my face. He was talking with his grandma. She was showing him some pictures. It didn't take long at all, but I could sense the daggers being slung in my direction. Sure enough, Casey was standing next to him. I either didn't notice her at first because I was entranced by him, or Grandma was blocking her from my view. Either way, Casey had a furious look on her face.

I swallowed and tried to muster my courage.

I am here. I was invited. I am okay, I reminded myself.

Rose pointed to the guest book, and we walked over there to sign it.

I was finishing signing my last name when I heard a familiar squeal. "Alli!"

It was Charlotte. She was running toward me with her arms open for a hug. I set the pen down and reached out in response to her. We embraced for the first time in months. Right then, I realized how much I'd missed seeing her too. I'd been so distracted with missing William that I hadn't realized how much I'd missed his family too. Well Charlotte and his mom anyway; his dad still scared me. Their mom was behind Charlotte, and I gave her a hug next.

"Hi sweetie! It's so good to see you!" She embraced me as well. They smelled like him.

"Hi Jenny, it's great to see you." I hugged her tightly.

"Let's talk later, Alli, before you leave." She squeezed my hands and I nodded. "Please, help yourself to the food and beverages inside. We have walking tacos, a meat and cheese tray, Pepsi, and more." She winked at me. I blushed, realizing even his mom knew my love for Pepsi. "I'll get Mother so you can say hi to Will. She's showing him photos of him from when he was younger. The same ones she shows every Christmas." Jenny shook her head but was smiling. "Follow me, you guys."

We did. I made sure to double check that Rose was right behind me though. She touched my elbow in acknowledgement.

"Mom," Jenny said, touching her mother on the shoulders and speaking up. "Mom, some of Will's friends are here and would like to say hi to him."

"Oh, yes. Don't mind me," she said in her adorable elderly voice. "I'm just showing William some pictures of him when he was younger. He looks so much like his grandfather when he was younger. He gets more handsome every year, don't you think?" his grandmother said, grabbing his chin playfully.

"Yeah, he does," Casey and I said in unison. We looked at each other startled. She instantly glared at me, and I averted my gaze in response.

"You see, I'm not the only one who thinks you're handsome. You have two beautiful women next to you who agree with your old grandmother."

You have no idea how true those words are, Grandma!

364

"Okay, Mom, I think you're embarrassing him. Let's go sit with Dad now. You kids have fun." His mom smiled at all of us politely but noticed the tension in the air that Grandma was oblivious to.

William stood up and hugged me. I wrapped my arms around him and squeezed tightly. He squeezed back a little bit to indicate he was letting go. I didn't want to, obviously, but I needed to. I stepped to the side so he could hug Rose next. I peeked over at Casey. If she had something sharper than daggers in her eyes, she was shooting them at me with full force.

"So, is this your guys' first party today?" he asked us.

I meant to answer his question, but all I managed to do was stare at him with my mouth partially opened.

When I still didn't say anything, Rose spoke up. "No, we've been to three already today."

"Oh cool. Who did you see?" he asked, looking at Rose since she was able to speak.

"We went to Anna Roberts' first, then Bonnie Grunger's, and we just came from Tucker O'Neil's."

"I'm hoping to swing by Tucker's at some point today," William said.

"That would be nice," I finally spoke. William looked at me and I continued to talk, and talk, and talk, because that's what happens when I get nervous; I babble on.

"It would just be nice because when we were there, there weren't many people. I mean there were some people obviously, but not as many as you have here, or that anybody else had at the other graduation parties we went to. Even if you were able to swing by after his party ended, I think he'd really appreciate that."

I could have kept going, but he held up his hand to stop me; he was chuckling. "Don't worry, Alli, I will definitely swing by his place today."

Casey stalked off angrily, but William ignored her and, in that instance, I felt at ease. I felt like me being here was actually okay with him.

More guests arrived, I'm guessing more family or friends of his family, because I didn't recognize anybody in the group.

"Well, like Mom said, food and drinks are inside. Help yourself. Everyone from our class is hanging out in the shed. Morris, you probably need to check on Peter soon, who knows what trouble he's causing or *thing* he is breaking as we speak. I'll be over in a bit when I can."

Like the good host he is, he wanted to make sure to greet everyone and talk to those he hadn't seen in a while. I selfishly thought I would fall into that category, but I would talk to him when I could.

We headed inside to scope out the food. I didn't realize how hungry I was until now. The entire morning I hadn't eaten anything because I was too nervous. Now that I felt better and a little calmer, I was famished. Charlotte was in charge of overseeing the kitchen. She refilled chips, toppings, or beverages when needed.

"Plates and forks are here, and drinks are over in the coolers." She indicated to the four Igloo coolers.

"Thanks, Charlotte, you are very professional. I think you may have a career in hosting ahead of you!" I said, making her smile more than what she already was.

"Thank you, but I'm going to be a singer, remember?" she corrected.

"Ah, yes that's right."

"Yup! I'm going to be even more famous than Taylor Swift, you'll see!" she said excitedly.

"You know what? I have a feeling you *are* going to be bigger than Taylor Swift. In fact, can I get your autograph now before you rise to the top?"

"Absolutely! You can be my first." She grabbed a napkin and a sharpie out of their junk drawer. She scribbled her name, which was three lines of pure chicken scratch, and handed it to me with pride. "I've been practicing writing my name really fast so I can crank out the autographs in the future," she explained.

"I appreciate you taking the time to socialize with the little people. Remember us." I winked at her, and she laughed.

We headed out to the shed with our plates of food to meet up with whoever else was there. All of William's friends whom I used to hang out with were here, Danny, Grant, Peter, and of course Morris. Naturally, Peter was the one to point out the obvious.

"Whoa, is that Alli Manex?! At Will's house, *while* Casey the girlfriend is here as well?!"

I rolled my eyes in annoyance while some of his friends laughed quietly. "Shut it, Peter."

"Is there going to be a cat fight later?!" he said, continuing in his teasing state.

"Of course not." I took a bite of my walking taco trying to ignore him and the eyes that were on me. The other people here were classmates of ours and one or two juniors William had class with. I remembered him telling me about them once. They're in his morning weightlifting class.

Thankfully William, followed by an upset Casey, came in and pulled up a chair. "What did I miss?" he asked, looking around at the now silent group.

"Nothing really." Peter shrugged, then added, "I think there may have been two cats fighting outside though. Did you guys hear anything when you came in?" He gave me the side eye with a stupid smirk. I glared back at him and looked at William to see his reaction. He thankfully was confused and said he didn't hear anything.

There was an obvious chair Casey could have sat in next to William, but oh no, she needed to mark her territory by sitting on his lap instead.

Was that a hint of annoyance on his face?

We sat in a group talking about what our plans are after high school. Danny and Grant will be attending the University of Kansas with me, Rose, Hayden, and of course William. Peter is going to attend our rival school of Kansas State University, while Morris will be going a lot farther away. He's going to be in New York studying theater.

Poor Rose. I know this has been on her mind a lot.

"I can't wait for when we play each other. We'll have the best tailgate party going on. All the chicks will be hanging out with us, and of course beer!" Peter enthused.

"Alli knows all about the booze. Don't ya?" Casey said, cocking her head to the side and looking at me with a smirk I wanted to rip from her face.

"Wait what?" Grant chimed in, completely surprised by Casey's snide comment.

I rolled my eyes directly at her. "It's nothing. I've been to a couple parties at the community college here in town."

"You drink?" Peter said, genuinely shocked.

"I have, yes."

He got up from his chair and gave me a high five. "Atta girl!! I didn't realize you were that kind of girl."

I was happy he wasn't giving me crap. I smiled over at Casey who was once again glaring at me; her plan to embarrass me was foiled.

"Yeah, well, she's an idiot drinker who drives drunk you know," Casey spat out.

"Casey, stop," William tried quieting her.

"Don't defend her. You were just as upset at her as I was. It's irresponsible and reckless! She could have killed somebody, an innocent person. She'll do it again too; all boozy people do."

The heat rushed to my cheeks and my hands were shaking again.

"First off," I started, trying to stay calm and not argue with her. "It was a major mistake. I own that and I will be the first to admit that, but it won't be happening again."

"Sure. That's what alcoholics always say."

Does she not know his uncle was a true alcoholic?? I can't believe she's talking this way in front of him.

I gave her a head nod and stayed silent. I wasn't going to fight with her, not during the first time I was actually hanging out with William again.

"Casey," William snapped at her, surprising the group and especially Casey.

It was dead silent. I think people were wondering how to change the subject. Naturally, Peter broke it by making a hissing sound, imitating cats. William took that as his cue to dismiss him and Casey to get back to the other party guests.

Thanks a lot.

Rose and I stayed for about thirty more minutes after that. I was ready to leave when William went back to the house, but I didn't want to be rude either. Things in the shed got back to normal and more of our classmates showed up. We repeated the conversation again about our college plans and got to hear theirs as well.

"Before we go, I need to say bye to William and his family," I told Rose.

"That's okay, take your time. I'll be waiting at the car."

She and Morris went left, and I headed right toward the house. I went through the front door this time instead of the garage. I didn't want to walk anywhere near Casey yet. I was still trying to calm my insides down after everything flared up. I found Charlotte and gave her a hug goodbye.

"Don't lose that napkin." She smiled.

"Trust me, I won't. Also, do you know where your mom is by chance?" I asked.

"She's upstairs showing off the house to some of her friends."

I sent a silent thank you to heaven above and then went upstairs to find her. They were in the master bedroom. I stood at the door and knocked, interrupting. The ten eyes looked my way, and Mrs. Mantel smiled at me in greeting.

"Alli, hi dear! Are you taking off?" she asked.

"Hi, sorry for interrupting. Yeah, I am," I said shyly in front of these strangers.

"Okay, stay right there, I'll be right out."

I turned around and took a few steps back into the hallway to give them their privacy once more. I heard her tell them to go and check out the master bathroom, and then she was in the hallway taking me into her arms for a hug goodbye.

"I'm probably overstepping as a mom, but I did want to tell you that Will hasn't been the same since you guys stopped hanging out."

Is that how he summed it up? That we just stopped hanging out suddenly?! I wasn't going to correct his mom though. I didn't need to tell my side of the story, despite wanting to.

"Really?" is what I said instead. My surprise was sincere. I figured he was doing perfectly fine without me.

"Oh, heavens no! Charlotte and I have noticed the change in him. Tom hasn't, but then again, he doesn't show emotions very well, let alone read the room he's in. Anyway, again, I just wanted to tell you that. I don't want to overstep any more than I already am. It was so wonderful seeing you. You look amazing. Where are you going to college again?"

"University of Kansas."

"Oh! So, you and Will just might have a class together! I wish you the best of luck. You're going to do great, sweetie."

I was touched by her sincerity. In fact, I could feel my eyes on the verge of watering, and I needed to suppress that immediately. I was not going to cry in front of her.

"There was one thing I was hoping you could do for me before I go," I hesitantly said.

"Sure, what is it?"

I pulled out an invitation to my graduation party from my purse and handed it to her. "Could you give him my invite? My party is tomorrow."

She brought it to her heart and responded, "Of course I will."

I hesitated once more before adding, "Could you do it when Casey isn't around? I don't want her to sway him one way or the other."

"Absolutely. I will make sure it's done in private." She reached out and touched my forearm in assurance.

I was confident she would deliver it discreetly. I turned around to head to the garage. I wanted to say goodbye to William regardless of Casey standing there. He was talking to Jack from school, and I knew I would be able to sneak in and say goodbye quickly.

I walked up to the three of them, William, Casey, and Jack. I stood there awkwardly for a second until Jack stopped his sentence and turned to say hi to me.

"Hi." I gave an awkward wave. "I didn't mean to interrupt, but I wanted to say goodbye really quick."

"Oh sure," Jack said, stepping to the side like a gentleman so William and I could say goodbye to one another.

He opened his arms for a hug. It wasn't as strong as it was when I arrived, but I still cherished it. I closed my eyes. I wasn't going to look at Casey.

"Thank you for coming, Poppy," he whispered into my ear.

"Thank you for the invitation, Hoppy," I whispered back.

I gave him a parting last look and then headed to Rose's car so I could go home and prepare for my graduation party tomorrow.

Now I'll wait and see if he comes or not.

CHAPTER 28

He didn't come to my graduation party. For the entire three hours, I kept thinking he would show, but it never happened. I checked my phone at least 100 times for a text saying he was running late or that he would swing by later that evening because he couldn't make it during the 11–2 timeframe that my party was at, but the text never came. Once again, I got my hopes up just to be let down.

It was finals week, and our last week at Greenwood High School. As a senior, we only need to show up for our scheduled finals, otherwise we don't need to be at school until Friday to practice for commencement.

I didn't see William at any point during the week. I thought maybe if I ran into him at our lockers he would apologize or give me a reason as to why he didn't show, but he was silent, and I didn't reach out to him. I was tired of being disappointed.

I wished I hadn't gone to his stupid graduation party. Well . . . that isn't completely true because I was able to talk to him and get two hugs which I loved. I suppose what I regret is that I invited him to my party. I gave him a hole back into my life again.

What if his mom didn't give him my invitation? No, she wouldn't do that. Of course she would have given it to him. What if Casey had found it first? She definitely would not have given it to him, or she could have shown it to him and forbade him from attending.

The worst thought I had, though, was that his mom gave it to him privately, and he decided on his own that he just didn't want to go. Maybe Casey wasn't a factor, and he genuinely just didn't want to see me.

But then WHY would he invite me to his party?! I don't understand him! I don't have time for this either. I have finals I need to be focusing on, not to mention graduating and coming to terms with the fact that I won't be seeing my best friends every single day anymore once summer ends. I need to focus on them. They're the ones that have been with me through thick and thin forever and they're not going to go anywhere, unlike somebody I know . . . well, knew.

On Friday, I learned two things about our commencement practice: it was an hour long, and we (like our locker assignments) were in alphabetical order by last name. Translation, I was stuck next to William for an hour, and it was awkwardly uncomfortable.

It wasn't supposed to be this way.

We didn't say anything to each other when they had us line up next to our walking partner. We ignored each other like the strangers we were. It wasn't until the third time we were practicing the walk-in portion that I couldn't hold back anymore.

"Why didn't you come to my graduation party?" I stared at him, but he wouldn't look at me.

"You know why . . ." was his response.

"Obviously I don't, otherwise I wouldn't be asking you right now," I snapped. I was trying to keep my voice down, but I knew the classmates in front and behind us could hear me. I needed to keep my temper, but I also wanted an explanation from him too.

He didn't say anything, so I persisted with my interrogation, "Did your mom give you my invite?"

"Yes."

"Did your girlfriend see it or something then?"

"No."

"So, then what? What made you decide that it was okay for you to invite me to yours, but that you couldn't attend mine?"

He inhaled and ran his fingers through his beautiful, brown hair. When he lifted his arm, I caught a whiff of his scent. I had forgotten how sweet it was. It made my mind spin for a second. I had to re-ground myself and remind myself what we were doing right now.

"I wasn't going to go to your party because Casey would have been even more upset at me than she already was. She was mad enough that I invited you to my party."

"So? You knew that when you invited me. That if I showed, she would have been pissed, but you invited me anyway. I don't buy that excuse. Why didn't you come?"

"I told her last night that it was my party, and I could invite anybody I wanted to, and I stood by that, but that didn't give me the right to go to yours," he explained.

That wasn't a good enough answer for me. I pushed on; I wasn't afraid of losing him anymore. I wasn't afraid of "pushing him away" either. He was already gone.

"It's still your own life, William. You can do what you want."

"Oh yeah, that's *great* relationship advice, Alli. Thanks," he sarcastically sneered, rolling his eyes at me.

We were sitting down in our seats now while our speakers practiced going on stage with their notes and making sure everything sounded okay.

I didn't say anything to his sarcastic remark. I wasn't sure what there *was* to say. It felt like we were dancing again. I thought he never wanted to see or hear from me again. I was coming to terms with that. It was slower than paint drying, but I was trying, and then there he went, inviting me to his party and hugging me as if he hadn't ripped my heart out and shattered me into pieces.

I didn't talk to him for the rest of practice, and he didn't attempt anything either. There was an iron wall between us again. When we were finally dismissed, we went to our separate friend groups to have lunch.

"That's such a stupid 'reason,'" Chelsea declared, putting air quotes around the word reason.

"He is confusing," Hayden chimed in.

"That's not okay. He should have come to your grad party, or he never should have invited you to his in the first place," Evelynn stated, and the girls nodded in agreement.

"Tell me about it," I said, swirling my fry in ketchup but not feeling very hungry.

"Do you think you'll be okay during the ceremony tomorrow?" Rose asked, touching my hand.

I shrugged in response, but I didn't say anything.

"This is supposed to be a monumental time in life!" Evelynn took it upon herself to try and cheer me up. "You have survived thirteen years of school. You're about to head to college with Rose and Hayden. You're going to meet a *ton* of new and cute guys, and you're about to have a career in a field you're extremely passionate about! Yes, tomorrow will probably be hard since you have to literally sit next to him, but after that, a new chapter starts for you, Sky."

Again, my friends nodded in agreement with her.

"Cheers to new beginnings!" Chelsea said, raising her glass of Mountain Dew.

We all lifted our drinks and clanked the plastic cups from the restaurant. I smiled in appreciation of them, but I was still aching inside.

My friends and I agreed we would all be wearing white dresses for graduation day. Mine was a solid white, short dress. It was fitted and had ruching throughout the entire dress. My mom wasn't a fan of it; she said it looked like the inside of a coffin. Evelynn's and Rose's dresses had lace on them. Evelynn's had an open back, while Rose's was a modest dress with lace sleeves. Hayden had on a high-low dress with some floral details throughout, while Chelsea's dress was covered head to thigh in glitter.

If these dresses didn't represent our personalities, nothing could.

Commencement was being held in Topeka at the Downtown Event Center. We needed to be there no later than 2:00 PM because our ceremony started at 3:00 PM. They wanted us there an hour early to check-in and take all the photos we wanted.

The buzz of excitement was intoxicating. People were laughing, jumping on each other's backs for pictures, and tears . . . all the tears! Thankfully, they had mirrors everywhere for those of us that needed to fix our make-up. I was one of them for sure. Once Evelynn started to cry, we all did. We dabbed our faces with the tissues her mom gave us and flapped our hands in front of our eyes to try and dry the tears before they hit our mascara.

We separated for a little while so we could take pictures with the other classmates of ours. I saw

William; he was taking a picture with Natasha Bert and her friends. Natasha was the one who asked him to our sophomore New Year's Dance, but he turned her down.

The dance that started it all . . .

I immediately had to stop my brain from going down memory lane. *I can't! Not here, not today.* I found Bonnie and hung out with her for a little bit. I knew she would talk my ear off, and that was exactly what I needed right now. I needed to focus and listen to anybody but myself.

Our principal whistled with his fingers at us to get our attention. I'm envious of people who can whistle extremely loudly. That has to come in handy (no pun intended) quite a bit. For instance, in this case where he needs to rally 500+ excited seniors who are graduating and will never report to him ever again.

It was time to line up, which meant it was time to stand next to William. I found our place in line first and stood where I was supposed to. He joined me, but neither one of us said anything externally.

Internally I wanted to tell him everything. I wanted to tell him how much I missed him and how I never imagined today would look like this. I wanted to tell him he looked great in his cap and gown, and I was proud of him. I wanted to take pictures with him, laugh, and reminisce about our last three (well two technically if you exclude 12th grade) years together. I wanted to cry tears of utter joy today! Now, as I stood next to him, my eyes started to tear up, but I had become accustomed to fighting them back.

I sniffled, trying to suck the tears back into my eyeballs as we started walking down the aisle. I tried to focus on the processional music to occupy my brain, but it wasn't helping. When we sat down in our chairs, we were practically rubbing shoulders.

I couldn't listen to our principal as he talked about the accomplishments our class had achieved. I couldn't listen to our valedictorian, who beat out Evelynn by 0.2 with his overall GPA. I counted to 3,000 twice. After that, I started to look for my family in the audience. When I did, I started to count the number of people around them. I needed to keep my brain occupied on anything besides the incredibly attractive and intoxicating guy next to me with whom I shared my best and worst high school memories.

I kept sniffling. It probably sounded like I was at a funeral instead of a graduation ceremony. Nothing was helping. As I was staring at my fingers, a white tissue was placed in my left hand. It was from William. I looked at him through blurry vision. He squeezed my knee once, and then turned his face back toward the speaker without saying a word.

That small gesture in this moment meant more to me than anything he had ever done for me.

Our class president wrapped up his speech, signaling it was now time to walk across the stage and receive our diplomas. Our school doesn't do it like they show in the movies. We're not getting our real diplomas today, but we are getting the protective booklet we will put them in once the school mails the actual diploma out to us.

One by one our classmates walked across the stage with the largest smiles on their faces I have ever seen.

They're using our full, full names. This is the first time we have heard everybody's middle names and holy cow, some of them were very unexpected.

"Mackenzie Gertrude Lindale. Kent Clyde Lonney. Matilda Rachel Lundgren."

I looked back at William in shock. He had the same expression I did. For thirteen years, we had always known her as Rachel, and now we were just finding out that had been her middle name all these years!

"Allison Sky Manex." I focused on picking up my feet so I would not be the sole person who tripped at graduation. I walked across the stage to shake my principal's hand. He smiled and told me congratulations. I then proceeded to reach for my booklet from our vice principal. She said something to me, congratulations I assume, but I was listening to the next name that was to be called.

"William John Mantel."

I turned around to look back at him as he shook our principal's hand. He was grinning ear to ear just as I was. He looked at me with the smile I love and nodded. I bit my lip and kept walking down the ramp. We got back to our seats and sat down. I didn't say anything to him. I didn't need to. Everyone was feeling the buzz of excitement once again.

The principal waited until James Atticus Zedder found his seat before addressing us one final time.

"Students, please stand and face the crowd. Everyone here today came to celebrate the milestone you have just crossed. May you always remember where you came from as you start the next journey toward who you are going to become. Family, friends, and guests here today, will you join me in recognizing the graduates who stand before us. It is my greatest honor to present to you, the Class of 2017!"

The loudest roar erupted. Some people threw their caps in the air, while others turned to their neighbors to hug. I turned toward William first naturally, and he opened his arms for me. I leaped into him with everything in me! My feet came off the ground and I squeezed with all the strength I had. He squeezed me back just as tightly. In fact, it was almost a little too tight for my breathing, but I wasn't going to stop him. I was going to hang here until he put me down, which he did sooner than I wanted.

I could have kissed him. If this were a movie, that's exactly what would happen. I would stare deep into his eyes, and he would feel the same electricity that was coursing through me. Passionately, effortlessly, and flawlessly, we would kiss until the screen went black.

Reality check, this wasn't a movie, and we did not kiss. He set me down on my feet and we smiled at each other before turning to the students who sat on the other sides of us. I hugged Enrique and he hugged Shantelle. The processional music started to play once more, as we fell into the same line we originally entered in.

Once we were behind the scenes, students were scattering like fireflies. William and I removed our caps and I turned toward him once more.

"Thank you, William," I said, smiling once more at him. This wasn't a giant smile. This was a small, but deep and strong smile.

"You're welcome, Al." He flashed his teeth at me.

If there was anything else I was going to say, it was tackled out of me by my friends swarming me with their arms in a celebratory motion. When I was able to look back, William was gone. He found his friends and I reveled in joy with mine!

We did it. We officially survived high school. Tears streamed down my cheeks, and I didn't try to stop them this time. These tears held every emotion I felt for the last thirteen years of my life. It was time to release them and let them go.

If there is anything I learned my senior year, it's that you can never predict what is going to happen in your life, no matter how much you might plan for something.

Exactly three weeks after our graduation ceremony, the band Blue Chalk came to perform in Topeka at an outdoor park. They're a local band

William introduced me to sophomore year. We were driving around town one night, just the two of us, when he played his favorite song of theirs, "Hazel." I immediately fell in love with it too. I listened to it on repeat the next day so I could learn all the words. I wanted to be able to sing it with William the next time I heard it.

Hayden, Chelsea, and I went to the concert. I knew William would be there too, but I figured there would be enough people I wouldn't bump into him. *Wrong.* My friends and I like to sit off to the side during the concerts and typically William does too. It was another small thing we had in common that blew my mind. With the concert being outside, there weren't any designated seats, you just stood or sat wherever you wanted to in the open grass area.

Hayden was the one to notice him first. She tapped me on the shoulder and pointed in front of us, to the right. He was about twenty-five feet away. My eyes drifted to see who he was with. There was a pair of fiery eyes glaring at me, along with Peter, Grant, and Danny who were also with him.

Of course she's the only one I made eye contact with. I rolled my eyes and turned back to my friends.

I could see other people from our grade here as well, but nobody I really wanted to talk to. Somebody was selling glow sticks as the sun set. My friends and I bought a few because who doesn't love glow sticks at a concert?

At 10:00 PM a bass drum started to beat. A few fireworks burst in the night sky, exciting the crowd. We started to clap our hands to the rhythm of the drums as the stage lights started to shine off the instruments. We were on our feet. A few more fireworks went off as the lead guitarist began to play. The four members played their parts perfectly in sync, creating a beautiful eruption my parents considered "noise."

I glanced down toward him to see his face. He had the largest smile, and a leech clinging to his body.

I wonder how much she has listened to Blue Chalk. Do they drive around like we used to, blaring his speakers? Is "Hazel" her favorite song too since it's his favorite? Gosh, I wish I were down there with him . . .

I sang along to every song and went back in time to where I was when I first heard it. "Crippling Time" —William's Jeep, "Winter Solstice" —my bedroom, "War Paint" —William's Jeep, "Meteorite" —William's Jeep, "Behind the Mirror" —Steve's Diner when Dave, Kim, and I were closing together. They weren't as big of a fan as I was, but they endured it because they knew I loved the song.

The crowd was alive with clapping, cheering, and singing. The lead guitarist, Jerry Denver, played the opening three notes I had been waiting all night to hear. It was the opening to "Hazel," the most perfect and soul-clenching ballad ever written.

Jerry started to sing,

"Photo after photo, you stand there like a soldier.
Posing as you're told to,
Smiling like you've been trained to do.
Are you happy with where your life is at?"

My body was swaying automatically, and my right hand was across my heart. Tears were stinging my eyes as Jerry continued to sing.

"Is this what you hoped for when we dreamed together all those years ago?
I see you there,
Standing next to your loved one,
That familiar smile spread across your face.
Is it touching your eyes?

Is it revealing your soul?
I need to know, are you truly happy though?"

Blue Chalk continued playing, but there was a weird popping noise. I ignored it and kept swaying to the music, feeling the bass of the drums beat through my veins. Again, I heard an odd popping noise; this one was louder. Jerry stopped singing and Bryan the drummer held his sticks in the air. They were looking around at one another with confused expressions. Quinton, who played bass, stepped off stage.

Then it happened, rapid fire. All hell broke loose as there was a string of popping noises that sounded like—

No! It CAN'T BE!

It sounded like gunfire.

A stampede of people who were originally by the stage was coming toward us like a tidal wave. My friends and I turned around and I couldn't help but to look toward William. I didn't see him. I didn't see any of his friends. I tried to hang onto Hayden's hand, but somebody knocked me onto the ground, and I lost her. I tried to stand up, but somebody stepped on my left hand, breaking my knuckles. I cried out in pain, clutching it to my chest. I knew I didn't have time to baby it, I needed to get going! If there really was somebody, *or multiple people* with guns, I was a sitting target. I didn't want to get trampled to death either.

I found my footing and started to run again. I didn't know where I was headed. The crowd was going in only one direction, and I moved with them. Even if I wanted to go a different direction, I wasn't going to be able to force my way through the sea of bodies. It was taking all the strength in me to stand my own ground as we crashed together, bouncing off one another with a force I never imagined.

It was louder now than at the beginning of the

concert. I guess fear trumps cheer when it comes to screaming for your life.

"CHELSEA?! HAYDEN?!"

I screamed at the top of my lungs, but I couldn't tell if they heard me or not. I also had zero idea if they were even in the same proximity as my voice anymore. I could shout until I lost my voice, but that wouldn't do me any good if they weren't going to be able to hear me.

I tried again though. "CHELSEA?! HAYDEN?!"

No response, at least not from the voices I wanted to hear. Sirens were in the distance now, but they didn't seem anywhere close to the madness yet. I wasn't sure if the gunfire was still firing or not. I was only able to concentrate on staying on my feet, running as fast as the crowd allowed, and attempting to protect my broken hand, while looking for my friends.

We were making our way toward the entrance of the park. The gate was coming into view over the bobbing of heads. I also could see the ferocious swarm of people trying to shove their way through the small opening.

Oh no! I'll never get through the gate in one piece!

"Alli?" I thought I heard my name. I slowed my pace, but I didn't stop. I would have been trampled immediately if I did. Not to mention, I'm sure there's multiple people here with a name that sounds like mine. I was still being shoved forward by the crowd. I didn't see anybody I knew so I kept going.

The last thing I remembered was being knocked to the ground again by a large body, and a sharp pain piercing my skull. The roar of the screams fell silent, my hand stopped hurting, and my vision was rapidly turning black.

Peace engulfed my body. For the first time, I didn't have any thoughts running uncontrollably through my mind. My brain finally understood how to "shut off," a feeling my anxiety has never been able to experience. I couldn't see anything. I couldn't hear anything, but I could feel something . . . warmth. A familiar warmth pulling me closer toward itself. Serenity consumed me within, setting on fire the few functioning nerves I had left from its touch.

"Come on, Alli," Darkness whispered into my ear.

There wasn't anything more intoxicating to me in this very moment. After everything I had gone through this year alone, all I wanted now was to be held by darkness, and so, I willingly succumbed to it.

TESTING LOVE

WILLIAM

"Alli, can you hear me?! Alli?! Come on now, wake up!"

I scooped her into my arms, trying to be careful of her broken hand. You didn't need to be a doctor to realize her bones were not in the correct position they should be.

I didn't have time to check for a pulse or her breath. I honestly don't even know if she's alive technically, but I need to get her out of here!

The crowd is still pushing and shoving, scared out of our minds.

"Is she okay?" A lady close to my mom's age was next to me, screaming over the crowd as we pushed forward.

"I don't know if she's breathing or not. I can't tell!" I yelled back.

"Let me see if I can feel for a pulse."

The woman took her first two fingers and shoved them into the side of Alli's throat while we were squished between bodies. Her fingers kept getting knocked off by others around us. I was busy trying to stay upright while making sure I didn't drop her. The only thing I could think about was Alli right now and wanting to protect her.

"It's faint, but I can feel it. I'm going to feel for breathing now," she stated, taking the same two fingers and resting them under Alli's nose, on top of her upper lip. "Her breathing is shallow too, but she's breathing. She'll come to, I'm sure," the stranger said, giving me a reassuring smile that I latched onto.

"Thank you!" I yelled once more.

She gave me a nod as we made it through the gate. *Thank God!*

I don't see any paramedics. Where are they?! She needs help!

More shots pierced through the air. I hunched my shoulders instinctively.

I ran into an alleyway and hid behind a garbage dumpster. I needed to set her down; she was becoming too heavy for me. I didn't want us to be a slow, easy target out there.

I gently laid her on her back and checked her pulse and breathing as well. I could feel it, but I was still terrified.

"Come on, Alli, open your eyes," I whispered into her ear. "Can you hear me?"

I was dripping sweat. I wiped my hands on my damp shorts, but I'm not sure it helped much. I took my shirt off and wiped my arms and face off too. My heart was beating a million miles per hour right now. My entire body was shaking.

I need you to wake up.

I brushed some hair from her face and moved my hands gently across her eyelids. They moved, causing me to hold my breath.

"Alli?" I whispered once more.

Her head slowly rocked to the right then back to the middle again.

"Groan if you can hear me," I whispered.

She rocked her head to the right once more and groaned softly. "Oww."

It was the most beautiful groan I have ever heard!

ABOUT THE AUTHOR

M adison grew up in Ankeny, Iowa and is proud
to call the fly-over state home. She attended the
University of Northern Iowa and graduated in 2016
with a degree in History Education endorsed in All
Social Sciences. Having majored in a degree she's
passionate about made class a lot easier to attend!

Madison started writing early in life in her elementary diary. During 10th grade she discovered
she enjoyed writing for others and kept a notebook
of her random thoughts to share with friends. To
date, Madison has written more than thirty poems,
two published in Lyrical Iowa Poetry 2019 and 2020
editions. Currently, she has written over 500 letters to
God, friends, and family. She will continue writing
letters and books for as long as she is able.

RIVERSHORE BOOKS

www.rivershorebooks.com
info@rivershorebooks.com